PRISONE

"What about Josiane? Di[...] [...]to the Crier?" Joan looked [...] [...] [...] breathe until he told he[...]

"No, I didn't find her," Mantle replied. Then, after a pause, he said, "Yes, I glimpsed something. I saw her... under water, as if drowned in a shallow pool."

"Oh God," Joan moaned.

"It could have been just a dream, rather than a sending. I don't know. But Josiane's taken my life, my memory. I want them back...."

Leave her, bury her, forget her, Joan thought, and Mantle heard it as if she had spoken to him in a soft whisper. Her pain became his own.

"What?" he asked.

"I didn't say anything."

He tried to embrace her, console her with himself, strengthen her, but she stiffened and drew away from him. He opened himself to her, and for an instant, a current flowed between them, revealing what could not be spoken. She smiled sadly at him, and left the room....

THE
MAN WHO
MELTED

Jack Dann

BANTAM BOOKS
TORONTO · NEW YORK · LONDON · SYDNEY · AUCKLAND

The author would like to thank the following people whose support, aid, and inspiration were invaluable:

Jeanne Van Buren Dann, Lorne Dann, Murray and Edith Dann, Ellen Datlow, Richard H. Dekmejian and Margaret J. Wyszomirski, Joseph Elder, James Frenkel, Perry Knowlton, Dr. Bon Yung Koo, Howard Lessnick, Barry Malzberg, the members of the Philford Science Fiction Writers' Workshop, Dr. Richard Normile, William Pizante, Victoria Schochet, John Silbersack, Robert Silverberg, Robert Sheckley, the staff of the Vestal Public Library and the Binghamton Public Library, Michael Swanwick and Marianne Porter, Susan Casper, Albert White, Roger Zelazny, and special thanks to Gardner Dozois, to whom this book is dedicated.

This low-priced Bantam Book
has been completely reset in a type face
designed for easy reading, and was printed
from new plates. It contains the complete
text of the original hard-cover edition.
NOT ONE WORD HAS BEEN OMITTED.

THE MAN WHO MELTED
A Bantam Spectra Book / published by arrangement with
St. Martin's Press

PRINTING HISTORY
Bluejay Books international edition published October 1984
St. Martin's edition published December 1984
Bantam edition / January 1986

The following portions of this book have appeared as short stories in the following:

"Amnesia" © 1981 by Jack Dann. Appeared in Berkley Showcase, Volume 3, edited by Victoria Schochet and John Silbersack.
"Going Under" appeared in OMNI Magazine, September 1981
"Screamers" appeared in OUI Magazine, October 1982
"Blind Shemmy" appeared in OMNI Magazine, April 1983

ISBN 0-553-25562-2

Published simultaneously in the United States and Canada

PRINTED IN THE UNITED STATES OF AMERICA

H   0 9 8 7 6 5 4 3 2 1

Our society may itself have become biologically dysfunctional, and some forms of schizophrenic alienation from the alienation of society may have a sociobiological function that we have not recognized.

—R. D. Laing
The Politics of Experience

The individuals that make up the crowd are called 'Screamers' or 'Criers'; only when these afflicted people gather into groups of a certain number do they become telepathic and develop mass empathy or a collective consciousness. When not in a group, the individuals exhibit the various schizophrenic patterns of behavior.

—Alain R. Lucie
The Collective Reality

Perhaps *you* are the seed crystal. Perhaps *you* are the focus around which the masses of the living and the dead will gather. And in that moment, the world will be drawn to you and changed forever.

Le Symbole de Crieur
(Annotated)

PART ONE

One

Raymond Mantle took a flyer to Naples, the fallen city. It looked as grim as he felt. Nemesius, one of Mantle's many sources, said that a woman fitting Josiane's description had been located here. He couldn't be sure, of course, because his *informatore* had mysteriously disappeared. After all, Naples had become a dangerous place since it had fallen to the Screamers.

But Mantle had to find his wife, Josiane. Nothing else was important.

He had lost her during the Great Scream, when the screaming mobs tore New York City apart, leaving thousands dead and countless others roving about like the mind-deadened victims of a concentration camp. With the exception of a few childhood memories, he couldn't remember her after the Great Scream. It was as if she had been ripped from his memory. Mantle's amnesia was not total; he could summon up certain incidents and remember every detail and everyone involved except *Josiane*. She inhabited his memory like a shadow, an emptiness, and he was obsessed with finding her, with remembering. *She* held the key to his past. She was the element that had burned out, plunging his past into darkness.

Nemesius' man, Melzi, met Mantle in the crowded Piazza Trento e Trieste, and they walked north on the Via Roma, past a gang of *sciuscias*—half-naked street arabs with implanted male and female genitalia on their arms and chests. It was not yet dark, but the huge kliegs were on, illuminating the alleyways in harsh whites and yellows—as if bright light could prevent a Screamer attack. Police vans passed back and forth through the noisy crowds of *elemosina*, those on the dole. They lived in the streets and on the beltways, in gangs and clans and families. During the rush hours, this street would look like a battle zone. But even here, even now, old,

3

familiar scenes caught Mantle's eyes: the shoeblacks and hurdy-gurdies and glowworms; the refreshment kiosks where a narcodrine could be sniffed for a few lire; the holographically projected faces of the holy saints which hung in the damp air like paper masks; and the ever-present *venditores* who sold talking Bibles and varied selections of religious memorabilia blessed by the Pope and sanctioned by the Vatican Collective which ruled the country. There were still strings of lemons hanging in shop windows; and lemon ices were being sold, as were *jettatura* charms, the coral horns and little bones everyone used to wear to ward off the evil eye. Now they were worn as protections from Screamers.

Here beat the heart of Naples, along the narrow, broken streets and crowded piazzas. Not far from here, though, small bands of Screamers still roamed, the last remnants of the mobs that had almost destroyed the city.

"We're going into the Old Spacca Quarter," Melzi said. He was a small man with thinning gray hair and a very clean-shaven face; he looked more like a clerk than a bodyguard. Most of the other men and women Mantle had to contact in the past were more obviously sleazy; they had the psychic smell of the streets all over them. "The woman who may be your wife is near Gesu Nuovo, off the Via Capitelli. Not a safe neighborhood. But we should not have any trouble finding the building. It is the only one that is not burned on the outside."

"Another one of Nemesius' whorehouses?" Mantle asked.

"We might as well walk," Melzi said, ignoring Mantle's sarcasm. "The beltways are not in good condition hearabouts, and we won't find a cab that will take us into Spacca."

Although they were still in a relatively safe area, Mantle was nervous. His whole being was focused on the remote possibility of finding Josiane; everything else was white noise. He was as haunted as the street arabs around him.

"You can still turn around and go home," Melzi said. "If the woman is a phony, *I* will know it." Mantle did not respond, and Melzi shrugged.

After they had worked their way through the crowds for several more blocks, Mantle asked, "How much farther?"

"You'll see, we are almost there," Melzi said. He carried his heat weapon openly now. Mantle kept his hands in his pockets; he always carried a pistol when he had to be on the streets.

The Via Roma, along which they were still walking, became less crowded. When they crossed over into Spacca, they found the alleyways and narrow buildings almost empty. Everything was dirty; ahead were the burned buildings scourged by Screamers.

A small, dangerous-looking crowd gathered behind Mantle and Melzi. Mantle took his pistol out of his pocket.

"Not to worry yet," Melzi said. "They're not Screamers. As long as they are behind us, we are relatively safe. They're nothing but *avvoltoio*." He spat the word.

"What?"

"Stinking birds. Scavengers."

"Vultures," Mantle said.

"Yes, that's it," Melzi said. "Now, if we engage a crowd up ahead, then we might be in trouble. But we are armed, and I would burn the lot of them. It would not be worth it for them to attack us. Some of them know me; they would not get anything of worth. You see" —Melzi extended his free arm and fluttered his fingers— "not even a ring. I have beautiful rings, that is my weakness. Especially diamonds, which are my birthstone. I wear one upon every finger, even the thumb." He made a vulgar gesture. "I might feel naked, but I'm not worried yet. Would you like to see them? My rings?"

"Yes, perhaps," Mantle said, annoyed. The crowd following Mantle and Melzi was unnaturally quiet; it unnerved Mantle.

"Maybe later," Melzi said. "If we do not have the luck to find your little bird."

Mantle fantasized smashing the little man's face. God, how he hated them all. All the filth from the streets. But if he could find Josiane tonight, it would be worth all the Melzis in the world.

"If the trash behind us were Screamers, *then* I would be worried," Melzi said. "You never know with them. They walk about in their little groups, looking just like the filth behind us. Then all of a sudden they decided to scour the street and you're dead. They're like junkies; you can burn them, fill them up with bullets, but nothing seems to stop them. And you can't even find them again, they just disappear. They're like centipedes. all those legs and one head." Melzi laughed at that, as if it were an original thought. Again he laughed, almost a titter. "I can smell them, you know. They smell different from *elemosina* or *avvoltoio*. Not like trash, just sick. You smell all right, of course. But there's a whiff, I don't know—"

"Shut up," Mantle snapped.

"Oh, I am sorry if I have hurt your feelings. Certainly, I did not mean any disrespect. Will you forgive me?"

They turned onto the Via Croce. A group of prostitutes, all hideously fat, sat on the steps of a palazzo and shouted, "*Succhio, succhio,*" as Mantle and Melzi passed. Melzi shouted obscenities back; he was more animated, nervous. There was much slave-marketeering hereabouts. Whores and old people, and especially children, were kidnapped and sold to those who would pay to hook-into their brains and taste their experiences, their lives. The black market catered to the rich. The dole was virtually nonexistent here; survival was the business of the day. Police and the other arms of government would not be found in these parts. This was free country.

"Now we must be a little careful, because this neighborhood is not so good," Melzi said. He made the gesture of being shackled by crossing his wrists. "Many slavers hereabouts; they look just like anybody. We would fetch a good price," he said preening himself. "I can imagine that you would be delicious to hook-into."

Someone shouted; there was another scream. There was a fight ahead in the square of Gesu Nuovo. Men and women and children were brawling, it seemed, over small metal canisters of some sort—perhaps food or drugs. Mantle glanced behind him; only a few *avvoltoio* were following, but still they made him nervous.

"We have a stroke of luck," Melzi said. "The fight will draw the *avvoltoio* and we can attend to our business."

"How close are we?" Mantle asked, excited.

"We are there, you see, that's it." He pointed to a palazzo which actually looked whitewashed, a miracle in these parts.

"Jesus."

"It is quite famous," Melzi said. "Like the Crazy Horse near where you live."

"I don't think you can compare—"

"What's the difference, except for the neighborhood? This palazzo is an attraction *because* of the neighborhood. Here you can find interesting pleasures; *polizia* do not make problems here." Melzi looked at the women fighting in the square and made a clucking noise of disapproval as he watched a young woman being disemboweled in the quaint broken fountain. Mantle hesitated, but Melzi took him by the arm; the little man was deceptively strong. "We are here to find your little bird, that's all."

As they neared the palazzo, the streets became crowded once again. It was like stepping into another, albeit dangerous, country, into an international oasis amid the lowlife of the street. Mantle could see well-dressed, and well-guarded, men and women stepping quickly among the street arabs, hawkers, pimps, and other assorted street people. One dignitary was actually enclosed in a glassite litter that was shouldered by four uniformed men.

A woman approached Melzi, and he burned a hole in her throat. Mantle lunged for Melzi's weapon, but Melzi deftly pulled it out of reach and continued to walk. *Elemosina* stepped over the dying woman as if she were a rock in the road.

"Scum," Mantle said, drawing away from Melzi. His flesh was crawling. "Murderer!"

"Now calm yourself," Melzi said, as if he were a bank clerk explaining why he couldn't accept a customer's credit. "That was just a precaution. She had evil thoughts in mind."

"Could you smell those, too?"

"You are not in Cannes, *Signore*," Melzi said. "And do not think you are safe here or now. Without me, it is doubtful whether you would ever get out of here alive, much less find your wife. Now do you forgive me? When last I asked, you ignored me." Melzi was playing him, and Mantle knew it. But he was so close. All that really mattered was Josiane. "Well . . . ?" Melzi asked.

"I forgive you," Mantle said, as if he were spitting up raw meat. Nemesius will pay for this, he thought.

"Thank you," Melzi said, not pressing it further.

Mantle followed Melzi, who walked past the white palazzo. The building was high and imposing; it was formed in the style of a Florentine palace, complete with rich embossing, curved frontons, projecting cornices, and ringed columns, most of which were broken or cracked.

"Where are you going?" Mantle asked, noticing that it was growing dark. They walked along a cobblestone close, which Mantle was afraid might also be a dead end. Could Melzi and Nemesius have set him up? Mantle felt a touch of panic. No, he told himself. He had dealt with Nemesius for too long.

"This is the best way to get in," Melzi said, "although I must admit, this alleyway does look dangerous." He pounded on a heavy, inlaid door. The door opened, but not before Mantle glimpsed that the shadows under the broken klieg at the end of the alley were moving.

"Meet Vittorio," Melzi said to Mantle as they entered a large pantry filled with canisters of foodstuffs and, from the look of it, rats. Vittorio was swarthy and as short as Melzi. He had almost transparent green eyes; waxed, curly hair; a kinky, short-cropped beard; and he wore a stained serge suit. He was missing a front tooth. Yet he bore himself as if he were presiding over a parliament of rich and respected *nubiluomo*.

"*Buona sera*." Then Melzi slipped him a package and Vittorio nodded to Mantle, mumbled, "*Mi scusi*," and walked off, presumably to hold court with the rats and kitchen cats.

"Well, come on," Melzi said. "He's going ahead to prepare her."

"Who is he?" Mantle asked.

"He's the proprietor, a very famous man. Don't be fooled by his teeth, he has many affectations. He owns this place and many more. And as you can see, he watches over his interests. That's the secret of success, is it not?"

Mantle followed Melzi out of the room and into a long, well-lit corridor. There was almost a hospital smell hereabouts, and Mantle shuddered, thinking of what might be going on behind closed doors. Josiane must be here, he told himself. He had to find her this time.

"We're taking a shortcut," Melzi said. "We're safer here than in the main rooms, which are, of course, much more interesting. But then that's the allure of a place such as this, is it not? I'm willing to bet you'd run into a pal in one of those rooms. You'd be surprised who risks the streets for a night at Vittorio's."

They took an elevator to the top story. Mantle was afraid

of elevators; they symbolized his life, which he could not control. They were driven, it seemed, by unseen forces. Once inside the box, you had to trust the machine. And the machine didn't care if it worked or not.

"You make it very hard for Nemesius, you know," Melzi said. "He has nothing but a few hollies of your little bird."

"The records were burned."

"Yes, how lucky for you Americans. Most of you got a second chance. Wiped the slates clean, so to speak. What *I* wouldn't give for such an accident."

"Come on, Melzi."

"One last thing, *Signore*," Melzi said. "You must remember that Vittorio is just a middleman, just like Nemesius. Just like me. It seems we've all become middlemen in these times." Melzi smiled at that, obviously satisfied with his philosophizing. "And you must also remember that there are *no* guarantees."

"I'll *know* if it's her," Mantle said.

They stopped at the end of the hallway and Melzi rapped twice on a metal door, which Vittorio opened. "She's right in here."

The room was a cell. It smelled of urine, contained an open toilet, a wall sink, a discolored bidet, a filthy mattress on the metal floor, a computer console and a psyconductor with its cowls and mesh of wires, and a wooden folding chair. On the pallet lay Josiane, or a woman who looked exactly like her. She was naked and perspiring heavily. Mantle almost cried, for her face and small breasts were black and blue. Her hair was blond and curly, although it was matted with dirt and clotted blood. She looked up at him, her limpid eyes as blue as his own; but she was looking through him, through the walls and the world, and back into the dark places of her mind.

"Well," Melzi said, sharing a glance with Vittorio, "that certainly looks like your little bird."

"Here are her papers," Vittorio said to Mantle in an American accent, which was the current fashion; and then he passed Mantle a large envelope. But Mantle just held it; he was lost. His memory was jarred, and he slipped back to the first time, in the old house in Cayuga, when there were still spruce and fir covering the mountain. But he didn't care about trees then. He was fourteen and Josiane was eleven—

but developed for her age—and she came into his room and they lay on the bed and talked and she jerked him off as she had done since she was eight or nine, and he rolled over on top of her, stared steadily into her face and entered her. Then stopped, as if tasting some kind of delicious, warm ice cream, and they just stared at each other, moving up and down, breath only slightly quickened. It was more a way of talking.

Another memory came back to him: the face of a young woman in a crowd. The same face as the woman on the mattress.

"*Signore*, come back to the world," Vittorio said, and Melzi chuckled.

Mantle shook his head as if he had slipped from one world to another and mumbled, "Josiane." Then he rushed to the psychoconductor, grabbed two cowls from the top of the console, and lunged toward her, intent on hooking into her thoughts; but Melzi caught him and pulled him away. "Are you that determined to burn your brain?" Melzi asked. "At least let me look at her first."

"We have many customers who wish to hook-into Screamers," Vittorio said. "But they must pay first. It's a policy of the house."

Melzi squatted beside the woman and examined her with an instrument that projected a superimposed holographic image of Josiane over her face. After several minutes, he raised the magnification and disappeared the holographic image.

"Whoever did this work was a real artist," Melzi said. "Her face corresponds exactly to the hollie. But you see, right there?" He indicated a dry area just below her earlobe. "You see, the pores are open everywhere else but in that tiny spot." He raised the magnification several more powers. "There you can see the faint thread of a suture. A recent job. He should have been just a *little* more careful and covered *that* up."

Mantle pushed Melzi out of the way and examined her himself. He felt anger and frustration burning through him, returning more violently than ever before. He began to shake. Once again he had tried to fool himself, this time with a burned-up Screamer, a *grido*, a *crieuse*—but she was not his wife!

"I don't think you would wish to hook-into that woman," Melzi said. "She is not—"

"But you must admit, *Signore*," Vittorio said, "she looks exactly like the hollies with which we were provided." Then Vittorio said to Melzi, "She was supposed to have been completely checked out by the man who brought her to me."

Melzi only shrugged.

"My contact is a reputable man; he will be very unhappy—"

Then Mantle snapped completely—it was as if someone, or something, had suddenly taken him over. He punched Vittorio in the abdomen before Melzi could stop him. At once, the door to the hallway slammed open and one of Vittorio's men entered. The man was big and had the dead look of the street about him. As Mantle turned, the man struck him hard in the chest and pushed him savagely against the wall. Mantle overcame his nausea and tried to free himself, but Vittorio's man was too strong.

Melzi watched, his mouth pursed as if he were amused. "You must forgive my client," he said to Vittorio. "He's not right in the head. He—"

"Now he *will* buy the girl," Vittorio said, still gasping for breath. He kept smoothing down his suit.

"Don't even argue," Melzi said to Mantle. Melzi nodded to Vittorio; and Vittorio, in his turn, told his man to release Mantle. Mantle made the credit transaction by applying his hand to the glass face of the computer console.

He had bought the woman.

"You realize that this is simply a transfer of funds from one account to another," Vittorio said, having recovered himself. "It cannot possibly be traced."

A matronly domestic entered the room with clothes for the woman and various messages for Vittorio.

"Get her dressed and let's get out of here," Mantle said impatiently.

"I named her Victoria. She'll answer to that if she'll answer at all," Vittorio said. He nodded curtly to Melzi and left the room. His man followed.

Mantle felt his flesh crawl. He was sure that Vittorio had abused her. "Let's get out of here. Now!"

"Let the girl finish dressing," Melzi said. "I am in no rush to be on the streets. Just a few minutes ago you were going to hook-into her and now—"

"Now," Mantle repeated. And he held out his hand to Victoria, who grinned at him, just as Josiane used to do.

The streets were empty—not a shadow moving, not a sound. It was dark, but the crooked, and usually deadly, intersecting streets were well lit, for anyone caught trying to break one of the kliegs would be torn limb from limb. The common folk had their own notions of law. However, enough lamps were broken to create a patchwork effect of white, black, and gray.

They were almost out of Spacca. Victoria seemed suddenly alert, her head cocked, as if listening to someone who was talking too low.

"I don't like this," Mantle said. His chest was aching, but he ignored it.

"It is very bad," Melzi agreed. "It's going to be a big one this time. I didn't expect anything like this to happen again so soon. I didn't think there were enough Screamers to do it. But you never know. All we can do is hurry. There's nothing to stop us, at least."

Mantle repressed an urge to slow down. He was curious, not really afraid. *That*, he knew, was dangerous. If Mantle was caught in a crowd of Screamers, he might not be able to resist becoming like them—very few could.

"The girl is slowing us down," Melzi said, grasping her arm and dragging her forward. "We don't have much time. The farther we are from Spacca, the safer."

"I don't see anything yet," Mantle said.

"*Jesù*, can't you feel it? Come on, hurry."

Mantle took her other arm. "Don't hurt her, Melzi," Mantle said. "You're *hurting* her, let go of her arm."

"She may look like your wife, *Signore*, but she's still a *grido*. She feels nothing. She's not in this world. I can smell that."

Victoria suddenly started dragging her feet. She shook her head back and forth, her eyes closed, face placid, as if listening to music.

"We can't drag her like this," Melzi said. "Come on, little bird, wake up." He slapped her back and forth on the face.

"Leave her alone!" Mantle said, bracing her arms as she

fell to her knees. Her head was cocked, and she began to smile.

"I'm leaving, and so are you," Melzi said. "I contracted to bring you home, and so I shall." He pointed his heat weapon at Mantle. "Please forgive me, *Signore*, but if you do not come along, I will have to kill her. The smell of *grido* is so strong all around us that I can hardly breathe. We've no time to waste. Now leave her be."

Mantle felt something in the air, electricity, as if a powerful storm were about to break, only its potential energy seemed sentient. Suddenly Victoria began to scream. Long, cold streamers of sound. Melzi—who was sweating profusely and looking around in nervous, darting movements as if he were about to be attacked from every side—shot Victoria in the throat, just as he had shot the other woman. Mantle shouted, but it was too late. He was overcome with hatred and disgust and sorrow. For that instant, it *was* Josiane whom Melzi had shot.

In return, Mantle shot Melzi, twice in the chest and once in the groin. It was as if Mantle's hand had a will of its own.

"But she will attract the others," Melzi whispered, referring to the Screamers. He looked nothing but surprised for a second, and then collapsed.

Mantle heard a distant roaring like faraway breakers. For an instant he was a child again, listening to the ocean calling his name. Then he saw the first Screamers running toward him, heads thrown back as they howled at the heavens like wolves. Thousands of them crowded the streets and alleyways, turning Spacca into commotion. Melzi had been right. The mob would converge upon them. It was a many-headed beast screaming for blood and Mantle, as if in response to Victoria's call.

Mantle had enough time to turn and run, but when he tried, Victoria rose before him like a ghost. She called to him, promised that she was Josiane. Her skin was translucent, her rags diaphanous, and her voice was that of the Screamers.

He heard Josiane's voice calling him, then a thousand voices, all Josiane's. . . .

The Screamers were all around him, pushing him, pressing against him, tempting him, a thousand sirens promising darkness and cold love. Mantle looked around, shaking his head in one direction, then another; and saw that *everyone* looked like Josiane. Then everyone turned into Mantle's dead mother, and an instant later, the features of every Screamer's face melted like hot wax. The mob took on the angry face of Mantle's dead father, then his dead brother. Every Screamer was changing, melting into someone Mantle had known or loved or hated.

"Stop it!" Mantle screamed as everyone turned into Carl Pfeiffer, an old friend and enemy. But Mantle was caught, another Screamer. He was running with them—south, past the Via Diaz, through the ruins of burned-out buildings and garbage-strewn streets, over the seamless macadam that covered the cobblestone roads once used by Romans. He screamed, lost in the mob. He could hear the thoughts of every other Screamer. Their cries and screams were the rhythms of fire and transcendence and death. He felt silvery music as the dark voices rustled his childhood memories like wheat in a field. He felt transformed, transported into the hot eye of a hurricane.

But a part of Mantle's mind resisted the dark, telepathic nets of the screaming mob, even now. Like a man pulling himself out of deepest sleep, he wrenched himself away. But he was only swallowed again, submerged in the undertow of minds.

Suddenly, he felt a blunt pain in his arm and shoulder—a Screamer running beside Mantle tripped and pushed him against the ragged stone side of the building. Although he couldn't stop himself from running or screaming with the others, he concentrated on the pain. He used it to close himself from the Circaen voices long enough to slow his gait until the mob was ahead of him. Then he fell to the macadam, exhausted and dazed.

Later, he would remember everything but the Screamer attack.

Two

The broadwalk creaked as Mantle walked, and the strong noontime sunlight turned the bistros, boardwalk feelies, and open-air restaurants white as bones in a desert. Once again he tried to remember what had happened to him last week in Naples, but his mind's eye was closed. Memory was lost in darkness.

He shivered as if he had remembered something painful, which quickly slipped away from him. He *knew* that he had been attacked by Screamers in Naples; he just couldn't remember. He remembered finding Victoria and shooting Melzi—he winced, just thinking about that—and then waking up in a hospital hallway that was lined with cots. He had suffered a mild concussion, and his arms and chest were black and blue. He had left the hospital as soon as he could to recuperate in the privacy of his hotel room.

Now that he was back in Cannes, he felt like himself again. Whatever had happened in Naples was like a dream. But he walked quickly, impatiently, as if he could walk his way through his amnesia: he was expecting an important phone call from Francois Pretre, a minister of the Church of the Christian Criers.

To his right was the ancient Boulevard de la Croisette, elegant but deteriorated, its rare gardens untended and its cement promenade cracked and broken. But still, it was the meeting place of the gentry, especially in the winter when expatriates, spies, political exiles, and reporters from all over Europe and the Americas would gather. Since Naples had first fallen to the Screamer mobs, the Boulevard de la Croisette had become what the Via Roma had once been: an informal center for intrigue and exchange of information.

The boardwalk ended, and Mantle crossed over to the boulevard. The computer plug whispered it was time for his pill. He felt a surge of anger and took the plug from his ear. He didn't need drugs to calm himself. He counted trees and inhaled the salty, decaying odors of the Mediterranean. Torn pieces of newsfax capered toward him in the wind like pigeons chasing bread. He passed an old woman cleaning the street in front of a dingy bistro called "Club California." She gave him a nasty look and stirred dust devils into the air.

He nodded to her and walked toward the old La Castre Museum. He would be home soon. The sea was behind him; the streets noisy with vendors and children and congregating neighbors. He passed his friend Joan's apartment and felt the old pangs of guilt. But he didn't stop. He would make amends later. She would understand. She always had.

He could feel a sort of electricity around him, as if a storm were brewing. Yet, there was not a cloud in the sky. But today would be a good day. It would bring him closer to Josiane. Perhaps Pretre would finally call to grant him permission to hook-into a dead Screamer.

Perhaps Mantle could find Josiane inside a dead man's mind.

Carl Pfeiffer stood outside Mantle's house in Old Town.

Mantle lived in a faded, dirty-looking yellow house with common walls and noisy neighbors—just under the clock tower, the grand machine that ruled ancient Cannes. Before the close-packed, tile-roofed, chimneyed houses were the square and the Church of Good Hope; then more houses and shops, less deteriorated and with a better view of the harbor and the misted island of Ste-Marguerite.

Before Mantle could change direction, Pfeiffer saw him and was shouting and waving his hands.

What the hell is he doing *here?* Mantle asked himself, already feeling trapped. Too late now to turn back on the Rue Perrissol, to try to find Joan and kill time until Pfeiffer grew tired and left. He wouldn't even have to miss Pretre; Mantle would have an excuse to call *him*.

"I've been waiting here for an hour," Pfeiffer said, taking a backward step as if Mantle had given him a push. Indeed, the thought had crossed his mind. "I left a message on your telie yesterday," Pfeiffer continued. "Haven't you been home? Don't you check the Net for messages?" He gave Mantle a condescending look.

The Reverend Pretre refused to leave any messages on the Net, so Mantle had not bothered to check it.

"You could at least pretend to be happy to see me," Pfeiffer said. "It's been a long time."

"This is a surprise, Carl," Mantle said, worrying his keys out of his pocket. His voice was still hoarse. "Yes, it has been a long time."

"You're still angry about the past, aren't you?" Pfeiffer asked—more a statement than a question. "After all these years, let things die."

"I can't remember the past, remember?" But Pfeiffer could, and Mantle hated him for that.

"Whatever you may think, I was always your friend."

"Let's not go into that." Their friendship had been ruinous, built upon the premise that Pfeiffer would succeed and Mantle would fail. Pfeiffer had always done his part. Now that Mantle's life had caved in, he was making an entrance.

"This is just a visit, not work-related at all," Pfeiffer said as if Mantle had asked a question. Again that condescending look, but that was Pfeiffer's way. He was a stout man with a boyish face and a shock of blond and silvery-gray hair. Pfeiffer looked like the successful reporter: expensive clothes that seemed slightly worn, sureness of manner, steady stare—an apple-pie, good-old-home-town boy, definitely a media man, not a shut-in newsfax technician like Mantle, but an actor, a holographic image seen every night in the millions of American living rooms. Pfeiffer was the good doctor who could make the daily dose of bad news palatable to his patients. Mantle, on the other hand, looked too menacing to deliver news. He had a tight, hard face, high cheekbones, deeply set pale blue eyes and a strong, cleft chin. He looked younger than his forty years.

Mantle was surprised that Carl had not yet recited his latest accomplishments and good fortune.

"I must say that things have been going quite well for me," Pfeiffer said as if on cue. "Have you seen any of my shows?" He picked up a thin brown suitcase behind him.

"Did you camouflage your bag?" Mantle asked, but Pfeiffer only chuckled.

As he followed Mantle up a flight of stairs, he told him of his recent books—he was a readable, if somewhat pedantic essayist, and sold everything he wrote to the popular fax magazines. It was depressing to think of Pfeiffer's gems of wisdom oozing out of every living room computer terminal in America. His collected essays were bound in hardcover, an honor indeed; and the best thing of all was that he had also been doing fiction again (his fiction was terrible); and of course, he was selling it under a pseudonym; and, yes, he had sold a novel, finally, and it would be in covers first and *then* go to fax for a huge amount of money; and he was taking a leave of absence to complete the book.

Are you still jealous? Mantle asked himself, or was that

burned out too? But that was unimportant now. Only one thing was important: Pretre must call today.

The hallway was dark, windowless except for the top landing, which had a yellow and red and orange-stained glass window, and, in marked contrast to the rest of the hall, was also clean. Mme. Acte and her flabby-fat daughter swept daily, but neither bothered to use a dustpan, and Mantle did not care enough to clean up the mess they left on his landing. They were his only tenants.

As Mantle opened the door to his flat, he excused himself and rushed into the living room to make a quick check of the computer for coded messages. There were none.

"It's all right, come in," he said to Pfeiffer who was waiting at the door.

"You did get my messages, didn't you," Pfeiffer said. It wasn't a question.

Ignoring that, Mantle said, "I'm afraid everything's a bit of a mess." Mme. Acte and her daughter used to clean house for him in lieu of rent, but he couldn't stand them fumbling about in his rooms, arguing, and fingering through his personal effects. They suffered the indignity of free housing by sweeping their dirt onto his landing.

Pfeiffer set his bag down in the middle of the living room (and surely he intended to stay as long as he could), then sniffed around like a tawny, compact animal. The room had large high windows that caught the morning light. Situated before the windows, upon a brightly colored drop cloth, were two easels and a ruined satinwood desk littered with broken paint cylinders and brushes. Piled upon and around a paint-smeared video console and the ever-present computer terminal were piles of books in covers, fax and fische, and disordered stacks of gessoed canvas boards.

The plaster-chipped walls were covered with Mantle's own paintings and graphics, with the exception of a few etchings and woodcuts by Fiske Boyd, a little-known twentieth-century artist. Most of the paintings were land- and seascapes; Mantle especially loved the perched villages, such as Eze and Mons. As he frequently traveled the old Esterel Road, many of the paintings depicted the red porphyry of the Esterel Massif and the Calanques, the deep, rugged inlets. Upon first look, some of his paintings appeared to be vague, almost smoky-looking, but shapes seemed to form as one stared into the milky canvases enclosed in heavy frames; they gained definition and color, as if the viewer were somehow superimposing his own imagination upon them. Then, for an instant, the paintings would appear to be as clear and defined as old photographs.

Mantle watched Pfeiffer inspect the room. Short, squat, freckled Pfeiffer with his baby face and widely set eyes and high cheekbones. How long have we known each other? It must be twenty years. All that hate and love wasted like a bad marriage. Now there was the old silence between them and all the walls of the past. Although he wanted to push through the barriers and reach Pfeiffer, kindle the warmth of the old days (and extract Pfeiffer's memories of Josiane like teeth), he felt repelled by this familiar stranger. Stymied, Mantle kept quiet, watched and waited.

"This one is very good," Pfeiffer said, staring at a large fantastical painting of a dead bird in the woods. It was centered on the far narrow wall of the living room. The painting commanded the space; one would not even notice the floral-figured easy chair beneath it.

Mantle laughed softly.

"What's so funny?" Pfeiffer asked, turning around, then back to the painting. "I think this is a very good piece of work, even though the subject matter is a bit depressing."

"I know the work is very good," Mantle said, walking across the room, taking the advantage. "That wasn't what I was laughing at."

"Well . . . ?"

"I was laughing at you, old friend." Pfeiffer scowled, as expected. "I painted this for you some time ago," Mantle continued. "You can take it back with you, if you like."

"Well, thank you, but I don't know." Pfeiffer's voice lowered in register. "Why did you laugh?"

"Because I painted it for you and, predictably, you took the bait. You nosed over to the Dead Bird without a hesitation."

"So what?"

"I'll show you," Mantle said. He stood before the painting; it was at eye level. "Look at the sky. There, where the dark, fist-shaped cloud meets the lighter one, what do you see?"

"I see two clouds. What should I see?"

"Step back a bit, and don't stare into the painting as if to burn a hole in it," Mantle said. "You see the black cloud as the figure and the white as the ground because there is so much more white area. That's a decoy. Try looking at the white area as figure and the dark as ground. Now what do you see? Don't strain to look: it will come into focus."

"I see letters, I think," Pfeiffer said.

"And what do they spell?"

Pfeiffer shook his head; it was more like a twitch. "T–O–D. *Tod*. Why, that's the German word for death. Is that really in there?"

"Yes," Mantle said. "It's part of a mosaic using *tod* and *tot*. If you look closely, you can also make out the words *death* and variants such as *deth*, over there." Mantle pointed to a shaded area in the sky.

"Why did you do that?" Pfeiffer asked.

"They're subliminal embeds. Surely you're familiar with them—"

"Of course I am," Pfeiffer replied, his voice a bit loud. "But why use death, or *tod*, or whatever—other than to be morbid."

"They're subliminal triggers. Your greatest fear was death, remember? You used to talk about it all the time." Mantle waited a beat. "Step back a bit and look into the forest—there, in the left corner where the crawlers are. What do you see?"

"Nothing."

"Look away from the painting," Mantle said. "Now look again."

"Why it's Caroline's face, I can see it. It's a real *trompe-l'oeil*." Pfeiffer's face seemed to darken. "What else have you hidden in there?"

"That you'll have to discover yourself," Mantle said. He couldn't tell Pfeiffer that the subliminal portrait of his wife was surrounded by genitals. Sweet, sexless, self-contained Caroline, radiant in a wreath of cocks.

"Then there are more subembeds?"

"Quite a bit more," Mantle replied, feeling relieved yet guilty. He was acting like a vengeful child. The past was dead, let it be, he thought.

"Do you really expect me to take that painting?"

"That's up to you." Mantle walked into the sitting room where he kept a small bar, and Pfeiffer followed. This room contained another desk, this one walnut with a drop front, several austere high-backed chairs, a discolored gilt frame mirror, and a blond Kirman carpet, which brightened the room considerably. This room had one small slat window; bookcases covered the walls. Mantle stepped behind the bar. "Fix you a drink?"

"You did that to hurt me, didn't you," Pfeiffer said— more a statement than a question. Pfeiffer the innocent, Mantle thought, and in a way it was true. Pfeiffer the paradox.

"Yes, I suppose I did. Old wounds heal slowly and all that. I'm sorry."

"Well, let's try to forget it," Pfeiffer said. "It was a long time ago that we had our trouble, wasn't it, although even now I'm not sure what happened, what was going on in your mind."

You sonofabitch, Mantle thought. You were feeding on me, that's what was going on in my mind. Don't take the bait, he told himself. Don't let him manipulate you into confession. It's the old trap. But the net that Pfeiffer dragged could still catch him. "Bourbon?"

Pfeiffer nodded, and Mantle poured him a shot. "Are all the other paintings like the Dead Bird?" Pfeiffer asked.

"They all contain subliminals, if that's what you mean," Mantle said, coming around from behind the bar. Shock the little fisherman and maybe he won't leave his bags, Mantle told himself. I don't need a guest tonight.

"And not all the triggers are visual," he continued. "There are some audio and olfactory sublims. I've even got several inductors hooked up; they're like very subtle tachisto-scopes."

"You're perverse," Pfeiffer said, but he craned his neck and looked into the other room. "Why are you painting that crap, you're a fine artist."

"I'm an illustrator, remember? A subliminal technician." He thought it a confession rather than a statement of fact. "And why should subliminals affect the quality of art? Rembrandt used embeds in the seventeenth century. Did that make him a lesser painter?"

"Well, it won't make you a better one."

Mantle laughed, and Pfeiffer said, "Don't beg the question. Why are you painting that stuff and keeping it in your house?"

"What does it matter?" Mantle asked. "You don't think they have any effect, anyway."

"I never said that, and you know it. I just don't think they have *much* effect. For the most part, we still choose products on the basis of quality, and like it or not, the same basic values remain. But I think you're crazy to expose yourself to subliminals like this."

"You once told me that you don't believe in the unconscious, either," Mantle said. "So these subs should have no effect on you."

Pfeiffer blushed, and Mantle found himself facing him. Too close, he could smell Pfeiffer's sour breath, see the faint chicken-lines in his soft face. And suddenly Mantle thought of Josiane. A flicker of memory, a flash: Josiane lost in a crowd, screaming. A complex of risors reflecting distant sunlight. Brooklyn swathed in grayness. But there was no emotional component; he had simply watched a few frames of a film that played in his mind.

Breaking away from Pfeiffer, he began to talk, hoping to jar his memory again. He was talking to himself; Pfeiffer was only a catalyst. "After Josiane was lost, I searched everywhere, did everything possible to find her. But she might as well have been swallowed up. I couldn't stand the thought that she might be dead, or that she might be only a mile away and I would never find her. It was all too close to me; that's one of the reasons I left the States."

"What were the other reasons?"

"One of my European sources found a woman who fit her description."

"Surely it was a hoax," Pfeiffer said.

Mantle nodded. "But I stayed on anyway. I couldn't face going back home. That was two years ago."

"Then you've given up." Pfeiffer stood in the doorway between the sitting room and living room and gazed at the painting of the dead bird.

"No, I never gave up." Mantle sat down in one of the uncomfortable high-backed chairs and watched Pfeiffer. Then he said, "I began painting privately as therapy. But I couldn't live with the paintings. I kept seeing things in them that weren't there."

"Like what?" Pfeiffer asked.

"I saw demonic faces, strange beasts, my own face, and people I knew," Mantle continued. "So I began turning my hallucinations into subembeds. Once I painted them into pictures, they no longer threatened me. And I supposed that, by painting my fears and visions, I could trick my memory."

"Did that work?"

"Not really," Mantle said. "I found bits and pieces, but not enough to make a difference." He regretted telling Pfeiffer anything. But Pfeiffer's presence had joggled his memory. For an instant, Mantle had *seen* Josiane; that was important, not what Pfeiffer thought. "I threw out a whole batch of those early paintings. I didn't even gesso them over; they could have been used again. But I had this crazy fear that somehow I would be able to see right through the gesso to the original painting. I couldn't live with them.

"I continued to paint in my spare time—I'm here on loan to Eurofax as a consultant, as you probably know. They kept me busy. Anyway, I traveled inland and all over the coast, but soon I wasn't painting for myself anymore. I began to pick up a lot of commission work. And, of course, I experimented with new kinds and combinations of subliminals, but I didn't use nearly as many as in the paintings you see around you." After a pause, Mantle said, "And I see you're still looking."

Pfeiffer turned away from the paintings. "Then for whom did you paint these?" he asked, making a gesture toward the living room.

"I started making paintings for every woman I slept with," Mantle said. "It became a kind of game. My work didn't frighten me as much as it had before—"

"What about the work you do for Eurofax?" Pfeiffer asked.

"What about it?"

"Didn't all that subliminal stuff upset you?"

Mantle chuckled. "I experimented with subs as a way of working out my problems, and most of the work I did translated easily into fax and other media. Made quite an impact, actually. On the whole industry. But translating my ideas for fax was a technical, not an emotional, problem. I'm old-fashioned: my inspiration still comes from brush, canvas, and the old masters."

Don't look so smug, Mantle thought. We *both* sold out.

"You were saying that your work didn't frighten you," Pfeiffer said.

"Oh, yes, not as much as it had before. So I began trying to trick my memory again by painting the past."

"But these are all landscapes. . . ."

"The real paintings are hidden under those you see," Mantle said. "They're models of my memory, sort of. There—" He stepped past Pfeiffer into the living room and pointed at a large painting in a simple metal frame. "That looks like the Cours Mirabeau—see the fountains and the plane trees and smoky sky? But the real picture is hidden in all that prettiness. Look at it long enough and you'll see a Slung City, then the fountains and trees will disappear. And finally, if I've done it correctly, they will both register. Memory works like that. You're gazing at the ocean and suddenly you're seeing a city where you once lived or a woman you've known."

"They're portraits of your past," Pfeiffer said, looking relieved.

"As an exercise," Mantle continued, "I painted some 'portraits' for friends, such as yourself. Some of the people I never expect to see; in fact, some are dead, or probably dead."

"Then why did you bother?"

"Anything might help me remember," Mantle said. "Even seeing you. If only I could remember, no matter how bad it might be, then maybe I could rest."

"But you know what happened to Josiane. She got caught up in the Scream. She's either dead or a Screamer. Same difference."

"And you are still a sonofabitch."

Pfeiffer looked taken aback, but Mantle recognized it as an affectation. "Jesus Christ," Pfeiffer said. "It has to be faced."

"I know it happened, but I don't know how it happened, or exactly what happened. I don't *remember*. I can't see it. . . ." For an instant, Mantle thought that Pfeiffer was gloating. Yes, he had seen that. Well, he had confessed, lapsed back into old patterns. It's my own fault, he told himself. But how Pfeiffer must have wanted that confession.

"You can't even remember the Scream?" Pfeiffer asked. "You *were* there."

"I don't remember any of it. What I know is what I've

been told, but it didn't happen to *me*. I can't even remember
Josiane." She's a holo on my desk, you sonofabitch, help me.

"It's the spider and the fly," Pfeiffer said, changing the
subject as if he had heard enough.

"What?" Mantle asked.

"Sympathetic magic. It's as if you thought that you could
bring us out of your past with a paintbrush."

"Perhaps I should have washed my brushes," Mantle
said, collecting himself.

"So you really did want me to come...."

Mantle walked around the living room, as if to gain
comfort from his paintings, then sat down on the divan. He
had to get Pfeiffer out of here. Pfeiffer sat down beside him.
"There's a painting for Caroline, too."

"Which one is it?" Pfeiffer asked, looking genuinely
surprised.

"Aha, that *you'll* have to figure out by yourself."

"Tell me," Pfeiffer said, a hint of anxiety in his voice. But
Mantle shook his head.

"How is Caroline?" Mantle asked. "Is she still taking
those crazy rejuvenation treatments?"

"I haven't seen Caroline for five months," Pfeiffer said,
his face turned away from Mantle. "We decided that a short
separation was in order, what with my work and—"

"You mean she left you."

So Caroline finally got up the nerve to cut herself loose
from him, Mantle thought, remembering. Caroline had been
trying to leave Carl since she was nineteen, but Carl needed
to care for his fragile flower, his little solipsist, as he called
her, lest she turn inward again and lose touch with the
world—the real world of Pfeiffer's books and Pfeiffer's career
and Pfeiffer's dreams: Pfeiffer, the maddened sleepwalker, the
man with no unconscious. Hadn't he started her on her career
as a novelist, didn't he correct and criticize all her work
didn't he rewrite her stories, didn't he provide the main
income and fame?—Never mind that Caroline had the critical
reputation, that her books were all in covers, and that
without any self-promotion. But Carl promoted her work,
made sure it reached the proper people.

"She didn't exactly leave me," Pfeiffer said, moving
closer to Mantle on the divan. Uncomfortable, Mantle edged
away. He felt that Pfeiffer was already suffocating him. Ironi-

cally, Pfeiffer had always kept a physical distance from Mantle, who needed less psychological space. Once, before they became involved with each other, they circled an entire room at a press club cocktail party, Mantle stepping forward to talk face-to-face, Pfeiffer stepping back, fumbling for an inhalor, excusing himself to check on Caroline and to freshen his drink.

"I can't imagine you two apart," Mantle said, excited and elated over Pfeiffer's misfortune. As the old guilt rose again, he tried to press it down like a cork on an opened wine bottle. "You'll just have to be strong."

"Oh, no, it's not like that," Pfeiffer said, defensive. "Separation was the natural thing. Our careers were moving in different directions; we began to have different interests."

"Of course," Mantle said, becoming fidgety, trying to think up excuses to dissuade Pfeiffer from staying. He sensed that a trap was about to close.

"But that's all in the past," Pfeiffer said, "and I'm using this time to acclimate myself to my new life."

"That's very good," Mantle said hollowly. "I'm sorry to have to cut this so short, Carl, but I have an engagement tonight and . . ."

"Jesus, I haven't seen you in five years. Is that all you can say?"

"Well, I'm sorry, Carl." *Take a goddamn hint!* He forced himself to look directly at Pfeiffer who, then, lowered his eyes.

"Would you mind if I stayed here with you for a few days?" Pfeiffer asked.

Horrified, Mantle heard himself say, "No."

Three

When Mantle finally received a call from Pretre, he was lying on his bed and watching Josiane move about his locked bedroom as she dressed. She kept turning toward him, gesticulating and speaking silently. Mantle had turned off the audio. He knew all the words: he had run this holographic sequence a thousand times.

He had this room redone as a duplicate of their old bedroom in New York. It was to Josiane's taste: an odd mixture of antiques and modern rounded architecture. There was almost something oriental about the room, Mandarin. On the walls were mirrors, fanlights, and a glazed and coved cabinet. The bed was beside a computer console built unobtrusively into the ornamented wall; above the console was a large, arched mirror. The slightly domed ceiling was a mirrored mosaic from which hung a chandelier of white crystal flowers. The rug, which Josiane seemed to glide over, was deep red and blue with a floral design that matched the ceramic tiles on the door and lower part of the walls.

It was a mausoleum, an untidy showcase of Josiane's oddments that Mantle had collected: diaries (both his and Josiane's), holos, old fische and photographs, old fax clippings, annotated calendars; even clothes, jewelry, and toiletries were strewn about the room as if Josiane had just left in a hurry. And hidden in drawers and pockets were letters, notes, and various papers; they were the keys to his memory, which he could not bring himself to trust to the computer Net.

Mantle disappeared Josiane when the telie buzzed.

The holographic image of a neatly dressed man appeared, as if seated naturally, in the center of the bedroom.

"Ah, Monsieur Mantle," Pretre said, mispronouncing the name. "Again I see you have not turned on your visual. If we are ever to meet, how will I be able to recognize you?" Pretre was dressed in brown with a white shirt buttoned to the neck; he looked, as he always did, uncomfortable.

"I'm not dressed," Mantle lied, "and everything is such a mess." He made an arc with his arm, as if Pretre could see. But Mantle wouldn't let *anyone* see or come inside this room. "I'm *sure* you'll recognize me when the time comes," Mantle said sarcastically. "Now tell me what you have."

"You realize that when I called earlier, I made you no promises."

"Yes, yes," Mantle said. "Now, is there going to be a plug-in service or not?"

"A deal has been made with the church to let you participate," Pretre said.

"A deal?"

"As I explained to them, you are a man of honor and truly interested in conversion. However, if you have second thoughts..." Pretre had the look of a zealot; to Mantle it seemed that all religious fanatics were incongruous-looking, too neatly dressed, hair too sharply trimmed, shoes too polished. They all looked uncomfortable, as if clothes and body were coffins for the soul.

"What do you want in return?" Mantle asked.

"As I said, if you have second thoughts. I really think we must conclude this—"

"Where shall we meet, then, and when?" Mantle asked.

"Of course, when we meet is contingent upon the demise of the one who is offering himself to the church," Pretre said, bowing his head slightly; oddly, the pious gesture did not seem pompous. "But, as is mostly the case, *le Crier* will die at the appointed time."

"Which is...?"

"Why don't you take a walk to the Quai Saint Pierre tonight at about eight o'clock," Pretre said. "It is still Festival, and very beautiful at night. Now, if you will turn on the visual for an instant so I will be able to recognize you—"

"I'm sure my holo is in your file," Mantle said, about to switch off the phone.

"Ah, but that is not fair, nor is it the way we do things. Now, I have been patient with you; it is your turn to do me the courtesy of proper introduction."

"All right," Mantle said, making an adjustment on the computer console so that only a sliver of the room could be seen. Then he struck the visual key much too hard and leaned forward.

Pretre smiled uncharacteristically and said, "Very pretty." Then the image disappeared, leaving the smoke flower, the symbol of the church, which dissipated into the room.

It had begun to drizzle. Thunder rumbled in the north; within an hour the wind would rise and the mists would be broken by pelting rain. But that would not dissuade anyone from going to Festival; the locals would splash about and let the rain dissolve their traditional paper clothes. Everyone else would be carrying rain repellors.

Pfeiffer had insisted on coming along with Mantle, at least as far as the quay; he had to pick up the rest of his bags at the old Carleton Hotel, anyway, and he was at loose ends. It was difficult to imagine Pfeiffer without his self-imposed regimen of writing and napping and watching the tube; in the old days Pfeiffer would work all night and never go out. Mantle had never gotten used to the constant clatterclack of Carl's and Caroline's old-fashioned typewriters; in more paranoic moments, he had entertained the idea that they were trying to make him insecure because he wasn't working.

And now the little fisherman has nothing to do, Mantle thought. Then he was seized with the aching loneliness that he associated with Josiane. As always, he could almost remember her; but even in those few childhood memories of Josiane that were left to him, she was out of focus.

They walked south toward the boulevard and the quay. The street was becoming crowded, and the sky was alight with color. The boom-boom of distant fireworks could be heard as the locals kept their holiday in the old fashion. Curfews had been temporarily lifted, and there were children laughing in the streets. Indeed, it was like the old days before the Scream.

"Where are you going tonight?" Mantle asked, regretting the question even as he asked it. He was making small talk because he was nervous about meeting Pretre, who could lead him to Josiane. He would fine her, even if it meant passing through the dead.

"More to the point," Pfeiffer said, "where are you going?"

"I was invited to a plug-in ceremony."

"Christ, you are morbid as ever. Going to a funeral service on Saturday night. Anyone I might know?" There was a touch of humor in Pfeiffer's voice. "Who is it, then?" he asked more seriously, but he didn't wait for an answer. "I think the plug-in ceremony is disgusting. It violates the dead."

Mantle chuckled, albeit nervously; if he weren't on his way to meet some unknown, dead Screamer (and if he weren't haunted by Josiane), he might enjoy the cool dampness of the evening and Pfeiffer's prissiness. It was raining hard now; a full moon could be seen as a bright smear in the mist above. But the rain didn't reach Mantle and Pfeiffer, who had activated their rain repellors and were walking along briskly, creating a wake like a ship at sea. "They're not really dead," Mantle said. "After all, psyconductors can't work unless there is some brain activity. So the person you're plugging into must be alive, at least clinically."

"But dead in the real sense," Pfeiffer said.

"It's no different than using a psyconductor in court or family counseling or, for that matter, for pleasure," Mantle said. "One can't get any closer than by touching another's mind. Brain activity is life itself."

"You sound like the man who directed my mother's funeral," Pfeiffer said. Mantle laughed; Pfeiffer had actually developed a sense of humor in the intervening years. Then Pfeiffer was serious again. "It's the same as necrophilia, this plugging-in with the dead. And plug-in necrophilia is actually becoming common at funerals."

"But you plugged into your mother when she died, didn't you?" Mantle asked, baiting him.

Pfeiffer blushed. "She insisted. When she first became ill, she begged me, and I promised."

"And was it so terrible?"

"I found it revolting, it makes my skin crawl to remember it." Pfeiffer quickened his pace, as if he could leave the memory behind. Mantle began to feel more anxious about meeting Pretre and entering the mind of a dead Screamer. Hooking into a Screamer, or anyone who was mentally unbalanced, could be disastrous, especially if one was prone to schizophrenia. The bicameral Screamers, just like our ancestors who heard the voices of the gods they worshiped, carried the voices and visions of their community in the right lobes of their brains. But to know one Screamer's thoughts was also to know, at least potentially, the thoughts and memories of every other, even those who had passed into the black and silver regions of death.

And one of those voices might be Josiane's.

When they reached the quay, it had stopped raining. The streets were comfortably filled with locals and visitors alike, everyone dressed in costume. A parade made its way down the boulevard like a great, colorful, segmented bug. Lightsticks burned in rainbow colors, held by all manner of demons and beasts and angels and religious figures. Children were up late and cavorting with the spirits, playing *jump-the-cross* and begging for the indestructible American money. Looking across the port, Mantle could see the festival floats covered with mimosa, roses, carnations, violets, narcissus, and hyacinth. The wetness seemed to make everything pellucid, preternaturally bright; Mantle was reminded of Mardigras in New Orleans. Indeed, Shrove Tuesday was not far away.

"You'd best get to the hotel for your bags," Mantle said to Pfeiffer as he looked around for Pretre, wondering if he would come at all.

"There's plenty of time for that," Pfeiffer said; he seemed to be enjoying the noisy Festival atmosphere. "Come on, let's take some wine before your rendezvous." Another touch of sarcasm there.

Mantle thought he glimpsed Pretre, who disappeared behind some people. "I'll see you later, then, at the house."

"Come on," Pfeiffer said earnestly, "we'll all have a drink together or, perhaps, something to eat. It is time." For all his bluster and show of independence, Pfeiffer did not do will alone except when he was writing—and even then he preferred to have people around so he could read his work aloud. "Perhaps I can join you. I can wait for you during the service, and then you can show me the town." He smiled. "I haven't had a woman in some time, you know."

Pfeiffer's false show of intimacy embarrassed Mantle. Again Mantle felt trapped, as if Pfeiffer really did have hooks into him. "Dammit, Carl, hasn't it occurred to you that I might not feel like seeing the town tonight? Or not feel like seeing you? I have something to do, give me some room."

Pfeiffer, ever the immovable object, said, "The funeral is only going to depress you. Going out will make you feel better."

"Fuck off," Mantle said wearily. "You haven't changed at all, have you? You still can't understand *no*."

"All right, Raymond, I'm sorry. But you can at least tell me what kind of ceremony it is that you can't take me."

"The ceremony is for a Screamer," Mantle said, watching for Pretre. "Now would you still like to come along?" he asked, turning to Pfeiffer. "Perhaps you could plug-in and meet your mother."

"I said I was sorry, Raymond." How Mantle hated the way Pfeiffer still used his full Christian name, as if Pfeiffer were a professor addressing a callow, pimply-faced student. "You don't have to reach to try to hurt me, especially with my mother. You were close to her once upon a time, remember?" Pfeiffer stood his ground, his presence suffocating Mantle more than the people around him. It was then that Mantle became aware that the Festival gathering was becoming dense, turning into a crowd which might become dangerous.

Mantle caught sight of Pretre and saw that Joan was with him. "Damn," he said under his breath, forgetting about Pfeiffer, who was saying something to him. What's *she* doing here? Does she think she's going along? Joan had introduced Pretre to Mantle as a favor—she had interviewed him once, she said; but never, never had she spoken of having ever been to a ceremony. He felt conflicting emotions. Seeing her again, especially now, excited him. He loved her more than he admitted, felt protective toward her, and didn't want her around as there might be trouble. But more than that, he didn't want to share Josiane with her. For a split second, though, he considered giving up the whole venture. He could have his own life with Joan; after all, the past was already buried.

Mantle waved at Joan and Pretre, who acknowledged by waving back. They made their way toward him through the crowd.

Could she have been a member of that fucking church all along? Mantle asked himself. Anger and anxiety began to boil inside him. Pfeiffer took his arm to get his attention. "You don't want to get involved with that sort of thing. What's the matter with you?" Pfeiffer asked—a bit too loudly, for an American couple nearby were staring at him. "Plugging into a Screamer is illegal and dangerous, and the fate of the Christian Criers is in litigation."

"You can't litigate faith," Mantle said, and then he turned to greet Joan and Pretre.

"Hello, darling," Joan said to Mantle. She appeared to be out of breath, but Mantle knew that as a sure sign of her nervousness. "I'm sorry we're late...the usual problems. Jesus, it's more crowded than we expected." She looked over at Pfeiffer and said hello. Pretre glared at Pfeiffer, then turned his gaze toward Mantle.

"Carl Pfeiffer, this is Joan Otur," Mantle mumbled. Ignoring Pfeiffer and Pretre, he asked Joan, "What the hell are you doing here?"

"I thought to come with you," she said, her eyes averted. "The first time can be a bit unhinging."

"Then you have done this before," Mantle said, feeling himself turning cold, and controlled. "And you never told me. Why?"

"I kept losing my nerve. I was going to try to tell you when you came back from Naples. I was going to try. . . ." She composed herself and looked him directly in the eyes. "It seems you have brought someone else, also," she said, then turned to smile at Pfeiffer who looked a bit embarrassed and bewildered, as did Pretre. But Pretre also looked anxious.

"Carl is not staying," Mantle said.

"I think, perhaps, I'd better leave," Pretre said curtly. "Another time."

"Oh, no, Francois," Joan said, taking Pretre's arm. "Stay, please." They made an odd couple: straight, stiff, squarely cut and uncomfortable Pretre; and Joan, who was tiny, with short-cropped hair, pale, full face, and an air of casual Midwestern sureness, if not sophistication. "Carl is a friend of Ray's. It will be all right, I pledge so."

Pretre seemed to relax a bit. He looked coyly at Mantle and said, "I do not know your Raymond, except for a momentary glimpse." It suddenly occurred to Mantle that, like Joan, Pretre was a poseur: the mock motions of fluttering and business, the ill-fitting, crinkle-neat uniform of the obedient convert were all protective guises. He suddenly saw Pretre as a survivor of the riots and burnings and camps.

"Joan, I want to speak with you for a moment," Mantle said, and he nodded to Pretre and left him standing awkwardly before Pfeiffer.

"You should not have come here."

"But I wanted to be with you, to share the past, to help you find it," she said, looking earnestly up at him. "You'll be different after you plug-into the Crier, and I want to be there to begin with you anew."

"You should have told me what you are. Liar."

"You weren't ready, and—can't you see?—I'm telling you now, just by being here, everything I've done—"

It was too late. "Does Pretre know why I want to plug-into a Screamer?"

Joan shrugged, her only affectation, and said, "Yes, I told him you are obsessed with the past; that—"

"It was a setup. From the beginning."

"There was no other way to do it. And it was what *you* wanted." It was to Joan's credit that she did not shrink from Mantle's stare. Poseur, he thought. User. Of course, subliminal engineers were always in demand, and most churches were evangelistic. Joan had done her homework. Well, he thought. It's fair. Mutual using.

"I don't want you along," Mantle said firmly.

"I do love you," Joan said, and, irrationally, Mantle believed her. But Joan was not Josiane. "We both have conflicting loyalties," she continued, "and secrets to be shared. But don't shut me out, not now. I came to help you, perhaps plug-in and share—"

"You can help me by getting Pfeiffer out of my hair."

"I don't think Pretre would permit that." Her voice lowered in register, becoming flat, cold. "He knows that plugging in could be dangerous for you."

"For *me*?" Mantle asked.

"Well," she said, shrugging again, then looking at him directly, defiantly, "you *have* admitted to right-brain tendencies. . . . I'm sorry, Ray. Let's stop this right now. Please, I want to be with you. It's no trick of the church."

"Is there anything you haven't told Pretre?"

"No," she said, and accepting the inevitable, turned to Pfeiffer. "Carl, would you like to accompany me to my club for a drink while these two attend to their business?" Pretre gave her a nasty look; unmindful, she took Pfeiffer's arm. Pfeiffer, who seemed interested in Joan, started to say something to Mantle, but thought better of it and said, "All right, but I think we should meet later."

You won't want to see me later, Mantle thought. He nodded and told them he would join them at the club or her apartment later if he could, although he had no intention of doing so. They didn't need him around to have sex. Mantle looked at Joan. There was a momentary awkwardness, shared sadness and regret, and then she and Pfeiffer left arm in arm, swallowed into the happy crowd as the old-fashioned fireworks boomed and spiraled in the windy air above.

Pretre silently led the way to the nearest transpod station. As they walked, the fireworks died away and the entire quay as far as La Castre became a huge videotecture. Lasers recreated the interior of Amiens Cathedral, which had been destroyed by terrorists; imaginary naves and chapels floated, as if in God's thoughts, above the Festival. People passed through the aisles and holy walls of the holographic structure like angels moving to and fro in heavenly reverie. The crowd was thick near the transpod station, everyone howling and halooing. As if on cue, hawkers appeared everywhere, selling their wares: holy inhalors with a touch of the dust of Palestine, shards of the true cross, magical silver amulets, and bone fragments of the true Christ. There was even an old woman dressed in rags selling dates, halvah, and plastic phylacteries.

It certainly was like the old days, Mantle thought.

"Come on, hurry," Pretre said, obviously disgusted with the goings-on around him. A car was waiting inside the small, glassite station, and a transpod rut descended into the ground a few meters away. The transpod looked like a translucent egg; it was computer controlled and driven by a propulsion system built into the narrow rut.

Pretre punched in the coordinates, opaqued the walls for privacy, and with a slight jar, they were off.

"Where is the ceremony taking place?" Mantle asked after a few moments to break the awkward silence. Pretre seemed to be lost in contemplation, as if he were deciding whether to take Mantle to the funeral after all.

"Near Plage du Dramont," Pretre said. "South of here."

A long pause, and then Mantle asked, "Has Joan told you why I want to attend the ceremony?"

"Yes," Pretre said matter-of-factly. "She told me of your lost wife, Josiane. A terrible thing, but a common problem these days."

"If you know that, why are you taking me to the ceremony?"

"So that you can see and believe that, but the grace of our Screamers, as you call them, we have not only found a new faith, but another, higher form of consciousness," Pretre said.

"And if I remain an unbeliever?"

Pretre shrugged. "Then at least you will owe us a favor.

Perhaps you will regain your memory, perhaps not. Perhaps this dying Crier can take you to your wife's thoughts, perhaps not. But I'm reasonably certain that you would not want to make public what you see tonight, as we could certainly affect your position with the newsfax. Given your previous record and your incarceration after you left New York . . ."

Mantle held back his anger; it would not do to spoil his chance at a plug-in now.

"We still have a bit of a ride," Pretre said. "If you like, I can give you a blow-job." That was said in his matter-of-fact voice, which was now without a trace of an accent.

"Why did you bring Joan?" Mantle asked, ignoring Pretre's polite suggestion.

"That was for your own safety. It was her suggestion—she's concerned for you. You know the chances of getting lost in another's mind, or you should. You might become a Crier yourself." Pretre smiled, enjoying the irony. "The presence of a familiar, sympathetic mind could help you, should you lapse into fugue. Now you take your chances. Whatever you might think of Joan now, she does love you, and has for quite some time. Of that I can assure you. I thought you treated her rather badly. Of course, that's none of my business. . . ."

"That's right," Mantle said. "It isn't." But Pretre was right: Mantle had treated her badly. He had always treated her badly. And now he was afraid of being alone. Suddenly, everything seemed hard, metallic, hollow. Mantle remembered his first experience with enlightenment drugs; how the trip reversed and he scammed down into the stinking bowels of his mind, through the hard tunnels of thought where everything was dead and leaden.

He might become lost inside the Screamer and still not find Josiane. At the thought, his insides seemed to open up, his heart began to pound, and he had a sudden rush of claustrophobia. Where was Joan to protect him . . . ?

"If you don't mind, I'm going to transparent the walls," he told Pretre as he pressed the appropriate stud.

"Are you all right?" Pretre asked.

"A touch of motion sickness, that's all."

They were above-ground now, near the city's edge. In a cold sweat, Mantle watched the tiers of fenestrated glasstex whiz past, studded with sunlights. The city blazed like noon under a night sky. A few moments later, they were rushing through darkness again, along the coast, through the ribbon of country. City lights were a mushroom glow behind them, stars blinked wanly overhead. Mantle's claustrophobia was replaced by vertigo.

"Some of the Esterel is still untouched by the cities," Pretre said, staring eastward in the direction of the ocean. "This used to be a beautiful country, full of flowers and grass and cathedrals."

Mantle smiled (did Pretre think cathedrals grew out of the ground like orange trees?), and then remembered his own country, remembered Binghamton and its hilly surrounds. As a boy, he had vision-quested for four days and three nights atop a hill near his home. How different that had been from his experience with enlightenment drugs. But that was a lifetime ago, before new Route 17 and the furious urbanization around the mechanized highway. That old vision-quest hill had been leveled as if it had never been. But the movement of the transpod calmed him, and Mantle fancied that he was a passenger on an old railroad train—he was riding the ancient Phoebe Snow, and he was heading into Binghamton.

Just then Pretre unnerved him by asking, "Your original home is Binghamton, isn't it?"

"Yes," Mantle replied, wondering for an instant if Pretre had read his mind. Coincidence, and his thoughts turned to Joan. She had told Pretre everything, he knew that. She was probably sitting down at a table with Pfeiffer at her club right now. He imagined that Pfeiffer would be holding forth about poor Raymond, what a waste, and Joan would listen intently and nod her head. Later, she would take him home to bed.

Until now, Mantle hadn't been possessive with Joan; he had not had those feelings since Josiane. Joan had always had other relationships, and Mantle even encouraged them.

It was Pfeiffer. He could not imagine her wanting to have Pfeiffer. The fat fucking fisherman! But that was another deception, and Mantle new it. He was simply afraid of losing her. It was the old, old anxiety surfacing.

Well, fuck her, he thought. She was loving me for the church. I must have sensed it, he told himself. Maybe that's why we made love so rarely. He felt himself getting an erection. Now he wanted her when it was too late.

"You look nervous, my friend," Pretre said. "Would you like a tranquilizer? It will calm you, but not affect your thinking. And it will wear off by the time we reach the beach." Pretre was staring at him intently, which did make Mantle nervous.

"No, thank you," Mantle said as he looked at the dark shapes and shadows whisking past like specters in a dream of falling. "I don't take any drugs if I can help it."

"Ah, since your incarceration, perhaps?"

"It has nothing to do with that." You faggot sonofabitch, Mantle thought. He still had an erection.

Pretre took another tack. His voice became louder, more hollow-sounding and the accent returned. "Binghamton was blessed with Criers, wasn't it? Consumed, as it were, by the Singing Crowds."

Mantle grimaced as he remembered returning to his old neighborhood, which had been ravaged by the Screamer mobs. They had killed his mother in her bed. Yes, he thought, again feeling a rush of anxiety and guilt, Binghamton was certainly blessed.

"But that should not have happened," Pretre continued, "because according to your theorists, the population density was nowhere near Beshefe's limit. Beshefe was his name, I think." The sarcasm in his voice was as thick as his accent.

"People become Screamers as a reaction to stress," Mantle said. "There are many ways to measure social stress, all approximations. Beshefe was a social scientist, not a physicist."

"Do you also believe our Criers are just schizophrenics?" Pretre asked. "Joan once believed that." He smiled, obviously toying with Mantle, who was in no mood for it.

It will soon be over, he told himself, while his thoughts darted from the past to present, back and forth, like fireflies in the darkness of his memory.

He remembered his first newsfax assignment in Washington, although it was hard to imagine that there were mobs and riots before the Screamers. He had worn a riot-cowl and had packed a small stun weapon that was little more than a toy. He had been so afraid that he'd kept saying "Jesus Christ" into his recorder. He could remember it as clearly as if he were still standing there in burning College Park, choking on the stink of explosives and burned flesh, listening to people scream. Like horses, they had tried to bolt, but everyone was trapped in the crowd. He remembered Dodds, who had been standing beside him and shouting into his recorder until half his face was blown away; and how for one eternal heartbeat they had stared at each other before Dodds fell and died. In that last moment, Mantle had felt nothing but surprise. But deep inside was one thought: that it would soon be over. One way or another.

I'll find Josiane, he told himself, confirming it.

"Well?" Pretre asked. "What do you think?"

"Schizophrenia is a reaction to stress," Mantle said. "But it's also a function of an individual's biochemistry and early environment. The Screamers are somewhat different, obviously."

"Ah, somewhat different," Pretre said. "Now tell me how they are different."

"Jesus Christ," Mantle said. "They're bicameral, they hallucinate instead of think, they're telepathic. You must know what I think about Screamers. Certainly Joan has told you. She's told you everything else."

"She doesn't know *everything* about you."

Mantle held back his anger; only his balled fist betrayed him. Was Pretre a Screamer? he asked himself. If not partially bicameral, he was certainly schizo—

"You probably think I'm mad, don't you?" Pretre asked as he stared vacantly ahead, his head cocked as if he were trying to hear something distant.

Mantle felt a chill. More than schizophrenic, he thought.

"No," he continued, "I'm just a bit deaf, as are all of us who belong to the Church of the Christian Criers." Pretre paused as if waiting for a cue from Mantle.

"Go on," Mantle said. He was nervous, as he always was in the presence of those who had slippery minds.

"When we're together in a ceremony, when we hook-into a holy Crier, then—for that precious short time—we can hear the voices of the other world which has been silent so long. We can hear the voice of any Crier who wishes to communicate, even if that Crier be dead."

Josiane! Mantle thought, almost saying her name aloud. For an instant, he thought he actually could see her face before him. It was such a beautiful face: strong yet delicate, framed in a halo of baby-fine, curly hair. I love you, my sister, please let me find you. . . .

He thought of Joan: such was his perversity. But her pleading face could not draw him back.

"Sometimes I can hear the whispering of the other world when I'm alone," Pretre said. "Sometimes I hear the departed Criers." He jabbed Mantle lightly in the crotch and, feeling an erection, let his hand linger. "And I suspect that you will hear a voice or two yourself."

Four

Joan took Pfeiffer to her club, which was within walking distance on the Rue de Latour-Maubourg, which angled off from the Boulevard de la Croisette. The club was a seedy bar called The Exchange, and was Irish. It was not a tourist spot as was Hell's Knell, with its sawdust floor and jazz bands, but just a hole in the wall where one could get a stiff drink and an American hamburger.

"I've heard of this place," Pfeiffer said, sliding into a booth as Joan took the opposite side.

"Is it what you expected?"

"I would imagine that its reputation is mostly a fake," he replied, looking toward the burly barkeep who was Irish, and then around at the booths and tables, not yet filled.

Joan smiled. Ray was right, she thought. Pfeiffer's lack of humor and subtlety was somehow endearing. For him, everything carried the same weight and deserved the same consideration. "Well," she said, "there was an incident once that made it a tourist attraction for a while. But now it's mostly fax people, bureaucrats, and an occasional diplomat."

"I'm worried about Raymond," Pfeiffer said, looking at her as if he needed to know everything about Mantle now, even before tasting a drink. As if on cue, the barkeep appeared to welcome Joan, make some small talk, and take their order—bourbon with a chaser for him, a Campari for her; then he left, thereby giving Joan a chance to recover from Pfeiffer's question. He was fishing: the least he could do was wait until she'd had a drink.

"I'm sure Ray will be fine," she said coolly, but she was anxious about him and wondered if he had plugged in yet. It's my own fault I'm not with him, she told herself. But he *would* be fine, she thought, only half believing it. In some ways Mantle was one of the strongest people she had ever met, and yet he was also one of the most insecure. He was open about it, accepted it, and guiltlessly used her to shore himself up from time to time. All those hours spent listening to him talk incessantly about his painting and subliminals and his fear of failure. He constantly compared himself to his peers, especially to Pfeiffer and his wife. There was something repellent about him when he was like that; perhaps it was because Joan needed him to be strong.

"I think this business with the Screamers is crazy," Pfeiffer said, staring intently at Joan. "And I think this cult of yours is even crazier." He paused, waiting for a reaction; receiving none, he said, "Raymond's always been on the edge, even before Josiane disappeared."

There was something about the way Pfeiffer said "Raymond" that Joan didn't like, but she didn't take the bait. Although she agreed with him about Ray being on the edge (and, perhaps because of that, also terribly sane), she made a disbelieving face.

"It's all in his medical records," he said, slumping down in his chair a bit, as if exposing Mantle's little secrets were a grave and difficult burden to bear. "He has definite right-brain tendencies. And his corpus callosum is slightly thicker than normal, which is the case with many schizophrenics and your Screamers. The corpus callosum connects the two hemispheres in the brain—"

"Jesus Christ," she snapped. "What's wrong with using your whole brain?" She caught herself and said, evenly, "You seem to've made quite a study of Ray. He must be very happy to have a friend who is so concerned."

"I am concerned," Pfeiffer said earnestly, seemingly missing her point, or possibly just ignoring her derision. Perhaps Ray was right: Pfeiffer might be the grand solipsist, wending his way around a world made for him, all the mirrors of the world reflecting only his own face. And yet there was something about him that reminded her of Ray.

"I'm afraid he *will* go over the edge if he plugs-into a Screamer," Pfeiffer continued.

"There's always that chance," she said evenly, but she was feeling panic. Her relationship with Mantle had been a series of small losses and loneliness leading up to tonight. It could have been different tonight, she told herself. I should have been with him. It's my fault. I've lost him now, really lost him. . . .

"But there's no chance of him finding Josiane," Pfeiffer said with finality. "She's probably dead or else she's running slack-jawed with a gang of Screamers somewhere in New York. Either way, she's beyond his reach."

"Perhaps not," Joan said, recovering.

"Bunk," Pfeiffer said, waving for a drink. There was a waiter on duty now, and a battered old Thring domestic robot keeping the back station where Joan and Pfeiffer were sitting. The club was becoming crowded.

"Do you want another drink?" Pfeiffer asked Joan as the robot hesitated beside their booth. The robot, although otherwise clean and burnished, had the flag of the old Irish Republic sloppily painted on its chest. It had a jolly, stereotyped Irish face on its video display; and it spoke in brogue. Although the robot moved smoothly on hidden wheels, it had the rectangular look of something that should rattle and squeak, like a twentieth-century automobile.

Joan and Pfeiffer ordered another drink, and the robot whispered off.

"Raymond won't find anything inside the Screamer but the last flickers of a dying mind," Pfeiffer said. "Did you know that Raymond had to be incarcerated in a sanatorium after he plugged into his psychiatrist?"

"What?" Joan asked.

"Ah, that he didn't tell you."

"I did know that he was in a private sanatorium for a time."

"Well," Pfeiffer continued, "it was an experiment to regain his memory—the idea being that the psych could gain access to whatever it was that Mantle was hiding from himself."

"And . . . ?"

"Raymond plugged into the psych, and then went over the edge when the psych started probing. Raymond must have had quite a stake in hiding the information, for he almost killed the psych before the connection was broken. And this doctor was supposed to be experienced in using the psyconductor with patients. The irony is that both of them ended up in the same sanatorium."

"You really don't like Ray, do you?" Joan asked, angry at the way Pfeiffer had told her the story, and angry at herself for being here, for not being with Mantle. And damn the church and Pretre for taking him away, she thought.

"Of course, I like Raymond. Christ, I've known him for twenty years."

"You don't seem to be much of a friend. You talk about him as if he were a thing, not a person."

"I'm sorry you misunderstand me. I know Raymond better than anyone else. I'm speaking of the things about him that worry me. Since I assumed you to be his friend too, I didn't think it necessary to review his good points, although I can do that if you wish." He gave her a wide, boyish grin, then bowed his head to disappear it.

"Okay," Joan said, *"I'm* sorry."

"Forget it."

You asshole, she thought. No wonder Ray hates him. She wondered how Pfeiffer would be sexually. Probably not very good, but then again. . . . He was probably not bisexual, probably fucked-up sexually.

"Do you really believe that Raymond can find Josiane by sticking into a Screamer?"

Another gibe, Joan thought, but she would play a game and take everything seriously, ignore nuance. She could excuse herself, get rid of him; but there was too much she wanted to find out about Ray, and about his relationship with Pfeiffer and Josiane.

"Yes," she said matter-of-factly, "I believe Ray has a chance of finding out about his wife." Smiling, she said, "And one doesn't 'stick-in,' one plugs-in."

Pfeiffer grinned, then his face became serious again, as if the muscles could only hold a smile for an instant. "Is that as bad as calling San Francisco 'Frisco'?" he asked, but the joke fell dead. "I don't think Raymond will ever find Josiane, and I think it's cruel for you and your fanatical friends to endanger him and give him false hopes."

"There *is* a chance," Joan said quietly, praying she was

right and that he wouldn't be harmed. After her holy initiation (she had also plugged into a dying Crier), her faith in the church and its methods seemed unshakable. Now she was having second thoughts. But I *must* believe, she told herself. "Many nonbelievers become converts after plugging in and contacting a lost relative. There are enough documented cases to convince—"

"And how many of your 'cases' went bonkers afterward? You sound like a rabid spiritualist from the last century."

"One cannot trick someone with a psyconductor."

"I'm not at all sure of that."

"And least of all Ray. Tricking people into believing things is *his* business."

"He's as vulnerable as anyone else," Pfeiffer said. "You should realize that. And as I understand it, the procedure won't work *unless* he's in a suggestible state."

"A trance can help you initially break with the world, which you must do when you plug-into the dead, especially into a Crier. But you can't locate a lost friend or wife or relative with a trick. Either the hook-in works or it doesn't. The psyconductor is a scientific instrument, and communicating with the dead is a common and indisputable fact." Joan caught herself, and her face became warm with embarrassment: she was anxiously singing the party song, and even to her, it sounded hollow and foolish. What she had felt as true—and, yes, profound—now sounded silly when put into words. She thought about Ray hooking into the Crier and remembered her own plug-in ceremony, the sense of expansion and uplift, of passing through the layers of the world and drifting through the black and silver spaces; and all she could communicate were a few trite phrases, true as they might be.

"He won't find her," Pfeiffer said. There was a strident edge to his voice.

"How can you be so sure?"

"I really don't think he wants to find her."

"Then why would he go to all this trouble?"

"To deceive himself, to give himself something to live for; maybe to forget his failings. He is, by his own standards, a failure. Surely you can see that."

"I see nothing of the sort," Joan replied angrily. "And don't you think you're being a bit too condescending? People who live in glass houses, and all that sort of thing. . . .?"

Pfeiffer smiled, this time genuinely, or so it seemed, for the smile passed slowly across his face. "Ah, so we return to maxims of great moral truth. You English are so fond of them."

Joan blushed. "The maxim does contain some truth. And I'm not English, I'm American, it's just that I've developed an accent from living abroad—"

"But for every maxim there's a counter-maxim," Pfeiffer said, ignoring her protest. "We aren't so removed from the medieval mind, after all."

"What do you mean?" Joan asked, content to let the conversation drift away from Ray for the moment. She would let Pfeiffer puff himself up.

"The Middle Ages were ruled by maxims and parables from history, legend, and Scripture. They contained all the great moral truths of the age, and were used to defend every action."

"Did you know that Ray has an interest in history?" Joan asked, feeling that she was on safe ground now.

"No, I didn't. He never showed much of an interest in the old days."

"Yes, he's fascinated by the twentieth century."

"Raymond always did have to have an escape."

"What?"

"Nothing."

"You really don't have a single good word for him, do you?" Joan asked.

"I'm sorry. It's not the way you think."

"Do you think yourself so much nobler and more in touch with reality than he? Is *your* profession so much better?"

Now Pfeiffer began to redden, although whether out of anger or humiliation, Joan could not tell. "I don't think of myself as noble, and I see the news medium as the filthy business it is. When I met Raymond, he was unformed but brilliant. Anyone could see that. I've watched him grow and develop and gain control over his craft. And watched him fail on his own terms. He wanted to be an artist, not an illustrator or, worse yet, a subliminal engineer."

"Glass houses. . . . ." Joan said.

"Well, I—"

Joan smiled, and Pfeiffer returned it. "Tell me about Josiane," she asked.

"What do you want to know?"

"Anything. I want to get a feel for what she was like." She watched Pfeiffer's hands as she spoke. He had the annoying habit of twiddling his thumbs, an American mannerism she had forgotten existed; it looked somehow obscene.

"You know, of course, that they're brother and sister."

"Yes."

"Actually, they look quite alike," Pfeiffer said, untangling his fingers and taking a sip of his drink, which was watered down by now. "You can't see it in holos, even if you set them side by side; only in the flesh. Perhaps it was because they had a similar sort of intensity. Of course, they had some of the same facial features. The same kind of bodies, I guess, too. Both long and lanky. But they had very different turns of mind."

"How do you mean?"

"Josiane was a scatter-head. Never finished anything. Very young and immature, really. Always falling in and out of love."

"But that was before she settled down with Ray." She said that like a question.

"Josiane never settled down. It was just that she and her brother shared a mutual romantic dream for a while."

"It seemed to have worked."

"For a while, and in its fashion, but there were always problems."

"As in any relationship," she said, looking into his eyes for a reaction. There was none.

"But Raymond was more stable," Pfeiffer continued. "Except in matters of the heart. Somehow he'd convinced himself that he was in love with his sister."

"She must have felt the same way."

"She was talked into it," Pfeiffer said. "But he had the talent. She was always a nice middle-class wife type."

"That's a sexist thing to say."

"But true, just the same. She was an anachronism. But she was also an actress, always playing one or another stereotyped role. Those I remember well. She and Raymond always played games; that's the way it seemed to me, anyway. At one time or another Josiane had pretended to be every other lover he had known, and played them quite well. Studied up on them, scanned their records, but she never went so far as to have face changes. She was quite an insecure woman."

Joan listened, certain that the bare facts were true; but Pfeiffer had none of the insides. Everything he said was couched in bile, somehow distorted. Pfeiffer was truly a faxmaster, as perverse as the crowds he tried to please.

"Most of that I know," she said. "Ray told me, but I wanted a different viewpoint, especially since you knew them both for so long."

"Josiane never really seemed to change, although she was, as I said, always playing at it. Perhaps that was what Raymond found interesting. At any rate, she was really quite charming. She had a definite charisma."

"So I understand," Joan said, suddenly feeling jealous of Josiane, desperately hoping that Ray wouldn't find her. "Did you think it unnatural for them to marry?"

"No," Pfeiffer said. "I'm not an old-line moralist. Why, does incest bother *you*?"

"I have trouble with it," she admitted.

Pfeiffer forced a laugh. "You are an anachronism, and I can see why Raymond likes you. Josiane had the same medieval bent of mind. She had a maxim for everything; she even named objects in her house."

Don't compare me with her, you bastard, Joan thought. "You've a nasty bent." Pfeiffer was a cipher, a bundle of facts, a storehouse of Raymond Mantle trivia distorted for television. No wonder Ray was always so frustrated around him, especially since his loss of memory. There was something in everything Pfeiffer said that seemed to tease rather than explain. But Joan would not give up.

"Ray hardly ever talks about his Indian heritage," Joan said. "Do you know anything about that?"

Pfeiffer looked disgusted. "Raymond's about as much an Indian as I am."

"Well, he told me—"

"He's got some Sioux in him, on his father's side, but all you need is a drop to play the game. His father was a failure who turned to religion; that's not surprising. But he shouldn't have pressed it on Raymond. All that nonsense about sweat lodges and fasting on top of a hill to find God. It was the worst thing that could have happened to Raymond, and is probably responsible for his being where he is right now."

"What do you mean by that?"

"He was fascinated by the Screamers, anything that smelled of the mysticism of his youth."

"You don't seem to really care that he has amnesia and has lost his sister," Joan said. It was easier for her to think of Josiane as Mantle's sister. She turned her glass in her hands as if she could read her future in the bottom.

"I am concerned for him," Pfeiffer said, "whether you believe it or not."

"Do you believe his amnesia's real?"

"Yes, that I know is real. I checked."

"Of course," Joan said in a nasty whisper.

"But there's something wrong with all of it," Pfeiffer continued, warming once again to the subject. He clenched his hands together, thumbs sticking up like stone dolmens. "You think that he was dependent on his sister, don't you; that he couldn't get by very well without her?"

"I think he loved her very much."

"Don't hedge."

"Yes."

"Well, I think that was *his* game."

"Why?"

"Because Raymond is, and always was, a loner. He's happiest by himself."

"He told you that?"

"I've lived with him, I know him; that's never changed. He uses people—not maliciously, perhaps—but he uses them just the same."

"And you don't?"

"I try not to," he said, and Joan wondered how much he had to do with the problems between Ray and Josiane.

"Are you saying that Ray knows more than he's letting on?" Joan asked. "Do you think he's lying?"

"I don't think he's lying, or realizes that he's lying, anyway. It's something else."

"And what do you think it is?" A real question. Answer it.

But Pfeiffer didn't answer. He looked down at his glass, examined his hands, then combed back a lock of gray-blond hair that had dropped across his forehead. At that instant,

Joan desired him. For all his boorishness, there was something attractive about him. He was almost pretty. Her thoughts wandered: Ray I love you lying beside a dead Crier, maybe lost in a dying mind, never to find your way out, you bastard. Damn the church.

Stop it, she told herself.

The bar had filled up, three-head deep, mostly reporters and diplomatic 'crats, although there were a few students and tourists standing about in groups. Joan knew most of the people, either from here or through the profession. A tall man nodded to her, was about to step out of the press and come over for an introduction, then thought better of it, winked at her and melted back into the crowd. There were few women, even in the booths, which was unusual. Boys' night out, Joan thought sourly.

"Do you want another drink?" Pfeiffer asked Joan. She shook her head, and he waved the robot away.

Someone in the next booth lit up a joint, and the sickly sweet smoke wafted over Joan and Pfeiffer.

"I hate that smell," Pfeiffer said. "Don't they have a ventilation system? Jesus! And there's enough people in here to make *me* claustrophobic." He tapped a switch on the wall above the table to activate the privacy guard.

"Don't do that," Joan said. She tapped the switch, disappearing what looked to be gray, vibrating walls, which would have made her claustrophobic.

"Well, excuse me," Pfeiffer said nastily.

"Just a local custom," Joan said. "Anyway, it gives me a headache."

Pfeiffer grumbled. There was something of the old fart about him, Joan thought. But, according to Ray, he had always been that way. He was of the type, she thought, that aspires to authority and claims the potbelly, balding pate, and varicose veins as badges of success, of having arrived.

"This place is a dump," Pfeiffer said, looking around quickly then hunching over toward Joan as if he were trying physically to block out the room. "Christ, you can't use the privacy guards—and it amazes me that they work at all—there's no ventilation, and the goddamned robot looks like it was stuck together with spit and paste."

"The ventilation system does work, sometimes."

Something passed between them, a look, a feeling; and

they both started laughing—nervous laughter, but even that was a touching of sorts. She had seen into Pfeiffer just a little, seen that there could be a wryness to his complaining, that perhaps he did not take himself so seriously all the time, after all. Perhaps it was because they both had something in common: nervous flutters about Ray, who might either be finding his dream's end or losing his way in the mazed mind of the dying Screamer.

When they stopped laughing, Joan found that Pfeiffer had taken her hand—but no, that wasn't true: she had instead reached across the table seeking his. There was an instant of embarrassment. She let go of his hand, but he held hers tightly for a beat before letting go. She felt the urge to laugh again, but bit her lip. The laughter was a release; she remembered an assignment in Washington, a park gathering which had turned into a riot. The image was before her now as if it were on video: she remembered faces, faces she would never see again, and the carnage of unrecognizable bits of bodies strewn about all the familiar places like the red and yellow leaves of that bloody autumn. Afterward, in a hole-in-the-wall bar like this, she had sat with her friends and other reporters making jokes about the riot until hysteria finally turned to fatigue. She had gone home with someone that night; she could remember being passive, too tired and numbed to satisfy him; but now she couldn't remember his name.

"Let's get out of here," Pfeiffer said, his hands clasped together again.

"We're waiting for Ray, remember?"

"He won't show up; you know that as well as I."

"He might, and it was you who suggested we meet him."

Pfeiffer rubbed the edge of the table, looked around the club, but would not meet Joan's stare. "I didn't want to be by myself," he finally confessed, "knowing what Raymond was going to do."

"You could have tried to stop him."

"It wouldn't have made any difference, no matter what I said or did. I would have made a fool of myself and, worse, him. He hates me enough as it is."

"Deserved?"

"Well," he said, "I've had enough of this. I can't sit here any longer."

"Why are you so nervous for him?" Joan asked. "Somehow it seems out of character. You two haven't seen each other for quite some time, haven't really been friends for longer still."

Suddenly, almost guiltlessly, he said, "I had nowhere else to go. It doesn't matter if we're friends or not, we've been through enough together to take advantage of each other." Joan believed that; it rang true.

"It sounds like something from *The Ghost Sonata:* psychic vampires."

"More like the spider and the fly," Pfeiffer said. Joan let that pass. "And, somehow, we're connected too, Joan, you and me. You can wait for him alone or with me."

"We could meet him at Darmont."

"No," Pfeiffer said instantly, as if afraid. "That would muddy the waters. This much I can tell you: if you want to keep him, he's got to return on his own time. Do you want to keep him?"

Joan nodded. She was being sucked in too quickly; already, she had offered that they travel together to find Ray. But she wanted to find Ray alone, without this misery from the past. No, that's wrong, she thought, looking at Pfeiffer, realizing how difficult it must have been for him to say what he had said. She began to get a feeling for Pfeiffer, touch a surface that wasn't smooth and oiled, find something about him that didn't repel her, that she could like—but never love. "Then what do you want to do?" she asked

"Something exciting and dangerous."

"Like what?" she asked, surprised at his manner.

"Organ gambling, for instance," he said, then slid out to the edge of the booth and deposited his credit card into an available slot. "Will you come with me?"

Joan sat, watching him and thinking. He had a nervous, hot-eyed look, just as Mantle had had at the carnival when he was trying to get away from her; there was something feral and frightened in that look. "I don't know of any casinos with that kind of game hereabout," she said.

"There are some in Paris Undercity."

"You and Ray *are* alike—you're both self-destructive."

Pfeiffer's face turned red, but he didn't reply.

"And what about Ray? Do we just forget about him?"

Pfeiffer replaced his card in his wallet, and Joan suddenly felt clumsy, as she always did when her mind and emotions were at odds, when she was in an unpredictable situation. Her hands felt hot and overly large.

"No, we don't forget about him," Pfeiffer said sharply. "I'm sorry I said it" —his shoulders seemed to lower slightly— "I should have known better. I'll give you my key to Raymond's flat, and you can wait for him there."

"Do you know that I've never been inside his flat?"

Pfeiffer stood up rather stiffly. "I just can't sit here and wait, especially since I don't believe he'll show up tonight. I can't explain it—I'm sorry," he said, looking awkward and embarrassed.

But Joan felt that something was amiss, as if the idea of Mantle plugging into a Screamer had touched off something in Pfeiffer, something irrational and dangerous, perhaps something suicidal. She did not imagine that he loved Mantle and was afraid for him, but that he was afraid for himself; and the only relief was to embrace danger and rush headlong into the controlled world of either/or, the gambler's microcosm. That was just the sort of mathematical, ideal world Pfeiffer would desire: a world where personal grief and fear could be transformed, where one could either win or lose and not have to face the tragedies of the in-between. If Pfeiffer was to succeed over Raymond, he had to walk the edge, outdo him, even now.

Joan felt the lure. She could not help Ray, but she could go with Pfeiffer, perhaps watch him be unmasked. . . .

"Okay," Joan said, "I'll come with you . . . but only to keep you away from the more dangerous forms of sport." She forced a smile. "Ray doesn't use an implant, but he does use a computer plug. We can leave a message on the Network for him. I hope he hasn't taken out the plug."

They left the crowded club immediately. Several people tried to speak to Pfeiffer on the way out, recognizing his face from teevee, but he dutifully ignored them. Outside it was sticky and oppressive. The wind was hot; mercifully, the streets were less crowded than before. Those still walking about looked like wraiths, ghost figures in a videotect. There was hardly any noise, and the occasional yowl or shout was cause for turned heads. Someone dressed as a plumed bird staggered out of an alley and mumbled something to Joan in pidgin French; Pfeiffer asked what he said, but Joan only shook her head.

It was as if night had claimed the carnival; and the people, dressed in shabby costumes, were wending their way home, embarrassed by the revelry of an hour ago. One would think that the curfews had not been lifted. But tomorrow was a workday. By dawn, the vendors would be out sweeping the streets, even though the machines would do the same job a half-hour later. It was a safe way of resisting the system, of tribalizing, enjoying the familiar and expected. While the vendors called to one another, dickered, displayed unsold produce, the world would seem wiped clean, as if there was nothing new under the sun.

"Do you believe in sympathetic magic?" Joan asked Pfeiffer. She smiled as she said it, but they were on a dark street and Pfeiffer couldn't see her face.

After a few steps, he said, "Yes. Tonight I do."

They would take a transpod to Mandelieu, and from there take a flyer to Paris. A quick shuttle.

Five

The ceremony was not being held on Dramont Beach, which was tar-soaked and dead, but around the ruins of the old watchtower that had been built during the reign of Queen Jeanne. Semaphores blinked on and off to warn passing ships of land. Clouds boiled about the moon, shadows flicked here and there, a ghostly mist pervaded. The ruins looked like natural formations, as natural as the monsters made of porphyry rock that guarded the Gulf of Frejus, or the rocks of Cap Roux, or Mount Vinaigre lost in the mists. Wind and pounding surf created a background of white noise that somehow made one imagine that there was no sound in this place, only the flittering of ghosts and gods. A perfect place for an oracle: here nature itself was dreaming.

There were at least two hundred people, mostly women, gathered in and around the ruins. They stood so still that one might mistake them for rocks in the veiling mist. Only the children moved about.

Pretre had left Mantle with Roberta, who had met them at the watchtower. She was a large-boned woman, tall and awkward-looking and attractive. Her face was rather long, yet delicate; its hard, sharp features were relieved by a full mouth and a halo of frizzy blond hair.

"The ceremony will take place over there," Roberta said, pointing west toward what looked to be dolmens at the edge of the olive trees.

"Why is everyone standing still as statues?" Mantle asked.

"They're praying, preparing a bridge from this world to the dark spaces."

Mantle frowned and asked, "And why so many women?"

Roberta squeezed his hand and asked, "Do you have something against women?" Mantle smiled, in spite of himself. "Women are not as lateralized as men," she said. "Unlike most men, we retain some residual language function in the right hemisphere of our brains. You work for the fax; you should be aware of that. Why do you think most of the Nouveau Oracles are women, as were the old? It's purely practical, I assure you. Women learn it easier." Her accent was light and her voice mellifluous, soothing as the drone of the surf and the sliding of shadows.

They walked toward the dolmens, and Mantle had the disquieting sensation that someone, or something, unseen was watching him.

"I know you believe we're all crazy," she continued, "but you should try to put yourself in the right mind for this if you want it to work. You'll have to let go, let everything that happens take you over, block yourself out—"

"I can't," Mantle said roughly, surprised at himself for blurting out the words. But the anxiety was growing inside him—that feeling of being watched by demons and devils as solid as stone who would collect him somewhere in the night, as if he were in a great maze. "I feel as if I'm being watched. I can't shake it."

"Then let yourself be watched," she said. "There are Criers hereabouts. Some alive and some dead, hovering between our world and the dark spaces. Their presence can be a comfort, as if you're riding on their thoughts. That's what those around us are doing. The Criers alone can induce visions, without any hook-in or—"

Mantle shuddered at the thought of so many Screamers, and something opened up inside him. He remembered. He flashed back to New York City. Remembered fighting the mind of the crowd. Being rent by screams and by thoughts as sharp and clear as breaking crystal. The crowd was telepathic, a many-headed beast trying to devour him.

"Come on," she said, pulling Mantle's arm around her waist, just as Joan often did. "You're thinking bad thoughts, I can feel it." She smiled, as if to make light of it, and said, "Let the Criers guide your thoughts. You'll be safer that way, and I'll stay with you, even hook-in with you, if you like."

"So I'm *your* ticket to hook-in," Mantle said, regretting his words and tone of voice. Even against his will, he had to admit that he felt safer with her. He had thrown Joan away—Wasn't that enough? he asked himself. But, like Pretre, Roberta had a slippery mind, which frightened him.

Mantle thought about Joan. Now he wanted her, now he needed her. I love you, I know you. . . .

"It's my time to hook-in," Roberta said. "With or without you."

"What's the danger of being discovered by locals?" he asked, changing the subject. They passed a group of long-haired *boutades*, faces rouged and lined. The boutadniks were naked, so as to expose the male and female sex organs implanted on their chests and arms. Standing beside the *boutades* were several children and a few locals in costume, probably the children's parents. Mantle gave the *boutades* a sour look and then turned his face, as if they represented everything he hated about the modern world.

"This is a religious area, and most of the gentlefolk protect us," Roberta said. "We have used this place since the incorporation of the church. It's holy. There are many Criers hereabouts, for death is a friend in holy places, and the police usually leave us alone. With the locals on our side, it's more difficult for them. . . . But, of course, there is always danger for us. We've been raided before and will probably be raided again. The police have sent some of us to the other side."

"You mean during a raid."

Roberta nodded, as if the words "safety" and "danger" could easily mean the same thing to her.

"Then why return to this place?" Mantle asked.

"Because the voices of the Criers are strong here. Why was there an oracle at Delphi, at Dodona, at Ptoa, at Branchidae, at Patara?"

"Perhaps it's the surrounds. . . ."

"Just believe that the voices are strong here," Roberta said. They stopped near the dolmen. Scattered rocks looked like the skeletal remains of a giant or a great fantastical beast conjured up by the elements and the play of shadows and wan moonlight. The converts were moving silently as specters now, gathering around the dolmen. They all looked like old men and women; even the *boutades* were hunched over, as if the foul, salt-heavy atmosphere had anesthetized them and they were gradually falling asleep on their feet. They seemed to fill up the night like cobblestones in a road.

"It's what happens inside you that's important," Roberta continued. "If you can feel something profound, does it matter what triggers it? Does it matter if it be the holy words of a prayer, the play of light through a window, or a plastic bauble sparkling on the ground? You must try to believe in what happens around you. Let yourself be focused into a trance; forget your left brain and your rational world. Live in the inside of things tonight. If you want to find your wife, you'll have to play along."

"Isn't the hook-in enough?" Mantle asked.

"No, you're dealing with Criers, remember? Our ceremony is a gathering on both sides like—on a mundane level—a seance. Those who have crossed into the dark spaces gather to accept you. Without a ceremony, they might reject you as an intruder; or hooking into the dying Crier might take you to places you have no desire to go, the edges, the dead places where you would be lost. Of course, there is always the chance . . ."

"That building looks like a tomb," Mantle said, feeling a chill. He was looking at the dolmen, which was a circular affair about three meters in diameter and four meters high. It was surrounded by a parapet of ocher-stained paving stones. Large rectangular stones jutted out from the ground around it like grave markers.

"It's both a tomb and a temple," she said, almost in a

whisper, as if she too were about to fall asleep. There was something palpable in the air, a silence, a straining, an anticipation of what was to come.

"Then a Screamer is inside?" Mantle asked. "When do we go inside and hook-in?"

"Pretre is making him ready," Roberta said, as if annoyed at being interrupted from a conversation that only she could hear. "These people around us" —and Roberta made a gesture with her arm— "have been purifying themselves here for days without food or drink, and they will not even be able to plug-in. But many will hear the voices, see into the dark. This ceremony is for them, too."

Now that Mantle was so close to possibly finding Josiane, he felt empty, as if it didn't really matter, as if none of this were real. It began to rain lightly, and then the rain turned to mist, which smoked on the ocean like steam from a demon's cauldron.

Yes, Mantle thought, trying to fight down the chill of fear, it's all typical: the spooky surroundings, the temple, the ritual, the bicameral paradigm, all here. But rational thought could not assuage Mantle's anxiety, which came from that part of his being that felt kinship with darkness and superstition and intuition. It was because of the darkness inside him that he was here.

The crowd began to chant, first in whispers, then louder, *Aria ariari isa, vena amiria asaria,* over and over, chanting louder now, and faster, then lower and slower, waiting to become possessed by dead Screamers, waiting for the gifted to become the vessels of the gods and pour out their incomprehensible words, the words of fire and wind.

Mantle was subvocalizing in time with the others. He caught himself and said, "Christ, are they speaking in tongues now?"

"Are you upset at being affected even a little?" Roberta countered. She was alert as a taxkeeper.

"This is a ragpicker's religion. Take a little from this religion, a little from that, mix it up for yourself. The Japanese would appreciate this."

"How does a Jew who is part Indian rationalize his prejudices?" Roberta asked. Mantle felt his face become warm, and he flashed back to Joan writing a dossier on him for Pretre. "If you want a healthy and successful experience with the Crier," Roberta said, "then you must stop being critical and loosen up. Or do you want to get lost forever inside our temple?" Her smile conveyed only irony.

Mantle noticed the statues scattered around the ruins between the gnarly, high-hatted olive trees. Now—all at once—he could see them, as if a subliminal engineer had been at work here. All the statues were alike: smooth stone heads entirely without features except for those created by shadows. He now noticed that the *boutades* and older people next to him were fingering small figurines, but he could not see them clearly; he guessed that they were smaller versions of the big smooth-faced statues.

The chanting became white noise to Mantle, as primordial and eternal as the surf churning behind him.

"Don't you find it difficult to accept the worship of idols?" he asked, genuinely curious; but a note of sarcasm had crept into his voice.

"I don't find it difficult," Roberta said, "but, then, I have heard them speak." Mantle groaned. "Would you feel better if I told you that the statues are merely devices for narrowing my consciousness?" She paused, then asked, "Do you believe that man has a soul, a divine spirit?"

Sensing a trap, Mantle said, "I don't know. Being a Jew, I've never given it much thought. Jews just die, they don't worry about heaven or the state of their souls."

"But Indians do," she said, flashing him a smile, giving him no escape this time. "All modern religions presume a soul, as did the ancients. It's God's breath, a speck of eternity carried within us. But what poor vessels we are to carry eternity! We sweat, shit, get sick, die, decompose. If even we can have a soul, flimsy flesh creatures, how much easier, how much more plausible, that perfect stone would be the vessel for the divine. It's virtually changeless, can be sculpted into the most beautiful forms, cannot be defiled by human passions, and is much more enduring than any flesh."

"Do you actually believe that?"

"I don't need to," Roberta said. "I look upon the stone and *see* it speak; I hear the Crier just as I hear you."

Jesus! Mantle said to himself.

"And Jesus to you," Roberta said, smiling.

The worshipers, the old people and *boutades*, the children, the townsfolk and well-kept men and women—these

representatives of different classes and cultures and styles—
were all shaking and crying and sweating and praying and
singing in tongues, passing between consciousness and trance,
seeing into the dark places, the dead places, without hooking in.

"Let it happen," Roberta whispered.

Mantle listened for what seemed only a minute, transfixed
by the pounding, persistent *aria ariari isa, vena amiria asaria:*
nonsense words that somehow meant something if only he
could find the rhythm, if only he could focus his mind. . . .

His thoughts were like sparks in the wind. He had not
been sucked into a trance: he could still analyze and catego-
rize and look ahead with dread and longing to the imminent
hook-in.

The music seemed to be all around him; he was being
carried along on the accented and unaccented syllables of the
Aria, which was as precise as poetry, but without sense—at
least without sense for the analytical left hemisphere of his
brain.

He was drifting in slow-time. His mind was clogged with
incomprehensible words. Roberta read my thoughts, Mantle
told himself, feeling a rush of anxiety which at the same time
seemed somehow isolated from him. But that was so long
ago, he thought.

He tried to shake himself loose from the mock-Screamers
around him.

"Have you dusted the air with hallucinogens?" he asked
Roberta.

"Would that help you?"

"That's no answer," Mantle said, looking around, trying
to keep everything in focus. He looked at the idols and saw
that they had faces now. Perhaps it was the face of the
Screamer in the tomb. A large stone near the dolmen had a
woman's face. It was Josiane's—it seemed to move, to stare at
him. The image was inside the stone and perfectly three-
dimensional. He blinked, and it disappeared.

"That's a cheap fucking trick," Mantle said.

"What's that?" Her voice rose in rhythm with *ariari isa*.

"The images on your idols: they're laser-projected. Are
you using a full complement of subliminals? Very sophisticated for such a *primitive* ceremony."

"Just let it happen," Roberta said, looking intently at
him as if he were one of the stone idols.

"Bullshit," Mantle said. Only an instant had passed. His mind was clear now. The rain, which had begun to fall again, felt good on his face. It was tangible and real.

Mantle and Roberta had been talking to each other in time with the rhythm, intoning downward at the end of each phrase, ending in a groan, then up again. Even Mantle's thoughts followed the rhythm, the rhythm of glossolalia, of fiery tongues, the same rhythm that could be found all over the world, from the Umbanda trance ceremonies in São Paulo to the Holy Rollers in Binghamton.

He had been trapped, duped. Now he was scamming down again into the hollow metallic regions of his subconscious, to the places he feared, that he only visited in his paintings, that he had shut off and bricked over since his bum trip on enlightenment drugs. There was no enlightenment, just bare metal. His skin was clammy and he was beaded with sweat.

"There *is* dust in the air, isn't there?" he asked angrily. "Sonofa*bitch*!"

"We didn't ask you to come here," Roberta said. "You've no right to anger, no matter what we do. You're using *us*. This is *our* ceremony." She was spitting her words now, or did Mantle only imagine that? Damn their drugs and subliminals, he thought. "We did not contract to take you by the hand and explain our service, point by point," she continued.

"Don't give me any holier-than-thou shit," Mantle said. "Your friend Pretre is already blackmailing me." The drugs isolated him, and he was afraid of being alone, of feeling that only he was real, that all the others were shadows. "I don't want to be drugged when I plug-in." He imagined that the mist had turned into veils which, in turn, were hardening like polymerized plastic around the laser-projected image.

"You want to find your wife and regain your memory," Roberta said. "What does it matter how you do it, straight or stoned? You should care only for the result." That said quickly, a glissando.

"Why did Pretre choose you to be my guide?" Mantle asked softly, changing the subject, leading her to safer ground. He knew that he needed her, for she alone was substantial; the others were shadows, ghosts—he thought that if he could keep her nearby, he could hold onto his thoughts and sanity even through the drug dust.

"Joan Otur was to be your guide; I was to help her as I could."

"It was my fault about Joan, she—"

"I'm sure she's fine," Roberta said, drawing nearer to him. Pretre must have told her what happened, Mantle thought, but he accepted her closeness and comfort.

"Why should Joan have needed help?" Mantle asked. "There's no one helping you."

Roberta smiled and said, "Actually, Joan wasn't much further along in the church than you are. Her own problems kept her back." Then she said, "I lost my husband, just as you lost your wife. And I suffered amnesia too."

"And that's why you joined the church?" Mantle asked. "To find him?"

"I attended a hook-in under the pretense of joining the church. Like you. But I joined the church out of belief."

"Did you find him?"

She shivered and said, "Tonight, I will meet him." Mantle could feel her close up; still, he pressed her. "And your amnesia—have you regained your memory?"

She ignored him and stared in the direction of the tomb. Mantle was alone now and vulnerable. The worshipers were quiet, waiting, twitching and swaying to an imagined rhythm as if they could see cloven tongues of fire and the rushing wind of holy spirits. Everything was quiet, or, rather, bathed in white noise.

Then Pretre stepped out of the tomb: an impressive figure, his face smeared with ashes or perhaps dirt. Standing naked outside the dolmen, he might have been an Olmec priest without cap and cape, or the gray bishop of Carthage, or a Judaic prophet, or an Indian Pejuta Wicassa. For an instant, he was all these things; then he was just another zealot, a foolish, potbellied upside-down man trying to return to a child's primitive world of authority.

Mantle saw him clearly, saw him as visionary and fool, one overlaid upon the other; and he was embarrassed for him and embarrassed for himself—and for Roberta and for all these worshipers who imagined that they could shake off their culture like a damp blanket. He felt sorry for them all, felt sorry for the mist and drug dust and idols and olive trees and transpods, for the very rocks of Cap Roux.

Sorry for the *rocks*?

And with a jolt, he realized that the drugs had taken him again.

He fought to hold himself together. He took Roberta's hand, hoping she would not pull away. She squeezed his hand in return, reassuring him. She seemed alert, unaffected by the hallucinogens, and the contact helped to clear Mantle's head. Or was that clearness itself a dangerous illusion?

"He's waiting for you," Roberta said softly, as if she were speaking directly to Pretre and not Mantle. She unzipped her clothes and stepped out of them. She looked chunky in clothes, but, naked, she was taut and well-muscled; only her overly large breasts broke the illusion of smooth lines. "Come on. Quickly," she said, turning to Mantle. "Get undressed."

"Why?" Mantle demanded, mouth full of brambles, and words spoken not conforming to the words in his head. For a second he thought he was speaking to Joan.

"Just get undressed."

But Mantle made no move to disrobe. Although he felt that public nudity was as natural as skin, he was suddenly shy and embarrassed.

"When you took your vision-quest, you went naked, as you must now," Roberta said. "Humble yourself, loosen your mind." Mantle's face burned. *Damn* Joan for telling them everything. He remembered sitting in the vision pit and dreaming of thunder beings and the mystery of the holy Cabala; he had been eighteen then. The vision-quest had been real, authentic; *this* ceremony was a sham. But no, that was bullshit, too: the vision quest had been a last attempt to hold onto childhood before his passage into civilized adulthood. He had hallucinated then, as he was hallucinating now; and that was all there was to either ceremony. But he didn't believe *that* either, did he? Inside, in the fearsome cellars of his mind, he believed in the old vision and all the spirits he had seen.

Even now he believed.

Mantle didn't really care that this ceremony was a sham, a paste-together of other cults and religions; what bothered him was that it was heretical. By participating, by taking off his clothes and plugging in, he was forsaking his old gods and accepting new ones.

He undressed clumsily, dropped his clothes in a heap,

and walked through the crowd to the tomb. The worshipers closed in behind him.

Roberta was waiting for him, and he followed her into the tomb, which was evenly lit and seemed larger than it had looked from the outside, no doubt an effect of its ziggurat-like structure. The stone walls were bare, and there were cracks in them large enough to see through. In the center of the room, beside the large and weather-worn console of the psyconductor, was the Screamer: a middle-aged man with a long, sallow face; gums drawn over even, capped teeth; and pale blue eyes that might have been piercing at one time but now were glazed. Mantle had the absurd notion that the eyes were porcelain, that he could have painted on them or tapped them with his fingernail without producing a single blink. The Screamer, who must have once been affluent to afford such a pretty set of teeth, was naked. Mantle could not help but notice that he had lost most of his pubic hair (and most of the hair on his head, although he was not completely bald) and that he had a formidable erection.

The other participants, looking skeletal and chicken-skinned, stared down at the Screamer, who was still alive and breathing shallowly. Mantle shuddered as he watched: they were all waiting for the Screamer to die.

There was a hospital smell in this room. Mantle felt miles removed from the ceremony and the crowd outside; years removed from the drug-induced euphoria of glossolalia. He was in a waiting room, simply that, waiting for a man to die so he could hook-in and then go home with a few memories to fill up his empty life.

"Where's Pretre?" Mantle asked.

"Outside with the other Criers," Roberta said in a whisper. "He'll be back in time."

We're vampires, he thought; Roberta smiled as if she had read his mind. "Shouldn't we plug-in before he's dead?" Mantle asked. "Help him over, so to speak?"

"We can't help him until he's dead. And then he's going to help us."

Mantle looked at the Screamer. Fuck him, he thought. If the man had wanted privacy, he would have died alone. Curious, this hatred he felt for the dying man. He wondered about that. Perhaps it wasn't so strange, after all. He was going to invade him, screw his mind, which was more physical and sensual than if he were engaged in a simple act of necrophilia.

He could imagine himself doing just that, debasing himself. He had reason: to find Josiane. But Joan—he could not imagine her sinking herself into the mind of a corpse. But she was going to do it for the church.

He felt a rush of hate for Joan, and desire.

With a long sigh, the Screamer died.

Six

Paris was below them.

But for the dymaxion dome of the Right Bank, Joan would not have been able to distinguish Paris from its suburbs. A city had grown over the city: the grid of the ever-expanding slug city had its own constellations of light and hid Haussmann's ruler-straight boulevards, the ancient architectural wonders, even the black, sour-stenched Seine that was an hourglass curve dividing the old city. Like silver mold, the grid had grown over Paris, even filled the dome, as if it were a Petri dish. Extending over the Seine and across the Left Bank, it would eventually grow around the dome itself and bury it.

But tonight, from the air, the dome looked like a child's transparent toy filled with specks of light. Indeed, the city seemed to extend forever, a great black field piled high with diamonds.

It will all be wrecked soon, Joan thought as she stared through the oval window of the flyer. Pfeiffer was leaning against her, was a little too close, craning his neck for a view.

"It's beautiful, isn't it?" Pfeiffer asked. The flyer was banking, making its descending curve toward the old Paris heliport on the Seine.

"No, I don't think so," Joan said, impatient with him and annoyed by his insipid remark.

"Aha," Pfeiffer said, "so now we're seeing politically."

"It reminds me of Christmas lights," she said, gently pushing him away, thinking of him as a cumbersome child. "One great string of pretty lights, that's the great grid."

"But pull the plug and all the lights go out, right?" Pfeiffer asked in a mocking voice.

"Yes, actually. Something like that." Asshole!

"And you're waiting for that, aren't you?" Now Pfeiffer drew away from her, as if one had to keep a distance to converse. "Isn't the Great Purging one of the tenets of your religion?"

"We don't have strict dogma," she said. "Some ideas they all seem to agree on, others not."

"They?"

"I meant 'we,'" Joan said, flustered. She checked her computer implant: still no word from Mantle. Well, it was much too early yet. . . .

"What do you believe?" Pfeiffer asked.

"There are members of the church who want the purging. They see every manifestation of psychosis as a step closer to the world inside, what you would call right-brain authority."

"I want to know what *you* think," Pfeiffer said.

There was that condescension, she thought. It was in his tone of voice. The empty sonofabitch. "I think they're fools, but there are fools everywhere," she said pointedly. "The cities are being torn apart because social reality is a sham. We've blocked over the internal world with a social one, the purpose of which is to keep us from ourselves."

"Surely you don't really—"

But Joan was carried on by her thoughts and insecurity. "It was built by and for those who haven't experienced anything but this world. The only relics of the old experience are the traditional religions, which have long been empty."

"Aha," Pfeiffer said. "So the Dreadful has already happened."

"What?" she asked, annoyed that he was trying to score points rather than trying to gain understanding.

"Something Heidegger said—"

But Joan had already subvocalized the question, and the computer was explaining: ". . . and Laing, R. D., a twentieth-century theologue, wrote that the Dreadful has happened to us all—that being the collective estrangement of modern man from the unconscious parts of his being."

"The Dreadful is a result of the old order," Joan said, "and the collective psychosis is merely a symptom of disease—"

"As are the Screamers, and your church."

"No," Joan said, feeling flushed and cornered. She had already said too much. "The psychotics can't adjust to a dysfunctional society. But the Criers have cut free, adapted themselves to an inner establishment."

"And the church is the authorized connection to the divine establishment," Pfeiffer said, smiling. "Spoken like a true fanatic."

He's right, Joan thought, turning to the window. But the Criers are real. As are the dark spaces. "You seem to place all your faith in science and its methods," she said, still looking out the window. "Consider what I've said as an untested hypothesis."

"And how do I test it?"

"By hooking into a Crier." She turned toward him, and she was right: she had caught him.

"We're in this mess because of politics," Pfeiffer said quickly. "What the hell do you think the famines in China and the flooding in Eastern America are all about? Or don't you believe in weather warfare, either?"

Joan knew just what Pfeiffer was getting at: viral warfare. But she didn't answer him. That, she thought, was probably the only way to stop him. Again, she checked to hear if there was a message from Ray; there wasn't.

"Your Screamers were most likely created in a lab somewhere, either by intent or mishap. You can explain it as vitalistic evolution or whatever else is fashionable right now, but it's probably some sort of virus that facilitates or blocks some neurohumoral action in the brain."

Jesus, not that old saw again. Joan thought.

". . . but you're caught in your own passivity," Pfeiffer said. "*That's* the collective experience." Joan felt herself stiffen, caught like a small animal. She had fought being passive all her life, and always seemed to lose. Could Pfeiffer have seen that? she asked herself. The sonofabitch was right-brained, she thought, but was so afraid of it that he proclaimed it nonexistent. "Your church is a manifestation of despair," he continued. "But none of this is new. All this cosmic-consciousness bullshit was prevalent in Germany once, before the Nazis came to power. That's your new consciousness—"

"I think we should continue this later," Joan said, nodding in the direction of a woman of about forty in the aisle before them. She was quite pretty, although overweight and dough-faced, as if she had glandular problems. She was staring, obviously eavesdropping.

The woman grinned and winked at Pfeiffer, who quickly turned away. But perhaps she had winked at Joan. . . .

"You don't seem to be the shy type," Joan said nastily.

"Cut it out," Pfeiffer said, looking unreasonably nervous. "We'll be landing in a few minutes."

"I'm not so sure. We're still circling at the same altitude. Perhaps something's happened below. Anyway," she said cheerfully, "there is still time for you to diagnose her illness."

"And what's that supposed to mean?"

"I'm also sure she's a Crier," Joan whispered.

"How do you make that surmise?"

"Just a feeling . . . the way she's looking at us. You see, if you'd use that right brain of yours a bit—"

"Ah, yes," interrputed the woman. "I have your right brain. Stare right at my forehead and you can imagine it right rightly." She was talking to Pfeiffer, or so it seemed. Joan leaned back in her seat, ready to enjoy what was to come.

"Dammit," Pfeiffer mumbled, "you're provoking her."

"But you're sitting beside her. Give her a chance."

"Jesus God. . . ."

"Ah, Jesus God," said the woman. "A religious man are you, but how can you be so without the right side of your brain?"

Pfeiffer ignored her.

"Come on, talky, talky. Alas, I forgot, you don't have your right side, but hear you may with the left. But I'll bet you can't sing. Sing 'Melancholy Baby.' Come on, sing, Mr. Pfeiffer."

Pfeiffer groaned at having been recognized.

"Be a sport," Joan said. "Play along, you might learn something."

"I've spoken to enough schizos—" he whispered angrily.

"But you don't *listen* to anyone."

"She's right about that," the woman beside them said. "But he can't really hear without his right side, now, can he?"

"Come on," Joan said, "play along."

"Why?" Pfeiffer asked, staring at his hands and blushing

like a little boy. He really can't handle this, Joan thought, curious.

"You might learn a few subtle gambits. Try a different point of view—remember old Kraepelin's servant girl?"

Pfeiffer paused, as he was listening to his computer implant explain the case of the early twentieth-century psychiatrist who had stuck pins into a schizophrenic girl during a clinical demonstration. A later school of psychology rightly claimed that it was only a matter of viewpoint whether one thought the servant girl or the psychiatrist crazy.

"Aha," said the woman. "Then you do have a double brain, quite correct." And she looked at Joan as a conspiratress.

"Quite right," Joan said. "He's got two left sides."

"Aha," repeated the woman. "One side for law, the other for order."

"What does she mean?" Pfeiffer asked Joan.

"Your computer implant, silly. Don't be so thick, talk to her."

"You do think I'm mean?" the woman asked, preening herself.

"I don't think anything about you."

"You're right to think me bad."

"But I really don't care—"

"Because he has no right," Joan said.

"Two lefts don't make a wrong," the woman said.

"You see, she does like you. . . ."

As the flyer made its descent, Pfeiffer sat stiffly, looking nothing but impatient to leave the plane. The woman across the aisle went back to reading with a tiny viewer, as if the conversation had never occurred.

When they debarked and were swept into the clamoring crowd of the airport, Pfeiffer said, "Don't ever do that to me again!"

"I just wanted to prove my point," Joan said, holding close to him in the crowd, "as you were so determined to prove yours."

"All that proved is you're both wigged-out."

As there were no transpods to be had, they took a beltway. The public means were uncomfortable and sometimes dangerous, but Joan had an access permit to one of the complexes at Grenelle which housed a private transpod station.

"It simply proves that you can handle only one modality

of thought," Joan said. She felt hot and trapped and claustrophobic in the press of people, as she always did. Above, like moving ceilings, were more beltways, speedier ones that were express. On either side of this slower beltway were others, all congested with people and their baggage. Since the Screamer attacks, everyone on the streets except the *boutades* were nervous and afraid. The crowds exuded fear like perspiration; and like the noise and stink and filth of undercity streets and ways, one never became used to it.

"That conversation was idiotic," Pfeiffer said.

"But you were positively alarmed, and quite unable to handle it. Don't you think that a bit odd—you, of all people, to get so upset over such an 'idiotic' thing?"

"I am not in the habit of talking crazy to crazy people. You were baiting me at the expense of that unfortunate."

"That 'unfortunate,' as you call her, wasn't any more schizophrenic than you," Joan said. "She was having it on you."

"Not on me, she wasn't. And I thought you were so convinced that she was a schizo?"

"I was having it on you, too. I wanted to see if it were true."

"If what were true?"

"That you can't handle anything that smacks of the right except, of course, your politics."

"That sounds like something you got from Raymond. Am I correct?"

"Correct." A group of *boutades* wearing identical one-piece suits jostled Joan as they were trying to jump off the belt onto the service catwalk below. They were all young and neatly dressed, and each one openly carried a weapon. All of them had shaven heads, which was the current unisex fashion.

"The skinheads will kill themselves," Pfeiffer said.

"Maybe break a leg, that's all. Didn't you ever jump the walks?"

Pfeiffer shook his head, and Joan said, "I thought not."

"You're a nasty bitch."

Joan reached for Pfeiffer's hand. It amused her that she really did like him. There was a sudden press of people on the beltway, for the six-hour shift was changing. As usual, the Rapid Transit System seemed to be working at minimum.

"Come on," Joan said, fighting her claustrophobia, which was worsening. "Let's get off the belt."

"And walk in the undercity?" Pfeiffer asked, surprised.

"It's not that bad, and I know the area."

"The crowd will thin soon," Pfeiffer said, holding on to Joan's arm.

"But I have to get off *now*," Joan said, pulling away from him. Pfeiffer followed, and they pushed their way onto the slowest-moving debouchment belt. Joan felt somewhat relieved. But Pfeiffer was buzzing. "It's crazy to walk around down here. Christ, we'll get ourselves mugged, at the very least. Couldn't you have stood the crowd for such a short time?"

"No," Joan said. "Leave it alone. I don't wish to discuss it right now." The street was crowded, but there was at least enough room to breathe. To their left were the ever-present beltways, a river of rollways and slidewalks. Like boats on water, vendor platforms and restaurants and pleasure hutches drifted slowly past as if they were isolated from the crowds and rollways.

Joan felt a need for a narcodrine: she wanted to open up, sail through the white spaces of her mind, be private and at the same time have Pfeiffer quietly make love to her.

"You said you know this area," Pfeiffer said. "How so?"

"It was here that the Criers first congregated—Surely you remember? It wasn't a large or a very destructive scream, but it was the first heard in Europe." She laughed. "They even rebuilt the area, which is a damn sight better than bombing them out as they did in Baltimore."

"The bombing was a mistake," Pfeiffer conceded, "but it was thought to be the only way to stop the Screamers. Christ, they burned almost—"

"Bombing them only made it worse. . . ."

"Well, this looks like any down-under slum to me," Pfeiffer said, changing the subject, looking about as he walked. He walked very erect, as if to make himself taller. Joan held his hand, which was a bit clammy, so they would not be separated. Pfeiffer tightened his free hand around the small heat weapon concealed in his pocket. Tiers and tiers of plasteel could be seen above; dark bones studded with lights, each hard, bright speck a modular living unit. The great grid was larger than any western arcology.

To their left as they walked was the oily, glassy water of the Seine. To the north, but not yet visible, was the destruction once known as the Quai d'Orsay: only the compounds remained. To the east were the floating cities, the cankers of Paris, as some called them. But this area, south of the Boulevard de Grenelle and the still-standing Palais de L'Unesco (now used by the military), had a fair share of police platforms and the imposing blue robots nicknamed bluebottles, blueblunders, or *bevve bule*. Everywhere could be seen the modular clusters, pastel-faded and filthy, beehive upon beehive of living space for the poor on the dole.

Paris had upwards of nine million people living on its levels.

"This area has become *de rigueur* for any self-respecting *boutade*," Joan said, nodding in the direction of a group of young people, all naked to the waist and obviously proud of the male and female genitals implanted on their arms and chests. Pfeiffer scowled at a boy of about nineteen who wore his long, blond greased hair in braids; his face was rouged and lined, and he sported one large breast. Joan walked along just behind Pfeiffer, a distant look on her face.

"Any news about Raymond?" Pfeiffer asked when she was beside him once again.

"I just checked. Nothing at all, which is to the good, I suppose."

"If there was any problem, you would be notified?"

"Yes, I would hope so, either by Pretre or Roberta. And my computer would pick up anything newsworthy on the Net. But I'm worried."

"I'm sure everything's fine," Pfeiffer said.

"You were right about waiting. If I'm wanted, I'll get a message." But something *is* wrong, Joan thought.

"Who's this Roberta?"

"Roberta Algaard. Pretre uses her in some capacity at most of his ceremonies. She'll probably hook-in with Ray to help guide him out of the dark spaces." It should be me, she told herself, not her.

"Then she's probably hooked in with him right now," Pfeiffer said.

Joan shuddered and said, "No, not yet." Pfeiffer was quite adept at finding the soft parts. But she would be calm about Ray and hold off her anxieties, for if she thought about

Ray and Roberta, she would certainly scam down. For all its disguises, her love for Ray was selfish. Just now, jealousy, rather than concern, was in the ascendant. As long as he wanted her, she didn't care about his other *ménages*. But he didn't want her tonight, when it was vital to her that they share his memory.

It just wasn't important enough to him, she thought. No, he's simply angry.

"Does that bother you?" Pfeiffer asked.

"What?"

"Roberta being with Raymond." Pfeiffer had queried his computer about Roberta and found only that the name was a nom de plume of a minor scandlefax writer. He was disgusted with the foolish secrecy that attended all the cults.

"You know," Joan said, upset, "I used to see a man who had been in love with a friend of mine. We would go out and then go to bed, but all he ever talked about was my friend. It used to upset me every time. I finally stopped seeing that man, although I thought quite a bit of him. So why don't we leave Ray out of our conversation until we have word of what's happened?"

Pfeiffer began to say something, stopped himself, and said, "Yes, of course. I'm sorry."

They walked. The streets had become quite crowded, but Joan could bear it until they reached the station. If only the undercity stink were not so strong here! Not even the huge air purifiers could combat the reek of food, perspiration, defecation, and death. "Christ," Pfeiffer said, "do they have to shit in the goddamm street?"

"Even with the dole, you'll always have those who prefer to live in the streets."

"For God's sake, why?"

"To escape the census, among other things."

"Doesn't make sense," Pfeiffer said, and Joan wondered if his pun was consciously made. "And why isn't the curfew being enforced here?" he asked.

"It *is* being enforced, for the most part."

"One certainly wouldn't think so."

"One would if one knew that these streets are not nearly as crowded as they used to be," Joan said. "Most people don't need a curfew to keep them at home."

"Then why isn't something done about . . . this?" And he

nodded toward a group of *boutades* who were shouting at each other.

"The police leave them alone, perhaps as a sop to those who have to live in the undercity. They're the modern-day folk heroes, like the cowboys and truckers of the nineteen hundreds. There's a certain attraction to that life, gruesome as it might seem. You're out of touch with what's happening, I think. That's what comes from spending too much time in diplomatic salons and corporate conferences." She smiled. "The real action's down here."

"That's a matter of opinion, and taste." Then, after a pause, Pfeiffer said, "And I'm certainly not out of touch."

Joan laughed and pressed closer to him, which he, quite correctly, guessed to be a gesture of condescension. But she was also overreacting to her claustrophobia. "These *boutades* are the last of the free," she said, a hint of irony in her voice. "They own nothing, yet don't have to go hungry."

"They'll be counted when they need medicine," Pfeiffer said.

"No, actually, most just get sick or die. You see, that's the stuff of which heroes are made."

"Crazy."

"All of these people are on the dole," Joan said. "It's a degrading life and they feel it. It gets a bit nasty hereabouts."

"Then let's get back on the belt," Pfeiffer said.

"That's just as dangerous, and we'll find a pod at Grenelle. We're almost there; I have an access permit."

"I think you're paranoid about the belts," Pfeiffer said.

"I don't think so. I was gang-raped last year during a rush on a main belt where I was doing a story, for God's sake. I had four technicians with me."

"What did they do?"

"What could they do? They saved their respective asses."

"What were you doing the story about?" Pfeiffer asked.

"The branglers who live on the belts and catwalks. They make up a whole subculture."

"Your heroes," Pfeiffer said sarcastically. He expertly shouldered his way through a tight spot in the crowd. Joan held onto him and tried not to gag.

"The branglers can't be classified as heroes," she continued—a true act of will. "Most of them are on the dole.

They pass their time on the belts, and barter." I'm almost there, she thought, looking above the crowd at what she knew was Grenelle Complex. The complex consisted of two risors, each five hundred stories high; the uppermost levels looked down upon the smooth surface of the dome of the Right Bank. In fact, the Casino d'Abbe Bellecour could be seen by a practiced eye from that vantage. "You *do* know about black-goods barter?" she asked Pfeiffer.

"Yes," Pfeiffer said, "I know what's going on down here. I just don't choose to rut about in it." He looked away from a smiling, toothless man shaking a turd out of his pant leg.

"Anyway, they pick up the droppings from the belts," Joan continued, oblivious to the bum as they passed—and lost—him in the crowd. "And, of course, some of them work the belts in tandem. Systemized muggings. Each clan's turf is, of course, clearly demarcated."

"I still think we'd be better off on the belts," Pfeiffer insisted.

"No need," Joan said. "We're here."

They crossed the avenue to deposit their identification cards into an unmarked door slot; after a short wait, the door slid open and they stepped into a small, foul-smelling cubicle where they were carefully scanned. But once inside the crowded, deteriorating, high-ceilinged station lounge, they had no trouble finding a transpod.

The pod was a transparent, albeit dirty, egg that swept them through a glassite tunnel and into the grid upon which was mounted the elevated Paris.

Before them was the dome of the Left Bank, and then they were inside it, past what had once been the Tuileries, past the Rue Saint-Honore, the Place Vendome, the wide, tree-lined Boulevard Haussmann, and the Place de Crieur. Pfeiffer could see no appreciable difference between Right and Left Bank, for the space between ground level and roof dome was filled with the uroboros of the grid network, passtubes, and living modules: it was like looking into the organs of a great glass beast. But here, in the pod, Joan seemed noticeably less nervous.

The Right Bank was a "safe zone"; its twin on the left was mostly slums. One was reminded of the Great Los Angeles Slums where it was difficult—at least, superficially— to tell the bad neighborhoods from the safe ones.

All around them was a vertiginous rush of line and object.

"This would seem the perfect place to make love," Pfeiffer teased, his mood elevated. "Right here, in the glass heart of the world."

Joan let him touch her face and breasts, but she was thinking about Mantle, who was dying, but not for her.

Seven

Mantle could hear the crowd screaming outside as Pretre fixed the metallic cowl over the dead Screamer's head. Two other cowls lay beside him: crowns for the converts. Mantle had expected to hook-in first—after Pretre, that is—but three others preceded him. Each hook-in was a quick affair, lasting no more than three or four minutes, after which Pretre would remove the cowl and replace it beside the Screamer. After hooking in, the three other participants slumped forward, either unconscious or in some sort of trance.

You can still get out of this, Mantle told himself, remembering his first Inipi ceremony when he was a child: sitting in the completely dark sweat lodge, listening to the medicine man explain what was to happen; that if anyone couldn't stand the heat to just say "All my relatives" and someone would lift up the tent covering and let you out; that it was no disgrace.

Roberta took his hand and led him to the Screamer. There was a faint smell of urine and feces. After all, the man *is* dead, Mantle told himself. Pretre stank, too; it was a nervous sweat, not the clean sweat of an athlete.

"Do you want me to hook-in with you?" Roberta asked. "It's up to you."

Mantle shook his head. I have to find Josiane alone, he thought, unwilling to share his past with a stranger. But I don't want to be alone. . . .

"All right," Roberta said, "just sit or lie comfortably, whichever you prefer." She caressed and calmed him as if he were a child or an impotent lover. "You'd be safer with me."

Mantle turned his face away from her. "You can still back out. It's not too late."

Mantle laughed softly and said, "All my relatives." Roberta gave him a queer look, then shrugged.

"Okay then," Pretre said. "We will all be with you." That said without sincerity. And he placed the cowl over Mantle's head.

A quick intake of breath, then complete silence, claustrophobia. It's only a machine, you nit, Mantle told himself, then suddenly realized that he had no clear idea of the position of his body. He tried to move his legs, wriggle his fingers, but he couldn't seem to locate them. His thoughts were skeins of thread, unraveling, knitting together, becoming more tangled with every breath.

Then he had the distinct sensation of looking down at his body; it was a shadow thing of black and silver. He could also see the Screamer's body beside his own.

He waited, as if an eternal river were purling around him, touching him, flowing on its way, at the same time still and in constant motion.

Something rasped. The sound jarred him but was somehow removed from him, miles away.

It's only Pretre talking to Roberta, he told himself, relieved. But then he wasn't sure. . . .

Suddenly Mantle felt a lurching, and images quickfired through his mind, all silver and black: a little boy lying in a casket, a small boat, a ribbon of beach in the distance, a twentieth-century ocean liner crossing the ocean, a gaming room, and sound of bullets ricocheting, a large stone mansion, *The Wizard of Oz*—and so the images flicked through his mind, all foreign, meaningless.

There was only black and silver, dark and darker; slowly, every so slowly, everything was becoming gray and indistinct.

The Screamer's memory was going.

Could it be that dull? Could the play of memory and reflection be that uninteresting? It was somehow ironic, this simple winding down. How much grander to believe that the end will be cathartic, that for those few last seconds colors will be brighter, experience will be compressed, all the juice and pith tasted one last time, one last great sucking at life and then a slow melting into darkness. . . .

Yet, images still flicked through Mantle's mind's eye: the

Screamer was still hallucinating, dreaming. Perhaps if there were at least some *color,* he thought . . . and then it struck him that this might be an accountant's examination of a past ledger, each column of memories being balanced in the cold light of reflection. It was as if he were being guided through a museum of extinct trivia.

Not with a bang but a whimper, Mantle thought. The old Nazi was right.

Mantle's point of view shifted again. He felt as if he were outside the tomb; he saw everything as black and silver, shadow upon shadow. The tall, silvery olive trees reached upward into a black as deep as he could imagine. Among the trees had gathered the Screamers, ghosts of the dead. Their thoughts were the darkness, their breath the silver wind that carried Mantle. . . .

He heard them calling to him, tempting him, and he awakened to them as if they had been talking to him all along but he had been in too deep a sleep to hear them. They were calling him home, telling him that he was part of them. That he was a seed about to blossom.

Another shift. Now Mantle was looking past the tomb, which was as silvery as the trees, and past the shadow-black congregation of the Crying Church to the guardians of the entrance to the Gulf of Frejus, called *The Lion of the Land* and *The Lion of the Sea*—beyond them was the sea, its waves like metal scythes, like blades cutting through the darkness.

Suddenly there was only darkness and silence.

Mantle was lost, adrift. If he *was* in someone's mind now, it was a completely dead mind, which would produce a straight line on an EEG: in the "eternal darkness," as his father used to call it when the covering of the sweat lodge was closed and everyone plunged into dark. He felt as if he were back in the sweat lodge. It was the same now, and the Screamers talked to him as if they were spirits. Indeed, they *were* spirits that took on the shape of his father, who now sat before him. "You must come back," he said. "Give yourself up and come home."

And Mantle felt himself being pulled away, gently but firmly: out of the imagined sweat lodge, past the Screamers among the trees, past the tomb and its congregation, past the guardian rocks and into the sea.

"Father, no," he screamed, trying to grasp onto something. "Help me." But he was weightless and powerless, a gossamer thing blown into the water. It was like awakening from a dream and finding yourself in a nightmare. His screams were silent streamers. There was only the sea—undulating, extending infinitely—and just under its surface swam all the hideous creatures of the soul.

They were swimming toward him.

It's only a machine, Mantle repeated to himself as he floated, trying to comprehend that he was "really" lying beside a dead Screamer inside a stone tomb. Then he saw Josiane. She was floating just below the surface of the water and staring unblinkingly at him. Although her mouth did not move, he heard her voice: "Give yourself up. Come home and remember."

"Josiane, I'm afraid."

"The sea is safe and calm as death," she said. "The creatures you see are your own fears. Leave them behind and come home."

"Are you dead?" Mantle asked desperately, but the snapping, silvery creatures closed in on him, swam around and beneath him, separating him from Josiane. "Josiane. . . ."

Growing bolder, hungry for their prey, they seized him with cold jaws and pulled him under.

"I'm here," Josiane said. "Don't turn away from me. Come back."

"I'm not breathing. Jesus God, Wakan Tanka. . . ." But there was the sense of the dream, of the self in the dream sensing the self outside the dream. There was also the realization that all the thoughts racing through his mind were not his alone.

I'm in the tomb beside the Screamer, Mantle told himself, trying to hold onto that and believe it, closing himself away from the voices he feared to hear.

The sea was gone. Only darkness remained, the hot, sweaty darkness of a sweat lodge. And Mantle felt as dead as the Screamer inside of whom he was trapped. He was afraid of bicameral thinking and schizophrenic breakdown, the melting of the soul; but it was an intellectualized, devised fear, almost mathematical. Indeed, he had left the living.

I will not die, he repeated to himself.

He remembered a doctor who had once said that Mantle was hot, that he had the look of someone about to go round the bend, about to be melted down and put together in a different way.

Again he was burning, melting, but alive.

"Let me go," he screamed into the darkness which was absorbing his life. He imagined that he had been passed from Screamer to Screamer, that he was now existing in the deadness between them, in infinite psychic space, all the dark spaces surrounding dreams, the countries of the dead.

Nothing was important now but light and color and sound, the rasping of breath, and constant knowledge of the small aches and pains of the body, blessed pain, living pain.

All at once he heard a deafening noise and felt himself falling. He had been held inside the Screamer's mind, inside many minds, and he felt the dark veils, the same dead stuff that he scammed into when he had that bad drug trip. Now the veils were tearing, and Mantle fell through—it was a jolt, coming back to life.

But he had seen Josiane. . . .

Roberta pulled the cowl from Mantle's head and shook him. "Come on, try to stand. There's no time." She pulled at him.

Cotton-mouthed, Mantle tried to raise himself, but his legs felt foreign; he tried to form words, but could only seem to make guttural noises. Everything was moving in slow-time. Pretre was curled on the ground beside him, his legs splayed on a bloodstained mat, his arm resting on the Screamer's neck as if caught between the bottom portion of the cowl and breastbone. But Mantle could not see a wound; irrationally, he thought it was Pretre's bleeding heart.

"Come on," Roberta said, helping him upright, then pulling him to the drop-curtained opening of the tomb. He staggered, stumbling, unable to find his footing. "Josiane?" he asked.

"Wake up. It's Roberta, not Josiane."

He heard a cracking, or perhaps something was popping. "Wh'issat?" he mumbled, surprised at the sound of his own voice. Moronic.

"Bullets."

"Then stay in here," Mantle tried to say, but his mouth wasn't working.

Roberta coaxed him to the drop curtain, and he suddenly

came fully awake, was finally pulled free of the black and silver world and thrown headlong into electric light.

"What the hell is—"

"Raiders," she said. "Now get out of here. Quickly." She tried to push him out of the tomb, but he grabbed her, pulled her to the ground and away from the opening. "Let me alone," she screamed.

"You can't stay in here," Mantle said. "Jesus, no one's even killed the goddamm lights."

"I'm here for a reason, and it's none of your fucking business."

"You're not going to hook-into Pretre or that Screamer. That's suicide. Now move."

"I'm staying here. My husband is—"

"He's *dead*!" Mantle shouted. "Now get us away from here or *I'll* kill you." He pushed her out of the tomb and crawled behind her along the gravelly edge of the dolmen, still unsure that any of this could be real: the rifle shots, dead bodies, the smell of earth and blood.

Someone close by called for help, but Mantle could do nothing but crawl on, a living machine.

I'm sorry, Josiane. I can't go back. . . .

Mercifully, the moon was hidden behind thunderclouds and everything was darker, as if masked; but it was a living darkness, one without the cold silver of the Screamers' mind spaces. Gradually, his eyes adjusted to the dark.

There was shouting, moaning, the sharp popping of gunfire, the sucking, wheezing, coughing sound of people dying. Mantle was acutely aware of every sound now, every movement, as he breathed heavily into the gravel and the damp, acrid-smelling dirt. It was all a wash of movement, every sight and sound and smell perceived and then immediately giving way to the next. For every instant, every bead of time was either/or: another few steps to walk or crawl, another few breaths and thoughts or a bullet smashing into tissue and bone. It was a hot, gland-exciting world, an extension of the moment before a suicidal jump or the pulling of a trigger; it was a complete compression of life and memory into survival.

Mantle guessed that the raiders were few but had automatic weapons. Rather than risk danger, they simply fired into the crowd. It didn't matter if some escaped—for the terrorist, it was the act, not the number of dead or wounded.

Suddenly the shooting stopped and a silence hung over the area, a heaviness that somehow excluded the distant pounding of waves and the occasional moan of the wounded.

Mantle and Roberta kept near the trees and made their way away from the beach where they might be trapped. But they were exposed, would be exposed almost everywhere hereabouts if the raiders had any kind of sensors. Still, they had to keep moving; the raiders might just be coming in close to clean up and make a neat job of it.

They came upon two male corpses lying facedown in the soft earth. Hurriedly, they stripped the clothes from the corpses and left, clothes in hand. Mantle swallowed vomit and remembered fighting in Ghana during the UN draft, remembered a night like this when his squad, all of them crazy from killing and hunger, ran through a burned field cutting off the fingers of the Ghaks, prying gold from their teeth, waving the charred bodies by their napalm-stiffened cocks like flags.

He felt the touch of that night again.

They stopped in a ragged copse to catch their breath and put on their new clothes.

"Where do we go from here?" Mantle asked.

"I know of an old road nearby. It's in disuse; not even the farmers ride it." Roberta pulled up the collar of the rough shirt and shivered in the mist. Everything was wet, saturated with miasma. Ironically, the clothes fit her quite well. "I have friends who might be waiting for me if *they* are in no danger."

"And if they're not there?"

"Then we find some good Campagnards to give us shelter or, perhaps, get caught."

A flash of lightning overhead, then a great blast of thunder, and finally pelting rain. They were soaked in a few moments—the trees could not provide enough cover. Tiny streams seemed to be flowing everywhere, a microcosmic Venice for worms and crawlers. With rain came more haze cover, and the pelting rain combined with the distant rush of the sea to, almost visually, cloak this night world in white noise. Everything seemed narrowed to the few feet of ground around them, and consciousness seemed to narrow also: here was a tuft of coarse grass; a worn, rounded pebble; gravel; a bit of moss atop the mud.

But the world looked as dead as the spaces Mantle had felt between the Screamers. He had the sensation that he had been left in the dead Screamer's mind, that he had never unhooked, that the sea would still claim him.

Roberta led Mantle beyond the northeastern edge of the forest and through a rock field. In the glow of the moon, jutting, sharp-edged rocks looked as if they belonged in a rock field in Urgap, Turkey, rather than in the south of France. It was as if this place had been sculpted—not into heads and faces by the left-handed thinkers who had ruined Mount Rushmore—but into masks and demon forms that danced with the play of shadows and only became solid and dead in the day. He could see Mount Vinaigre as a dark fist. The mist wasn't continuous, it was spotty. Although reassuring in its appearance of heavy cover, it was just that: illusion. If those with the rifles have infrared . . . Mantle thought.

Only the rocks are friends, he told himself, remembering an Inipi ceremony when he was told that the glowing, almost translucent stones were the rock people; that even though they were broken by the fire to make steam, they would grow again, grow in their own time, layer after layer, and once again give themselves up so the Indians, the Natural People, could follow the traditional way.

The rain stopped.

Mantle heard thunder in the distance, then realized it was rifle fire. Am I still drugged? he asked himself.

"Oh God," Roberta moaned. "Oh sweet Christ."

"What is it?" Mantle asked, stopped inside a small crown of rocks. He could see that Roberta was about to snap now that they were removed from the immediate danger. "Those last shots were farther away," he said. "I'm sure they're moving off. But we can't stop now. We may not be out of danger yet, even here."

Mantle rested his hand on the small of her back, and she wriggled closer to him, pressed against him, her face under his chin as if she were a frightened animal burrowing into safety. He had an instant image of himself on top of her, pounding in and out of her while she called to him, dug her nails into his arms, shook her head back and forth as Joan used to do, and dissolved herself in the mind-deadening moment. He wanted to rut, to taste salty skin. Instead, he patted her neck, shushed her, and ignored his erection.

"Jesus God, Jesus," she moaned, as if to herself. "Francois, oh God, Francois. . . ." She was losing it, tripping into shock.

"Who's Francois . . . ?"

"Pretre, you idiot!" She spoke loudly and seemed to be out of breath. "He's dead, how could that be? Not inside the tomb, not there, it's—"

"Stop it," Mantle said, shaking her hard, trying to reach her before she went over the edge.

"All the others lying dead on the ground, and I was supposed to plug-in. My husband is waiting for me on the other side; it's your fault; it was *my* time to die."

"Shush, don't think about it, don't think about anything now," he whispered. She tried to pull away, but he held her tightly until he thought he would crack her bones, as if he could squeeze out her fear and stop her from trembling. Then he released her.

"I'll be okay now," she whispered, "and I'm sorry I called you that name."

"You don't need to apologize," Mantle said.

"But how could he be shot *inside* the tomb? It's made of stone." Her voice rose as if following the shape of her anxiety—which threatened to turn into panic again.

"A fluke," Mantle whispered. "One of the terrorist *boutades* fired into the cracks of the tomb, a stray bullet."

"Why Francois?"

Better me instead? Mantle thought, angrily. But he remained silent, for there was really nothing to say and he couldn't bring himself to mouth platitudes, all the old bullshit which, ironically, was as valid now as it had always been.

"Francois was special," Roberta said. As if that could bring him back, Mantle thought. Roberta inhaled sharply, held her breath, then said, very slowly and carefully, as if each word were a coin and could not be taken back, "I should not have acted this way. I have seen enough to know better—" Then she cocked her head, just slightly, and Mantle knew that she was looking inward; in fact, for an instant, he felt the black and silver spaces. He tried to remember what he had seen when he had hooked in, but he couldn't remember anything except the black and silver.

Josiane, did I find you?

Mantle heard a whisper that he couldn't make out, and he felt himself jump as one does sometimes when sleeping.

"Roberta," he said, shaken. "Roberta!"

She caught herself, returning his intense stare and said, "Forgive me. I heard my husband calling me."

"You pulled me back there, as if we were plugged-in—"

"Sometimes that happens, even without a psyconductor or a ceremony," Roberta said. "I'm tied to the dark by my husband. Promised, as it were."

"I don't want to go back again," Mantle said firmly.

They started walking, careful not to slip on the wet rocks.

"The rocks here are so strange," Mantle said.

"It's been bombed," Roberta replied. "A man-made Delphi." She smiled, as if recovered from the shock of the last half-hour; but Mantle looked away, as if he were a soldier returned home only to find it had been destroyed. "That tablet commemorates the landing by your army," she said, pointing to what looked like a chiseled headstone.

"What?"

"The Second World War, in 1944."

"Why isn't it on the beach?"

She shrugged. "Maybe we don't like to remember being saved, we have enough problems, we have lost enough face. Can you understand that?"

Mantle heard a faint scream, joined by others, a distant wailing. Then four long bursts of automatic-rifle fire followed. Roberta shuddered.

"That was closer," Mantle said. It began to rain harder.

"Probably *Gendarmerie*."

"Won't they run the terrorists off?"

"No," Roberta said softly, "they'll shoot over the heads of the *boutades* and claim they all got away. They're probably doing the mopping up. I'd take my chances with the *boutades* first."

They worked their way east, toward the bay of Rade d'Agay; and finally caught sight of the old road that Roberta said ran parallel to Highway 1. As if they were suddenly in another country, the rain stopped and the moon was visible and clear, as were a few bright stars. Mantle could even see the beach below: in the moonlight the sand looked black, but it was red, as were the rocks, the porphyritic evidence of an ancient geological upheaval. The beach was dead and the land was sick: this whole area had once been forest country, a dense world of pine met by sea; now it was a deadland, a filthy, oil-smeared lip.

They followed the road for a half mile. The cover became better, the land healthier, although the trees were as thin and gnarled as those in Pennsylvania.

"There," Roberta said, pointing toward a curve in the road. "I see a car."

"I don't."

"Well, I *do*."

"It might be police," Mantle said. "Or—"

"It's not. Now come on, hurry." And Roberta ran down a rock-strewn bank toward the road.

Eight

The casino, like almost every other structure in central Paris, had common walls; but it was distinguished by heavy, inlaid, fifteen-meter-high oaken doors which, after being activated by scanning units, opened into an ample, stone-paved courtyard hung with plants and flowers. It was a veritable greenhouse, and the effect was striking: trees and flowers, bush and bud—all combined into an artist's palette as if Ernst and Rousseau had combined their considerable talents.

A young man who reminded Joan of an upright (if possible) Bedlington terrier led them through the courtyard. He spoke with a clipped English accent and had tufts of woolly, bluish white hair implanted all over his head, face, and body. Only his hands and genitals were hairless.

"He *has* to be working off an indenture," Pfeiffer said sharply as he repressed a sexual urge.

"Shush," Joan said as the boy gave Pfeiffer a contemptuous look—in Parisian culture, you paid for the service, not the smile.

They were led into a simple but formal entry lounge that

was crowded but not uncomfortable. The floor was marble; a few pornographic icons were discreetly situated around the carefully laid-out comfort niches. The room reminded Joan of a chapel with arcades, figures, and stone courts. Above was a dome from which radiated a reddish, suffusing light, lending the room an expansiveness of height rather than breadth.

But it was mostly holographic illusion.

They were directed to wait but a moment and then presented to the purser, an overweight, balding man who sat behind a small desk. He was dressed in a blue camise shirt and matching caftan which was buttoned across his wide chest and closed over with a red scarf. He was obviously, and uncomfortably, dressed in the colors of the establishment.

"And good evening, Monsieur Pfeiffer and Mademoiselle Otur. We are honored to have such an important guest . . . or guests, I should say." The purser slipped two cards into a small console. "Your identification cards will be returned to you when you leave." After a pause he asked, "Ah, does Monsieur Pfeiffer wish the lady to be credited on his card?" The purser lowered his eyes, indicating embarrassment. Quite simply, Joan did not have enough credit to be received into the more sophisticated games.

"Yes, of course," Pfeiffer said absently. He looked around; there was not a robot to be seen. Hogs, he thought. Conspicuous consumption. He felt guilty and anxious about feeling a thrill of desire for that grotesque boy.

"Well then," said the purser, folding his hands on the desk, "we are at your disposal for as long as you wish to stay with us." He gestured to the Terrier and said, "Johnny will give you the tour," but Pfeiffer refused. Johnny ushered them into a central room, which was anything but quiet, and—after a wink at Pfeiffer—discreetly disappeared.

This room was as crowded as the city ways. It was filled with what looked to be the ragtag, the bums and *boutades*, the street people, the captains of the ways. Here was a perfect replica of a street casino, but perfectly safe. This *was* a street casino, at least to Pfeiffer, who was swept up in the noise and bustle as he whetted his appetite for the dangerous pleasures of the top level.

Ancient iron bandits whispered "Chinkachinka" and rolled their picture-frame eyes in promise of a jackpot, which was immediately transferred to the winner's account by a magnetic sleight-of-hand. The amplified, high-pitched voices of pin-ball computers on the walls called out winning hands of poker and blackjack. A simulated stabbing drew nothing more than a few glances. The room was mostly filled with telefac booths, which gave it the uncomfortable air of a medieval cemetery on picnic Sunday; the tombstone booths were filled with figures working through their own Stations of the Cross. Hooked in winners were rewarded with bursts of electrically induced ecstasy; losers writhed in pain and suffered through the brain-crushing aftershock of week-long migraines.

And, of course, battered robots clattered around with the traditional complement of drugs, drinks, and food. The only incongruity was a perfectly dressed geisha who quickly disappeared into one of the iris doors on the far wall.

"Do you want to play the one-armed bandits?" Joan asked, fighting her growing claustrophobia, wishing only to escape into quiet; but she was determined to try to keep Pfeiffer from going upstairs. Yet, ironically—all her emotions seemed to be simultaneously yin and yang—she also wanted him to gamble away his organs. She knew that she would feel a guilty thrill if he lost his heart.

She checked her computer implant for news of Mantle: still nothing. Then she pulled down the lever of the one-armed bandit; it would read her finger and odor prints and transfer or deduct the proper amount to or from Pfeiffer's account. The eyes rolled and clicked, and one hundred international credit dollars were lost. "Easy come, easy go. At least this is a safe way to go. But you didn't come here to be safe, right?" she said mockingly.

"You can remain down here if you like," Pfeiffer said, looking about the room for an exit, noticing that iris doors were spaced every few meters on the nearest wall to his left. The casino must take up the whole bloody block, he thought. "How the hell do I get out of here?"

Before Joan could respond, Johnny appeared as if out of nowhere and said, "Monsieur Pfeiffer may take any one of the ascenseurs, or, if he would care for the view of our palace, he could take the staircase to heaven." He smiled, baring even teeth, and curtsied to Pfeiffer, who was blushing. The boy certainly knows his man, Joan thought sourly.

Am I jealous? she asked herself.

"Shall I attend you?" Johnny asked Pfeiffer, ignoring Joan.

"No," said Pfeiffer. "Now, please leave us alone."

Indeed, there was a narrow, winding staircase with a twisted iron balustrade which seemed to curl up into a roseate dome such as the one they had seen in the other room. A palace of domes this was, with the *boutadish* pleasures at street levels. Above was the promise of quiet rooms, stylish conversation, and cool-handed gambling: the ancient, venerable pleasures of Hoyle.

"Well, which is it?" asked Joan. "The elevator would be quickest, zoom you right to the organ room."

"We can take the stairs," Pfeiffer said, a touch of blush still in his cheeks. But he would say nothing about the furry boy. "Jesus, it seems that every time I blink my eye, the stairway disappears."

"I'll show you the way," Joan said, taking his arm.

"Just what I need," Pfeiffer said, smiling, eliminating one small barrier between them.

"I think your rush is over, isn't it? You don't really want to gamble out your guts."

"I came to do something and I'll follow it through."

The stairwell was empty, and like an object conceived in Alice's Wonderland, it appeared to disappear behind them. "Cheap tricks," Pfeiffer said.

"Why are you so intent on this?" Joan asked. "If you lose, which you most probably will, you'll never have a day's peace. They can call in your heart or liver or—"

"I can buy out, if that should happen." Pfeiffer blushed, but it had nothing to do with his conversation with Joan, to which he was hardly paying attention. He was thinking about the furry boy . . . and Mantle.

"You wouldn't gamble them if you thought you could buy out. That's bunk."

"Then I'd get artificials."

"You'd be taking another chance, with the quotas—thanks to your right-wing friends in power."

Pfeiffer didn't take the bait. "I admit defeat," he said. Again he thought of the furry boy's naked, hairless genitals. And with that came the thought of death.

The next level was less crowded and more subdued.

There were few electronic games to be seen on the floor. A man passed by dressed in medical white, which indicated that deformation games were being played. There were a good number of dice games being played for high, but safe, stakes: bird cage, chuck-luck, craps, hazard, liar dice, and yacht. There were also the usual traditional roulette tables, and card games such as vingt-et-un. On each floor, the stakes became higher: fortunes were lost, people were disfigured or ruined, but—with the exception of the top floor, which had dangerous games other than organ gambling—at least no one died. They might need a face and body job after too many deformations, but those were easily obtained, although one had to have very good credit to ensure a proper job.

One each ascending level, the house whores, both male and female, became more exotic, erotic, grotesque, and abundant. There were birdmen with feathers like peacocks and flamingos; children with dyed skin and implanted, overly large, male and female genitalia; machines that spoke the language of love and exposed soft, fleshy organs (such machines could be found wheeling about in all the ancient ruins of Western Europe and America); amputees and cripples; various drag queens and kings; natural androgynes and mutants; cyborgs; and an interesting, titillating array of genetically engineered mooncalves. But none disturbed Pfeiffer as had that silly furry boy. He wondered if, indeed, the boy was still following him.

"Come on, Joan," Pfeiffer said impatiently, "I don't want to waste any more time down here."

"I thought it was the expectation that's so exciting to seasoned gamblers," Joan said.

"Not to me," Pfeiffer said, ignoring the sarcasm. "I want to get it over with." With that, he left the room.

Then why bother at all, she said to herself. She stood by herself, ignoring a skinny, white-haired man and a piebald, doggie mooncalf coupling beside her in an upright position. Lost in thought, she visualized Pfeiffer as Mantle. Both men were obsessed with themselves, with their true natures, which were buried in the darkest parts of themselves.

But it was Pfeiffer, she sensed, who somehow held the secret. A geisha—perhaps the one they had seen downstairs—walked past Joan and nodded, as if in recognition that they were both servants of the house. Joan remained aloof, surprised at the woman's (if she was a woman) lapse of grace and manners; and yet, for just an instant, Joan was happy to be part of *something*, anything—and she knew that that was one of the reasons she had joined the Crying Church and why, too, she was a phony.

She took a lift to the top level.

It was like walking into the foyer of a well-appointed home. The high walls were stucco and the floor inlaid parquetry. A small Dehaj rug was placed neatly before a desk, behind which beamed a man of about fifty dressed in camise and caftan, the blue and red colors of the establishment. He had a flat face, a large nose that was wide but had narrow nostrils, and close-set eyes roofed with bushy brown eyebrows which were the color his hair would have been—had he had any.

Actually, the room was quite small, which made the rug look larger and gave the man a commanding position.

"Do you wish to watch or to participate, Monsieur Pfeiffer?" he asked, seeming to rise an inch from the chair as he spoke.

"I wish to play," Pfeiffer said, standing upon the rug as if he had to be positioned just right to make it fly.

"And does your friend wish to watch?" the man asked as Joan crossed the room to stand beside Pfeiffer. "Or will you give your permission for Miz Otur to make your connection." His voice didn't rise as he asked the question.

"I beg your pardon?"

"A psyconnection, sir. With a psyconductor." A note of condescension crept into his voice. "That would cost approximately—"

"No, I don't want that," Pfeiffer snapped, then moved away from Joan, who was not surprised that she could hook-in with Pfeiffer. In fact, that was just what she had hoped for.

"Oh, come on," Joan said. "Let me in, too."

"Are you serious?" he asked, turning toward her. Caught by the intensity of his stare, she could only nod. "Then I'm sorry."

"Afraid?" she asked. The thought that crossed her mind at that moment was that if the Dehaj rug could fly, then Pfeiffer would most certainly lose his balance and fall off.

"If you will, then yes. I'm not a window for you to stare through."

"Have you ever done that with your wife?" she asked. I can't be mindfucked so easily, she thought. But she immediately regretted the words and the thought. Could it really be jealousy? she asked herself. For this puffed-out fisherman? Or was it simply that Pfeiffer's mind was an entrance into Ray's past? She would take her chances to find out what Pfeiffer knew about him.

The man at the desk cleared his throat politely. "Excuse me, Monsieur, but are you aware that *only* games *organes* are played in these rooms?"

"Yes, that's why we've . . . ah, I've come to your house."

"Then you are perhaps not aware that all games are conducted with psyconductors on this level. If you will—"

"I think I will not," Pfeiffer said, taking a step backward. Joan was surprised when he, looking perplexed, said, "Well, perhaps you'd better explain this to me."

"Of course, of course," the man said, beaming as if he had just won the battle and a fortune. "There are, of course, many ways to play, and if you like, I can give you the address of a very nice house nearby where you can play a fair, safe game without hook-ins. Shall I make a reservation for you there?"

"Not just yet," Pfeiffer said, resting his hand, knuckles down, upon the flat-top, Louise XVI desk. His feet seemed to be swallowed by the floral patterns of the rug, and Joan thought it an optical illusion, this effect of being caught before the desk of the casino captain. She made another check for possible messages from Ray, Roberta, or Pretre, but there was nothing yet: all were on answering service. Suddenly she felt the urge to run, to take fliers and transpods, to leave this suffocating place and drive down the Esterel to find Ray, to break in on him, tear him apart, suck on his sweet mouth and bitter prick and mother him.

Instead, she stepped toward Pfeiffer. Perhaps he would let her slide into his mind.

". . . it is our rule, however," said the man at the desk, "that you and your opponent, or opponents, must be physically in the same room."

"Why is that?" Joan asked, feeling Pfeiffer scowling at her for intruding.

"Well," he said, "it has never happened to us, of course, but cheating has occurred on a few long-distance transactions. Organs have been wrongly lost. So we don't take chances. None at all." He looked at Pfeiffer as he spoke, obviously sizing him up, watching for reactions. But Pfeiffer had composed himself, and Joan knew that he had made up his mind.

"Why must the game be played with psyconductors?" Pfeiffer asked.

"That is the way we do it," said the captain. Then, after an embarrassing pause, he said, "We have our own games and rules. And our games, we think, are the *most* interesting. And we make the games as safe as we can for all parties involved."

"What do you mean?"

"We—the house—will be observing you. Our gamesmaster will be hooked-in, but, I assure you, you will not sense his presence in the least. But if anything should go wrong, or look as if it might go wrong, then *pfft*, we intercede. Of course, we make no promises, and there have been cases—"

"But anything that could go wrong would be because of the hook-in."

"Perhaps this *isn't* the game for you, sir."

"You must have enough privileged information on everyone who has ever played here to make book," Pfeiffer said.

"The hook-in doesn't work that way at all. And we are contract-bound to protect our clients."

"And yourselves."

"Most certainly." The captain looked impatient. "You would have to be scanned, anyway: it is a rule in all houses."

"And downstairs?"

"The stakes aren't as high; and when they are, we require a quick connection."

Pfeiffer suddenly laughed and glanced at Joan. Of course, the bitch certainly knew the nature of these games. All this to mindfuck me for Raymond. As if I would give her his past.

"If you can both read each other's minds," Pfeiffer said to the captain, "then there can be no blind cards."

"Aha, now you have it, Monsieur." At that, the tension between Pfeiffer and the desk captain seemed to dissolve. "And, indeed," the captain continued, "we have a modified version of chemin de fer that we call blind shemmy. All the cards are played facedown. It is a game of control (and, of course, chance), for you must block out certain thoughts from your mind while, at the same time, tricking your opponent into revealing his cards. And that is why it would be advantageous for you to let your friend here connect with you."

Pfeiffer groaned, and Joan smiled, amused now by the captain. Obviously, he didn't have to sell his game to his customers.

"Please clarify," Pfeiffer asked, certain now that he was right about Joan.

"Quite simply, while you are playing, your friend could help block your thoughts from your opponent with her own. But it does take some practice. Perhaps it would be better if you tried a hook-in in one of our other rooms where the stakes are not quite so high." Then the captain lowered his eyes, as if in deference, but in actuality he was looking at the CeeR screen of the terminal set into the antique desk.

Joan could see Pfeiffer's nostrils flare slightly. The poor sonofabitch is caught, she thought. "Come on, Carl, let's go back and wait for Ray."

"Perhaps you should listen to Miz Otur," the captain said, but the man must have known that he had Pfeiffer.

"What games would be open to us?" Pfeiffer asked, turning toward Joan, glaring at her. She caught her breath: if he lost, then she knew he would make certain that Joan lost something, or someone, too.

"If you wish, you can play what we call 'Vite,'" replied the captain. "It is a simple game in which you must make your play quicker than your opponent upon seeing the draw. It is a much better game for amateurs, especially if you are loathe to have anyone make the connection with you."

Joan knew instinctively that that was a game Pfeiffer would not play.

"I wish to play blind shemmy," Pfeiffer said.

"I have a game of nine in progress," the captain said. "There are nine people playing and nine others playing interference. But you'll have to wait for a space. It will be quite expensive, as the players are tired and will demand some of your points for themselves above the casino charge for play."

"How long will I have to wait?"

The captain shrugged, then said, "I have another man waiting who is ahead of you. He would be willing to play *a bon chat bon rat.* I would recommend you play him rather than wait. Like you, he is an amateur, but his wife, who will be connected with him, is not. Of course, if you wish to wait for the other..."

Pfeiffer accepted; and while he and Joan gave their prints to the various forms, the captain explained that there was no statute of limitations on the contract signed by all parties, and that it would be honored even by those governments that disapproved of this form of gambling.

Then the furry boy appeared like an apparition to take them to their room where they would be given time to practice and become acquainted.

The boy's member was slightly engorged, and Pfeiffer now became frightened. He remembered his mother, and her last filthy thoughts.

The furry boy led Joan and Pfeiffer into the game room, which smelled of oiled wood, spices, traditional tobacco, and perfume. There were no holos or decoration on the walls. Everything, with the exception of the felt atop the gaming table, cards, thick natural carpet, computer consoles and cowls, was made of precious woods: oak, elm, cedar, teak, walnut, mahogany, redwood, ebony. The long, half-oval gaming table which met the sliding partition-wall was made of satinwood, as were the two delicate but uncomfortable high-backed chairs placed side by side. On the table before each chair was the psyconductor cowl, each one sheathed in a light, silvery mask.

"We call them poker faces," the boy said to Pfeiffer, and he placed the cowl over Joan's head. He explained how the mechanism worked, then asked Pfeiffer is he wished him to stay.

"Why should I want you to stay?" Pfeiffer asked, but the sexual tension between them was unmistakable.

"I'm adept at games of chance. I can redirect your thoughts, and without a psyconductor"—and he looked at Joan and smiled.

"Put the mechanism on my head and then please leave us," Pfeiffer said.

"Do you wish me to return when you're finished?"

"If you wish," Pfeiffer replied, and Joan watched his face

redden ever so slightly. Without saying a word, she had won a small victory.

The boy lowered the cowl over Pfeiffer's head, made some unnecessary adjustments, and left reluctantly.

"I'm not sure I want to do this," Pfeiffer said, faltering.

"Well," Joan said, "we can easily call off the game. Our first connection is just practice—"

"I don't mean the game. I mean the connection."

Joan remained silent. Dammit, she told herself, I should have looked away when he made his pass at the furry pet.

"I was crazy to ever agree in the first place to such a thing."

"Shall I leave now?" Joan asked. Trump the fucker, or get off the pot and wait for Ray. She stood up, but did not judge the distance of the cowl/console connections accurately; the cowl was pulled forward, bending the silvery mask.

"I think you're as nervous as I am," Pfeiffer said.

"Make the connection right now. Or let's get out of here." Joan was suddenly angry and frustrated. Do it, she thought to herself, and for once she was not passive. Certainly not passive. She snapped the wooden toggle switch, which activated both psyconductors.

There was no scamdown into the black and silver places, the soothing death-hollow corridors. Instead, she was thrust into vertiginous light. It was all around her, as if she could see in all directions at once. But she was simply seeing through Pfeiffer's eyes. Seeing herself small—even in his eyes, small. After the initial shock, she realized that the light was not brilliant; on the contrary, it was soft and diffused.

But this was no connection at all: Pfeiffer was trying to close his mind to her. He was thinking "slut," projecting images of her trying to mindfuck him, digging into him with nail and claw. He let her know that he had been taught by brainwash psychs to stonewall dangerous thoughts and memories.

But she saw that, until now, he had never been put to the test. . . .

Pfeiffer appeared before her as a smooth, perfect, huge, sphere. It slowly rotated, a grim gray planet close to her, forever closed and hiding Ray's secrets.

"Are you happy now?" asked Pfeiffer, as if from somewhere deep inside the sphere. It was so smooth, seamless.

He really doesn't need me, she thought, and she felt as if she were flying above the surface of his closed mind, a winged thing looking for any discontinuity, any fault in his defenses.

"So you see," Pfeiffer said, exulting in imagined victory, "I *don't* need you." The words came wreathed in an image of a storm rolling angrily over the planet.

She flew in sudden panic around his thoughts, like an insect circling a source of light. She was looking for any blister, crack—any anomaly in the smooth surface. He would gamble himself away without her, that she knew, unless she could break through his defenses, prove to him how vulnerable he was.

But she only needed entrance to that country of memory where Ray's past was buried. After that, it wouldn't matter. . . .

"So you couldn't resist the furry boy, could you?" Joan asked, her thoughts like smooth sharks swimming through icy water. "I would not think you a pervert if you were not such a hypocrite. Does he, then, remind you of yourself, or do I remind you of your mother?"

His anger and exposed misery were like flares on the surface of the sun. In their place remained an eruption of Pfeiffer's smooth, protective surface. A crack in the cerebral egg.

Joan dove toward the fissure, and then she was inside Pfeiffer—not the outside of his senses where he could verbalize a thought, see a face, but in the dark, prehistoric places where he dreamed, conceptualized, where he floated in and out of memory, where the eyeless creatures of his soul dwelled.

It was a sliding, a slipping in, as if one had turned over inside oneself; and Joan was sliding, slipping on ice. She found herself in a dark world of grotesque and geometric shapes, an arctic world of huge icebergs floating on a fathomless sea.

"Where is Ray?" she demanded, and Pfeiffer responded by closing imaginary ice walls around her, barring her from his memories of Mantle, trapping her. . . .

And for an instant, Joan sensed Pfeiffer's terrible guilt and fear.

"Mindfucker, slut," Pfeiffer screamed, projecting those words in a hundred filthy, sickening images; and then he smashed through Joan's defenses and rushed into the deep recesses of her mind. He found her soft places and took what he could.

All that before the psyconnection was broken. Before the real game began. As if nothing had happened.

Nine

The car was dark, an ancient four-door Chevy Steamer.

"*Vite, vite,*" someone said impatiently in the front seat of the car: a male voice, deep and scratchy.

The car lurched forward as soon as they climbed in, before Mantle could even close the door, which locked with a sigh.

They drove north, away from the shooting. There were two men in the front seat. Mantle guessed the driver to be in his fifties; the other man, wearing a peaked cap, looked considerably younger. Campagnards, good peasant stock. A woman sitting beside Roberta twisted around to look out the back window.

The driver negotiated a series of broken back roads without turning on his headlights, and then suddenly they were on the highway, speeding along at an easy seventy miles an hour. Mantle could hear the woman speaking to Roberta and the men in the front seat in quick French, but he ignored it and watched the trees whiz past, glaucous green, as if lit by floodlights hidden in their branches rather than the headlights of the auto. Beyond the trees, everything looked milky with moonlight or shadow dark. Mantle imagined that they were rushing through a tunnel, and felt once more as if he were hooked in, felt the pull of the other side, of the Screamers.

He fought the feeling, tried to hold on, to stay sane and swallow the fire of his heart. He couldn't go over the edge. Instead of asking Roberta what was going on and who these people were, he waged silent war with himself.

Plugging in had not helped him remember Josiane: it

was just another scalpel, cutting and tearing, not restoring. He stared at his hands, which were clenched together, fingers intwined. When he released the pressure, he saw Josiane's face in the hollow made by his palms. The same face as in the stone, but this was not a holo.

"Oh, Christ," he whispered.

"What?" Roberta asked, pressing close to him.

He didn't answer her. This was the way it had happened before, when he went over the edge, he thought: first, hallucinations, whispering, incomprehensible voices, then the heat and rushing sensations, the feeling of falling through the layers of the world, of isolation and helplessness.

Maybe I'm just still stoned, he told himself. It will wear off. . . .

"Everyone has episodes after a hook-in," Roberta said. "You've had a perceptual overload; think of it that way." The woman beside Roberta was staring intently at him. "You haven't closed down yet," Roberta continued. "That's not such a bad thing. You can hear more. See more. Isn't that so? You're more alive."

"Don't condescend to me," Mantle snapped. Then, after a pause, he mumbled, "I feel more dead now than alive." Stop that! he told himself. Fight it, goddammit, don't indulge it.

"Well, you're not dead. Don't fight it. Let it take you where it will."

Back to the hospital, he thought, carried by anxiety. I should have left well enough alone, left Josiane alone instead of following her down the hole. But something told him that he wasn't only searching for Josiane. There was something else down there, buried inside him, hidden in a mesh of lies and dead memories and false clues.

He was covering up his past, and dredging it at the same time.

"It wouldn't do any good to fight it," he said to Roberta.

"That's good. I'm here, and so are the others." She raised her face to the woman beside her as an indication. The woman was dark, pretty, with a long face, deep-set eyes and shoulder-length hair. She was as thin as an American model. "Danielle has been in the dark spaces; she can hear the voices," Roberta said. "She will help you, and perhaps you will become *more* sane." That said with a smile, a flash of irony which disappeared as she pursed her lips.

"You must work your way back to this world from the dark spaces," Danielle said. "It is the same for all of us." Her accent was heavy and provincial; but it wasn't so much the way she rolled her r's as it was the way her voice lifted when making a statement, as if it were a question. "If you fight what is happening, you cannot get on and make your passage."

Mantle had a sudden flash of a great ship, a four-stacked liner cutting the sea; and then he imagined he saw a gaming table and players wearing silvery masks. Dammit, he told himself, but he stopped trying to fight the noise in his mind. She's right, he thought: get it over with. It has to be, either now or later. "There is one thing, though," Mantle said, a note of pleading discernible in his voice.

"You needn't ask it," Roberta said. "We won't take you to a hospital under any circumstances. That is a promise."

He felt an instant of relief and realized that, like it or not, these were kinspeople by common circumstances, a dark family; and like family, they would blackmail him. But it was too late to worry about that now. He had only to get through the night, and the next day, and the day after. . . .

A police van passed, going in the opposite direction, its siren blaring and lights blinking. Mantle felt a surge of relief as it passed, as if he had escaped the form-destroyer, foiled death, beaten the odds once again. Just then, he became aware of the slight lump in his back pocket. It was a wallet, a very thin one: a reminer that the owner of these clothes was a ghost and perhaps Mantle hadn't escaped after all.

Mantle opened the window and threw the wallet out: he would keep the confidence of the dead man. Neither Roberta nor Danielle said a word. He subvocalized into the computer, and it told him that Joan and Pfeiffer had left him a joint message and were waiting for him to call. They were sure that everything went swimmingly and they would meet up with him at his flat later. They had gone to Paris on a whim, but were checking through the Net every half hour in case he left a message.

Mantle scowled, annoyed and surprised. He would not leave a message. Let them have a good time, he thought, and experienced vertigo. He closed his eyes for a second and hallucinated the gaming table again—a monochromatic image seen through the same eyes as when he had been hooked in.

Afraid, not wanting to drop back into the black and silver world, he tried to keep control of himself. But it was inevitable that he would have to pass through the dark places if he was to become whole again. He shuddered at the thought, and subvocalized.

The computer plug whispered in his ear.

The year he lost Josiane, Mantle had been keeping a diary. The entries were brief and served as pegs to jog his memory. Although he knew most of the entries by heart, Mantle had become obsessed with working over every shred he could find from the past.

"July 8, 2112," the computer plug whispered. "Congressional faxphotos retouched and symbolized, finally. Message from mother. Josiane dancing again. With reputable company. Pfeiffer called about rave review for his novel. Fight with Josiane. Still can't make love."

Mantle could remember that hot, dry day in July—the anxious message from his mother about his father, "who was getting into that Indian business again," and Pfeiffer droning on endlessly about how much *The Times'* reviewer Bjornson had appreciated the subtleties and significance of his novel—but he couldn't remember Josiane inside that day. He couldn't remember what the fight with her had been about, or why he couldn't make love.

He couldn't remember how she had looked or tasted or smelled.

"July 11, 2112 . . ."

The computer whispered the days to him, and the words became a litany, a personal mantra. But he wasn't listening to the words. He was drifting backward to the still-vivid, yesterday memories of childhood and adolescence.

While growing up, he shared his bedroom with his sister. He could remember that old room as well as he could his present bedroom in Cannes: the battered wooden furniture, which would now be worth a fortune—a daybed; long black dresser; a captain's chair that slid into a built-in desk; holos of Duchamps and Van Gogh and LeFere permanently lit on the walls. But Mantle had a habit of keying the computer to light the whole room with paintings and statues, or to blow up a painting three-dimensionally so he could walk around the figures, live in the painting, or change it to fit his taste. His favorite was Pollock's *Number 29*, an impressionistic abstract of shells, string, wire mesh, pebbles, and oil paint on glass, which appeared to hang in the air and fill the room. Mantle had made love to his sister inside that painting.

That he could remember.

He had often lived in that painting since.

"What are you listening to?" Roberta asked.

"Perhaps voices," Mantle said.

Roberta smiled. "I think not. But why do you use an earplug?"

"Is that so strange?"

"Usually only old people use computer plugs. Implants are so much better."

Mantle took the plug from his ear and dropped it into his shirt pocket. "You see, I'm no longer plugged in. You can't do that with an implant."

"You don't need to, you simply don't have to use it."

True, Mantle thought. But you're still connected, without the real privacy of isolation. . . Isolation, the black and silver. Mantle shivered, and stopped his train of thought.

"Are you so afraid of being tied-in?" Roberta asked. "It seems your most important connection is with a past you cannot remember." She laughed. "A disconnection."

"Fuck you," Mantle mumbled, disliking her as he had often disliked Joan for that same sarcastic kind of probing, the armchair psych bullshit. But it felt good to be angry again, even just a little; at least he didn't feel drugged. It was like turning on a light in a dark room, waking up to see that the night monsters were dreams. But still the dark closed in, all around him, inside him. "I'll probably have the episode soon enough," he said to her as he looked out the window at the secondary road they were now traveling. The luminescent trees looked like old crones and gargoyles reaching for the car. "Must you hurry it?"

"You're not hot enough yet," Roberta said; and she placed her left hand over her mouth, and with her right she jerked out a tooth. "Now we're both disconnected. Does that make you feel better?"

To Mantle's surprise, it did.

*   *   *

They reached a large, rambling stone house a half-hour later. The sky had cleared, and the moonlight softened the night to something less than twilight. Nearby and to the east was ocean. But the familiar trees beside the road were sparse here; in their place was the kind of exotic vegetation one might find in Africa, India, or the Orient. There were oleanders, arbutus, aligousiers, amelanchiers, aloes, eucalyptus, pistaches, jujube trees, acacias, lemon trees in variety, and sweet and bitter orange trees. It was like breathing perfume; Mantle could smell eucalyptus and pine, and the flowers: jasmine, violets, roses.

"I'm not ready to go inside, to be with anyone," Mantle whispered to Roberta as they got out of the car. After a brief conversation, the others went on ahead to the house.

"Our clothes are filthy and damp," Roberta said. "Come into the house with me."

"Why don't you go inside with the others? I'll be in after a while."

"I'm going to see it through with you," Roberta said. "Is that all right?"

Mantle nodded, discovering that he was glad for her company, and asked, "What is this place?"

"We are just outside Boulouris—"

"No," Mantle said, "that's not what I meant. All this strange vegetation" —he gestured with his arm— "and the fragrance, is it real?"

Roberta, who had looked pensive and vulnerable, suddenly began to laugh, then excused herself, apologized, and said, that, indeed, it was all real. Did he think it was a videotect with olfactories? Granted, that would have been cheaper than the real thing....

Mantle walked to the edge of the circular driveway and found a cobbled footpath leading through the trees.

"It's all transplants; originally, from Hyers, surely you've heard of 'The Bosphorus of the Côte d'Azur,' alas, the very place that—" She paused to draw breath, as if she was not quite sure whether to go on in this new, but perhaps more comfortable role. "The very place that Pompignan dreamed up the Zephyr who 'with his soul ablaze covers his swooning beloved with audacious kisses and in this precious moment

the whole plain is perfumed.'" She took his hand then, and
they both laughed, a touch of hysteria in their voices. They
walked together. The air, heavy with natural perfume, had
become cloying. It was hot and humid, as if the full moon
above were a wan sun sending out heat but little light.

Mantle stopped, for the path turned to dirt and seemed
to be swallowed ahead by brush and vine and trees. He was
almost glad to see an olive tree, its characteristic shape
lending reality to the grotesque, alien vegetation growing
around it. He stared into darkness.

"Your friends were very kind to leave us alone," Mantle
said. "But you must go back to them. I know how upset you
must be, you need—"

"Shush," Roberta said. "It's my business to be with *you*,
and that helps me."

"But—" Mantle stopped himself as he felt her grip
loosen on his hand. "I asked you to tell me about this
place . . . and these people."

"This house is something like a church," Roberta said,
"and something like a commune. Some of us live here, and
some, like myself, visit."

"Who owns it?"

"You Americans are always interested in who-owns-it.
You'll meet them soon enough, as soon as we go inside. Are
you ready?"

"Not yet," Mantle said, but they walked back toward the
house, stopping when it was in view. "Is the owner a priest,
like Pretre?" He regretted that as he said it, but too late—

Roberta looked at him, but seemed to show no pain, as if
Pretre had not really been killed and she would see him
tomorrow. "No," she said after a pause. "Faon is no priest,
just an indefatigable servant of the church."

"What?"

"You'll meet Faon. She and her husband *own* the house."
Roberta smiled, as if to herself, and then said, "You know, it
never occurred to me to think of Faon as a priest. Perhaps
she is. . . ."

"You mean you don't *know*?"

"You're not afraid now, are you," Roberta asked, but it
was more a statement than a question.

"No," he said, surprised that he wasn't. "I feel good
here. Perhaps I won't have that episode, after all." A thin, hot

breeze brushed his face. He put his arm around Roberta and they leaned against each other.

"All episodes don't have to be bad, you know."

"Yes, I've heard the party line."

"And yours—they were very bad?"

Mantle didn't answer.

"Well," Roberta said, "I have had bad and I have had good. Since the church, always good."

"Like tonight?" Mantle asked. She stiffened, and he said, confessing, "I still can't remember what I saw when I was hooked in. Only that everything was black and silver... and an ocean, falling into it." Anxiety began to rise, as if it had been lying dormant inside him and was now expanding again.

"That is not unusual," Roberta said, but she looked worried. "You'll remember, it's just the shock of a new experience. Don't worry and don't fight it."

Mantle looked back at the house, which looked more like a fortification erected by an impoverished noble. It was constructed in the style of Puget, who was considered to be the heir to the Roman stone-cutters. The great stones, each of a different size, fitted together perfectly. The roof was made of curved, graduated pantiles, and a correct fit demanded a craftsman with a great deal of manual intuition. Still, it resembled a great barrack, even with the obviously more recent addition of a colonnade; yet it was a dignified house and at least four hundred years old—as was attested not only by its style, but by the splotches of plastup used to mend the walls. An outside lawn lamp illuminated the front face of the house; the rest of the house lamp illuminated the front face of the house; the rest of the house seemed to merge into the shadowy, exotic growth around it.

"Do you think you're ready to go inside now?" Roberta asked.

Mantle nodded.

They entered the house, first into a stucco-walled anteroom which was bare and yellow-streaked, and then into a large, arched sitting room from which he could see a circular staircase to his left and other rooms ahead and to his right. He imagined room after room, an infinity of rooms, an infinite hotel for all the guests of heaven and hell. He stopped himself from thinking that way, but the house did have a museum quality of decay about it, heightened by the rich wallpapers, crenations, period furniture, paintings, tapestries, bronzes, and porcelains. Some of this, he thought, had to be holos. A lovely Limoges enamel miniature caught his eye, as if the tiny plaque covered the entire wall leading into the sitting room. In the miniature, two costumed women were reading what was obviously a love note, while a young man eavesdropped; they were all caught in the translucent enamel, closed in the bronze frame.

But the house seemed alive, he thought. It was like the insides of a seashell, winding round and round from mystery to mystery, a living concretion.

As they approached the stairs, Mantle could smell the perfumed tallow of candles. A woman in her forties, hair pulled back, eyes direct, stepped out of a nearby room and left the paneled door ajar. She wore a simple, loose-fitting black dress; her appearance was severe, perhaps prim. She nodded to Roberta, smiled warmly at Mantle and said, "Hello, I'm Faon. Welcome."

Mantle thanked her for her hospitality, but could not help looking over her shoulder and into the room she had just left. Everything inside was suffused with yellow.

Faon turned to the room and asked, "Would you like to see our candle room?"

"Perhaps he should wait until tomorrow. . . ." Roberta said.

"Yes, I would like to see it," Mantle said, and Faon led him into the room. Roberta followed.

Candles were flickering and guttering everywhere: along the floor, set side by side to create the illusion of aisles; upon sideboards and desks and silver serving trays; in crystal baskets; in girandoles and sconces on the textured walls. The black parquet floor, which reflected the candles darkly, made the room feel large and cold. It was like looking down at a river from a bridge at night and seeing the city lights reflected.

Mantle felt as if he had just walked into the chapel of a wealthy but Campagnard-style sect. There were so many sects. . . .

On the far side of the room, lifted high above the floor like a bier for a miniature Greek hero and surrounded by candles, was a small, open casket. Mantle walked over to it.

A little boy lay in the casket, brocade all around him, folds of red velour touching his calm face. He could not be more than eleven or twelve; his hair was white-blond and cut very short. He was dressed in a black, gauzy gown. Fascinated, Mantle stared into the casket.

This is familiar, he thought, excited. I have seen this boy before! Be careful. "Why do you do this?" he asked.

"It's custom," Roberta answered. "This little one is passing across to the other side. Our custom is to have someone watch over the passage. We all take turns."

"Something like in the Tibetan Book of the Dead," Mantle said.

"Something like that," Faon said, smiling.

"Is this your child?" he asked her.

"No, he was given to us after his mother and father were lost."

"Given?"

"Have you heard the voices?" Faon asked.

"No," Mantle said wearily.

"Last year during a ceremony," Roberta said, "we were told where to find this child."

"By whom?" Mantle asked.

"By the voices you can't seem to hear," Faon said.

"Was he a Screamer?"

"I prefer the word Crier; and, yes he was. Stephen's parents were lost in the first Panic in Saint Raphael. They couldn't stand in both worlds, ours and that of the Crier. They simply lost their bodies before they died."

"Stephen told us that he was going to follow his parents, which he did," Roberta said, gesturing toward the casket.

"Didn't you try to help me...him?" Mantle asked Roberta.

Faon smiled, as she seemed to look right through him, excoriating him. Mantle blushed, but there was nothing to do but return her stare. "An interesting slip of the tongue," she said, exchanging a glance with Roberta. "No, there was nothing we could do to *help* him. He knew what he wanted to do, what he had to do, and we promised him that we would guard his passage, as we say." Mantle frowned. "You still don't understand. He knew what he was doing. He was not committing suicide, as you think. He had a place to go. Just to die, without help, without others on the other side waiting to pull you up—that is suicide."

"I know I've seen that little boy before," Mantle said,

blurting out the words. Roberta stepped closer to him, offering security.

Faon nodded, as if that were not out of the ordinary, and said, "Perhaps when you were in the dark spaces."

"I saw him in the casket," Mantle said, "when I plugged into the Crier at Dramont. And I glimpsed this house." He remembered as he talked, his words the catalysts of memory. "But I'd never seen it before."

Faon made a clucking sound and said, "You make much out of nothing. Of course you could dream the house. But what about your wife? Did you find *her*?"

"No," Mantle said. "I can't remember." And he couldn't.

Suddenly, Faon slapped him squarely in the face with her open hand. It stung and drew blood from his nose and mouth. But he saw Josiane's face, as if in her hand. It was as if Faon had struck him with Josiane herself.

Mantle swore and raised his hand as if to block another blow or to strike back, but it was only reflex. He was too surprised even to feel anger.

"Now do you remember?" she asked.

Mantle hesitated an instant, and before he could answer, she struck him again. This time he grabbed her arm roughly, and she—pulled off balance—was pulled against him, her face against his chest.

"Do you remember?" she asked, her voice only slightly muffled.

"Yes!" he said, his teeth clenched. When Faon struck him last, it was as if he were back in the tomb again, plugged into the dead man; and again he saw Josiane floating just below the surface of a dark sea, saw her staring unblinkingly at him, heard her voice calling him home. It was Josiane. It was. And home was New York. He resolved that he would return to the States. He would find her. She was there—he felt that—and she was alive.

Then Mantle began to shiver as if he had been thrown into icy water. Suddenly he knew he was going to have an episode. He could feel the pull of the dark spaces, the hollow places. It's going to happen again, he thought. Sonofabitch!

Faon pulled away from him and said, "You've had a rather rough time." She looked at him with a directness that seemed to be hers alone. "I'm sorry. But the transition crisis which you've been experiencing will bring you closer to reality, to true seeing. . . ."

Mantle's hands felt clammy and he was drenched in cold sweat. Faon's voice was echoing in the room, or so it seemed to him. "Excuse me," he said, "but I think I'd like to go outside."

Roberta took his hand, as if to draw him out of the room.

"It's close," Mantle said to her. "I can feel it on me. Just leave me alone and—"

"We'll go upstairs right now," Roberta said. "I'll see it through with you, share it."

Mantle tried to conrol his anxiety and said, "I'll be all right on my own hook."

"You don't have to be embarrassed, not here, not with us," Faon said. "We've all been through it. You're not a freak here. Go with Roberta; it will make it easier for you."

"Come on," Roberta said. "Quickly."

Mantle followed Roberta up the stairs, along a rather narrow hallway lined with paintings of dusty woodland scenes—some of which certainly had to be facsimiles, for Mantle saw a painting of trees bending toward swampy water that looked like the work of Van Ruisdael, a melancholy artist of the mid-seventeenth century. Even the paintings alarmed him, not because of the incongruity of possession, but because they seemed to reflect the tones and textures of his own thoughts, those thoughts which were driving him over the edge.

Roberta led him up another flight of stairs and into a room that was virtually empty except for a simple bed, chairs, and the ever-present computer console. This was more a monk's cell than a guest room.

"Take off your clothes and try to relax," Roberta said gently. "Do you want a narcodrine?" Mantle shook his head: he had had enough drugs. He sat down on the bed, which was hard, and suddenly felt removed from Roberta and everything in the room, as if skeins of invisible material were separating him from the real world of people and things. It was almost as if he were in two places at once. He shuddered to think about the other place.

Roberta bent over the computer console; then, as if she had just remembered, turned to Mantle and said, "There's a dry shower in the bathroom, there." She pointed to the door on the far wall. "Why don't you slip in; I'll follow you." Then she turned back to the computer and keyed in a program. Mantle jumped as the room dimmed slightly and became full of colored streamers and splotches, bits of shells, string, and wire mesh; and he remembered Josiane with the clarity of hallucination, remembered her bending over him in their old bedroom (she a child with budbreasts and a tight, unwrinkled face) and screwing him, watching him impassively as he stared at the holographic objects of Pollock's painting hanging in the air.

"How did you know about that?" Mantle asked. The tremors were beginning again, even now, with the familiar all around him as if he had captured the past.

"Not yet," Roberta said. "I'll tell you after we shower. Now a word until I'm clean." She stepped out of her clothes, leaving them in a bunch on the floor, and went into the bathroom. Mantle followed, and, indeed, felt better after showering, although he still didn't feel entirely clean. His hair was fluffy and his skin tingled.

"There's a marvelous shower down the hall," Roberta said. "A real antique with I-don't-know-how-many water nozzles, which spray you from every direction. It's better than anything we've got now, I don't care what anybody says."

They sat on the edge of the bed. "Well," Mantle asked, "how did you know about the painting?"

"I thought it would calm you. Doesn't it?"

"It was just a shock at first," he said, as if from across an abyss. "But how did you know to pick that—"

"I read over your records. Joan made an entry about it. So . . . Raymond?"

"Yes," he answered, feeling calm and deadened, not caring about Joan or Pfeiffer or Roberta; and Josiane was only a perfect idea, a form for his thoughts, as dead as he. He now felt that time was subtly, but definitely, slowing down, unwinding; and when it stopped he would be left in the eternal black and silver spaces with the dead.

Fight it, you sonofabitch, he told himself.

"Why didn't Joan come with you?" Roberta asked, as if she could not see that Mantle was losing it, slowly sliding over the edge into himself.

"I wanted to do this alone." Talk to her, keep her talking, touch her, help me, Josiane.

"But she would have wanted to be with you." Mantle didn't reply. "Do you love her?" Roberta asked after a pause.

"Yes, I suppose I do," Mantle said, answering the question as if by rote, his thoughts far away, glimpsing shadows of Josiane, feeling time running down. "But in a different way." He was talking as if to himself now. "Without the passion and longing, without the sickness."

"Sickness?"

Mantle shook his head and touched her hand, which was resting on her lap. He ran his fingers over her knuckles and through her pubic hair.

"Do you think passion is sick?" she asked.

"No. That's not what I meant."

"But what you said. Do you consider your feelings for your sister as being *sick*?" She turned to face him, and he touched her shoulders, her arms, her face. He noticed that her nostrils were flared. He felt slightly repelled. She was so far away now, mile upon mile; and yet he could touch her as if his arms were a thousand kilometers long and he could stretch them across the void. And he could answer her questions now, perhaps even more objectively than before. He was burning from the inside with thoughts and memories that he could not give form. But the outside still retained its appearance.

"No," he said after a long pause. Time distending and contracting. "I don't think of my feelings for Josiane as sick."

"Do you want me to call Joan for you?" Roberta asked, somewhat anxiously. "She could be here—"

"No, again."

"It's like with Josiane, isn't it?"

"What do you mean?" Mantle asked, seeing the smooth pit before him, the silver and black exit inside him, that had always been inside him. He felt the burning, the cold fire, turning him to ash, giving him escape.

"Josiane serves to hide something; Joan was a way of finding it." The words seemed isolated, a metallic mobile hanging in a dark room.

"I don't understand any of that," Mantle said, and the room seemed elongated, hard and hollow, as he began to scam down, falling through the thinnest layers of the world as vision changed from eye to mind's eye, as colors faded to silver and passed into darkness.

Mantle caught himself, tried to hold himself back. A last clinging to the world.

"Where are you from?" he asked Roberta, as if the mundane could hold him back from the pit.

She smiled now, a nostalgic smile, that of one lover saying good-bye to another, and said, "I'm from Missiri, above Saint Raphael, but I grew up and went to school in England. But I am French...."

And it began. A long, rushing relief, a tearing away. Better to fall through the world and die, get it over with.

Then Roberta was on top of him. She felt cold as metal, as if she were a silver construct, a perfectly molded, moving embracing icon of a woman. Her hair, now dark as the pit through which he fell, hid her face; and she made him hard and, without foreplay, pressed him into her, then pumped him, this strong metal being moving up and down upon him, a silver spider planted squarely above him, heavy as lead.

She watched him, her face impassive, and shrank into Joan. Became smaller, a child, and Mantle took her with him as he slowly fell.

And she changed again, into a woman thing with knots on her arms and face and body, and still she pumped, and changed again and again, as long as he watched: she became the leaden spider, and a scorpion, and then transformed herself into other women he had known; but the scorpions and spiders were wriggling inside them, only to crawl out their mouths in ecstasy.

Later that night, Mantle awakened. The room was dim, the videotect still hung in the air—a shadowy mass without weight—and still everything was black and silver and in between grays; still he saw with his mind's eye from one world into another. This was the real world, he thought, the bottom of everything, the inside, the underpinning, and on the outside was flesh and color and life—all sham, an intricate illusion. Here was where the Screamers lived, in the dead places, the empty places; but Mantle heard no voices, remembered only falling.

This episode was only emptiness. Where were the monsters of his soul, the phantoms, the demons, the seraphim and cherubim, the powers and dominions? Where were the apparitions, Josiane's face, and the Screamers themselves?

Where were the voices, the whistlings and rustlings, the ululations, the glossolalia of words almost apprehended?

He tried to remember, but remembered only emptiness.

He tried to remember being plugged in. He tried to remember what had happened during this episode.... Roberta's metallic touch. Something about that....

Roberta moved in the bed beside him, both hands clasped together upon the pillow, her face resting on them. She slept in fetal position, her knees together and just touching Mantle. He turned toward her and found her staring at him, her eyes as large and hard as the dark stones of an icon.

Again he awoke, and found Danielle in bed with them: Danielle, silver-gilded, with her long, dark hair and delicate, yet openly sensual, face. She and Roberta were beside him, facing and comforting each other, resting their weight on their knees, and they felt each other's breasts and sucked on each other's fingers and kissed.

Mantle propped himself up on one arm and watched them. He felt their distance—even though they brushed against him—yet welcomed their presence. He was seeing and reaching across an eternity, looking through a window into a world of flesh and life, even if everything around him was dead and silver.

He reached across the abyss and touched the small of Roberta's back, felt a tuft of soft hair, while Danielle leaned across her and took Mantle's penis into her mouth. Her lips felt cold as a crypt.

Mantle was not afraid. He had passed through life into death and found nothing: no Screamers, no specters, no horrors, just emptiness. Perhaps this would be an easy passage, even if he awakened to find that this episode was a blind, leading nowhere. He had no desire for the world. He wasn't falling anymore. He would simply wait out this episode, no matter how many subjective eternities it might take.

He was as hard as the walls now, a part of the underthings, no longer flesh.

As Danielle, who had a good, earthy, sour smell, ran her mouth up and down his penis, Mantle watched her work like some intricate machine, hard and impenetrable; and then she changed, became scaly, grew row upon row of teeth like a shark. She hurt him with her cold mouth, and Mantle, grateful for the emptiness and surcease, was carried through the dead places.

He swam through the dark spaces where everything drifted in an eternal Now, where past, present, and future were one and the same.

Josiane was calling him, or so he thought. . . .

And he was an eyeless shark, caught, and being reeled in.

Ten

A man and a woman wearing identical cowled masks sat across from Joan and Pfeiffer. The partition had been slid back, revealing the oval shape of the gaming table and doubling the size of the wood-paneled room. The dealer and the gamesmaster sat on each side of the long table that lay between the opponents. The dealer was a young man with an intense, roundish face and straight black hair cut at the shoulders; he was most likely in training to become a gamesmaster.

The gamesmaster's face was hidden by a black cowl; he would be hooked into the game. He explained the rules, activated the psyconductors, and the game began. Joan and Pfeiffer were once again hooked in, but there was no contact, as yet, with the man and woman across the table.

Pfeiffer cleared his mind, just as if he were before lasers or giving an interview or teaching. He had learned to cover his thoughts, for, somehow, he had always felt they could be seen, especially by students and those who wanted to hurt him politically and on the job.

White thought, he called it, because it was similar to white noise; he had once told Raymond about his technique, but the crazy fool could only use it as a title for one of his techtonic sculptures.

Pfeiffer could feel Joan circling around him like the

wind, but he could hide from her. Although he couldn't conceal everything, the most dangerous thoughts were safe: the psychs had given him a lock on his mind. Joan was a tough, elastic bitch, but Pfeiffer could use her, just as she could use him. They had reached an accord via mutual blackmail. Somehow, during their practice hook-in, Joan had forced herself into Pfeiffer's mind; shocked, he had attacked her.

So now they knew each other.

They built a simple symbol structure: he was the world, a perfect sphere without blemish, made by God's own hands, a world as strong and divine as thought; and she was his atmosphere. She contained all the elements that could not exist on his featureless surface. She was the protective cloak of his world.

They built a mnemonic in which to hide, yet they were still vulnerable to each other. But Pfeiffer guessed that Joan would remain passive: she had the well-developed conscience of a mystical liberal. She would not expose him to danger to gain her selfish ends. He had seen that—or thought he had.

Pfeiffer congratulated himself for being calm, reinforced his calmness. Perhaps it was Joan's presence. Perhaps it was the mnemonic. But perhaps not. He had the willpower; this was just another test. He had survived all the others, he told himself.

Joan rained on him, indicating her presence, and they practiced talking within geometric shapes as a protective device—it was literally raining geodesic cats and dogs.

When the gamesmaster opened the psyconductor to all involved, Joan and Pfeiffer were ready.

But they were not ready to find exact duplicates of themselves facing them across the table. The doppelgängers, of course, were not wearing cowls.

"First, Mesdames and Messieurs, we draw the wager," said the dealer, who was not hooked in. The gamesmaster's thoughts were a neutral presence. "For each organ pledged, there will be three games consisting of three hands to a game," the dealer continued. "In the event that a player wins twice in succession, the third hand or game will not be played." His voice was an intrusion; it was harsh and cold and came from the outside where everything was hard and intractable.

'How do they know what we look like?' Pfeiffer asked, shaken by the hallucination induced by his opponents. But before Joan could reply, he answered his own question. 'They must be picking up subliminal stuff.'

'The way we perceive ourselves,' Joan said. The doppelgängers became hard and ugly, as if they were being eroded by time. And Joan's double was becoming smaller, insignificant.

'If we can't cover up, we won't have a chance.'

'You can't cover everything, but neither can they,' Joan said. 'It cuts both ways.' She noticed a fissure in the otherwise perfect sphere below, and she became black fog, miasma, protective covering. Pfeiffer was afraid, and vulnerable. But she had to give him credit: he was not hiding it from her, at least.

'Did you pick up anything from them, an image, anything?' Pfeiffer asked.

'We've been too busy with ourselves, but they can't hide everything. We'll just wait and be ready when they let something slip out.'

'Which they will,' Pfeiffer said, suddenly confident again.

From deep inside their interior symbolized world, Joan and Pfeiffer could look into the external world of croupier, felt-top table, cards, wood-covered walls, and masked creatures. This room was simply a stage for the play of thought and image.

Pfeiffer was well acquainted with this sensation of perceiving two worlds, two levels: inside and outside. He often awakened from a nightmare and found himself in his living room or library. He knew that he was awake, and yet he could still see the dream unfurl before him, watch the creatures of his nightmare stalk about the room—the interior beasts let loose into the familiar, comforting confines of his waking world. Those were always moments of terror, for surely he was near the edge then and could fall, just as Raymond had.

The dealer combined two decks of cards and placed them in a shoe, a box from which the cards could be slid out one by one. He discarded three cards: the traditional burning of the deck. Then he dealt a card to Pfeiffer and one to his opponent. Both cards landed face up. A Queen of Hearts for Pfeiffer. A Nine of Hearts for his opponent.

So Pfeiffer lost the right to call the wager.

Just as the object of blackjack was to draw cards that added up to twenty-one, or as near as possible, the object of blind shemmy was to draw cards that added up to nine. Thus, face cards, which would normally be counted as ten, were counted as zero. Aces, normally counted as eleven, became one; and all other cards had their normal pip (or face) value—with the exception of Tens, which, like Aces, were counted as one.

"Monsieur Deux wins, nine over zero," said the dealer, looking now at Pfeiffer's opponent. Pfeiffer was Monsieur Un and his opponent Monsieur Deux only because of their positions at the table.

'A hell of a way to start—' Pfeiffer said.

'Keep yourself closed,' Joan said, turning into mist, then dark rain, pure sunlight and rainbows, a perceptual kaleidoscope to conceal Pfeiffer from his enemies. 'Look now, he'll be more vulnerable when he speaks. I'll cover you.'

'Your choice,' said the gamesmaster. The thought was directed to Pfeiffer's opponent, who was staring intently at Pfeiffer.

'Look now,' Joan said to Pfeiffer.

"Since we both turned up hearts, perhaps there is where we should begin," Pfeiffer's opponent said, speaking for the benefit of the dealer. His words felt like shards of glass to Pfeiffer. "They're the seats of our emotions, so we'd best dispose of them quickly." Pfeiffer felt the man smile. "Do you assent?"

"It's your choice," Pfeiffer said tonelessly.

'Don't let anything out,' Joan said.

Pfeiffer couldn't pick up anything from his opponent and the woman with him; they were both empty doppelgängers of himself and Joan. 'Pretend nothing matters,' she said. 'If you're to see his cards and look inside him for weaknesses, you must be removed.'

She's right, Pfeiffer thought. He tried to relax, smooth himself down; he thought white thoughts and ignored the knot of anxiety that seemed to be pulling at his groin.

"Cartes," said the dealer, dealing two cards from the shoe, facedown: one to Pfeiffer, the other for his opponent.

Another two cards, and then a palpable silence; not even thoughts seemed to cut the air. It was an unnatural waiting. . . .

Pfeiffer had a natural nine, a winning hand (a Queen and a Nine of Diamonds), and he looked up, about to turn over his cards, when he saw the furry boy sitting across the table from him.

'What the hell—'

'Call your hand,' Joan said, feeling his glands open up, a warm waterfall of fear. But before Pfeiffer could speak, his opponent said, "My friend across the table has a natural nine. A Queen and a Nine, both diamonds. Since I called his hand and I believe I am correct, then . . ."

The dealer turned Pfeiffer's cards over and said, "Monsieur Deux is correct, and wins by call." If Pfeiffer's opponent had been mistaken about the hand, then Pfeiffer would have won automatically, even if his opponent held better cards.

The dealer then dealt two more cards from the shoe.

'You're supposed to be covering my thoughts,' Pfeiffer said, but he was composed, thinking white thoughts again.

'I'm trying,' Joan said. 'But you won't trust me. You're trying to cover yourself from me as well as your opponent. What the hell can I do?'

'I'm sorry,' Pfeiffer thought.

'What are you so afraid I'll see? Your memories of Ray?'

'This is neither the time nor the place.' His rhythm of white thought was broken; Joan became a snowstorm, aiding him, lulling him back to white blindness. 'I think the gamesmaster is making me nervous, having him hooked in, privy to all our thoughts. . . .'

'Forget the gamesmaster,' Joan said.

"Monsieur Un, will you *please* claim your cards," said the dealer. The gamesmaster nodded at Pfeiffer and thought neutral, papery thoughts.

Pfeiffer turned up the edges of his cards. He had a Jack of Diamonds—which counted as zero—and a Two of Spades. He would need another card.

'Don't think about your cards,' Joan exclaimed. 'Are you picking up anything from the other side of the table?'

Pfeiffer listened, as if to his own thoughts. He didn't raise his head to look at his opponent, for seeing his own face—or that of the furry boy—staring back at him from across the table was disconcerting, and fascinating. An image of an empty hollow without any organs, formed in his mind. He imagined her as a bag somehow formed into human shape.

'Keep that,' Joan said. 'It might be usable.'

'But I can't see his cards.'

'Just wait.'

"Does Monsieur wish another card?" the dealer asked Pfeiffer. Pfeiffer took another card, and so did his opponent.

Pfeiffer had no idea what cards his opponent was holding; it promised to be a blind play. When the cards were turned over, the dealer announced, "Monsieur Deux wins, six over five." Pfeiffer had lost again.

'I'm playing blind,' Pfeiffer said anxiously to Joan.

'He couldn't see your cards, either,' she replied.

But that gave him little satisfaction, for by losing the first two hands, he had lost the first game. And if he lost the next game, he would lose his heart, which, white thought or not, seemed to be beating in his throat.

'Calm yourself,' Joan said, 'or you'll let everything out. That was the easy part...'

'What?'

'If you trust me, and stop throwing up your defenses, I can help you. But you've got to let me in; as it is, you're giving our friends quite the edge. Let's make a merger.' There was laughter in that thought, but Pfeiffer was in no mood. His fear was building, steadily, slowly.

'You can fold the game,' Joan said. 'That is an alternative.'

'And give up organs I haven't yet played for!' The smooth surface of Pfeiffer's sphere cracked, and Joan let herself be swallowed into it. The surface of the sphere changed, grew mountain chains, lush vegetation, flowers, deserts, all the mingled moods of Joan and Pfeiffer.

Pfeiffer was no longer isolated: he was protected, yet dangerously exposed. Inside him, in the human, moist dark, Joan promised not to take advantage of him. She caught a fleeting thought of Pfeiffer's dead mother, who had been a fleshy, big-boned, flat-faced woman. She also saw that Pfeiffer hated his mother, as much now as when she was alive.

In the next hand—the opening hand of the second game—Pfeiffer held a Five of Clubs and a Two of Spades, a total value of seven points, which wasn't bad. He would not take another card unless he could see his opponent's. But when he looked up, Pfeiffer saw the furry boy, who blew him a kiss.

'You're exposed again,' Joan said, and they thought themselves inside their world, thought protective darkness around themselves, except for one tiny opening through which to see into the enemies.

"Concentrate on that image of the empty woman,' Joan said to Pfeiffer. 'She has to be Monsieur Deux's wife or woman. I can't quite visualize it as you did.' But Pfeiffer was trying to smooth down his emotions and the dark, dangerous demon that was his memory. The image of the furry boy sparked memories, fears, guilts. Pfeiffer remembered his father, who had been a doctor. There was always enough money, but his father extracted emotional dues for every dollar he gave his son; and, as a result, the young Pfeiffer had recurrent nightmares that he was sucking off his father. Those nightmares began again after his mother died: she had seen that homosexual fantasy when Pfeiffer hooked into her on her deathbed.

Pfeiffer still had those nightmares.

And now, the image of him sucking off the furry boy passed through his mind, drawing its train of guilt and revulsion. The boy and his father—somehow one and the same.

'You're leaking,' Joan said, her thoughts an ice storm. She could see her way into Pfeiffer now, into those rooms of buried memories. Rather than rooms, she thought of them as subterranean caverns; everything inside them was intact, perfect, hidden from the harmful light and atmosphere of consciousness. But she could not find any memories of Ray.

Pfeiffer collected himself and peered into his opponent's mind. He thrust the image of the organless woman at the man.

It was like tearing a spiderweb.

Pfeiffer felt the man's pain as a feather touching flesh: the organless woman was Monsieur Deux's permanent wife. Pfeiffer had broken through and into his thoughts; he could feel his opponent's name, something like Gayah, Gahai, *Gayet*, that was it, and his wife was used up. Gayet saw her, in the darkness of his unconscious, as an empty bag. She was the compulsive gambler who had spent her organs; and Gayet hated gambling, but she possessed him; and he hated her and loved her and was just beginning his self-destructive slide.

Now she was using him up. She was gambling *his* organs.

'She's used up,' Pfeiffer thought at Gayet. But Pfeiffer could only glimpse Gayet's thoughts. His wife was not exposed.

Nor was she defenseless.

She thrust the image of the furry boy at Pfeiffer, and Pfeiffer felt his head being forced down upon the furry boy's lap. But it suddenly wasn't the furry boy anymore. It was Pfeiffer's father!

There was no distance now. Pfeiffer was caught, tiny and vulnerable. Gayet and his wife were swallowing him, thoughts and all.

It was Joan who saved him. She pulled him away, and he became the world again, wrapped in snow, in whiteness. He was safe again, as if inside Joan's cold womb.

'Look now,' Joan said an instant later, and like a revelation, Pfeiffer saw Gayet's cards, saw them buried in Gayet's eyes with the image of his aging wife. In that instant, Pfeiffer saw into Gayet and forgot himself. Gayet's wife was named Grace, and she had been eroded from too many surgeries, too many deformation games. She was his Blue Angel (yes, he had seen the ancient film), and Gayet the fool.

The fool held an Ace of Hearts and a Five of Diamonds.

Now Pfeiffer felt that the odds were with him. It was a familiar sensation for gamblers, a sense of harmony, of being a benevolent extension of the cards. No anger, no fear, no hate, just victory. Pfeiffer called Gayet's hand, thereby preventing Gayet from drawing another card, such as a Lucky Three, which would have given him a count of nine.

Pfeiffer won the hand, and he thanked Joan, who was a constant presence, part of his rhythm and harmony; and she dreamed of the victorious cats that padded through the lush vegetation of Pfeiffer's sphere.

The cats that rutted, then devoured each other.

Pfeiffer won the next hand. Thus he won the second game; Pfeiffer and his opponent were now even. The next game would determine the outcome. Pfeiffer felt that calm, cold certainty that he would take Gayet's heart. This obsession to expose and ruin his opponent became more important than winning or losing organs; it was bright and fast flowing, refreshing as water.

He was in a better world now, a more complete, fulfilling plane of reality. All gamblers dreamed of this: losing or winning everything, but being inside the game. Even Joan was carried away by the game. She, too, wanted to rend, whittle away at the couple across the table, take their privacies, turn over their humiliations like worry beads.

Joan knew it as Junkie's Revenge, this harmonizing of destructiveness. Pfeiffer blocked out her thought, for she was also thinking about Ray. Deep down, in the quick of his unconsciousness, Pfeiffer knew he would lose joyously and follow his friend Raymond to a dark, mutual epiphany.

Everyone was exposed now, battle-weary, mentally and physically exhausted, yet lost in play, lost in perfect, concentrated time. Pfeiffer could see Gayet's face, both as Gayet saw himself and as Grace saw him. A wide nose, dark complexion, low forehead, large ears; yet it was a strong face, and handsome in a feral, almost frightening way—or so Grace thought. Gayet saw himself as weak; the flesh of his face was too loose.

Gayet was a failure, although he had made his career and fortune in the Exchange. He had wanted to be a mathematician, but he was lazy and had lost the "knack" by twenty-five. Gayet would have made a brilliant mathematician, and he knew it.

And Grace was a whore, using herself and everyone else. Here was the woman with great religious yearnings, who had wanted to join a religious order, but was blackballed by the cults because of her obsession for gambling and psyconductors, who would never plug-into another Crier. Who yearned for the dead, for the dark spaces. But Pfeiffer could only see into her a little. She was a cold bitch and, more than any of the others, had reserves of strength.

This last game would be psychological surgery. Tearing with the knife, pulping with the bludgeon. Pfeiffer won the first hand. This was joy; so many organs to win or lose, so little time. Let Raymond have his corpses, he still won't find Josiane.

Pfeiffer lost the next hand. Gayet exposed Joan, who revealed Pfeiffer's cards without realizing it. Gayet had opened her up, penetrated all that efficiency and order to expose anger and lust and uncontrolled, oceanic pity. Joan's emotions writhed and crawled over her like beautifully colored, slippery snakes.

Pfeiffer had been too preoccupied to protect her.

Joan's first thought was to expose Pfeiffer, but Pfeiffer opened up to her, buried her in white thought that was as cold and numbing as ice, and apologized without words, but with soft, rounded, comforting thoughts. She accepted it, but couldn't trust him; he was hard inside, and as damaged as Ray.

The dealer gave Pfeiffer a Three of Diamonds and an Ace of Clubs. That only gave him four points; he would have to draw again. He kept his thoughts from Joan, for she was covering him. She could attack Gayet and his whore, expose them for their cards. Gayet's heart was not simply his organ, not now, not to Pfeiffer. It was his whole life, life itself. To rip it away from him would be to conquer life, if only for a moment. It was life affirming. It was being alive. Suddenly he thought of Raymond, who was embracing a corpse to find his past.

'Close yourself up,' Joan said. 'You're bleeding.' She did not try to penetrate his thoughts of Mantle—that would have exposed Pfeiffer even more dangerously.

'Help me,' Pfeiffer asked Joan. This hand would determine whether he would win or lose the game . . . and his heart. Once again she became his cloak, his atmosphere, and she weaved her icy threads of white thought into his.

Pfeiffer couldn't see Gayet's cards, and nervously asked Joan to do something. Gayet was playing calmly, well covered by Grace, who simply hid him. No extravagance there.

Joan emptied her mind, became neutral, unseen; yet she was a needle of cold, coherent thought. She prodded, probed, touched her opponents' thoughts. It was like swimming through an ever-changing world of dots and bars, tangible as iron, fluid as water. As if Gayet's and Grace's thoughts were luminous points on a fluorescent screen.

And still she went unnoticed.

Gayet was like Pfeiffer, Joan thought. Seemingly placid, controlled, but that was all gingerbread to hide a weak house. He was so much weaker than Grace, who was supporting and cloaking him. But Grace was concentrating her energies on Gayet; and she had the fever, as if she were gambling her own organs once again. Undoubtedly, Grace expected Joan and Pfeiffer to go for Gayet, who had read the cards.

So Joan went for Grace, who was in the gambler's frenzy as the hand was being played. Joan slipped past Grace's thoughts, worked her way into the woman's mind, through the dark labyrinths and channels of her memory, and into the dangerous country of the unconscious. Invisible as air, she listened to Grace, read her, discovered:

A sexual miasma. Being brutally raped as a child. After a riot in Manosque. Raped in a closet, for God's sake. The man tore her open with a rifle barrel, then inserted himself. Taking her, just as she was taking Gayet, piece by bloody piece. Just as others had taken her in rooms like this, in this casino, in this closet.

And Gayet. . . . Now Joan could see him through Grace: imperturbable Gayet who had so much money and so little life, who was so afraid of his wife's past, of her lovers, and the liberations he called perversions. But he called *everything* a perversion.

How she hated him beneath what she called "love."

But he looked just like the man who had raped her in that closet so long ago. She could not remember the man's face—so effectively had she blocked it out of her mind—yet she was stunned when she first met Gayet. She felt attracted to him but also repelled; she was in love.

Through Joan, Pfeiffer saw Gayet's cards: he had a Deuce and a Six of Clubs. He could call his hand, but he wasn't sure of the Deuce. It looked like a Heart, but it could just as easily be a Diamond. If he called it wrong, he would lose the hand, and his heart.

'I can't be sure,' Pfeiffer said to Joan, expecting help.

But Joan was in trouble. Grace had discovered her, and she was stronger than Joan had imagined. Joan was trapped inside Grace's mind; and Grace, who could not face what Joan had found, denied it.

And snapped.

Joan, realizing she was fighting for her life, screamed for the gamesmaster to deactivate the game. But her screams were lost, for Grace instantly slipped into the gamesmaster's mind and caught him, too. She had the psychotic's strength of desperation, and Joan realized that Grace would kill them all rather than face the truth about herself and Gayet.

Instantly Grace went after Pfeiffer. To kill him. She blamed him for Joan's presence, and Joan felt crushing pain as if she were being buried alive in the dirt of Grace's mind.

Grace grasped Pfeiffer with a thought, wound dark filaments around him which could not be burned away by white thought or anything else; and like a spider, she wrapped her prey in darkness and looked for physiological weakness, any flaw, perhaps a blood vessel which might rupture in his head. . . .

Joan tried to bring herself away from the pain, from the concrete weight crushing her. Ironically, she wondered if thought had mass. What a stupid thought to die with, she told herself, and she suddenly remembered a story Ray had once told her about a dying rabbi who was annoyed at the minions praying around him because he was trying to listen to two washerwomen gossiping outside. Later, Ray had confessed that it wasn't a Jewish story, it was Buddhist.

She held onto that thought, remembered Ray laughing like a little boy after his confession. The pain eased as she followed her thoughts.

. . . If thought had mass.

She was thinking herself free, escaping Grace by finding the proper angle, as if thought and emotion and pain were mathematical.

That done in an instant.

But if she was to save Pfeiffer's life, and her own, she had to do something immediately. She showed Grace her past. Showed her that she had married Gayet because he had the face of the man who had raped her as child.

Gayet, seeing this too, screamed. How he loathed Grace, but not nearly so much as she loathed herself. He had tried to stop Grace, but he was too weak. He too had been caught.

As if cornered, as if she were back in the closet with her rapist, she attacked Gayet. Only now she had a weapon. She thought him dead, trapped him in a scream, and as if he were being squeezed from the inside, his blood pressure rose. She had found a weakened blood vessel in his head, and it ruptured.

The effort weakened Grace, and a few seconds later the

gamesmaster was able to regain control and disconnect everyone. Gayet was immediately hooked into a life-support unit which applied CPR techniques to keep his heart beating. But he was dead.

Joan saw that. . . .

As Gayet died, a tunnel seemed to open up inside him. It was silver, and it was also black. It was felt rather than seen. It was the fabled silver cord, the dead connection; and Joan was too close, for she could barely keep herself from being plunged into its narrow confines, sucked through its vortices.

She could resist the dark spaces only because of her connection with Pfeiffer. Because he would not let go of her. . . .

Suddenly, like electricity passing through an outlet, a familiar presence came through the tunnel and smashed into their thoughts.

It was drawn to Joan through the dark spaces like a fleck of metal to a magnet.

It was Mantle, and he thought he had found Josiane.

For an instant, Joan and Pfeiffer and Mantle fused together, incandescently merging souls and selves. But before they could fuse inescapably, Pfeiffer recoiled, released his psychic grip on Joan and protected himself behind skeins of white thought, as he had been trained to do.

Without Pfeiffer, Joan was sucked into the tunnel like a leaf carried by a dark current. She could feel Mantle slip past her, another ghost in the dark. Now she was adrift in the black and silver places. Alone. 'Help me, Ray,' she screamed, looking for him, unable to find her way back to life. 'Where are you? I can't find you.'

Then she heard him, his thoughts made cold and thin by the dark spaces. But he was calling Josiane. . . .

'No,' she screamed, drowning in distance. 'Come back.' But he could not come back, and she could only hate him for leaving her because she was not Josiane. But her emotions began to evaporate like sweat. She was made of dark stuff now.

I'm dead, she told herself, and the thought swallowed her; and she, in turn, swallowed the thought, becoming smaller and smaller in the process, lifting and falling through the layers, through the thermoclines of the dark.

Still she called to Mantle.

But her pain and hatred became one long silvery-dark thought.

Toward morning, just before the edge of the sky turned gray, Mantle dreamed that he heard whispers.

He listened and heard his name.

Lost and crying for help, too distant to be heard closely, Josiane whispered to him. She wandered through the hidden reaches of his mind, dredging up memories.

But it wasn't Josiane calling. It was Joan.

With a sudden shock of recognition, Mantle sat up in bed. He blinked away the last vestiges of his dream and looked around. He was alone; Roberta and Danielle had left the room sometime during the night. "Joan?" he said aloud, then again, questioning. He remembered searching the dark spaces for Josiane . . . remembered being drawn to her as if he were a speck of iron and she the magnet. Then he remembered being pulled right out of the darkness into blazing, blinding light and smashing into another presence. But it wasn't Josiane!

Overwhelmed, he had escaped back into the quiet rustlings of the dark spaces.

Now Mantle was certain that Joan, and not Josiane, had been calling to him in his dreams. But that was impossible. Yet he remembered smashing through her thoughts like a rock thrown into a fire. The damp bedsheet clung to his sweaty legs and abdomen. He called her again. "Joan . . . ?"

The word seemed suspended, as if made of light like the videotect, which loomed above him.

PART TWO

Eleven

The morning light was dim and gritty and filled Mantle's room like dust. He felt the need to urinate, but he lay where he was, staring out the arched arcade window, listening to the morning sounds of birds, distant chatter, and laughter; the long buzzings of the heat bugs, promising a hot day; and the crunching of leaves and twigs as a handyrobot weeded and planted somewhere in the great gardens. He felt as if he had been very ill and had just broken the fever. He was exhausted, his mouth was dry, and he could smell his own sour odor. But he felt at ease, secure in this morning world. He had had his schizophrenic episode, scammed through the black and silver spaces, made the transition into the dark world and back into the light. He had come full circle, or so he thought. He had not discovered himself, nor had he found any hidden tele-pathic talents. He could not summon the dead nor guide them through Gaol. He had simply been sick. Now he lay on the bed, alone, his head propped against a sweat-stained pillow. His arms and legs were outstretched, as if he had been on a raft in a stormy sea, and although it was calm now, he was still afraid of losing his hold and being tipped into the deep.

He went to the bathroom, relieved himself, and then, instead of taking a dry shower, walked down the hall to stand under the old multi-nozzled shower until he became faint from the heat. He returned to his room and found a stylish pair of brown slacks and a matching open-collar shirt in the dresser. He dressed, found the soft boots that had been placed just under the bed. On impulse, he looked around for the filthy clothes he had had on last night, but they were not to be found. Jesus, Mantle thought, remembering, my clothes and wallet are somewhere in Dramont. If *Gendarmerie* find the wallet, I'm done. I'll have to find it—perhaps it hasn't been picked up.

There was a knock at the door.

"Yes?" Mantle asked, distracted.

"It's Roberta. May I come in?"

"Yes, of course." He would ask her about the wallet.

She came inside and stood by the door, somewhat awkwardly. She was dressed in a pale blue skirt made of a silky, clinging material and a white, sleeveless blouse in the American style. Her frizzy blond hair was pulled back and tied; it looked gauzy in the sunlight. "How do you feel?" she asked.

"Like I've been stepped on." Mantle stood up. "Well, are you coming in? I've got to talk to you." Then he realized something was wrong: Roberta was upset. And Mantle suddenly remembered a voice calling him in a dream. "What's the matter?" he asked.

"It's Joan. She's here."

"Well, I'm very pleased that—"

"She's in a coma," Roberta said, softly kicking the door shut.

Mantle was touched by a vague, uneasy memory of smashing into Joan in the dark spaces. It was last night's fever dream remembered.

Mantle stared at her.

"What happened?"

"Joan was attending your friend Pfeiffer, who was organ gambling—"

"Jesus Christ, I didn't know they were going organ gambling. Well, I guess she was bound and determined to hook-into someone."

"—and she had an accident."

"What?"

"She was hooked into Pfeiffer and his opponent, and she lost it. It was a pretty bad show: Pfeiffer's opponent died in the hook-in."

"Jesus. If she's in a coma, why isn't she in a fucking hospital, getting proper care?"

"We had her taken out of the hospital and brought here."

"Why?"

"Because she's better off here. If it comes to reaching inside and pulling her back, she's safer with us."

"So we'll have to hook-in?"

"If we'd let the hospital psychs at her, she'd end up brain-burned—Is that what you want? She can just as easily rest here—we have adequate medical facilities. She might come out of it by herself. We thought you might be able to help."

"Where's Carl?"

"Carl?"

"Pfeiffer, the man Joan was with."

"He contacted us. I left a message on the Net for Joan, and he had sense enough to trace—"

"Where is he now?"

"It seems that he made the arrangements and left."

"I'm sure he wanted her out of the hospital. He's always looking out for his own ass."

"What?"

"What happened to you last night? Why didn't you stay?" Mantle was suddenly afraid, as if the dark spaces were claiming him again. He couldn't bear the thought of being alone. He felt as if he was being *watched*.

"You told me to leave, remember?"

But Mantle didn't remember.

He went into Joan's room alone. It was in the old wing of the house which had probably served as servants' quarters in bygone days. Joan was lying on a bed near the far, plaster-cracked wall; and a robot, lifeless as stone, stood in its recess and stared at her. The life-signs monitor murmured as if talking to itself. Joan was breathing deeply and evenly, as if in a deep, dreamless sleep. Her face was smooth, calm, except for a nervous tic beating its rhythm inside her cheek.

"Joan," he whispered as he leaned toward her. He watched her and listened, but she was all silence and distance, lost. "Joan, can you hear me?" he asked, louder. "It's Ray. Come on, please try." No response. Sunlight cut into the room as if it were a solid block of yellow. Dust motes did their Brownian dance. It was a lovely young afternoon; there wasn't a shadow in the room.

But once again Mantle felt that he was being watched. Then a voice whispered to him, just as it had in his dream this morning. It was Joan's voice, but Joan was sleeping, not speaking. He felt the small hairs on the back of his neck rise. Automatically, he looked for the robot in the recess. It was still, dead until needed.

"Joan," he said anxiously, "wake up." He could feel himself being pulled into the dark spaces, see the sunlit room turn to silver. Terrified, he turned away from her, as if to run. But the voice called him again, wrapping him in a waking dream. He could not run, he was drugged with it.

The voice seemed to have direction now. It was near the door, a discontinuity, calling. Whispering.

He went to the door. The voice seemed to be ahead, calling him into the doorway. It led him on, turned into the *Aria ariari isa* that he had heard at the hook-in ceremony. Whispers became tongues of fire, every word a punishment. Joan had finally found him, just when he thought he was free, when he thought his episode was over.

He walked through the light-flooded, expansive rooms and hallways of the great house, following her voice as if in a trance. It was as if the sunlight were only an illusion, a superimposition upon the raw, ever-present reality of darkness.

The voice led him down, through the house, winding, wending from floor to floor, into the cellars, which were rough-hewn, ancient, and damp. They smelled faintly sulphurous. He walked through wide and narrow passageways and down stone steps. His heels clicked on the stone, something scurried ahead, and Joan's voice murmured like a cold stream rushing through the corridors and rooms.

If a house could be said to have a soul, this is where it would reside. If the house had a memory, it would be here too: in the dark, mazed corridors; the crypts, caverns, and recesses. Mantle felt as if he were being led into a cold womb. To dig, to climb into the earth, to be at one with the dark places and protected from the hot-blooded beasts above: those were his elemental urges.

Corridors gave way to natural rock formations, stalactites and stalagmites, but human artifice was always present in the subtle, indirect lighting.

The voice led him into a cavernous room a grotto which contained a still, transparent lake. Mantle stood at the edge of this subterranean pool and began to wake up. Shocked, he looked into the grassy lake and saw what seemed to be descending galleries of blue-green amphitheaters below its surface. It was very deep, and the preternaturally clear water glowed with a dim, nostalgic light.

Here was the secret of the house.

"Jesus," Mantle mumbled, feeling as if he were standing on the edge of a ledge, looking at the world below. He felt he would fall, and stepped backward. Water dripped in the distance, in another room, worlds away.

And something moved in the water. At first it was a shimmering; then, a vague shape in the deeps. It was a drowned woman, rising. The surface rippled, dividing everything below. The woman floated upright toward the surface.

It was Joan.

Mantle screamed.

She rose out of the lake before him as if she were a statue standing upon an invisible platform. She was hard, dead, unforgiving. Her face and body were stone white and mottled blue; her wet, short-cropped hair a helmet.

She rose slowly, as if in slow motion, and her dreaming eyes stared into his.

Then she stepped across the water toward him.

She came to him like a lover and dragged him screaming into the icy, transparent lake.

Twelve

Normally, Carl Pfeiffer could have easily slept through the morning noise of neighbors gossiping from window to window and house to house; the sounds of cleaning machines making their second pass down the street below, children playing and laughing and speaking a delightfully idiomatic French punctuated with jarring Americanisms, and the vendors calling their wares. After all, he had been up most of the night. But he got out of bed, rubbed the sleep out of his eyes, and crossed the room to the front window, which he opened fully, as if to let in the concentrated life of the streets.

The bedroom smelled of Pfeiffer, of anxiety and cold sweat.

I did everything I could for Joan, under the circumstances, he told himself; but the old guilt gnawed away at him. I had to let her go, he thought, remembering the deadly tunnel created by Gayet's death. He had tried to hold on to her, to her thoughts, but something had happened. Joan's mind had snapped, for she hallucinated Raymond Mantle. Pfeiffer saw and felt that: he was hooked into her. But the hallucination had the effect of a shock of electricity. As if by reflex, Pfeiffer buried himself in white thought and cut himself off from Joan. After all, he *had* to protect himself. And with the connection broken, poor Joan must have been sucked into the dark spaces.

Still, something niggled away at him, as if there were more to the incident than he could remember.

Surely, Joan had only projected Raymond. . . .

Pfeiffer leaned out the window and took a deep breath, as if to clear his insides of the past. He watched some of the boys in the street below playing nail-the-cross, a game he had known as a child, although his parents, being very religious, had forbidden him to play it. Women shouted at each other across the street. Fish and produce mingled with the particular dusty odor of old Cannes in the morning. It was an odor with which every child was familiar, the unique smell exuded from two stones being rubbed together. Perhaps it was caused by the friction of feet and wheels on the cobbled streets. The smells—and the sensation of the sun warming him—seemed to evaporate the anxiety left over from the restive night.

He turned away from the window to wash and dress.

Feeling refreshed, he passed Mantle's bedroom, which was locked, keyed-in breakfast in the kitchen, and then padded through the sitting room into the living room. The high windows caught the morning light; this was a perfect place to work, or so it seemed to Pfeiffer. He set his tray of food on a sideboard, which he pulled over to the couch; he sat down to eat. The omelet was lousy; the fine herbes were dried. But what did he expect? Raymond could afford much better, but evidently didn't care. Raymond would never change. He would always slide from this to that. Yet he always managed to keep working, even if he wasn't doing good work. But this recent stuff was quite good, Pfeiffer thought as he chewed noisily. He was alone and could suck the juices out of his food, something he could not do when he was in public—nor, for that matter, when he dined with Caroline, his wife.

After placing his tray in the disposal, he took another cup of coffee and returned to the couch. The living room was cozy, and he felt secure in the niche of protected space formed by wall, couch, and sideboard. Then he placed a call to Joel Bose, a little stump of a man who seemed to be everywhere and in touch with everyone (and yet was *not* a public personality). Pfeiffer and Joel had been logrolling and pork-barreling for years. This would even things up, for Pfeiffer had done more than his share for Joel over the last five years—had, in fact, kept Joel anonymous in a few dangerous situations, and helped elect five of Joel's toadies—good men, really, but it didn't hurt to have patronage in the right places. That was not only good business, but good ethical sense, because he could not be of use to his public if he didn't constantly mend political fences. It was a sadomasochistic game: every newsbreak, every good story, made and destroyed friendships. Keeping in the middle was also expensive. Pfeiffer always made some sort of remuneration to anyone he had to victimize.

Except Raymond, he thought. Jesus, did he owe Raymond. . . .

Joel's image appeared in the living room at a comfortable distance from Pfeiffer. It was a bit fuzzy, the image, but then Joel always used a scrambler.

". . . it's all taken care of," Joel said, "but, Christ, was it a fucking massacre, and you know goddamn well that those fucking *gendarmes* were getting their rocks off, and the fuckers hadn't even taken anyone into custody, said the terrorists weren't local, couldn't be found, the old bullshit—"

"Yes, yes, I heard the news from Max. What I'm interested in is—"

"It's done," Joel said. He had a hard, handsome face. He made a sucking noise with his lips and cheek, one of his characteristic expressions of satisfaction. What could not be seen on the hollie, however, was that Joel was very overweight; yet, the fat had not yet padded out his face. "Your friend left his clothes lying about; we collected them. Everything's tidy; we recovered his wallet, too."

"Wonderful," Pfeiffer said, relieved.

"Yes, it certainly was. The wallet, dear Carl, was already in the hands of the police, just in case you thought it was easy work."

"Well, I guess that evens us up. . . ."

"More than that, I would say."

"Then I'm in your debt again," Pfeiffer said, smiling.

"You certainly are. I'll let you know what the damage comes to. A fuck of a lot of money had to change hands."

"Well, my . . . client can afford it," Pfeiffer said, nodding, indicating that he was about to break the connection.

"Carl?"

"Yes, Joel."

"I heard about what happened at the casino. Did everything work out?"

"Yes, fine," Pfeiffer said. He hadn't expected the news to spread that fast through the grapevine.

"And your lady friend?"

"All taken care of, thanks."

"Carl, one last thing."

"Yes . . . ?"

"You are aware of the *Trouble;* it is conceivable that you could be implicated if—"

"Max gave me the word," Pfeiffer said. "But I appreciate the thought."

"If there's anything I can do . . ."

"What are *you* going to do?"

Joel smiled one of his engaging back-room smiles and broke the connection. Pfeiffer stared at the space where Joel's image had been. Things would work themselves out, he told himself. He sat very still; he was satisfied with himself and took the time to enjoy it. He would take time for everything now, he thought. He was going to start living. But first he had to set his past in balance; then he could get back into the world. It would be a new world, and he would be a new man.

But his old fears rushed back to him like a crazed mob that had found its witch. He knew he was going to suffer. He would pay. The room suddenly darkened as a cloud passed across the sun, and then it was bright again. He was living and breathing Mantle's world now; it was deep and layered, as comfortable as an oriental carpet. Pfeiffer floated upon his thoughts. He became the rational part of himself, the observer, and his fear became only a small, tangible thing. And he could handle "things."

He was worried about Joan and Raymond, especially Raymond. He would call Boulouris again and inquire; but first he called Max back, and then confirmed his passage on the *Titanic*, which was docked in a special berth in Southampton harbor, awaiting its final voyage.

Thirteen

It was like awakening from a dream and still being touched by it. He remembered Joan rising out of the lake to pull him into the icy water as if she were death herself. He was choking, drowning, trying to tear himself awake.

And again he felt someone watching him.

"It's all right, Ray, be calm. You're fine," Faon said, her voice soft, almost a whisper. She sat in a chair beside the bed and caressed him.

"Get away from me, Joan, get—"

"It's Faon. Look at me."

For an instant, Mantle didn't recognize her, and then everything began to come into focus. Faon's gray-streaked hair was loose and reached to her shoulders, framing her face in a V. She was wearing jeans and a tight-fitting short-sleeve shirt.

"Jesus, I must have been dreaming," Mantle said, recognizing that this was the room in which he had slept with Roberta. "I must be having another episode—Jesus, I'm losing it, going crazy."

"You're *not* going crazy, you're fine."

"But the dream was so real, I dreamt—"

"I know all about it."

"What?"

"It was not a dream, Raymond, it—"

Mantle sat bolt upright, his legs swinging over the side of the bed. He caught his breath. Yes, he thought, he had slipped back into the dark spaces, and somehow Joan had tried to kill him. His throat ached. "Jesus, I am losing it."

"Only if you allow yourself to do so," Faon said. "May I give you an injection?"

"Of what. . . . Why?"

"A very mild sedative to calm you. But I promise you it won't make you drowsy or impair your thinking."

Mantle permitted her to give him the sedative—anything to keep him away from the dark spaces—and after what seemed like a few moments, he asked, "Do you mean that Joan actually rose out of that pool and—"

"No, but that's what you saw. You were in the Blue Pool, which is what we call it, and you were drowning. It was Joan who rescued you: she broke out of her coma, ran downstairs, and pulled you out of the pool."

Yes, Mantle did remember. But how could that be: Joan had tried to drown him! He remembered choking, and then a robot extruding an aspiration catheter down his throat. That was why his throat felt sore now. "But Joan tried to kill me, or that's what I dreamed," he said. "How could she try to kill me and save me at the same time?"

"You were connected to each other, as if under a hookin," Faon said. "And you were reacting to Joan's thoughts and feelings as if they were physical things in the world."

"But we *weren't* hooked in."

"But you both *were* hooked into others. You hooked into the holy Crier and then moved in and out of the dark spaces during your transition, your passage. And Joan was hooked into a group in the casino. Because of your intense feelings for each other—love, need, call it what you will—you were drawn together and made a connection."

Once again Mantle remembered the dream of smashing into Joan in the dark spaces. Perhaps they *had* made a connection.

"Your experience is not uncommon, you know," Faon continued. "Connections are possible outside the dyadic hookin. They're referred to as *circuits fantomes*." She explained that the phantom connection between Joan and Mantle was an anomaly in the ebb and flow of the dark spaces, which could be thought of as a collective unconscious. "Directive synchronicity," she called it.

"My God," Mantle whispered. "How she must hate me to try to kill me."

"Remember," Faon said, "she also saved you. She loves you very much."

"Then why—?"

"She wasn't in her right mind, she was lost in the dark spaces, she—" Faon stopped herself and then said, "I think she loves you too much. Maybe she thought you didn't love her enough."

"So she was going to kill me for that."

"I told you she wasn't in her right mind," Faon said. "But she's well now; it's all in the past."

"I *do* love her," he insisted . . . and it was true. The sedative blunted the edges of his fear, but he still felt guilt and remorse. He shouldn't have closed her out. She deserved better than that.

"Both of you will need time together to work this out, and that you must do, one way or another, for you have made a connection."

"What do you mean? That we are still connected?"

"That is possible, yes."

"Where's Joan now?" Mantle demanded. "Are you *sure* she's all right?"

"Yes, she's fine, and she'll be down to breakfast right along. Breakfast has been waiting for you all morning."

"What time is it?" Mantle asked.

"Almost twelve."

"How much time have I lost?"

"A day and a night. It was the day before yesterday when we found you and Joan by the pool."

"Was I drugged all this time?"

"Yes, we thought it best. And by now you should be ravenous."

"I am hungry," Mantle confessed.

Faon brightened and said, "We can talk again later, if you wish. But now you must let the daylight evaporate your anxiety, which it will, believe me. You must give yourself up to the daylight world, just as you gave yourself to the dark spaces. You must pretend that everything's back to normal. Don't think bad thoughts or try to order and understand everything that has happened," she warned, "or you might initiate another transition."

Mantle felt a chill feather up his spine. He was still vulnerable to the dark spaces, and to Joan. . . .

"Now that your passage is over, which I'm sure it is, you should be with people," Faon continued. "The sedative should help you, too. Can you feel it?"

"I don't know . . . I'm not sure."

"Then it's working."

"But that business by the pool feels like a dream," Mantle insisted.

"Are you afraid of Joan right now?" asked Faon.

"No, I don't think so."

"The drug will keep it all at bay until you can handle it. But it wasn't a dream. Now, everybody's waiting for you—Do you feel up to coming downstairs?"

"I suppose—if they can accept that I'm still wonky."

"Pardon?"

"Still unsteady," Mantle said, remembering that American slang had only recently become faddish again and would not reach the coast for another few weeks. He dressed quickly, and they went downstairs to the southern side of the house where he had first entered the stucco-walled anteroom and large, arched sitting room that contained the Limoges miniature. Faon guided Mantle through a bright parlor, down a short hallway radiant from high, pink stained-glass windows, into a large, formal dining room and out onto a veranda where a table had been set up.

"Everyone, this is Raymond Mantle, whom we all met when he was in a slightly more disordered state," Faon said.

Everyone laughed, and two men—the same two who had rescued him in the car—stood up and shook hands with Mantle.

Mantle saw that Joan wasn't at the table, but the drug lent him patience.

"The older one with the ugly scar is Charles, my husband, and this pretty young thing is Peter, who is married to Danielle whom you already know, I think." Faon's introduction was light, without a hint of sarcasm or *double entendre*. Danielle waved to him to sit beside her, which he did.

"She always steals the men," Faon said, passing him a tray of chocolate brioches, croissants, orange tea rolls, and raised muffins. He took a croissant, and Faon pushed the butter and jam toward him. The food was warm and smelled delicious. Although his throat ached with every swallow, he ate a fresh quiche filled with shrimp and lobster. The coffee was strong and good.

Mantle felt as if his senses were suddenly heightened, and a dark heaviness seemed to slough away from him; it was as if everything around him were somehow more real, and he was grateful for the company and the food and the warmth of the late-morning sun. He finally felt that he had come through the dark spaces. He was the man who, having been saved from drowning, suddenly discovers that what had previously been mundane is now poignant and poetic. The clouds were thin, so many white smears against the pale blue sky; it would be a clear afternoon after the clouds were burned away and the last of the dew-dampness left leaf and soil.

"And Roberta, where is she?" Mantle asked, having taken the edge off his hunger. This was a roundabout way of asking after Joan.

"She'll be along," Faon replied.

"Are you sure she's all right? After the slaughter at Dramont . . ." Once again, just by remembering, Mantle became vulnerable to the dark spaces, to the black and silver that he now sensed as strange angles in his peripheral vision. Blundering on, he said, "I understand that Monsieur Pretre was—"

"Monsieur, please!" Faon said. Then, softly, as if she had lost control for only a second, she continued: "Roberta has been attending Joan, who had as much need of her ministrations as yourself. And we don't grieve for our dead, at least when we are in our right minds. If you think back to our meeting the other night when you saw dear Stephen in the candle room, you will understand why." With a touch of irony in her voice, she said, "We have more important things for which to grieve."

"I apologize—"

"No, no, it's going to be a beautiful, warm day, and we must celebrate for you. Your passage, as it were, but I warned you not to dwell on the past, lest the dark spaces . . ." She paused, then said, "Become part of this day; give yourself to it."

It occurred to Mantle that this house and its tended grounds were themselves celebrations of both the bright and dark spaces. Perhaps one could learn to live in both worlds, make daily transitions. He thought of Joan and what had happened in the pool—that was simply a bad dream. He would leave it at that. And this place . . . it was like the surface of the moon: scorched by the sun in the day, cold and dead at night.

"I understand you're an artist," Peter said as he poured himself another cup of coffee.

"Actually, I'm an illustrator," Mantle said, distancing himself from the past, trying to be just in the here-and-now. But Joan was still a ghost swimming through his mind, waiting to pull him under again, kill him. . . .

"Then you do most of your work on computer?"

"Some, not all. But advertising is almost entirely computers and cybernetics now. It's quite sophisticated, I'm told."

Peter chuckled and said, "But your recent work seems to have had a profound effect on the field."

"Watch him," Danielle said. "He's manipulating you into giving him a painting."

"I would do no such thing. I only wish him to sell me a painting."

"You shall have one," Mantle said. "It would be my pleasure."

"What did you do?" asked Faon.

"Pardon me?"

"Peter said you profoundly affected the field of advertising. How did you do that?"

"I'm afraid that's quite an exaggeration. With all due respect."

"I shall let you off this time," Peter said. "But don't let it happen again." Mantle smiled back at him. Peter was dark and extraordinarily handsome; he looked like an Israeli travel poster with his deeply set eyes, long, straight nose, narrow mouth and strong chin. He was thin and probably would not look as good naked, Mantle thought. But for all the geometry of his face, there was something weak about him: a hint of the spoiled child in his movements, and a whine in his voice. Surely it was he who depended on Danielle, probably both financially and emotionally. But perhaps he had family money— he could well be Arabian with those looks.

"I really didn't change anything," Mantle said to Faon. "I

was doing a lot of painting and experimenting with some of the techniques of the old masters, and I naturally introduced some of this into my work. I had no idea it would take on as it did, but it's just a fad, that's all. It will be over in another month or so, maybe two. People are amused right now at seeing and feeling nonrealistic representations of their favorite drug or whiskey or toilet paper, but that will change. It swings back and forth."

"But it's *your* style, the way *you* see the world," Danielle said. "Surely that is what sells the products. 'Products' is such an ugly word, isn't it?"

Mantle took another croissant, although he wasn't hungry. Where was Joan? He had to see her.

"Our friend is a genius, an artist, of the sublime," Charles said.

Mantle laughed, but it was forced. "I've never heard it put quite so well." He was sure that Charles had done his homework. After all, Pretre had made it very clear that Mantle would have dues to pay. But did he owe the church anything after the debacle at Dramont, where he had almost lost his life?

"No, I mean that," Charles said, "and without all the irony you're reading into it."

"Just take a half-portion of it," Peter said as he put his arm around the back of Danielle's wicker chair.

"You've done marvelous things with subliminals in your private work too, no matter how much your commercial style has changed the market." Charles glanced at Faon quickly, as if for support, but that was a private conversation to which Mantle was not privy. Charles and Faon were a real couple; they lived in each other's private worlds, something most couples cannot manage. Danielle and Peter, although they looked perfect, seemed almost two-dimensional.

"I didn't think my private work was that well known."

"We have a few paintings right here in the house," Charles said, smiling.

That took Mantle aback. "Well, I'm very flattered. Where, may I ask, did you purchase them?"

"From various private collections. Your best work—to my mind, at least—was either given to your friends or sold to collectors. You see, I'm a Raymond Mantle connoisseur."

"I can see that. From *whom* did you purchase them?"

Mantle regretted giving away, much less selling those paintings, for if one knew how to read them, they laid bare his deepest fears, anxieties, and hate.

"You seem disturbed," Faon said to Mantle. "Please don't be. Charles has been interested in your work long before you met Francois Pretre. You must not think he was trying to pry into your private life—"

"Except as a collector," Charles interrupted. "Please believe that."

"But surely you realize that we had to have information, that when you decided to attend a ceremony—"

"That's enough of that!" Faon said to Peter, who nodded and accepted the reprimand. "We will always be honest with you, even if you do not approve of what we do or how we feel. Charles bought your paintings for his own aesthetic uses and not for the church. All the information is in the computer; you may have the code if you wish. However, all the information was made available to Pretre when he requested it."

"But after hooking in, you revealed yourself to those on the other side," Danielle said.

"You'll soon see that we're all in the same situation, more or less," Faon said.

Just then Joan stepped onto the porch with Roberta. "But most of us don't have to worry about being murdered by jealous lovers *after* we've hooked in and are trying to ascend from the dark spaces," Joan said.

Mantle jumped, as if he had seen a wraith; but this woman wearing borrowed blouse and pants was surely Joan. She looked exhausted; her eyes were puffy, her skin white and drawn, and her hair, which was usually brushed out, looked stringy and thin. Suddenly, Mantle remembered how well Pfeiffer seemed to look when he, Mantle, had needed emotional support; and his heart went out to Joan, who looked so vulnerable and spent. Seeing her now evaporated his fears.

Charles and Peter stood up, as did Danielle an instant later. "We must get something done today," Charles said, exchanging a quick glance with Faon. "And I think you'll be more comfortable alone just now."

"No, that's not fair," Joan protested weakly; and she sat down beside Faon, her attention fixed on Mantle. Roberta took Danielle's chair. "You can stay, you know," she said to Danielle.

"I think it will be better without . . . strangers." Then she waved good-bye, linked arms with the two men, and they were off.

"How do you feel?" Mantle asked Joan, trying to press through the awkwardness of the moment.

"How do *you* feel?" she asked—and then, as if she were looking through him, she said, "Christ, I'm sorry, Ray. I don't know why I tried to . . . would want to kill you. Jesus, I know why. Oh God, it's all me."

"Stop it," Roberta said. "We've been over that and—"

Faon shushed her and said to Joan, "Now, you know it wasn't your fault; it wasn't anyone's fault. Is it your fault if you have a dream?"

"But it was real. It wasn't a dream and can't be undone."

"Even if it was real, it was like a dream. You couldn't help that."

"Yes I could, I tried to kill him," Joan said.

"But you also saved him," Faon said. "You broke out of your coma, out of the dark spaces, to rescue him—"

"From myself," Joan said to Mantle. But something passed between them, an understanding, a shared grief, a sad, sweet laughter. Then, as if oblivious to Faon, Roberta, and the preternaturally bright afternoon, she asked, "Are you afraid of me . . . *now*?"

"No," Mantle said hollowly, even as he remembered the cold, dead being that had tried to kill him.

Fourteen

Midafternoon, and as promised, it was hot.

Joan and Mantle lay on a faded, flower-patterned blanket and looked out at the quiet turquoise sea which was limned with pearl. The sky was clear. Everything seemed to shimmer in the windless heat. To their left, curving away from the small, private beach, were the scraps of red porphyry—they looked like rough-cut shields of Viking giants. Behind them was a wall of the same rock; this place was seemingly inaccessible, unless you knew the path which led out of the pine forest to the hidden perron cut into the rock where the slope was more gentle. The beach was gray shingle, the only drabness in this sunlit place. The blue water swirled gently around the stones, and cicadas kept up their daylong melody.

Mantle's sedative had worn off, or so he thought. He was nervous now, but in control, as if he had put the dark spaces behind him.

"Do you know we've never been naked together, except in bed?" Joan said, turning from her stomach to her side, nervously looking at Mantle and resting her head on a tight little fist. They had been silent since they had undressed; both the silence and being undressed were awkward.

"Well, that's the usual place for people to be naked, don't you think?" Mantle said.

"You're a Puritan."

"I most certainly am not." Mantle brushed a black fly away from his face; there was a swarm of them. He grinned, but it was awkward. The whole world seemed to be at a standstill, hanging on each word and gesture, ready to crash. Mantle and Joan were afraid, each afraid of breaking the other with a word or gesture.

"Christ, this is worse than being together for the first time, isn't it?" Joan said.

"I don't know where to start. It's as if we've known each other too well; I've done too many things to you, hurt you too many times."

"No, it's me who—"

"Let's not start that game of whose fault everything is and who's more to blame than the other."

"Then you want to break everything up before I can even—"

"Stop it, Joan," Mantle said, sitting up. He knew he should put his arms around her, but he felt emotionally paralyzed: a vision of Joan pulling him into the pool passed through his mind. "I'm not breaking anything up, but Christ, look what we're doing to each other."

"That's my fault, not yours."

"You don't believe that, so stop it—"

"I tried to kill you, I know that. I saw you when I was hooked in with Pfeiffer at the casino, but you thought I was Josiane; and when you saw it was *me*, you left. I hated you and needed you, I wanted you to be dead so you couldn't hurt me again. . . ." She motioned with her hands as she talked, which was out of character for her; but she wasn't really talking to him. She was talking to someone, or something, only she could hear. "I love you and I wanted to kill you—"

"Stop it," Mantle said; and then in a whisper, "I'm sorry, I'm sorry. . . ."

"Yes, I did, it was all my fault." She began to shake as if she were wrestling with her self, or selves. She whispered angrily, "Stop it, you unworthy cunt, let him go."

Mantle suddenly became frightened: not for himself, but for her. Joan was not just having an episode. She might lose herself—not in the dark spaces but in the crushing mechanisms of her own frightened mind. Mantle could feel her anxiety; it was palpable, cloying, suffocating. Forcing himself against her thoughts, he embraced her, caught her, and she responded as if he had pulled her back into the world, back to an imperative, immediate reality.

And once again he felt caught in her mind.

They rolled off the blanket onto the hot shingle, which was uncomfortable against Mantle's back and legs. Joan was on top of him, kissing and biting him, as if by taking his essence she could blot out what had happened ealier. Mantle felt anxious, as if this were all wrong, but slowly he became excited by her, by her thoughts, her intense need. His own thoughts were a distant voice telling him that Joan was his way out, his chance to stay out of the dark. If she was strong, she would help him. He became aggressive, lost himself in the sweaty, gritty rutting.

It was ironic, but they were both more comfortable with their clothes on. Mantle had stepped back into his boxer style swimsuit, and Joan wore a flesh-colored bikini. As long as they lay naked, they couldn't talk or expose their thoughts, and Mantle was more comfortable with this Joan whom he knew intimately. Even their telepathic flashing during love-making didn't frighten him now, as he lay beside her. But the woman he had just coupled with was someone else, someone who was crawling with exposed instincts and drives—not the controlled, giving woman whom he thought of as wife (although she wasn't) and confidante.

He felt spent and languorous in the sun, which seemed to beat down upon him in waves. When he opened his eyes, tiny, shimmering motes appeared on the edges of his vision as if they were the very atoms of the world and could only be seen now, when Mantle felt no fear and need of the world. But each second comprised a thousand events: the flap and noise of gulls; the background rushingshushing of the city (which could be heard if one put an ear to the ground, for the nearby undercities growled with teeming life); the insects, the bees, midges, and hornets; the lapping of water; the crack of a shuttle above; the short bleat of a skimmer on the water. Yet, everything was still suspended, eternal, ageless, as if every sight and sound were composed, as if time and event were art rather than hazard. Joan was lying beside Mantle, but she kept a comfortable distance, as if she were able to gauge exactly his psychological space.

"You know, it's almost silly..." Joan said, sitting up and blinking in the light. A long, white ship crawled across the smooth sea in the distance: a toy on a piece of cellophane.

"What's almost silly?"

"This."

"What do you mean?"

"That fucking made it all right, at least for the moment. It's as if all that we do reduces to that, that all we can ever do—"

"I do love you," Mantle said simply, and he meant it, although that surprised him. "I'll try to make it different this time. I'm ashamed that it almost took losing you for me to realize how much I do need you. And not the way it used to be, not just as a friend, but physically."

"You didn't just then."

"What do you mean?"

"You fucked me because I needed you."

"At first—"

"Yes," Joan said, picking at the pebbles and then tracing the design of the blanket with her finger, "I felt the change, and I love you for that."

"But...?"

"What about Josiane? Did you find her when you hooked

into the Crier?" Joan made cabbage folds with the edge of the blanket.

"No, I didn't find her," Mantle replied. Then, after a pause, he said, "Yes, I glimpsed something, but Faon had to smack my face before I remembered it." Joan's expression changed; she looked at him intently, as if she could not breathe until he told her. It was like being hooked into Pfeiffer: she could glimpse a stray thought, but could not penetrate him directly. "I saw her... under water, as if drowned in a shallow pool."

"Oh God," Joan moaned.

"I wasn't going to tell you. So much for resolve."

"Weren't going to tell me? Jesus Christ—"

"It could have just been a dream, rather than a sending. I don't know. But Josiane's taken my life, my memory. I want them back. Yet after the episode... the passage—if that's what you want to call it—everything feels different. It's as if my compulsion to know, to find Josiane, has lifted. As if I could start again with you, unencumbered."

"You don't believe that!" Joan said. "You were always honest with me, at least about those things that directly concerned me. I knew what you were, what you are. Perhaps that's why I let myself become involved with you: you were safe; nothing could come of it, or so I thought." She laughed. "But you are not being honest now, neither with me nor yourself."

"If I had any real strength—"

She touched him lightly on the leg, and that stopped him in midsentence, another signal they both understood. Just now, as he stared out into the lambent water, sparkling because of a breeze breaking its surface, he understood that his relationship with Joan was something apart from both of them, an autonomous entity, a thing-in-itself that came into being because of them. It could not be broken now; it would live on in spite of Mantle. He felt that somehow the relationship was the world; and if he chose, he could hide inside it, secure. He knew its parameters. Everything would be all right—except for Josiane.

'Leave her, bury her, forget her,' Joan thought, and Mantle heard it as if she had spoken to him in a soft whisper.

"What?" he asked.

"I didn't say anything," Joan said, blushing.

"But I felt the connection." Mantle felt her pain and it became his own. He tried to embrace her, console her with himself, strengthen her, but she stiffened and drew away from him.

"You're going to have to find out about Josiane, one way or another," Joan said flatly, her face still burning. "I never thought otherwise. I would not want you like this forever, but if it's to be, I'll take that."

"But, Jesus, it's like taking leavings. You're better than that."

She laughed, this time bitterly. "You've got a talent for being 'the loved.' Someone has to be it."

"Just as Josiane was for me," Mantle said. "Is that what you mean?"

"Was she?"

"So I've been told."

"Anyway," Joan said, "at least I'm becoming aggressive." A smile reflected the irony in her voice. "That, you see, is a function of the lover."

If I end it here, I hurt her again, he thought, and hated himself. This much he understood: he would not be able to leave her unless the relationship threatened to destroy her sanity or he found Josiane. He would not, could not, end it until the last shallow gasp.

Again, Mantle was looking out to sea. It still frightened him, especially now, when everything was clear, pellucid; the ocean was a proper blue, meeting the sky at the horizon, but such a great expanse—no one could feel claustrophobic on such a day. Yet that was it: the security of space, the sunlight that could never give way to darkness—it was too beautiful, and hence two-dimensional. He could, by just taking a wrong direction of thought, fall right through this world; and the ocean, that beautiful blue swelling, was illusion. Its reality was depth and darkness. It was the sea he had been plunged into when he was hooked in.

"Let's talk about what happened in the pool, and our connection," Joan said.

"No, it's too early for that. Let's settle back together for a while, I still don't have my bearings. Jesus, I don't even know if I'm out of the woods yet. I might have another passage. I don't know when I might go crazy again, and that episode by the pool... thinking about that now is a sure way to—"

"I don't think you have to worry now," Joan said. She caressed his leg, twisted the dark hairs as if to make tangles out of tangles. "It feels over."

"What makes you say that?"

"Just a sense I get from you, a feeling. It's no great mystical thing, you know. Most anyone who knows you as well as I do could sense the difference."

And Mantle remembered how once, long ago, when he was having an anxiety attack, Pfeiffer actually ran out of the room. He left Mantle with Caroline, who talked him back.

"I'm not going to try to convince you that you weren't sick for a part of your episode," Joan said. "You probably were, I mean in a psychotic sense."

"It's better for you if I stop it dead right here, isn't it?" Mantle asked. "Break all the connections except the natural ones."

Joan laughed softly, then said, "No, it's better for me if you leave yourself open to me. It's better for me if you find her and remember your past. At least until then, I'll stay with you. What happened at the pool will never happen again. But what I did. . . . Christ, you're right, there's nothing more to say, nothing I can say. I love you and I'm sorry. Maybe it won't separate us, maybe it will. Yet, some good could come of this. . . ."

"How do you mean?" Mantle asked.

"We're still connected, as if we have a room all our own locked up inside us, a place of safety, a hiding place, but you have to be willing to make the shift. You don't ever have to, of course. . . ."

Mantle nodded, remembering Joan rising dead and naked out of the lake.

"Or you can see it as a curse, that we could glimpse each other, hurt each other—that's what you think, isn't it?"

"No, it's just . . ."

"Such a nakedness. You don't have to be naked, you can wall yourself in—I couldn't see. And what happened at the pool—"

"I'm just afraid," he admitted.

"I know you're going back to New York, I saw that."

"What?"

"Josiane. You've got to find out, isn't that right? In the dark spaces you saw her . . . there."

"Yes, I did," Mantle said, relieved. She knew, and he didn't have to fake it for himself. He felt as if they were part of this sunlit world again, together. And with that thought came bone-aching fatigue, but not the slippery fatigue of anxiety; rather, the sense of having come through the fire. He had felt it when he was taken out of combat, and when he had learned that his mother would survive a particularly virulent form of cancer (one of the *new* varieties)—he had been at home when he had heard the news, and had fallen asleep with the video on, even before the doctor could finish his explanation.

But Mantle wouldn't be able to sleep now; he needed to talk and savor the bright world.

"Well, are you going to take a walk with me or not?" he asked.

When he returned to his room, he found a thick, well-thumbed book on the neatly made bed. Faon had left it for him. Embossed on the imitation cloth cover in rough boldface was only the title *Le Symbole de Crieur*.

He picked it up, then dropped it back on the bed. He paced back and forth across the room, from the door to the window. He couldn't sleep. He didn't want to read. He wanted Joan, but she wanted to be alone to "sort things out," as she said; and he was to do the same. That was unlike Joan, though. Perhaps she was having second thoughts, also. She could certainly do without him; maybe she had finally come to terms with it. After all, she would have Faon and Roberta and this house and her religion to bolster her. He felt shaky again his thoughts were feverish, and he followed them as if he derived some bitter enjoyment out of giving form to his fears.

It was dusk, always a bad time for him. He lay down on the bed, propped himself into a comfortable position, and dipped into the book, skimming, stopping to reread a passage here and there, alternately turning from the thick serif print of the first quarter of the book to the footnote-size print that followed. Mantle was not really interested in the scriptures, which were oddly incongruous intercessory prayers, all derivative. The bulk of the book was annotation. Some of the annotated material was very perceptive, but there was too much of that annoying "divine irradiation from other worlds" business. The annotations were a hodge podge of different styles, a botch of the common and the sublime. They were not written in any scientific spirit, but were rather anecdotal, after the fashion of most nineteenth and twentieth-century writing on psi phenomena and the occult.

But it did seem that his experience with Joan was not uncommon. The book told of *circuits fantomes* and *circuits autonomes*, connections that could exist outside of and after the dyadic hook-in.

Without retaining a word, he automatically read the next few paragraphs on Raudive voices, the recordings of the dead—a controversy that was not resolved until the invention of the psyconductor.

Once again he remembered Joan rising out of the water, grabbing him.

Jesus, if something like that could happen again. . . .

It was their intimacy that would tear the relationship apart. The irony was not lost on Mantle, who tossed the book onto the floor. It must have hit just right, for it began to speak. A touchtape had been activated.

"*I believe in the wave that is One curling toward the shore of Unity*.

"*I believe in the crystal and the seed that turn the many into the One*.

"*I believe . . .*"

Later, he dreamed that he heard Josiane's voice calling him.

"Come in," Mantle said. His room was dark. The book glowed on the floor; it was the color of the water in the Blue Grotto in Capri.

"It's getting late; they're holding up dinner for you." Joan sat down on the edge of the bed; Mantle changed position to give her room. She reached over to the console beside the bed and turned on the lights. "Sometimes I wonder if you paint in the dark."

But Mantle could feel her anxiety, her distance.

"I'm intruding, aren't I?" she asked, but it was more a statement than a question. "It's Josiane."

Mantle nodded. He could not bridge the distance; perhaps it was him.

"I'm going downstairs," Joan said. "We'll leave tomorrow morning if that's agreeable to you. We owe them the night, at least. And Faon wants to talk to us again, kind of a counseling session to ensure that we won't kill each other with love." She laughed at that, her bitterness as plain as a pikestaff, and stood up to leave the room.

"Joan . . . ?" Mantle asked.

She paused at the door, then turned to him. Mantle tried to open himself to her, and for an instant, a current flowed between them, revealing what could not be spoken. She smiled sadly at him, and left the room.

Fifteen

Joan awakened the next morning in Faon's bed. Curtains were drawn across the windows, and the room was dim. Faon moaned, said something incomprehensible in her sleep, and moved closer to Joan, who was staring at the jigsaw puzzle of cracks in the ceiling. Joan looked at Faon, lying naked beside her, and thought about Ray.

You tried to be the perfect fiancé last night out of guilt, didn't you, Ray. But your thoughts were already centered on Josiane. You've slipped away so easily again. I was warned that this might happen, but I didn't expect it to be so soon.

I hate you. . . .

Stop it, you slut, you tried to kill him once, isn't that enough for you?

"Joan, relax, it's all right," Faon said, her voice hoarse. She was a heavy sleeper and snored during the night.

"I'm sorry I woke you," Joan mumbled.

"You're shaking, what's the matter?"

Joan sat up, leaned back against the pillows and headboard, and brought herself under control. The shaking subsided. "I should have been with Ray last night."

"Well thanks for the compliment," Faon said, smiling.

"I didn't mean it like that," Joan said, remembering how Faon had kissed and caressed her.

"I know you didn't."

"But Ray didn't want me last night: I read his thoughts. He was thinking about Josiane."

"You both needed time away from each other," Faon said. "The connection that you have with Raymond will take some time to adjust to. And you'll just have to get used to glimpsing his thoughts of Josiane. He can't help thinking about her. She represents the past, his—"

"I know that! But I'm afraid. I'm afraid I'll hurt him again" —she shuddered— "or kill him, as I tried to do at the pool. But I don't want to lose him. I *can't* lose him." Joan started shaking again, and Faon touched her hair, her face.

"Of course you can lose him, just as I could lose Pretre," Faon said softly.

"It's not the same," Joan said. "You didn't kill Pretre."

"Nor did you kill Raymond."

"But I tried to, God forgive me."

"You're slipping back into old ways of thinking," Faon said. "The church wants Raymond, the Criers in the dark spaces are calling him. You can't hold yourself responsible for what happened at the pool. You would not have tried to kill Raymond if the Criers on the other side had not prompted you and used the strength of your emotions."

"It was *me*, not the Criers."

"You must understand that Raymond is, inevitably, on his way to the dark side," Faon said. "He made himself vulnerable to the Criers to find his wife."

"No," Joan said, "he's not promised to the church. What happened at the pool had nothing to do with Screamers. It was *me*!"

"So now you call them Screamers, as if you were an outsider."

"That's how I feel," Joan said, drawing away from Faon.

"I know this is all happening too fast for you, but you must believe in the church."

"Believe in the church?" Joan asked, her voice rising and cracking. "After you just told me that the fucking Criers tried to kill Ray?"

"Stop it!" Faon said. "If the Criers take Raymond, there will be no death for him. *That* should be what you want if you love him in a proper way. If you lost him now, you'd have him forever."

"I can't believe that anymore," Joan said.

"But you've seen the holy Criers and the dark spaces."

Joan was silent.

"You can't save him without the church," Faon continued. "He's like a raging volcano. He's dangerous to you and others and himself. Only the Criers can help him."

"*I* can help him," Joan insisted.

"He will say that he's going to stay with you always," Faon said, "but the compulsion to find Josiane will come back and he'll leave you. There's something odd about his amnesia. It seems to me that he's using it so as not to face something terrible. You must be careful."

Joan stared at the patterns in the ceiling. She felt lost, isolated, as if everything and everyone had receded from her.

"If you need me, I'll always be there for you," Faon said. "And you will always have the church, no matter how you feel about it now."

"I know that."

"Then you must help him," Faon said. "You know what he is."

Joan closed her eyes, as if she could forever blot out Faon, the church, and the Criers who ruled the dark spaces.

"He is a seed crystal," Faon said, and then she leaned over and kissed Joan good-bye on the lips.

Joan and Mantle rode silently in the transpod. The sunny day and breathtakingly beautiful countryside seemed like a huge joke at her expense, as if the world, which was usually so distant and ugly and foreboding, could appear so superficially friendly when she felt sick to death of it. Although she didn't show it, Joan was exhausted. Normally, her face became pale when she was tired, but the flush of yesterday's sunburn was a camouflage.

It was a short walk from the station in Cannes to Mantle's house in Old Town. A painter was putting the last touches on the trim; the entire house had been painted exactly the same stil-de-grain yellow it had been before, but now it looked clean. Although Joan had never been inside the house, she had often passed it, as if proximity could salve her heart. It was masochistic, she had always told herself, for she always felt worse when she lost control and did that; he would be inside doing who-knows-what, thinking about anything and anyone but her. During those times, she never felt more alone, or more isolated. And then she would become angry with herself, tell herself that she wasn't seventeen and in love, and go home or to the club to pick someone up, a friend who would at least be familiar in bed.

"The house looks nice," she said, nervous now that she was about to enter it. Everyone else had been inside, she told herself. Why should you give a fuck? Everyone but me. The houses on either side of Mantle's looked dismal by comparison.

"Sonofabitch," Mantle said. "He never gives up."

"Well, it does look nice."

"Now the neighbors will expect me to paint their houses, just to keep faith. He knows that." And Mantle smiled and said "sonofabitch" again under his breath.

"Why are you giggling?" Joan asked, feeling shaky; that old feeling of awkwardness, of swelling hands. Suddenly she realized that she didn't want to go inside, that she had wanted him to keep his home as secret as he wished. What she wanted would not be found there, not now. But, somehow, she did want to see it, but alone, not when Pfeiffer was waiting for them. Not to have it pushed into her face that he had got there first.

"He's just paying back an old debt," Mantle said, pausing at the steps. "When we were schoolmates, I painted his apartment. He complained bitterly for the entire semester that he liked it better dirty. You see, I had painted it with a rather loud color that made it nearly impossible for any of us to study there for any period of time." He chuckled again. "We all took to working in the library after that." Then he climbed the stairs; Joan followed. Through all that hate and estrangement, he still loves him, Joan thought.

More than me, she thought as she climbed the stairs behind him. The hallway's depressing. God, I don't want to go inside. If he'd wanted me to see it . . .

"Well, the prodigals return, safe and sound," Pfeiffer said. She couldn't see him yet; he was standing just behind the doorway. The light from the apartment cut smokily into the hall; obviously only available light from the windows. "How do you like the new facade?"

"The elephant never forgets," Mantle said, stepping into the living room. He turned to Joan, who was standing in the doorway, nervous about coming into the apartment. As soon as she saw Pfeiffer, she had begun to blush.

Something passed between her and Mantle.

Jesus, he doesn't need my okay to talk to Pfeiffer, Joan thought as she walked into the room.

"You're looking well," Pfeiffer said to her, but she could not meet his stare.

"What the hell were you doing organ gambling?" Mantle asked Pfeiffer. "That's—"

"That's not like me, is it?" Pfeiffer said. "Well, I'm not the stuffy book you think me to be. Even I need to take chances, to feel alive. Frankly, I was worried about you."

"And that's what made you organ gamble," Mantle said.

"Yes, in part. . . ."

"Then why did you fade out and leave Joan in the hospital?"

"I made the arrangements, I . . . wait a moment, I'll be right back." And Pfeiffer left the room. He returned a few seconds later and handed Mantle a wallet. "You left this near the ruins, my friend. I believe I've saved your ass."

"Roberta told me that everything had been taken care of; I thought she had someone in the police. . . ."

"Well, I'm the someone," Pfeiffer said. "So, you see, I didn't just 'fade out.' Anyway, everything has been wiped, all records, and you owe me quite a sum. I went into the hole for this."

"So what do you want, a medal?" Mantle asked.

"I thought a simple 'thank you' would have been sufficient."

Mantle turned and went into the sitting room where he kept a small bar, and returned with a Campari for Joan. She accepted it, although she really didn't care for a drink. A narcodrine would have been better, but she had promised herself never to take another one. Once, she had scammed down so low that she attempted suicide; not so long ago. . . .

"Carl, a drink for you?"

Pfeiffer shook his head, and Mantle did not fix a drink for himself. Something was in the air, something ancient and human. They were reenacting the mythology of their relationship. The telepathic images of Mantle's anger and envy and love and hate were palpable, and Joan closed herself from him, for she was embarrassed and repelled. She didn't want to glimpse the ugly pettiness that underlay his strength and goodness. Instead, she sat down on a comfortable sofa and looked at the paintings that filled the walls, the portraits that seemed to instantly appear as if seen from one angle and then another. She saw herself in one of them; it was in an ornate frame. An oceanscape, of all things. She looked away from it, somehow terrified to study it any longer, afraid of what she might find. Jesus, she thought, this is his world, how he sees it, and us. . . .

"You never gave anything away for nothing in your life, Carl," Mantle said as he leaned against a bookcase opposite Joan.

"That's wrong, especially coming from you, and unfair." Pfeiffer paced around the room, then stood beside a floral-figured easy chair to stare at a fantastical painting on the wall above it. "You really haven't changed: you're still as paranoid as you used to be."

"But *I* don't spend my sleeping hours walking about and shouting that the ceiling's caving in."

"I must still do that," Pfeiffer said, turning toward Mantle, "because just last night I found myself hanging out the window over there." He pointed toward the bedroom where he slept.

Joan looked at Pfeiffer; that didn't sound at all like him.

"So now we've both lost someone," Pfeiffer said, as if out of the blue. "Can we stay here together until I must leave?" Pfeiffer looked at Joan for an instant, as if to include her in his plans.

"Jesus Christ, Carl, I think you've gone over the edge," Mantle said.

Pfeiffer laughed and said, "That sounds familiar."

Joan felt Mantle's frustration and ambivalence.

"I propose a vacation to resolve the past and cement the future," Pfeiffer said, and he produced three cardboard tickets, faded pink. "Joan, come over here. Now, perhaps, I can tell you that I was very worried about you. I'm very pleased Raymond brought you back."

"What are they?" Joan asked, walking over to Pfeiffer to examine the tickets.

"Look closely."

"They look like old cinema tickets—why, they must be ancient," Joan said. "These are steamship tickets for the *Titanic*," she said, genuinely impressed.

"That they are, for a voyage on the Royal Mail Steamship herself. This is going to be the media event of the year, and I have a ticket for each of us to New York harbor."

Joan felt something from Mantle, the feather touch of a thought, his old fear of being unmasked and betrayed. How could Pfeiffer know of his plans to return to New York?

Coincidence, Joan thought, trying to communicate that to Mantle. But Joan wanted Mantle to accept Pfeiffer's offer. There were *three* tickets. Joan would have Mantle for a little longer, and every moment was precious, for he might change, he might stop looking for Josiane—anything was possible. Joan closed herself to Mantle and thought about him. She couldn't let him go. . . .

"Of course, you know the story of the *Titanic,*" Pfeiffer said, excited as a schoolboy, as if the great ship were a little toy.

"Didn't it sink sometime in the eighteenth century?" Joan asked. "And was raised by some treasure hunters?"

"It sank in the beginning of the twentieth century," Mantle said, edging toward Joan and Pfeiffer. "But I thought the Saudis had bought it and were using it as a hotel."

"They did, almost a hundred years ago to the day," Pfeiffer said. "They bought it from the Titanic Salvage Group for an exorbitant amount of money to embarrass the English. It was completely restored, exactly as it was, and kept in the harbor at Salwa as a sort of pleasure palace for dignitaries. But over the years the Saudis lost interest, and they sold it to an American conglomerate this year. Now it's getting a new lease on life, so to speak.

"And as if by a miracle, I managed these three tickets," Pfeiffer continued. "Will you accept them?" He looked at Mantle, then at Joan. "Raymond, the past is done. I need to be with you, I need company, help, whatever you want to call it. You came to me once in a similar situation—"

"I don't remember."

"You lived with me for more than a month until you resolved your differences with Josiane."

"I don't remember."

"Yes, you do," Joan said. "You just don't remember Josiane, but you once told me that you stayed with Carl, that he kept you together. You said it was in your diary."

"It was Caroline who offered help—"

"You said it was Carl."

"Do you want him to stay?" Mantle asked her, talking about Pfeiffer as if he weren't there.

"Do you want *me* to stay?" Joan asked, feeling as if everything had suddenly collapsed again, that she had no business meddling, or even being here. But she had caught something from Mantle. She knew he was lying, lying to Pfeiffer and himself; and there was something else too, something she couldn't quite put her finger on, but something she sensed, about Pfeiffer: when they had hooked in at the casino, Joan was certain that Pfeiffer was hiding something, was afraid of her seeing what he had buried. And he had been successful in keeping it from her. It was as if a professional psych had done the job—a common practice, especially in those industries where brainwashing was often used as a last resort. Perhaps that was it, Joan thought, just a piece of dangerous political or corporate information lying there like a bit of undigested pork.

"I've asked you to stay, isn't that enough?" Mantle asked.

"Yes, of course it is, and I love you for keeping yourself open to me. But I feel you're not being honest with yourself, and with Carl, for all your disagreements and misunderstandings in the past. Where *is* Carl?" she asked, looking around. But without waiting for an answer, she said, "I think it would be good for you to be with him, for all your misgivings. I sense that something might come of it." She was talking in a whisper.

"What do you mean?" Mantle asked, stepping even closer to her.

"Something during the hook-in at the casino. I'm probably just adding fuel to the fire. But he does need you; perhaps this is the time to finally make repairs."

"What did you feel during the hook-in?" Mantle asked, insistent.

"Something he's afraid of. Perhaps you can help him."

"Then you care about him."

"Don't you?"

"Did you make love with him?"

Joan nodded, relieved that Mantle had sensed something of a relationship between Pfeiffer and herself other than a cordial sticking-it-in.

Pfeiffer appeared in the living room, his bag in hand. He

walked over to the doorway leading to the stairs and said, "I think I've had enough, and I'm sorry I've imposed. Actually, though, this wasn't a bad scene as our scenes go." He smiled. "Remember the time we had an argument and I ran into the bedroom, you ran downstairs, and Caroline had no idea what was going on?"

"I believe she said that we should have gotten married, rather than you and she," Mantle said. Then after a pause: "Stay, Carl, I owe you that."

"Not for debt," Carl said, but he placed his valise on the floor. "Too much blood under the bridge for that. Not even for old time's sake. For real or nothing. I came here first because we always saw each other without masks." He laughed. "I guess we've known each other too long, seen each other step on our respective dicks too many times. But I've options. You know me, Raymond. I've *always* got options." Then to Joan: "And thank you. I can't explain it, but Raymond knows why I went organ gambling. I'm only sorry I caused you pain."

"Cut the bullshit," Mantle said, though not very seriously.

"What does he mean?" Joan asked.

"When Josiane left me the first time, I went to a place in—"

"Kabul, in Afghanistan," Pfeiffer interrupted as he left his valise by the door and walked to the center of the room. "I found you in a hospital there, remember?"

"I used to have quite a fondness for gambling. I played something called *Solitaire muliter*. All the odds are against the player, which was why I played it, I guess."

"Jesus Christ," Joan said, surprised. He was walled-in as he talked; she had only his words, none of the textures of his thoughts. Perhaps never would again, she feared.

"I was mutilated quite badly. Carl can tell you the rest some other time."

"But . . ." Joan stopped herself. Whatever the mutilation was, he would have had it repaired surgically. Then she felt a blast of dark thought, a dart, an angry steel-scratching, and she felt his disgust mingled with her own. He had had his cock razored. "I shouldn't have come," she said. "I should have kept my mouth shut, mind your own business, slut. . . ."

Mantle and Pfeiffer led her to the couch, sat down beside her.

"You shouldn't have been put in the middle of this," Pfeiffer said.

"It was my doing. I knew you had things to work out between yourselves. I should have known better than to come. It was selfishness on my part."

"No, it wasn't," Mantle said, "or if it was, it was the right kind of selfishness."

"We shouldn't have played out the past before you," Pfeiffer said.

"We had a similar fight once, which Caroline witnessed," Mantle said, and Joan felt a change of mood. "Do you remember that one, Mister Ego?"

Pfeiffer said, "I still think I was in the right," but he smiled as if it was of no consequence, a joke at his expense. "Now, do you remember the umbrella?"

"The what?" Mantle asked.

"It was with Caroline, long before I really fell in love with her, before I found out how fragile she was."

"Not as fragile as you suspected, though."

Pfeiffer was silent for a few beats, and then he said, "I think not, but the wheel turns, and she'll begin having episodes again. She might be fine for a year, two, or—who knows—maybe ten."

"But that's physiological, treatable. Certainly you're not still deluding yourself about that," Mantle said.

"Say what you will, but she's untreatable, at least over the long run. She adapts to her illness, so as to return to that state, just as we adapt to wellness."

"Bullshit," Mantle said.

"The umbrella?" Joan asked, sensing that there lay some sort of closure among them.

"Well?" Pfeiffer asked Mantle, and Mantle smiled distantly, for he was remembering past events; Joan felt the touch of his thoughts, warm and also distant, as if coming from someone like Ray, yet different: younger, freer, happier.

"Yes, I do remember," Mantle said. "Jesus, it seems so long ago, so many relationships modeled upon it, partaking of it afterward."

"For you, not for me," Pfeiffer said fussily.

"It was simply a *ménage à trois*," Mantle said. "But we all knew each other intimately anyway, that I suppose it was natural. You were particularly set on the idea, if I recall, because you were afraid of Caroline."

"Only to do that," Pfeiffer said. To Joan he said, "Believe it or not, I was a virgin."

"She'd believe it," Mantle said, chuckling. "That was quite a while ago, before we even reached university level. We were neighbors then—at least, Carl and I were. Caroline lived in Ithaca. Suburbia."

"It was more than a *ménage à trois*," Pfeiffer said. "Don't demean something that was good and innocent. It was protection from the rain, from life. Remember when we went out into that rainstorm naked, shouting we had our own umbrella?"

"You're dating us," Mantle said.

"How do you mean?"

"Umbrellas? That's like ice boxes." There was no laughter, but it was somehow in the air, as the past was reaffirmed and Carl and Ray were revealed, shorn of the barnacles of the last years, healed of the myriad acid-bites of hatred and jealousy that had undone their friendship.

"Does it upset you to talk about Caroline?" Joan asked.

"Yes, but not just now. Not inside the umbrella." He looked at Mantle tentatively, as if needing some familiar response, but nothing was spoken. Suddenly, Joan realized that she was trying desperately to talk, even to make small talk, because she felt that whatever was happening—whatever she had, in fact, instigated—was centered on her and would overwhelm her. She was afraid.

She did not remember, after that, who had begun. She was fondling, and being fondled by, both of them. Undressing and being undressed. Kissing, sucking, caught inside the eye of a hurricane of soft words and quick breathing. She opened herself to it all, her mind quietly, carefully analyzing, reaching out to touch another filament of thought, as she was entered by Pfeiffer, or perhaps it was Mantle. It didn't really matter, for she was listening to Mantle, using Pfeiffer to bring her closer to him, to Mantle. They played themselves out, and Joan felt Mantle, knew him as Pfeiffer did, as a young man, all potential.

Pfeiffer was the glue, she thought, frightened. If Ray really loved me, he wouldn't be doing this. An umbrella is for two. . . .

"I love you, Ray," she whispered. Her eyes were closed, her own feral noises distant; all this fucking was geometrical, a premise she didn't understand being proven. But in some last instant before descending into exhausted sleep, she felt both their thoughts. Pfeiffer was full of anxiety and ego, but she knew that. Mantle, on the other hand, was composed, as if, like herself, floating above experience. He was thinking of the *Titanic* and Josiane's face just below the surface of a pool of dark liquid.

And Joan thought she could hear Josiane's distant voice calling him.

PART THREE

Sixteen

Mantle stared at the painting of Joan that he was working on. It was all wrong, somehow. Although it was technically brilliant, he simply could not bring the image to life. After the *ménage à trois* was under way, he had set up his studio in the vacant first-floor apartment, which had been his original intent when he bought the house. The light was actually better here than in his apartment, and now everyone had more room upstairs, especially Pfeiffer, who tended to spread his books, papers, clothes, and personal articles everywhere.

Joan and Pfeiffer were both staying with him now.

"Well, are you going to go?" Joan asked as she sat on a stool before a row of high windows. She was posing for him, and, naked, she was bathed in the cool morning light. "You've really got to give him an answer: the ship leaves from Southampton in just a few days."

"I can't paint here," Mantle said, disgusted. He leaned back in the armless chair in which he always sat to paint and looked at Joan over the left side of the canvas.

"That doesn't answer the question," Joan said. She walked over to the windows as if oblivious that she was naked. The windows were situated high above the street, and she could not be seen except from other windows, perhaps.

"I don't know what I want to do."

"If you must go to New York, the ship will give you some more time to think things out, give you a chance to reconsider. . . ." She talked as she stared out the window onto the street. The street was empty; it was ten o'clock in the morning, the first hiatus of the day, the time when the streets became the quiet ruins of a past age.

"Do you *want* to go?" he asked.

Joan laughed—a short, bitter explosion. "Do you mean it's my choice whether you stay here or go to New York? If that's it, then I want to stay here forever. With you. My choice is to bury the past and make a future." She looked at him, into him, and Mantle felt their connection. "There's no future for the United States now," she continued in a low voice that was almost a whisper. "The country is sinking into the dark spaces."

"I don't believe that for a moment," Mantle snapped. "The Screamer attacks have been contained."

Joan shook her head. "It's only a matter of time. . . ." After a long pause she said, "Ray, I know that you made reservations to fly to New York alone."

Mantle could only lower his eyes.

"If you have to go to New York," Joan said, "then I want to be with you, and I want to take the ship. Yes, I want the time, and you owe it to Carl."

"I don't *owe* Carl anything."

"I think you do, or feel that you do. He needs you, and from what I understand about you two, you've been waiting a long time for that."

"You're a nasty bitch."

"And you're a bastard, but I love you."

"Everything's gone wrong. I'm sitting around here, waiting; I can't paint: that's a bad sign. . . ."

"I know," Joan said. "You tell me that every day. And yet, so much has felt right to me. For the first time ever."

"That's the triple."

"You sonofabitch," she said. "Can you really believe that?"

Mantle stood up and walked over to Joan. He put his arms around her while she stood stiffly facing the window, a warm icon. "I'm sorry. It's because of *us*," Mantle admitted. "Carl, the whole *ménage à trois*, was the excuse."

"It's a shame we needed 'an excuse' to love each other and take the time. You've never loved me so much, or so often." She smiled, but as it was bright outside, Mantle could not see her reflection in the window.

"All right," Mantle said. "I'll go with Carl . . . and you."

"I'd rather we didn't go at all."

"We'll stay under the umbrella until the bitter end," Mantle said, as if to himself.

"Don't talk that way."

"There's nothing in this for you," Mantle said. "You

should go back to Boulouris, spend some time with Faon and—"

"No!"

"You haven't even called her since you've been back here."

Joan pulled herself away from Mantle and picked up her clothes from the floor. She pulled a pale blue sweater over her head, then stepped into loose-fitting jeans. "I don't want anything to do with them . . . not now, not yet, maybe never."

"Why?"

"We've been over it. I don't trust them, what they did to you. . . . I don't know. I just need some time, some time with you and away from them."

"You've got it all confused and distorted. They gave me a chance to find Josiane—"

"They wanted you for their church," Joan snapped.

After a pause, Mantle said, "Faon called."

Joan looked at Mantle, waiting.

"She asked me to do some work for the church."

"You see?"

"She asked that we both take a visit. I think it would be a good idea. We could be alone, see if *we* could work without the umbrella."

"No," Joan said flatly, fumbling in her pockets for an inhalor. "We're the umbrella, with or without Carl."

"I thought you'd stopped taking narcodrines," Mantle said.

"Think again."

"Well, I'm going. I've got some questions, some things that are driving me crazy."

"Then talk about them with *me*," Joan said. "You don't need Faon. *We're* the connection, remember?"

"Yes, of course I remember, but you've somehow got all wound around yourself. I know it's my fault, but I can't stand it. You're so afraid of everything. You're suffocating us."

"That's not true."

"It is true, and the umbrella has kept us together because we've been submerging everything for Pfeiffer."

Joan sat down on the floor near Mantle's easel. "What do you want to discuss with Faon that you can't discuss with me?"

"You know what's been bothering me, but you pretend it doesn't exist. You, of all people, should be able to see it."

"What?" Joan whispered, afraid and certain of what was coming.

"I've the constant sensation of being watched. I feel it, dammit, I feel that the Screamers are coming for me, coming through the dark spaces. I hear them calling me in my dreams, and when I'm awake. I hear them, even now. I can feel the dark spaces touching me. Don't tell me you haven't felt any of that. . . ."

Joan turned her face away, as if by not looking she would not hear. She was terrified of losing him, caught up in her obsession. They were both deaf and blind to each other. "Then all the lovemaking, the good feelings, the shared thoughts, they were all phony."

"No, of course not. We're too close; you've—"

"You're using Pfeiffer and me; you're using me because you're afraid of what you're going to find in New York."

"Joan, stop it." But she had caught him with that, caught him dead. He was fighting the dark spaces, and Josiane. Josiane called him, tempted him, was the very substance of his thoughts. But he was afraid and confused, and fighting for survival. So he turned to Joan as if she were Josiane, the Josiane of the bright spaces.

"Stay here, Ray, please. We'll talk about whatever you want. I'll try; it will be different."

"Joan, you led me to the church, remember? It's one thing to quit, to decide it's not for you, but you're overreacting. You're lying to yourself."

"So are you."

"About what?" Mantle asked.

"If you're afraid, and I know you are, maybe it's for good reason. I'm afraid for you, too. Maybe you should trust yourself and be rid of Josiane."

"Jesus *Christ*—"

"And then maybe you won't be afraid to let me into your locked bedroom that you once shared with her."

"I can't," Mantle said. "I'm just not ready to do that yet."

"I think the Criers are just using the idea of her to lure you into the dark spaces. I've seen your dreams, I've seen that. And if you accept the church, even a little bit, then you accept the dark spaces. That acceptance brings them closer to you. Sucks you in. Into death, Ray. Death. You must fight it."

"I am."

"No, you're not, not enough, not by going back to Boulouris. And certainly not by going back to New York."

Just then, Pfeiffer appeared. He had been in and out of the house all morning, had been unusually nervous; now he seemed happy, as he used to when he finished a project.

"Am I disturbing something . . . ?"

As soon as Mantle left, Pfeiffer went upstairs and turned on the telie in the living room. Joan stayed in the studio; Pfeiffer knew enough to leave her alone.

The living room seemed to dissolve, and was replaced by hollies. A thousand Muslim men, women, and children watched and listened to a white-bearded, ferocious-looking old man who stood on a podium and harangued them in a thin voice. He stretched out his arms, as if to Pfeiffer.

Pfeiffer had activated all the tactiles and olfactories, and he had the crushing sensation that the crowd was pressing in on him. He could hear hoarse whisperings and huzzahs behind him, could smell the sweet and acrid odors of food and sweat as surely as if he were really in the midst of a Muslim crowd listening to Islam's new charismatic leader: the Mahdi of the Sudan.

To Pfeiffer the Mahdi said: "Know that I am the Expected Mahdi, the Successor of the Apostle of God. Thus I have no need of the sultanate, nor of the kingdom of Kordofan or elsewhere, nor of the wealth of this world and its vanity. I am but the slave of God, guiding unto God and to what is with Him. . . ."

Disgusted, Pfeiffer switched channels. A voice droned on about the success of containing the Screamers while Pfeiffer had an aerial view of the bombing of Long Beach, California. It was a rerun; he had seen it before. Then the scene changed to an on-the-street view of New Orleans, which was still burning. Pfeiffer deactivated the audio and watched the silent Screamers and felt the blasting heat.

"Are you still watching that shit?"

Pfeiffer jumped, not expecting Joan. "It is my business to know what's going on."

"By watching the telie?" Joan laughed, switched off the television, and sat down on the couch.

"Raymond's not coming with me, is he," Pfeiffer said.

"Yes, as a matter of fact, he is."

"Well, that's wonderful."

"Yes, it's certainly wonderful."

"What's the matter, then?" asked Pfeiffer. "Aren't you coming?"

"Yes, we're all going."

"Why didn't you go back to Boulouris with him?" Pfeiffer asked, his tone of voice changing. "I don't trust them with him, I—"

"*You* don't trust them . . . ? Haven't you anything better to do with yourself than eavesdrop?"

"I wasn't eavesdropping," Pfeiffer said.

"What do *you* call it?"

"Listening." Pfeiffer smiled, and the tension broke. Joan settled back into the couch; Pfeiffer sat down beside her.

"God, I'm worried," Joan said. "Ray's deluding himself about the church and Faon and . . ." Her voice just trailed off.

"He's going to be just fine," Pfeiffer said.

Joan didn't reply for a moment. The curtains were drawn over the windows, and the sunlight edged in through cracks and spaces like smoky swords. She stared at the curtains and then said, "You had a bad time last night again."

Pfeiffer stiffened. "Was I talking in my sleep?"

"Yes, you were."

"Jesus."

"You see," Joan said softly, "you're as much of a throwback as I am."

"I'm sure I don't know what you're getting at."

"You kept crying 'Johnny' in your sleep. He was the furry boy, remember?"

"I'm not a homosexual; I can't stand it in myself."

"You're afraid of the idea, not the act," Joan said. "Remember when you told me I had a medieval bent of mind? I guess we're both cut of the same cloth." Pfeiffer smiled wanly, and Joan continued; "If you like, you can pretend that I'm the furry boy, and—"

"And you can pretend that I'm Raymond, isn't that right?" Pfeiffer asked.

"I'm sorry, it was supposed to be a joke."

"I'm not jealous of your love for Raymond."

"I need to break through to *somebody*, connect somehow," Joan said. "I'm sorry I used you. I wasn't trying to hurt you, I just wanted to be close. I wish I didn't love him, Carl."

Pfeiffer put his hand on her lap, caressed her legs, and said, "I have a present for Raymond."

"What is it?"

"You'll both have to wait until we board the *Titanic*," Pfeiffer said, already pretending that she was, indeed, the furry boy.

Faon had expected Mantle, and she met him in front of the great house, which looked even more monolithic in the strong afternoon sunshine. They walked through the shaded, perfumed gardens beyond which were stunted trees, scrub, rocky inclines and, finally, white ocean sand so smooth that it looked tended, imported.

They sat on a stone bench, one of three which were positioned around another garden: a rondelle of smooth, raked pebbles and large rocks. Upon first glimpse, the rocks seemed to be randomly placed. It was a classic rock garden, and perfect.

The nearby ocean was only a salty scent, one among many.

The silence was awkward.

"I saw the overload mosaic commercial you did for a Senator Florio, I think that's his name," Faon said. "Charles, my husband, has been explaining your work to me. He says you combined traditional mosaics with a mirroring technique so the viewer would unconsciously associate himself with the politician. The viewer would actually see himself as this politician—and who wouldn't vote for himself?" Faon smiled. "Now, do I have all that right?"

"I can see you've memorized all the right things," Mantle said, surprised. "Did you really call me here to work for you?"

"Did you really come here to work for me?"

Mantle stared at the rock garden as if it were some sort of mandala, as if he could find answers in the sharp edges of the rocks and the stop-motion ocean of pebbles. "I came because I'm afraid."

"I can see that," Faon said. "You look like you've been seeing into the dark spaces."

"I need answers."

"And Joan, I would expect—"

"I've tried to talk to her," Mantle said, "but she won't listen."

"She's afraid for you."

"I tried to talk her into coming, but she refused."

"I know."

"She won't even talk about the Screamers."

"Criers," Faon corrected. "It will take time for Joan."

"And what about me?" demanded Mantle. "I can't stand what's happening to me."

"Just what *is* happening to you?"

"I feel that I'm being watched, constantly, by Criers. If I let down my guard, I'll be pulled into the dark spaces, I'm sure of that. Every night they call me, pull at me, suck me in, and—"

"What about Josiane?" asked Faon.

"That's what I came here to ask you."

"Have you seen her, heard her?"

After a pause, Mantle said, "Yes, she calls to me, but it's a trick, for I've heard my father call, my mother and brother—all tricks of the other side."

"You could have found out the truth," Faon said.

"How? By letting them take me?"

"You look for Josiane, and when you find her, you turn away or forget or make excuses."

"That's not true."

"It is," Faon said. "Why haven't you left for New York? Why are you waiting?"

"Why are the Criers after *me*?"

"I don't know," Faon said, relaxing, easing the tension. "Not exactly, that is. Have you ever heard of Seed Crystal?"

"Yes, I do remember something about that, it was in that prayer book you left me when I was staying at the house. There was something about the many changing into one, I can't quite remember."

"The line was 'I believe in the crystal and the seed that turn the many into the One.'"

"That was it," Mantle said. "Now what are you getting at?"

"There are those of us who are seeds around which things and people crystallize. They focus things and people, act as principles or archetypes."

"I think that's bullshit," Mantle said.

"Think what you like. You didn't believe in the dark spaces, either, until they swallowed you and you saw Josiane."

"I'm not even sure if I saw Josiane."

"Ah, so it's *all* hallucination. Did Joan hallucinate you down by the Blue Pool, then? Is your *circuit fantome* hallucination, too? If it's all hallucination, you're just going crazy. See a psych."

"I came to see you," Mantle said.

"I don't have the answers you want, none of us do," Faon said. They were both looking at the circular garden as if talking to it rather than to each other. "Perhaps some of what you saw, or thought you saw in the dark spaces, was from your own mind. That happens. It's difficult to separate the real from the other."

"Have *you* seen her in the dark spaces?" Mantle asked.

"Yes," Faon admitted, "but I don't know if she's alive or dead. No more than you know."

"What can I do?"

"Can you live without your past, without knowing?"

"No," Mantle said. "It's as if I'm being constantly pulled; I have to know, one way or another."

"Then that's what you'll have to do," Faon said.

"That doesn't help me with the Criers."

"It's all one and the same; dead or alive, Josiane is certainly not living in the bright spaces. And the Criers will take you."

"You've seen that?" Mantle asked.

"I know they want you; so do you. Whatever you do is good for the church."

"What's that supposed to mean?"

"If you are a focus, a crystal," Faon said, "you will have to burn brightly. It may be ironic, but the more you fight the Criers, the more you become a crystal."

"And if I do nothing, I'll simply be pulled into the dark spaces," Mantle said quietly.

"You said you came here for answers. I'm giving you the truth. Perhaps that's *not* what you wanted. However, I don't know how things will actually work out, I only see what I'm supposed to see, I think."

"I don't believe it," Mantle said.

"Good."

"This was no help at all," Mantle said, standing up, still watching the garden as if it were a live, round being. He felt helpless, and suddenly terribly tired.

"If it's any consolation, we're all going to melt," Faon said. "In the eye of the crowd, the many do become one. We'll all become the One."

"Not me!"

"Good," Faon said. "Fight it."

They walked along the path they had taken back toward the house. One of its Spanish-tiled roofs could be seen, a glinting above the trees. Joan was right, Mantle thought. He shouldn't have come.

"You know," Mantle said, "the thing I can't stand is the condescension."

"You mistake condescension for submission. You asked, and I told you, what I believe. You only lose if you hang onto this shared reality of the bright spaces. It's killed us, truly. You've seen another reality, one without death. But realities are waging war inside you."

"I'd like to see Roberta before I leave," Mantle said as they approached the house. "If that's all right. . . ."

"She's dead," Faon said matter-of-factly.

"What?" Mantle stopped walking.

"Why, she joined her husband. Surely she told you of her intentions."

"She said something after the ceremony," Mantle said, stunned.

"Do you remember Stephen, the little boy in the casket?" Faon asked softly. She stood close to Mantle, as if offering him security now rather than the cold edges of truth.

"Jesus, I can't believe that she'd—"

"Are you seeing into the dark spaces?" Faon asked.

"No!" Mantle said. "I think you're trying to fuck up my head, throw me into the dark spaces, is that it?"

"Do you really believe that?"

"I don't know," Mantle said.

"You are my responsibility as well as those on the other side," Faon said. "I don't want you to die—please believe *that*."

"But you don't care if I physically die, is that it?"

"Yes, that's it. But you could die, in the old sense, if you do not accept the other side. You affect reality, whatever you might think about that right now."

"Why did you mention Stephen?" Mantle asked. "Roberta had her wits about her; she wasn't a shell waiting for physical death."

"She was promised, and she was waiting," Faon said.

"Are you trying to say that *I'm* promised?"

"Have you ever been a Crier?"

"No, of course not."

"Then you're not promised," Faon said. "Just wanted, perhaps."

"But you're intimating that I am the other. Promised."

"I sense that about you, yes," Faon said. "But there's something broken about it, something wrong, almost perverse. Perhaps when you find your memory...."

Mantle started walking again. As they approached the house, he said, "I don't believe you."

"What do you mean?"

"I don't believe Roberta's dead."

Faon chuckled. "Would you like to see her? She's in the candle room. Well...?" She stopped before the house, in front of the stone portico.

"No," Mantle said, "I'm not coming in."

"Charles would love to see you, and I'm really not trying to inveigle you into working for the church." She smiled softly.

"Thank you, no." Mantle turned and walked down the driveway, away from the house.

"Raymond, I'll be seeing you."

Mantle paused for an instant, but did not turn around.

Seventeen

The next two weeks were an agony for Mantle. Perhaps it was just another manifestation of the fear and tension that had begun to pervade Europe since the recent Screamer attacks and containment bombings in the United States, but he simply couldn't paint. He had lost it as surely as his memory. He felt that he was being watched, felt the cold edges of the dark spaces even during the day. And he couldn't stand the nights, which had become empty and dreamless—couldn't stand waking up in a cold sweat, and not remembering.

He had begun to hate the idea of Josiane. She was pulling him into the dark spaces. He had to find her, and it was killing him. If only he could forget Josiane, forget the past, and lose himself in Joan. Joan was good, Joan was pure. She could help him. . . ,

But something was beating in his head, louder and louder, a code he could not decipher.

It was almost with relief that he found himself on the RMS *Titanic*.

Eighteen

She was beautiful; huge even by the measure of the Twenty-second century; and graceful as a racing liner. She was a floating Crystal Palace, as magnificent as anything J. P. Morgan could conceive. Designed by Alexander Carlisle and built by Harland and Wolff, she wore the golden band of the Ismay line along all nine hundred feet of her. She rose one hundred and seventy-five feet like the side of a cliff, with nine steel decks, four sixty-two-foot funnels, and over two thousand windows and sidelights to illuminate the luxurious cabins and suites and public rooms. She weighed forty-six thousand tons, and her reciprocating engines and Parsons-type turbines could generate over fifty thousand horsepower and speed the ship over twenty-three knots. Because of her sophisticated system of watertight compartments, the journal *The Shipbuilder* had once pronounced her "practically unsinkable." She had rooms and suites to accommodate 735 first-class passengers, 674 in second, and over 1000 in steerage. She had a gymnasium, a

Turkish bath, squash and racket courts, a swimming pool, libraries; and lounges and sitting rooms. The grand *salon* had cathedral windows, which were artificially lit; and plush-carpeting and rich paneling could be found everywhere. One first-class restaurant had its own *boulevard*, as if it were a French streetside cafe. And, remaining true to historical demands, there were twenty lifeboats and rafts. Each boat could carry fifty-eight people, including a crew of eight.

A steward named Vincent escorted Pfeiffer, Joan, and Mantle to their suite, which was more like a hotel room than a stateroom. It had a parlor and a private promenade deck with Elizabethan half-timbered walls. The plush carpeted, velours-papered bedroom contained a huge four-poster bed, an antique night table, and a desk and stuffed chair beside the door. The ornate, harp-sculpture desk lamp was on, as was the lamp just inside the bed curtains. A porthole gave a view of sea and sky.

"Are we, then, all supposed to sleep in one bed?" Pfeiffer asked.

"No sir," the steward said. "If you will please come with me, I will show you the *other* bedroom." And Pfeiffer followed the steward from room to room. There was a knock at the door, and Vincent directed two boys dressed in uniform to put the valises in the bedrooms. As they left, he said, "I shall, of course, put everything away for you." He actually polished a veneer piece on the bed with his handkerchief.

"Perhaps later," Pfeiffer said, "but I don't want any bags opened just yet."

"As you wish, sir. I will be at your service at any hour, Mademoiselle and Messieurs. If you wish, you can explore the ship."

"How much time do we have?" Joan asked.

"Over an hour. We're scheduled to leave at noon. Would you care for a cocktail? Should you wish to remain—"

"Yes," Mantle said, "I'm going to stay here."

"Well, I'm going to tour the ship," Pfeiffer said.

"I'll be back in a few moments," the steward said, and in true valet style, backed out of the room, neatly clicking the door behind him.

"There'll be plenty of time to sightsee," Mantle said, looking disturbed; indeed, he wanted to be alone. The *ménage* was a farce, he told himself. He had hoped he could gain some purchase on his past with Pfeiffer's help—by reliving the old relationship, the old *ménage*. But this was phony, and he couldn't trick himself into remembering. And Pfeiffer was altogether too composed, too quick to look away, to believe that the past had returned.

"Do you remember when we rented that yacht at Bahia Mar?" Pfeiffer asked, smiling.

"Yes," Mantle said, "I do." He remembered Lighthouse Point, Pompano, Lauderdale, and their intercoastal waterways that reminded him of the canals of Venice—they were just as beautiful and polluted. "We couldn't afford it, but you were intent on having a vacation in Florida. You even convinced Caroline it was a good idea, if I recall."

"She didn't need much persuading," Pfeiffer said. "How many years ago was it?"

"At least ten years," Mantle said. "Sometime around oh-nine, I'd say."

"And do you remember when we left you and Josiane off on that island because you both claimed you had to pee . . . ? And we found both of you trying to set a record for the world's fastest quickie."

"No, I don't," Mantle said.

"We all went on that trip together," Pfeiffer said.

"I remember the sights."

"Josiane was with us."

"Yes, I'm sure she was," Mantle said.

"It was supposed to be a belated double honeymoon," Pfeiffer insisted.

After an uncomfortable silence, Joan said, "I think I'll unpack."

"Aren't you going to tour the ship with me?" Pfeiffer asked.

"Ray's right; there'll be plenty of time to see the ship later."

"Well, I don't have plenty of time. I have work to do," Pfeiffer said. He enunciated his words carefully, as he always did when he didn't get his way. Joan could not help but smile as Pfeiffer left the room, almost slamming into the steward who was carrying a bouquet of flowers and a tray of drinks.

"I brought refreshments in case you wished to remain," the steward said. "A Campari on ice for the lady—isn't that correct?—and a finger of Drambuie for you, sir. I will leave Mister Pfeiffer's bourbon, in case he returns."

"You certainly do your homework."

"Thank you, ma'am." And he opened the door to leave.

Before he could slip away, Joan asked, "What do you do for a living? I mean, certainly there's no great need for ship's stewards nowadays. And this ship is only sailing this once."

The steward's expression changed. His face became hard.

"Oh come on," Joan continued. "Be a sport. We won't tell. It would make me feel much better about this trip."

The steward closed the door and took a step into the room. "In real life, if you will, I am a valet. There are still quite a few of us, believe it or not—a thousandfold more than there were when this girl we're riding was built. And the reason I'm on this ship, ma'am, is because I'm an enthusiast. The *Titanic* is more than a dead legend to some of us; most every member of the Titanic Historical Society is on the ship. We've been granted passage for this voyage in return for acting as consultants. We know this girl better than anyone. And we'll wish her a proper good-bye. If you wish, I can give you the society's address after—" He looked embarrassed, but continued. "Then we might talk more informally. Now, please don't ask me to return to this century until our voyage is finished." With that he left, as if he had just scolded naughty children from an important family.

As soon as the door closed, it was quiet. Mantle was uncomfortable; Joan fidgeted with the bedspread, folding a corner and then smoothing it out. "You've been closed since you went to visit Faon," she said. "I'm sorry I couldn't help you then. And even before then. And I'm sorry about Carl, about the whole damn *ménage*. It was wrong to have him, to take this trip with him, to try—"

"None of this is your fault," Mantle said. "It's me." He sat down beside her on the bed. "I thought that by trying to relive the past, or a facsimile of it, I would remember...."

"Let's leave the ship, take a flyer to New York next week. I have a bad feeling about the whole thing."

"No," Mantle said.

"Why?"

"We should play out the *ménage*."

"At first I really thought you wanted to let Pfeiffer in," Joan said. "That he could help you remember the past. And I thought it would augment our feelings as it once had yours and Carl's. But then you slipped away from me—was that the way you were going to let me down easy?"

"No, the *ménage* happened, that's all. Naturally, just as naturally as it happened once long ago with Caroline. And I wanted Carl in. Yes, I did, not just to extract information, but perhaps to relive the past, the past I could still remember."

"And you used me to do that."

"Do you believe that?"

"Yes," Joan said, "I do. But I allowed the *ménage* to form around me; I suppose I instigated it. Ray, open the connection. Let me in. Please." But the connection was broken, perhaps dead.

"You wanted the *ménage* too," Mantle said.

"No . . . yes, I suppose so, but only because Carl interested me; but not to separate us, you and me. I thought he might help me *keep* you. . . ."

"We're not separated," Mantle said gently.

"Then let me in."

"I can't explain about Carl and me, through all the hate—"

"You don't have to, just let me back in."

Again, the silence. They sat together, only breathing. At another time, they would have made love, confirmed what they felt for each other; but to do that now would distance them even further. Then there was a sharp knock at the door. "We leave in ten minutes," called the steward. "There's been a change in the departure time, we're sorry for any inconvenience." Then the clickclick of his footsteps and, far away, another sharp rap and "We leave in ten minutes," as if it were an echo.

"The ship's probably drawing too much of a crowd," Joan said. "The authorities are very nervous since the American upheavals."

"Yes, I suppose," Mantle said. "Well, come on. We shouldn't miss this."

"Raymond . . ." Joan asked as Mantle stood up. "Let's end the *ménage*. Now."

He extended his hand to her and pulled her from the bed. "It's whatever you want."

"I want you."

"That you have, as much as—"

"But you still want the *ménage*."

"Yes," he said. "At least until New York. As phony as it may be, it's comfortable."

"Because Carl doesn't have the upper hand anymore."

"Perhaps he does. But you must believe that I love you, and trust me."

Bullshit, she thought. You sonofabitch. But it's your own fault, you stupid bitch, you should have known; you knew, cunt. . . .

"It's not bullshit," Mantle said, reading her. She jerked backward slightly as the *circuit fantome* was restored.

They walked down the corridor, which was empty, and then took the stairs to the Upper Promenade Deck, which was crowded, but only with passengers. As they didn't expect to be standing on deck for very long, neither Joan nor Mantle bothered to clip on a mask. With or without masks, the Southampton air would be fetid. It was humid, windy, and hazy; the sky was beautiful, though, a blaze of crimson and yellow. A heavily policed crowd cheered ashore as the passengers threw colored ribbons that snaked and coiled in the air down toward them; and at least fifty cameras hovered and sailed around the ship like rectangular kites, transmitting this event to millions of television viewers. This was major media, and the world was watching.

"There you are," Pfeiffer said, making space for Joan and Mantle by the rail. It seemed a long way down to the gray, foamy water. "I thought you two were intent on missing everything."

"Not everything," Mantle said, and then bells began to ring and the ship's triple whistles cut the air.

"What's that antique ship dong over there?" Joan asked when the noise let up. An old hulk of a steamer was berthed beside the *Titanic*.

"For history," Mantle said.

"Ah, I remember!" Joan shouted, excited; and again they all felt what they called "the umbrella." Even Pfeiffer, who was an outsider in every other respect, was a part of them again. Josiane and hot, dream-ridden sleep was far away now. Only the present in its favored immediacy remained. The *ménage* was an avenue back to the immediacy of childhood, to long moments that never need end, a way around the rotting body of old friendships and into the firm flesh of what was. For an instant, Joan shuddered, feeling Mantle's thought and afraid that this wasn't a reliving of a past, but a death. All these relationships were dead, they were all dead.

Another shout from the crowd below, and the ancient tugs began pushing as the *Titanic*'s triple-expansion steam engines could be felt thrilling throughout the great ship.

Then with a terrible crack, the hawsers mooring the antique steamer *New York* broke and whipped into the air. The crowd, like a mass of colored beetles, moved out of the way.

The steamer was being sucked directly into the path of the *Titanic*. But just when collision seemed imminent, one of the port engines was revved and the backwash gently pushed the *New York* away. There was another cheer, and the ship slowly moved out to sea. It seemed that the land, not the ship, was moving. The whole of England was just floating peacefully away while the string band on the ship's bridge played Oskar Straus's "The Chocolate Soldier."

"Well, you two have nothing to do for the next four days but relax and have a good time," Pfeiffer said with just a hint of condescension, as he was one of the few official reporters on assignment. He fished inside his jacket and produced a guest list. "Neither of you is on the list, I'm afraid. Now, if Raymond would have made up your minds earlier, then you too would have a memento." Pfeiffer was smiling; it was all in fun; but Mantle felt uneasy about it. "Do you wish to accompany me as I interview some of our fellow guests?" Pfeiffer asked Joan.

"Are there any familiar names such as Isidor Straus or Mister Guggenheim?" Joan asked.

"No," Pfeiffer said, "this is to be an experience of our own, not just a re-creation. Everyone here is real, all the names are real."

"Do we know who's going to die?" Mantle asked.

"Now, that wouldn't be cricket, would it?" asked Pfeiffer.

"To be sure," Joan mumbled. She looked at Mantle and then said to Pfeiffer, "But I'm having second thoughts about this whole thing."

"This will only happen once," Pfeiffer said. "Would you really miss it?" When Joan didn't respond, he said, "If you'd like, we could do the *Titanic* story together, a double by-line."

Joan looked surprised.

"Now, that's what she's been after all along," Mantle said lightly, knowing that it was nevertheless true.

"Jesus, I don't know what to say. I'm not prepared, and—"

"I can assure you, it's the chance of a lifetime."

Joan turned to Mantle, who said, "He's right. I'd go along with him if I were you."

"I can't *see* you, Ray."

"Just go," Mantle said, trying to soften his voice.

"We should figure out an original angle for the story," Pfeiffer said to Joan. "Ray, would you like to join us? We're going to the Café Parisien. I was there earlier, it's quite nice."

"I think I'll stay on deck awhile," Mantle said. Joan looked distraught. "I'll be fine," he said to her.

"But—"

"I do need to be alone," Mantle said; and after a beat, Joan reluctantly left with Pfeiffer.

Mantle stood by the rail as the ship slipped through the curtains of Southampton's smog. Sky and sea seemed dark and smooth, as if made of some tinted, striated glass. Toward the west, the ocean was a green expanse turning to blue toward the horizon. But Mantle looked back toward Southampton, as if he could discern the shapes of his past in the unclean water and air.

"What did you mean when you said you couldn't see Raymond?" Pfeiffer asked.

"Nothing," Joan said. "Nothing at all."

Nineteen

When Joan and Pfeiffer returned to the suite to dress for dinner, they found Mantle asleep in the curtained four-poster. Although Joan was not in the mood for sex, Pfeiffer was; and he insisted that they make love in the same bed with Mantle for the sake of the *ménage*. Joan obliged him while Mantle slept fitfully, once again dreaming of Josiane.

When they were finished, Pfeiffer questioned Joan about Mantle, about his dreams. He most often questioned her, rather than asking Mantle directly.

"What do you want from him?" Joan whispered. She had not yet caught her breath; after their initial few times together, Pfeiffer became more and more sexually passive, and Joan exerted herself far more than he.

"I don't want anything from him, I want to help him."

"That old saw."

"Believe what you will, but it's true."

"What do you know about Josiane?" Joan asked.

For an instant, Pfeiffer seemed taken aback, and Joan caught her breath and waited for his response. Carefully, he got up from the bed.

"Where are you going?"

He waved his hand, walked across the room, and opened his suitcase, which he had left in the corner and refused to unpack. He took out a white box and returned to the bed. "You know, I realize that Raymond took me in because he thought I could help him remember."

"And you, in turn, wanted to question him."

"That's not true! Stop it. I know also that it wasn't entirely that he thought I could help him find the past—it was to relive the past, bring it back, have it again, have each other again. We've watched too much of our blood pass under the bridge to let each other go."

"What's in the box, Carl?"

"Yes, what's in the box?" Mantle asked without opening his eyes.

"I thought you'd be awake," Pfeiffer said. "Anyway, I appreciate what both of you have done for me."

"It wasn't charity, for God's sake. We wanted to be with you," Mantle said.

"Because you find me extraordinarily sexy, I know." Pfeiffer grinned; Joan did not.

"Because we care about you," Joan said.

"I had this made for you," Pfeiffer said to Mantle, "if you would care to open your eyes and look at it."

Mantle sat up, then propped himself against a wall that was contiguous with the bed. Leaning forward he said, "Jesus, you can hear the damned engines through the pillows and bed and walls. It's enough to give anyone a migraine."

"That was one of the problems that the Ismay line didn't have a chance to iron out," Pfeiffer said smiling, and he handed Mantle the package. "This should explain all my impertinent questions. I'm sure that Joan has also complained of them to you. . . ."

"You're a bastard, Carl," Joan said.

"But it's programmed as best as I know how; it has as much of the past as I could find; it's as correct as I could make it—"

"Then I'd better open it, hadn't I?" Mantle said, picking up the box from the bed.

Suddenly, Joan didn't want him to open it. But it was too late. He opened the package and pulled out something wrapped in gauze. Pfeiffer leaned over and unveiled it.

It was Josiane's head.

"Jesus Christ," Mantle said, almost dropping it to the bed. Then, sickeningly, the face came alive. It moved and changed expression, eyes narrowing, mouth pursing slightly, just as Josiane's used to do.

"Are you so afraid of me, Ray?" it asked.

Then Mantle did drop it on the bed, and drew away from it, shuddering. Joan found herself standing beside the bed. She laughed, half out of embarrassment.

"Make it stop," Mantle said tightly.

"Just place it—or we should really say 'her'—back in the box, which is real cedar, incidentally. It will be quiet, or rather she will be quiet."

"Please don't put that gauze around me," said the head. "Don't put me away," it pleaded. "I'm afraid of the dark—"

Quickly, Mantle shut the head inside the box, closing the lid. The gauze wrap lay across his pillow.

"What *is* it?" Joan asked.

"A talking head," Pfeiffer said matter-of-factly. "These are going to be all the rage in the next few months. They aren't on the market yet, but you can imagine their potential for both adults and children. They can be programmed to talk and react very realistically. The next logical step from talking books, don't you agree?"

"I think you're a sadist," Joan said.

Pfeiffer looked genuinely shocked and turned to Mantle, who was holding the box and staring at it. "She is as authentic as I could make her. I thought it would help. It wasn't meant as a joke or as a toy, I can promise you that. It was expensive as hell and took a lot of time to—"

"I understand, Carl," Mantle said. "Thank you." Then, looking at Joan: "Maybe it will bring something back."

"I'm sorry," Pfeiffer said.

"No need to be, really."

"Even if it might be painful at first, I thought—"

"You thought correctly," Mantle said.

"There is a party being given by the captain in the smoking lounge before dinner," Pfeiffer said. "We're all invited. There should be some interesting and influential people there." Pfeiffer showered and dressed quickly. He wore a black tuxedo with tails, studs, fluff shirt and diamond-initial cuff links. Joan and Mantle sat on the bed, Mantle opening and closing the box, peering at the head; and Joan watched him.

"Well, I can see you're not going to make the party," Pfeiffer said, after going into the bathroom to take one last look at himself in the mirror. He reeked of expensive perfume. "I thought you'd find her interesting. If you have any flashbacks, remember that I get the credit. She's my creation. You see, you're not the only artist."

"Carl, why are you giving me this *now*?" Mantle asked. "Wouldn't it have been more, ah, theatrical to have waited until we parted?"

"First of all, that's not a nice way to put it. You're always looking for motives. I once told you that I had no unconscious, and there's more truth to that than not." He smiled. "It's simply because we're going to different destinations after our . . . accident."

"Then you're not going to New York?" Joan asked.

"Not right away, I'm afraid. Now, if you two can manage to dress each other, I'll meet you for dinner."

"You know," Joan said to Pfeiffer as he opened the door, "you're not dressed properly."

"What do you mean?"

"We're supposed to be wearing the period clothing provided by the ship."

"That's an option, not a requirement," Pfeiffer said stuffily. "And, at any rate, it would not apply to me." With that, he left.

"Well, I suppose he's back to his old self," Joan said to Mantle.

"You never knew his old self."

"I think I can take credit for knowing him a little. After all, I was hooked into him, remember?"

"Who knows," Mantle said, "maybe this thing will help."

"I'd be careful," Joan said.

"I'll check it out on the computer—I brought my plug. It's just a question of asking it—her—the right questions."

"I'd check for subliminals, too."

"Thank you, Miz Otur, I'll make a note of it."

"I don't trust him, Raymond."

"Stop calling me Raymond." Mantle looked up at her and smiled. "I don't either . . . trust him, that is. Now, why don't you shower and dress? Maybe you can make the party."

"And you?" Joan asked.

"I've got some questions to ask Josiane."

After considerable coaxing, Joan left, and Mantle took the head out of the box and placed it on the desk. Even under the harsh illumination of the desk lamp, it looked like a living head.

And it was Josiane—that lovely, mobile face, arched eyebrows, narrow nose and faint joylines drawn from the corners of her painted lips to flared nostrils. Her hair was a halo around her face, more silver than gold under the light. "Ray," she said, "I'm afraid. Even now in the light, I'm afraid of that . . . coffin, it's so dark."

"Do you know how you got here?" Mantle asked.

"Where am I?"

"You're on the table in my stateroom on the ship *Titanic*."

Josiane looked from side to side. "I can't move my head, I can't feel my body, I'm—" And then her face relaxed, as if she were about to go unconscious, and she continued. "I know what I am, but I'm me and not me. I am Josiane, and I'm alive."

"Until I put you back."

Josiane shut her eyes for a second, then looked at Mantle as if she were the old Josiane—that intense stare that could rivet Mantle as no one else's could. That couldn't be faked, Mantle said to himself suddenly remembering. It was working. He was beginning to *believe* that this construct was Josiane. "You've been a lot of things, Ray," Josiane said, "but never cruel. It was always me who was cruel, who made mistakes. . . ."

Mantle found himself almost saying, "No, you were never cruel." She could push the old buttons, elicit the old responses. "You're not Josiane," Mantle said flatly.

"I am, please don't say that. I *am*. I *feel* the same, even though I know what I am. But it's me, and this is a terrible nightmare. It's as if I've been thrown into hell, and you, of all people, are my tormentor. Ray, I love you. I know you, I'm the only one, remember?"

"Then tell me what happened the day I lost you," Mantle demanded.

"I went shopping; that's all I remember. It was on a Friday—I always shopped on Fridays, remember? The next thing I knew I was feeling your hands on my face and then falling."

"When was that?" Mantle said, excited.

"I don't know, my time sense seems to be gone," Josiane said.

"Perhaps during the Great Scream, perhaps I had found you . . . ?" Mantle asked, pleading, forgetting he was talking to a construct.

"The gauze was removed, I remember that," Josiane said, "and then I remember the softness of a blanket, I guess it was. You looked at me with such horror, Ray."

"Damn you," Mantle said, standing up and pacing the room. "That was a few minutes ago, when I took you out of the box. That's no answer. What do you *remember*?"

"What I told you."

"Well, it's a piss-poor job of programming, then."

"I remember when we went to Florida with Carl and—"

"Oh, shut up," Mantle said, disgusted. "Carl's fed you what he knows, which isn't much. Sonofabitch!"

"Ray . . . ?"

Mantle paced slowly, back and forth. "I should put you away and meet Joan and—"

"Who's Joan?" Josiane asked. "Is she your wife? Oh, God, I never even thought of that. I'm really dead, aren't I?"

"You're a construct."

"Ray, help me. Whatever you think I am, I feel the same way I did about everything when I was . . . as I was . . . as . . . "

"Say it," Mantle said, sitting down before the desk again.

"I know what I am, but I can't believe it. Help me."

"Pfeiffer made you up to help *me*, remember?"

"No, I don't remember. Some things are clear, but time is all mixed up for me. How's Mom? I thought she came through the operation really well. Remember, we were both in the room, waiting for her in the hotel—I can't remember the name of it—and the doctor called and you fell asleep right on the phone. But I don't remember anything else. Ray . . . ?"

She *was* there, Mantle thought. He had glimpsed it, just now, remembered that it was she who woke him up after everyone else had left, after she had taken the phone from him and found out that Mom was all right. They had gone to Le Cygne for dinner and then spent the night sitting at Mom's bedside. He remembered making love to Josiane in the hotel room—no, it was a suite. The furniture was all cream-colored, and there was a living room and, God, he could taste and smell Josiane right now; he remembered.

"Ray?"

"Yes," Mantle said, sitting back. He had been staring into Josiane's face. "Mom's dead. She died in a Screamer attack."

"Oh my God." And Josiane began to cry, softly, as she always had. Tears leaked from her eyes. "God, this is hell, I'm in hell."

"Stop it," Mantle said softly. "I'll try to make it easy for you; I can imagine what you're feeling."

"Can you?" she asked, sobbing.

"I'm sorry, but I have to know what happened to you; I've got to find you . . . Josiane."

"Then you still love me."

"I love her, yes. And I can't remember."

"I'll help you," said the head. "Please let me help you."

Sighing, Mantle said, "You know only what Pfeiffer knows."

"I remember the ice cream," Josiane said, trying to smile. Her tears made lines down her face, and she was sniffing.

"What do you mean?" Mantle asked, but he smiled in spite of himself.

"The first time, when we were kids, and we used to call it making ice cream. And I remember that you used to always want to do it with those stupid videotectures hanging all over the room in the air. And I remember how you used to come to me when you were afraid, and make love to me. Ice cream." She closed her eyes as if to squeeze out the last tears, and whispered, "I can't believe Momma's dead."

"Stop it," Mantle said, oddly embarrassed that he could react to the head as if it were Josiane. "I'll try to make it as easy as possible for you, but I can't believe you're Josiane, no matter how you feel or think you feel. You're a construct. Believe that and it will be easier for you. And perhaps if I don't take you out, then—"

"No," she said, fear transforming her face. "Don't put me back in the box. I'm afraid of the dark, just as you are. Oh my God, no. Just leave me, but don't do that to me." Then suddenly her face became calm, just as it had before. She closed her eyes, then opened them. "I suppose I have emotional fail-safes," she said. "So you see, I can't throw a tantrum and get my way as I used to." She smiled, but the eyes looking out from that sad, incredibly realistic face were Josiane's. They reflected the loss.

Mantle lifted the head from the table, suddenly forgetting that her emotions were mechanical, that she was a construct, wired and grown.

And he had to fight the urge, the compulsion, to kiss her before he gave her back to the dark.

Twenty

Shaken after his talk with the head, he went to the Café Parisien for a drink. He couldn't bear to sit at a dinner table and make small talk with the other guests; and he wasn't ready to answer any of Joan's inevitable questions about his conversation with the head.

The cafe was almost empty, although a small dance band was playing a waltz, as if for the edification of the walls. There were a few Europeans and Americans sitting quietly in clusters, but the majority of the passengers on the ship were Africans and Asians, and they were punctilious observers of proper social custom; hence, they were all at dinner.

Mantle took a table away from the others; he sat in a large wicker chair that faced an ornately trellised wall. A waiter took his order, and Mantle was left to himself, the music, and his thoughts. He would not easily forget the look on Josiane's face when he put her into the box. He had vowed not to take her out of the box again—for both their sakes.

"Well, hello," said a familiar voice behind him.

"What are you doing *here*?" Mantle asked, shocked to find Faon standing beside him. She looked different than when he had last seen her, younger somehow, as if she had cast all her troubles to the sea. She was appropriately dressed in turn-of-the-century French fashion, which was in vogue when the ship first sailed. She wore a white silk dress under a pink and red flowered caftan, matching red bracelets, a fur-trimmed coat—as it was nippy outside—and an oval-shaped hat covered with a willow plume.

"Is that any way to greet a friend?" Faon asked, smiling.

"You're the last person I would expect to find on this ship," Mantle said as he stood up to pull out a chair for her, but a waiter rushed over, took her coat and her order for a drink.

"Are you glad to see me, then?"

"Yes, of course . . . but—"

"But Joan will be upset—Is that what you're thinking?"

"Yes," Mantle said. "She's frightened of you and the church, she—"

Faon sighed and said, "I know what she thinks. She'll just have to deal with it, won't she?"

"That doesn't sound like you. You seem different."

"I am."

"What's happened?" Mantle asked. "What are you doing on this ship. How did you know we were taking it?"

"My, are you the egoist."

"You did know," Mantle insisted.

"Yes," Faon replied. "Of course I did." She paused, then said, "I had a sending when I was hooked into Roberta."

"Yes?"

"I was told to keep my promise."

"What do you mean?" Mantle asked.

"I'm promised, just as Roberta was. It's my time to die and shift over to the other side."

"And where's your husband?" Mantle asked, suddenly angry and anxious.

"In Boulouris; it is not his time yet."

"Why die here?" Mantle asked. "Why not at home?"

Faon lifted her face to Mantle, and suddenly she looked

older, as if once again she were carrying some great invisible weight. "I don't know, exactly. Perhaps to help you, perhaps Joan . . . perhaps to serve as an example."

"Of what?"

"Of what it means to cross over to the other side. You too, are promised, Raymond. Remember what I told you about the Seed Crystal?"

The waiter brought Faon a cocktail, asked Mantle if he wished another, then bowed and left.

"I think you're all crazy," Mantle said. "Joan was right."

"Yes, until it's time, I am going to be crazy." Faon smiled flirtatiously at him. "And remember what I told you when you last came to visit me? It doesn't matter what you think."

"I want to know why you're here," Mantle said tightly.

"To show you how the world will end," Faon said. "Now, will you dance with me . . . ?" The band was playing a fox-trot.

Twenty-One

The great ship hit an iceberg on the fourth night of her voyage, exactly one day earlier than scheduled. It was Saturday, 11:40 P.M., and the air was full of colored lights from tiny splinters of ice floating like motes of dust. "Whiskers 'round the light'" they used to be called by sailors. The sky was a panoply of twinkling stars, and it was so cold that one might imagine that they were fragments of ice floating in a cold, dark, inverted sea overhead.

Mantle and Joan were standing by the rail of the promenade deck. Both were dressed in the early twentieth-century accoutrements provided by the ship—he in woolen trousers, jacket, motoring cap, and caped overcoat with a long scarf; she in a fur coat, a stylish "merry widow" hat, high-button shoes, and a black velvet two-piece suit edged with white silk. She was fidgeting with a small camera, which she usually wore in her hair or upon her dress. This trip had made her career. It was Pfeiffer's idea that she interview the most interesting passengers, predict who would opt to die, and why; and then give her predictions to the millions of Pfeiffer's faithful viewers. She conducted a poll several times a day, and the viewers responded immediately. They loved her. She was creating new heroes and heroines for a tired and jaded public, and effectively upstaging Pfeiffer.

"Why are you going to throw Little Josiane away?" Joan asked Mantle, who was resting the cedar box containing the talking head on the rail.

"The dreams are becoming worse."

"Then stay away from Faon," Joan said. "I'm sorry, we promised not to talk about her and—"

"You could have at least spoken to her," Mantle said. "She certainly approached you enough times."

"No, I couldn't. You know what she's here for."

"And just what *is* she here for?" Mantle asked.

"You."

"She's here to die."

"And to try to take you with her," Joan said. "I'm afraid of her; I'm afraid for you."

"I'm afraid, too," Mantle confessed.

"The dreams?"

Mantle nodded. "I keep seeing Josiane just below the surface of a shallow pool. And I heard her voice, I hear it every night."

"I hear it, too," Joan said cautiously.

"How . . . ?"

"You're open to me at night, just as I am to you, no matter how much you close me out during the day."

"I'm sorry, Joan, I know I've hurt you—"

"Stop it, please."

"But I have to find out about Josiane, I have to know."

"What does Faon have to say about it?" Joan asked.

Mantle shuddered. "She thinks that I'm in the dark *and* bright spaces, and I will have to choose one or the other. And she thinks that I'm promised."

"Oh, God. . . ."

"And the dreams of Josiane—it's as if I can't really wake up from them. I feel the dark spaces, and I'm afraid. I've got to find Josiane, but I don't want to die to find her. . . ." His hands tightened around the box. "Joan, I need you to help me. Faon can only help me to die."

Joan drew closer to him, then rested her weight against him. "But I don't understand what this has to do with throwing the head away."

"I questioned her," he said, referring to the talking head, "and I checked it out on the computers."

"And what did you find out?"

"Mostly oral sublims, some pretty sophisticated, although I have no doubt that Carl programmed her himself."

"And?"

"The doll, in all her subtle ways, is trying to tell me that she—that Josiane—is dead."

"That's quite possible; it must be faced."

"Of course I know that," Mantle said, "but I just can't believe it, not after the dreams. And if she was dead, why would she call me home?"

"I don't know," Joan whispered, shivering in the cold. The sea was black, and as forbidding as anything she'd ever seen.

"Carl programmed the head to manipulate me," Mantle continued. "I won't let him do that to me . . . again. And this thing, this doll, somehow makes me grieve for Josiane, yet still I can't remember. I can't stand it."

"Then throw it away," Joan said.

Mantle brought the box to his chest as if he were about to throw it overboard, and then slowly placed it atop the rail again. "I can't."

"Do you want me to do it?" Joan asked, realizing that was a mistake even as she said it. He would blame her for doing it, even upon his authority.

"No," Mantle said.

Joan exhaled in relief. "I wonder why Carl didn't wait until after the . . . accident to give you the head."

"It doesn't matter when, really. He told me to let the purser have it, along with any other personal items; that the purser would make sure they arrived in New York unharmed." He toyed with the box, moving it back and forth against the rail as if he had to somehow align it. He chuckled and said, "I guess I'll just let nature take its course."

"What do you mean? Oh, the ship."

Just then someone shouted and, as if in the distance, a bell rang three times.

"Could there be another ship nearby?" Joan asked.

"Jesus, there it is," Mantle said, pulling Joan backward, away from the rail. An iceberg as high as the forecastle scraped against the side of the ship; it almost seemed that the bluish, glistening mountain of ice was another ship passing, that the ice rather than the ship was moving. Pieces of ice rained upon the deck, slid across the varnished wood, and then the iceberg was lost in the darkness astern. It must have been at least one hundred feet high.

"Oh Jesus," Mantle said, rushing to the rail and leaning over it.

"What is it?" Joan asked.

"Little Josiane, I dropped her when I pulled you away from the iceberg. I feel as if I've killed someone."

"She was a machine," Joan said. "A machine. . . ." Then, changing the subject, she said, "The iceberg, it almost looked like a ship. Like a sailing ship, an ancient windjammer. But I didn't feel a thing when we hit, just the scraping noise and—"

"No, the engines seemed to lose a beat, I felt that," Mantle said, recovering. But still he leaned over the rail and looked down at the dark water.

"Ray, open up to me," Joan whispered. "I *need* the connection. Don't grieve for a machine, help me."

"I need the connection, too," Mantle said, putting his arm around her. "But it doesn't seem to work that way. I can't open it, I've tried."

"Could this really have been an accident?" Joan asked abruptly, as if she didn't want to hear what Mantle had to say. "That would serve us right, wouldn't it, hubris and irony and the gods and all that. We were supposed to collide with that thing *tomorrow*."

"It's no accident, I think, just a little something to throw everyone off, to make the trip more interesting," Mantle said. "I have a feeling that our little vacation is going to become all too real in the next few hours. Now, come on, let's go inside. My face is freezing off, and you don't even have gloves on."

"Ray?"

"Yes?"

"I thought that being together, all of us, would somehow help you." Joan rested her hands for an instant on the rail, which was so cold it was sticky to the touch, and then put her hands into her pockets. "I didn't trust Carl . . . don't trust him, although I like him, maybe even love him in a way. But I saw something when Carl and I hooked in at the casino: that he needed you."

"You told me that already, early on."

"I know," Joan said, "But it's more than that. When I saw that iceberg, I remembered how I felt when I was hooked into Carl. I can't help but feel that Carl's done something terrible, or is going to do something terrible. I remember his fear and his guilt, and I'm frightened."

"Joan, let's go inside. It's freezing out here. . . . We're both shaken up, seeing that iceberg, the—"

"I'm afraid for you," Joan said. "I think Carl's going to hurt you." Once inside, she shivered and said, "I suppose I'm as bad as Carl. This trip is my version of organ gambling." She laughed, as if this were a change to lighter topics.

"What do you mean?"

"The poll, of course. I know you disapprove—I certainly would if you were engaged in such foolishness. You're right about everything becoming real . . . real and dark and dirty."

"It was your chance," Mantle said. "You'd have been a fool not to grab it."

"I couldn't stand being closed out, not being able to feel the connection, except at night when you slept and dreamed of Josiane. My weakness, I suppose." Josiane leaned against the stairwell bannister and looked down the scuffed stairs. "It was knowing that you were with Faon instead of with me, knowing what she was trying to do. I knew that if I tried to argue, to fight for you, I would certainly lose you."

"You don't have to be more than you are," Mantle said. "You're stronger than me, and, please believe me, you did the right thing, no matter how it turns out. You did everything for me; that's more than I could do for you, for anyone. I couldn't do anything else but fail you, but you didn't fail yourself or me."

"I did it out of anger," Joan said. Standing in the harsh light of the stairway, she looked vulnerable, drawn, thin, and small beside Mantle. Yet her face was strength itself, supported, as it seemed, by her high cheekbones. "I was mimicking Faon, who makes a circus of death, who has given herself up to it. But you didn't notice. . . ."

"Yes," Mantle said, "I noticed." For an instant their *circuit fantome* was restored, as if by its own accord; and

Mantle felt bathed in her faith and love and strength. Indeed, he felt that, like a vampire, he was drawing it from her. When the connection was broken, Joan looked pale and weak.

"I want us to be together; I want the connection back," Joan said.

"I don't think it works like that. It seems to have its own life, and its—" But Mantle was interrupted by a group of burly crewmen who rushed up the stairs and out onto the deck. They were, in turn, followed by a steady stream of passengers. "It's going to get crazy up here soon," he said.

"You're going to see Faon, aren't you?" Joan asked, her face tight with fear, anger, and hurt.

"Neither one of us is going to die on this ship," Mantle said. "I, too, want us to be together. You must believe that. But, whatever you think, I can't let Faon die without saying good-bye."

Joan nodded.

"Go find Carl, and I'll meet you back here within the half-hour. He may be in the stateroom, and we'll need that bag we packed for the lifeboat. I don't know how long it's going to take this old lady to sink, so let's conserve our time."

"No," Joan said, stepping closer to Mantle. "Carl will meet us here. We're all taking the same lifeboat." Then after a pause, she said, "You and I will see Faon together. If I'm going to be able to live with myself, I should see her before she dies."

And suddenly the ship became unnaturally quiet. The engines had stopped.

Faon had a stateroom on C-deck. It was a smallish room with a large bed, stuffed chair, washbasin, and writing desk. A mirrored chiffonier stood against the wall opposite the bed, looking for all the world like a rococo robot made of wood. Faon was sitting comfortably on the neatly made bed when Mantle knocked and entered with Joan.

"I've been expecting you," Faon said. "Both of you." She wore a simple nightdress, and her thick, gray-streaked hair was loose, but pulled away from her high forehead. She held a small brown bottle tightly in her hand.

"We've hit the iceberg a bit early," Joan said awkwardly.

"Yes, the steward banged on my door." Faon motioned

Joan and Mantle to sit down beside her. Although Joan remained standing, Mantle sat down on the bed. "Anyway, the deed is already done."

"What do you mean?" Mantle asked nervously.

"I guess I'm a coward; I took the pill." She gave the bottle to Mantle, who swore and stood up. He tossed the bottle onto the chiffonier and paced back and forth.

"You didn't have to do this," Mantle said quietly.

"What else did you expect?" Faon asked, looking surprised. "Didn't you come down here to wish me good-bye?"

"Yes, of course," Mantle said. "I'm sorry."

"Why did you *really* come to see me?"

"To tell you—"

"You came because I promised to show you the end of the world, remember?" Faon smiled as if remembering a private joke. "You two came just in time," she said, looking up at Joan. "I would guess I'll be dead in a few minutes." Then she turned to Mantle and said, "But even if I were already dead, it wouldn't make any difference. I could, and will, make good my promises."

"Faon," Mantle said gently, "I came to say good-bye, and Joan came to make amends. . . ." Then Mantle took a step backward and looked around the room anxiously, as if he had just seen something that frightened him.

"Faon, I—" Joan said, but she was unable to finish her sentence. She felt the electric jolt of a connection, then sudden terror—Mantle's terror—and knew that she had to get Mantle out of this room. Through him, she could feel the cold edges of the dark spaces.

The *circuit fantome* had come alive again.

And Joan remembered what had happened to her when Gayet died, how a tunnel seemed to open up inside him, how she had been sucked through it into the dark spaces, as if into a vacuum. "Ray, let's get out of here. Right now."

Faon lay back on the bed, her head resting against the paneled wall. She closed her eyes and said, "Raymond, stay with me, please. . . ."

"I can't, Faon," Mantle said, but even as he said it he took a step toward her.

"No, Ray," Joan shouted as she tried to reach him. She broke out into a cold sweat and trembled, but she couldn't move, not even for Mantle. It was as if there was a deadly presence in the room, a great dark bird of prey silently beating its wings, ready to swoop down upon her. If she took a step toward Mantle, who was so close to Faon, she was certain she would be sucked into the dark spaces. Faon was the tunnel...she was the dark spaces...the bird of prey...she was death itself. ...

Oh God, I'm afraid, Joan thought as she screamed to Mantle to turn away from Faon.

But no sound cut the air. The room had filled up with the stuff of the dark spaces as if with heavy black smoke, or a gas, paralyzing them. ... They were both dreaming the same dream, breathing and thinking each other's thoughts... both caught. ...

An instant later, Faon stopped breathing.

Then the transformation began: Faon seemed to rise from the bed and float in the air as if gravity had no effect—just as Joan had risen from the pool in Boulouris to try to kill Mantle. Faon began to spin, faster and faster, spinning just in front of Mantle's eyes, spinning and turning into Josiane, as if she were being created on a lathe...slowing until she *was* Josiane, staring into Mantle's eyes, *connecting* with him, becoming a tunnel for him; and Joan saw through his eyes, sensed with his mind, saw that he was transfixed, searching for the truth and his past, even as he was trying with his whole being to turn away, to run, to escape. ...

Just then there was a sharp rap on the door, and suddenly it slammed open, jolting Joan and Mantle instantly from their mutual dream of Faon and the dark spaces. And the black and silver, the stuff of the dark spaces, dissipated, dissolved as if a spell had been undone.

"Everyone up to the boat deck," shouted a harried-looking steward. "Ship's going down. Not much time if you want a lifeboat."

Joan and Mantle did not wait to be caught again. Still woozy and not yet completely free of Faon's dream, they stumbled out of the room into the corridor.

Twenty-Two

Although it felt vague and distant, the *circuit fantome* was still open. Mantle and Joan had recovered, and did not speak of the incident in Faon's room, both wishing to put it behind them. Still, the image of Faon spinning herself into Josiane remained with them.

It was bitter cold, and they were looking for Pfeiffer.

The boat deck was filled with people, all rushing about, shouting, scrambling for the lifeboats; and, inevitably, those who had changed their minds at the last moment about going down with the ship were shouting the loudest, trying the hardest to be permitted into the boats, not one of which had been lowered yet. There were sixteen wooden lifeboats and four canvas Englehardts, the collapsibles. But they could not be lowered away until the davits were cleared of the two forward boats. The crew was quiet, each man busy with the boats and davits. All the boats were now swinging free of the ship, hanging just beside the boat deck.

"We'll let you know when it's time to board," shouted an officer to the families crowding around him. The floor was listing dangerously. At this rate, the ship would be bow down in the water in no time.

Mantle and Joan checked the bow and starboard side— there were eight boats to be lowered on each side—but still no sign of Pfeiffer. They rechecked the first-class lounge, where the *Titanic*'s band of seven was playing ragtime. Most of the passengers waiting here for the boats were calm, as they had only come along for the ride. All were dressed warmly in greatcoats and furs.

Not finding Pfeiffer, they went back outside to the boat deck.

"He could be anywhere on the ship," Mantle said, thinking that Pfeiffer was probably on one of the lower decks, recording the group suicides. Mantle had heard about such parties, and there would be the normal run of drugs and orgies, all spurred on by the excitement of imminent destruction.

But they found Pfeiffer in the gym off the boat deck, big as life, riding one of the stationary bicycles, as he pedaled, he was watching red and blue arrows chase each other around a white clock on the wall. "I thought I'd make myself easy to locate," he said to Mantle and Joan.

"We've been looking for you for most of an—"

"I had work to do, still do. How's it been going?"

"I've been frantic," Joan said.

"No, I mean the work. This is a golden opportunity." Pfeiffer got off the bicycle and put his arms around Joan and Mantle. "You should at least take a few pictures, do an interview," he said to Joan.

"I can't. I'm ashamed of myself."

"It's no different from any other assignment, except the routines," Pfeiffer said, removing himself from Mantle and Joan, looking suddenly very tired and drawn, as if he had been pumping himself up and was now collapsing under his own weight. "The public wants the either/ors, the lifes and deaths."

"But this is different," Joan said. "No need for any of it, no—"

"It's no different from what happens in every other house or apartment on the street. Here you're privy to it, that's all. *This* is what it's about; this is what goes on all around us. The dead pile up and are carried safely away without anyone's being the wiser. That's why my . . . our viewers love this voyage and why so many have taken it. The doers and the voyeurs, we're all here."

"I chose this," Joan said. "It's not like an assignment."

"So you did," Pfeiffer said. "My point."

A young steward, looking nervous, came into the room and said, "Mr. Pfeiffer, the boats are going fast now. Most are already lowered." He looked at Joan and said, "You know the rules, sir, the women must go first."

"I think we should still have a few minutes," Pfeiffer said, giving the steward a knowing look.

"Yes . . . a few, sir."

"Call us again, just before it gets dangerous."

"Very good, sir." The steward left. The ship seemed to

groan below them, and the list became a bit sharper. A gaily colored ball rolled across the floor.

"The boy's probably happy for an excuse to get into the warm," Pfeiffer said; and then, "Don't worry, Joan. They've got to make sure of our safety."

"Well," Joan said, "if you want to make the most of this, why are you sitting here, why are we sitting here?"

"Because I have something I want to tell you."

"Here it comes," Joan said to Mantle in a low voice as they all moved to the wicker chairs, which had all slid against the far wall. The blocked linoleum was terribly scuffed, as if horses had been galloping around the room.

"It shouldn't be a surprise," Pfeiffer continued, "especially after I gave you Little Josiane."

"Well?" Mantle said tightly.

"Josiane's dead," Pfeiffer said flatly. When Mantle said nothing, Pfeiffer added, after a pause, "That's what I came to Cannes to tell you in the first place."

Mantle's face still hadn't moved. His anger was a cold band tightening around his chest. "And what about Caroline?" Mantle asked at last, as if ignoring what Pfeiffer had just told him. "Your breakup?"

"That happened, and I found out about Josiane at the same time. Another irony, I suppose. You see, we're always linked in sadness, especially in sadness. But it's better for you to know, so that you can stop searching."

"There are other ways to be alive," Mantle said, remembering—and sensing—the dark spaces once again.

"You don't believe that shit, do you?" Pfeiffer asked.

Ignoring that, Mantle finally asked, "How did she die?"

"A brain hemorrhage, of all things. But it was natural causes. Meadowbrook Hospital on Long Island has all the records, she—"

"Did she die in the hospital?" Mantle asked quietly.

"No, she was brought in DOA."

Mantle felt the cold band tighten around his chest. He didn't feel grief, just anger; cold, dead anger toward Pfeiffer who had waited until now to tell him this. Joan was right, he thought, the little fisherman is up to something. The sonofabitch never stops. . . .

The band grew tighter.

"She was found in Hempstead," Pfeiffer continued, "in

the Hofstra ruins with some other Screamers. She was also... I don't know if I should tell you this. . . ."

"Go on," Mantle said. "You know you're going to tell it."

"She was also shot, but that's not what killed her." When Mantle gave no response, Pfeiffer said, "I'm sorry, Raymond, truly I am."

"How was it that *you* found all this out, that *you*—"

"I loved her too, you know, and my connections are better than yours. After all, it's my business."

"I never asked you to—"

"You never needed to."

There was a dead silence in the room, which seemed to absorb even the squabbling and shouting outside—as if the world, like the ship, had suddenly stopped. Joan was sitting beside Mantle, leaning toward him, as if by being closer she could hear his thoughts.

"She's not dead," Mantle insisted.

"What's that?" asked Pfeiffer. He glanced at Joan, but she fixedly ignored him. "I'm not doing this to hurt you, Raymond, but to help you. You *must* believe that."

"Then why didn't you tell me before? Why did you wait until now?" Mantle asked, his voice as cold as the air outside.

After a pause, Pfeiffer said, "I came to Cannes to tell you, but you seemed to be in such a shaky mental condition... I felt it would be better if I took the time to prepare you. You must believe me, Raymond. It's all I have left to offer you."

Mantle looked sharply at him at that, but Pfeiffer stood up suddenly, as if he were about to bolt.

Just then the door opened again, letting in the frigid air, and the steward said, "They're lowering away the Englehardts. You must leave *now* if you're going to leave at all."

"All right," Pfeiffer replied distractedly, as if the steward was merely calling teatime.

"Come on," Joan said. "We'd better get out there."

As they left the comfort of the room for the cold deck, a rocket was fired from somewhere on the starboard side, one of many; and it exploded far above the spars and netting of the *Titanic*, a cold, white phosphorus light that exploded into sparks dropping toward the sea.

"Jesus, we *are* late," Joan said. She was frightened as she looked around at the empty davits and the angry crowd milling around boat C. A few men rushed the ring of officers and seamen guarding the boat, and were beaten with an oar wielded by a mean-looking member of the crew. There was a gunshot, then another, and two men fell to the ground.

"My wife has changed her mind!" shouted a man in the crowd, but the voice melted into the others and the band on the deck played even louder, as if mocking those still on the ship.

"I can hear her calling me," Mantle said to Pfeiffer as they stood away from the remaining boat and the crowd.

"It's in the hospital records, you must believe . . ."

"I can hear her!"

"Ray, stop it," Joan said.

"Oh, God," Pfeiffer said. "There's no time. Come on, let's get you into that boat."

"What do you mean?" Joan shouted as Pfeiffer dragged her into the crowd. Then the young steward, who was remarkably strong, grabbed her arm roughly and said, "She's all right."

"Him too," Pfeiffer shouted at the steward, indicating that Mantle was to go next.

A crewman shot a passenger who tried to push Joan out of the way and take her place. Joan screamed, tried to break free of the steward.

"Put her on the boat!" Pfeiffer commanded.

"What the hell are you doing?" Mantle shouted.

Pfeiffer leaned close to Mantle and said, "I elected not to take a lifeboat. That's why I told you all this when I did; that's why I wanted you to be with me on this trip. I've stayed alive as long as I have for *you*, to give *you* new life."

"That's crazy!" Mantle said. "Are you killing yourself for Caroline?" For *Caroline*?"

"And for me, there's nothing else to be done, but when you're picked up by the airship later, there'll be a tape waiting for you. It will explain everything. . . ." And then Pfeiffer turned and disappeared into the crowd.

"I'm not leaving you to—"

"Come on," said a burly crewman as he grabbed Mantle tightly from behind. "Like it or not, you're supposed to live. That's what the mother computer says." Another crewman laughed, and Mantle was picked up by the both of them and thrown into the collapsible.

"What is Carl *doing*?" Joan cried, pushing past a fat woman to be closer to Mantle.

But Mantle ignored Joan. Grabbing the davit line before it could be lowered, he pulled and swung himself back onto the ship. He took the heavyset crewman by surprise and punched him sharply in the kidney. Then he pushed himself through the crowd.

Joan shouted to him and someone else said, "Lower the fucker away, let the stupid sonofabitch drown."

Mantle caught sight of Pfeiffer and ran wildly across the deck after him, pushing people out of his way.

He could not believe that Pfeiffer would kill himself. Never, that was unthinkable.

Pfeiffer pushed through a set of high glass doors and disappeared inside the ship. Mantle followed, chasing him down stairs, through lounges and corridors. After a while, he stopped shouting at Pfeiffer. It only slowed Mantle down.

After almost losing him, Mantle caught up with Pfeiffer in one of the restricted forward storage areas. There was water up to his knees; it was green and soapy. Soggy boxes floated in the water and collected against one of the walls. The ship was listing to port.

Pfeiffer stopped long enough to shout, breathlessly, "Go back up, save yourself." He looked frightened, and then, as he turned and headed toward an exit, there was an explosion that pitched them both into the water.

The wall behind Pfeiffer gave way, and a solid sheet of water seemed to be crashing into the room, smashing Mantle, pulling him under and sweeping him away. He fought to reach the surface. A lamp broke away from the ceiling, just missing him. "Carl," he shouted, but he couldn't see him, and then he found himself choking, swimming, as the water carried him through a corridor.

Finally, Mantle was able to grab the iron curl of a railing and pull himself onto a dry step. There was another explosion; the floor pitched; yet the lights still glowed, giving the submerged corridors and rooms a ghostly illumination. As Mantle looked down at the water that had taken Pfeiffer, he realized that he had been hearing Josiane's voice... was hearing it now. Or was it Joan's...?"

The ship was quiet. Through the corridors and rooms, Mantle made his way up, walking like a ghost, as if the ship were already submerged and he would relive its last moments forever. In the great rooms, chandeliers hung at angles; tables and chairs had skidded across the floors and seemed to squat against the walls like wooden beasts. Still the lights burned, as if all was quite correct, except gravity, which was misbehaving.

Mantle walked and climbed, followed by the sea, and then there was a lurch and a crashing below, and Mantle shuddered as he thought of Pfeiffer and Faon floating in the illuminated water below, just as Josiane floated in his dreams.

Twenty-Three

The twenty-six-foot collapsible with its high side-canvas floated low in the icy cold water.

It was almost like a picnic in the boat, for it was early, and the passengers were still excited by watching the listing *Titanic*. They passed around food and flasks while the crewmen quietly rowed them away from the great ship. It was a still night, only broken by the faraway sounds of ragtime being played by the ship's band. Everyone remarked how smooth the sea was, "like glass"; the oars hardly seemed to disturb its surface.

The *Titanic* was brilliantly lit, every porthole afire, even those parts that were submerged, as if under glass. The bow was low in the water, and although it was not quite noticeable minute by minute, the ship was going fast.

Once again Joan begged the crewmen and passengers on the lifeboat to go back to the ship for Mantle. He was *supposed* to be under the protection of the ship's company, he had not signed a protection waiver.... Once again, they refused. She screamed and threatened, and then—helpless and frustrated and angry—she just stared at the *Titanic*, saw the tiny figures swarming near the rail, blinked back tears as a rocket exploded into searing white light, unmasking the dance of death on the decks.

She tried to find Mantle, searching for his thoughts; trying, somehow, against all hope, to pull him back, to save him, as she had done once before.

She called his name.

Surely he would need her now. He had to. But the *circuit fantome* seemed once again to be dead... unless, God forbid, Mantle was....

And then, for a harrowing instant, she saw him, felt him, heard him calling her. "Oh God," she screamed, "he's drowning," and she called back to Mantle, but the connection was dead, silent....

The others ignored her, as if she were raving. But a heavy woman who sat beside Joan wrapped her blanket around her, tried to console her. "I hope they're enjoying the view," the woman said as she looked up at the huge airship floating silently above them. It could only be seen by its tiny running lights, which looked like red stars in the sky, and the occultation of stars as it passed overhead. It was the dirigible *Californie*, a nuclear-powered luxury liner.

"I'm sure they are," Joan said quietly.

Then everyone gasped as the *Titanic*'s lights flickered and the bow dipped and the stern rose. The strains of the song "Autumn" seemed to float, evanescent, and all was quiet, as if this were all taking place under the dark, cold dome of a cathedral. Then there was a roar as the stern of the ship swung upward and the entrails of the ship broke loose: anchor chains, the huge engines and boilers, pianos, trunks, crystal. One of the huge, black funnels fell, smashing into the water amid sparks. But still the ship remained brilliantly lit.

Once, long ago, the sinking *Titanic* had been described as a finger pointing at the sky, but to Joan it was like an arm... Mantle's arm... reaching out of the sea.

The dark water slowly swallowed the ship; it lapped over her red and green running lights, and the noise of the ship breaking apart internally seemed to be reaching a crescendo, drowning out even those screaming passengers who had jumped into the freezing, twenty-eight-degree water.

Then the noise suddenly stopped and the ship simply slid into the sea, into its own eerie pool of light.

Joan screamed and tried to climb over the side of the boat, but the heavy woman sitting beside Joan, who was surprisingly quick, restrained her.

But all Joan could hear or feel was Mantle screaming inside her head.

Twenty-Four

When Mantle made it back up to the boat deck, he found it partially submerged. Almost everyone had moved aft, climbing uphill as the bow dipped farther into the water.

The lifeboats were gone, as were the crew. He looked around, afraid now. Men and women were screaming, "I don't want to die," while others clung together in small groups—some crying, others praying, while there were those who were very calm, enjoying the disaster. They stood by the rail, looking out toward the lifeboats or at the dirigible which floated above. Many had changed their clothes and looked resplendent in their early twentieth-century costumes. One man, dressed in pajama bottoms and a blue and gold smoking jacket, climbed over the rail and just stepped into the frigid water.

But there were a few men and women atop the officers' quarters. They were working hard, trying to launch collapsibles C and D, their only chances of getting safely away from the ship.

"Hey," Mantle called to them, "do you need any help up there?" He knew that he was really going to die unless he did something.

He was ignored by those who were pushing one of the freed collapsibles off the port side of the roof. Someone shouted, "Damn!" The boat had landed upside down in the water.

"It's better than nothing," shouted a woman, and she and her friends jumped after the boat.

Mantle shivered; he was not yet ready to leap into the frigid water, although he knew there wasn't much time left, and he had to get away from the ship before it went down. Everyone on or close to the ship would be sucked under.

Perhaps it was his recurrent dream of Josiane floating in a pool of water as calm as this ocean that stopped him from jumping. He crossed to the starboard side where some other men were trying to push the boat "up" to the edge of the deck. The great ship was listing heavily to port.

This time, Mantle didn't ask. He just joined the work. No one complained. They were trying to slide the boat over the edge on planks. All these people looked to be in top physical shape—Mantle noticed that about half of them were women wearing the same warm coats as the men. This was a game to all of them, he suspected, and they were enjoying it. Each one was going to beat the odds, one way or another; the very thrill was to outwit fate, opt to die and yet survive.

But then the bridge was under water.

There was a terrible crashing, and Mantle slid along the floor as everything tilted. Impossibly, there was music coming from somewhere, an Episcopal hymn. He just then realized that the band had been playing ragtime all along.

Everyone was shouting, and Mantle saw more people than he thought possible to be left on the ship. People were jumping overboard. They ran before a great wave that washed along the deck as the stern of the ship swung upward.

"She's going down," someone shouted as the icy water swept Mantle away. Mantle panicked and swam toward the crow's nest, which was not yet under water. Then he caught himself and tried to swim away from the ship, but it was too late. He felt himself being sucked back, pulled under. He was being sucked into the ventilator, which was in front of the forward funnel.

Down into sudden darkness. . . .

He gasped, swallowed water, and felt the wire mesh, the air shaft grating that prevented him from being sucked under. He held his breath until he thought his lungs would burst; he called in his mind to Joan. Water was surging all around him, and then there was another explosion. Mantle felt warmth on his back as a blast of hot air pushed him upward. Then he broke out into the freezing air. He swam for his life, away from the ship, away from the crashing and thudding of glass and wood, away from the debris of deck chairs, planking and ropes; and especially away from the other people who were moaning, screaming at him, and trying to grab him as a buoy, trying to pull him down.

Still, he felt the suction pull of the ship, and he swam, even though his arms were numb and his head was aching as if it were about to break. Then the noise stopped, the crashing and even the shouting and howling, and Mantle knew that she was going down. He swam harder. In the distance were other lifeboats, for he could see lights flashing. But none of the boats would come in to rescue him; that he knew.

He heard voices nearby and saw a dark shape. For a moment it didn't register; then he realized that he was swimming toward an overturned lifeboat, the collapsible he had seen pushed into the water. Suddenly, someone grabbed him from below, and he felt himself being pulled down. It was Joan! he thought, pulling him under, and his mind seemed to open up as he screamed and fought and pushed himself away from whoever was drowning, who never reached the surface again.

There were almost thirty men and women standing stop the overturned boat. Mantle tried to climb aboard and some-one shouted, "You'll sink us. We've too many already."

"Find somewhere else."

A woman tried to hit Mantle with an oar, just missing his head. Mantle swam around to the other side of the boat. He grabbed hold again, found someone's foot, and was kicked back into the water, which was freezing him, leaching away his will, drawing him down. . . .

"Come on," a man said, his voice gravelly. "Take my arm and I'll pull you up."

"There's no *room!*" someone else said.

"There's enough room for one more."

"No, there's not."

A fight threatened, and the boat began to rock.

"We'll all be in the water if we don't stop this," shouted the man who was holding Mantle afloat. Then he pulled Mantle aboard.

"But no more, he's the last one!"

Mantle stood with the others; there was barely enough room. Everyone had formed a double line now, facing the bow, and leaned in the opposite direction of the swells. Slowly the boat inched away from the site where the ship had gone down, away from the people in the water—all begging for life, for one last chance. As he looked back to where the ship had been, Mantle thought of Pfeiffer and Faon. And desperately, he wanted to be with Joan, to have her take him in her arms.

A swimmer who was not wearing a life preserver came alongside the boat and called for help. Mantle hunkered down, took the man's hand, and said, "If you can survive the water, I'll keep you afloat."

The man squinted his eyes, then closed them and nodded.

The cries for help could be easily heard across the water. In fact, the calls seemed magnified, as if meant to be heard clearly by everyone who was safe as a punishment for past sins.

"We're all deaders," said a woman standing beside Mantle. "I'm sure no one's coming to get us before dawn, when they have to pick up survivors."

"We'll be the last pickup, that's for sure—that's if they intend to pick us up at all."

"Those in the water have to get their money's worth."

"And since we opted for death. . . ."

"I didn't," Mantle said, almost to himself.

"Well, you've got it anyway."

Mantle felt the man in the water lose his grip. He tried to pull the man up, but it was no use. Mantle was too weak.

There was nothing to do but let him go and watch him fall slowly downward.

"You must go back now," Joan said to the crewman at the tiller. "The ship is gone, surely it's safe, surely—"

The heavy woman sitting beside Joan took her hand and squeezed it.

"We're staying right here," said the crewman.

"He's going to die out there. We're his only chance."

"He may be dead already, ma'am," said another crewman rowing opposite her. "We can't take the chance, not yet, anyway, not with so many people still out in the water still—"

"You mean still alive!"

"That's right, ma'am. They'd overturn the boat, and we'd all end up dead. These people didn't pay for that now did they?"

"You've got to help him," Joan mumbled, as if to herself.

"And the chances are that he's already dead, why—"

"Shut up," said the woman beside Joan.

"He's alive," Joan said. "He's got to be. . . ."

"Well, I'm afraid that I'm for staying right where we are," someone said. "I've had more than enough excitement for one night. I had no idea it was going to practically kill us."

"It's a shame about your friend, honey," the heavy woman said to Joan, "but he knew the conditions of this trip. We all took it for the element of chance—you too, I daresay."

"Well, we're staying right here until we're picked up," the man at the tiller insisted. "Those are my orders."

"After all," someone said to Joan, "it wouldn't be fair to those who are trying to beat the odds on their own, like the man you interviewed yesterday."

"That's an idea. . . . Why don't you interview *us*?"

Sometime later, Joan heard Mantle call to her from the chill and silent darkness. . . .

Mantle's teeth were chattering, and his hair had frozen to his scalp like a helmet. He watched the dirigible for a while, as did the others. He fought the numbness, the cushiony feeling of cold comfort, and forced himself to move his limbs as much as he could. It seemed colder yet. Certainly the sea was rougher than it had been; only the stars and the dirigible above seemed to be still.

The hours passed. If he could just last until dawn . . .

Mantle was numb, but no longer cold. As if from far away, he heard the splash of someone falling from the boat, which was very slowly sinking as air was lost from under the hull. At times, the water was up to Mantle's knees, yet he wasn't even shivering. Time distended, or contracted. He measured it by the splashing of his companions as they fell overboard. He heard himself calling Joan, as if to say goodbye. To open the gate. To let her know that he did, indeed, love her.

And Joan flooded him with warmth and words and thoughts, and he jerked upright as first light seemed to be melting upon the choppy waves. He had her words inside him, keeping him awake and alive for hours.

His first thought, muddled by the cold, was that he was on land, for the sea was full of debris—cork, steamer chairs, boxes, pilasters, rugs, carved wood, clothes, and, of course, the bodies of those unfortunates who could not or would not

survive—and the great icebergs and the smaller ones called
growlers that looked like cliffs and mountainsides. The icebergs were sparkling and many-hued, all brilliant in the light,
as if painted by some cheerless Gauguin of the north.

"There," someone said—a woman's hoarse voice. "It's
coming down, it's coming down!" The dirigible, looking like a
huge white whale, seemed to be descending through its more
natural element, water, rather than the thin, cold air. Its
electric engines could not even be heard.

In the distance, Mantle could see the other lifeboats.
Soon the airship would begin to rescue those in the boats,
which were now tied together in a cluster. As Mantle's
thoughts wandered and his eyes watered from the reflected
morning sunlight, he saw a piece of carved oak bobbing up
and down nearby, and noticed a familiar face in the debris
that surrounded the lifeboat.

There, just below the surface, in her box, the lid open,
eyes closed, floated Little Josiane.

She opened her eyes then and looked at Mantle, who
screamed, lost his balance on the hull, and plunged headlong
into the cold, dark water.

Twenty-Five

Mantle awakened in his stateroom on the dirigible *Californie*.
It was a small but comfortable and well-furnished room. Joan,
looking haggard, sat on the edge of his bed and tried to smile
at him. He was looking stronger now; his eyes no longer
looked glazed. But Joan felt alone, lost. She remembered
Mantle's thoughts when he lost his balance on the lifeboat
and fell into the water. He had seen Josiane! And then the
connection faded.

The *circuit fantome* was broken.

"It's like being back on the ship," Mantle said. "I can
hear the thrum of the engines . . . and everything creaks, just
like on the ship."

"Haven't you ever been on a dirigible?" Joan asked, hating the small talk. But she couldn't ask him about Pfeiffer . . . or Josiane. Not yet.

Mantle shook his head and then, after a long pause, said, "Always thought of them as being so slow." He shivered. "Jesus, I can't get rid of the chill."

"It's the injection the doctor gave you. You'll feel cold for a while, but you should have your strength back now."

"Except for the chill, I feel fine."

"Do you want to talk about—"

"Yes," Mantle said, shivering. "Let's get everything out in the open. God, I'm sorry. You look as if *you'd* been standing on a lifeboat all night." He reached for her hand, and she moved closer to him. Her hands were hot, perspiring; his were cold. "Thank you," Mantle said.

"For what?"

"For the connection, and all your love. For being with me out there. I can see what a strain it was, what it did to you. And I know how you had to pressure the captain to rescue us first."

"I couldn't let you drown," Joan said. "I—but how did you know about the captain?"

"Through the connection."

"The connection's dead," Joan said flatly. She felt herself trembling. After being so close to Ray, thinking his thoughts through the *circuit fantome*, she felt that she had lost part of herself when the connection was broken. Like scamming down, she thought. God, I'll never have him back.

"Joan?"

"I'm sorry. I guess we've both had a rough night." Then, as if she had bricked over her bad thoughts, she resumed conversation. "Do you know how I talked them into rescuing you? I told the captain and his officers that you were a reporter working with me and—"

"So Carl saved my ass one last time." Mantle smiled, but his face seemed filled with hate or, perhaps, loathing. "I saw him die. I left him, there was so much water and—"

"You tried," Joan said, "and almost lost *your* life trying to save him. You can't expect any more from yourself than that. But Carl just didn't seem to be the type. But then, who is the type?"

"Jesus, the message!" Mantle said suddenly. He sat up

and activated the computer, which was built into the wall near the head of his bed. The computer asked for the usual identity check; Mantle pressed his palm against the silvery face of the computer and recited his identity and code numbers.

"What are you looking for?" Joan asked, worried.

"Carl told me that he left a message for us."

Joan stiffened.

The messages were projected holographically before Mantle, as if a CeeR screen were floating beside the bed. There were several "red" messages—red messages could only be read once; then they were scrambled and automatically erased. Mantle told the computer to run the message from Hilda, and the computer requested an identity check of Joan if she were going to be present.

"Who's Hilda?" Joan asked, after giving her prints and identity number to the computer.

Mantle smiled sadly. "You know, just now I miss him. I suppose it will take time to hit me—just as Josiane's death will—that my past is forever—"

"Ray, you can do this another time, when you're feeling better."

"When we were in college, Carl and I used to send letters—not fax, mind you—to each other. He used to sign his letters 'Hilda Snatch.'"

Joan laughed, an edge of hysteria in her voice. "What did you call yourself?"

But Mantle didn't answer, for a hollie of Pfeiffer appeared before them as if Pfeiffer himself were sitting in the center of the room. The image had the telltale fuzziness of the scrambler. Pfeiffer was wearing an open shirt and neatly pressed white pants—an outfit he had often worn at Mantle's home in Cannes.

"Hello, Raymond—and Joan, if you are present, which I assume you will be or, rather, are." Pfeiffer looked down at his folded hands for an instant, as if to consciously stop himself from twiddling his thumbs, and then continued. "I think you deserve an explanation for what I've put you through, old friend. I knew that I wouldn't have much time and, quite frankly, I wanted to spend the last hours with you, and you too, Joan. . . ."

Pfeiffer seemed to be looking directly at Joan and Mantle, as if he were really alive. Mantle shuddered, for he knew better.

"I was involved in the Watergate to dethrone the Mahdi of Afghanistan. I was *very* much of a peripheral person, but nevertheless involved. I had nothing to do with the actual assassination attempt, however. Anyway, the deal was already in several weeks ago to prevent a war. Our president and his cabinet—which means *everyone* with affiliation, according to the new Salah al-Din al Ayyubi—must be dishonored and thrown over; that's all that will satisfy him. Of course, what we consider to be an honorable apology and then stepping down will do. The government will make it look good and iron it out. After all, there is a precedent for this sort of thing. I imagine that by the time you hear this, the vice president will have already taken over. However, the Mahdi demanded that everyone else be put to death. . . ."

"Jesus," Joan murmured.

"Our government is afraid of a repetition of the Paropamisus Executions," Pfeiffer continued. "You remember how the Mahdi executed the brothers, sisters, mothers, fathers, cousins, and then the *friends* of the 'Traitors of Islam' until the men he was after either gave themselves up or were found. Either way, they were executed. The Mahdi and his people are fanatics; our government will comply. So I was given a choice." Pfeiffer smiled grimly and said, "I do—or did, rather—have friends in power. I chose to take an ocean voyage—it's best for everyone involved. Caroline is living in San Francisco, you might call her for me. I'm sure this will have shaken her up. But, as you know, we were finished. I suppose I used up her portion of love for me, just as I used up your friendship. There, you see, confession." Pfeiffer paused, then said, "And I still owe you one, Raymond. I'm sorry that I had to pressure you into coming along with me. But even though you don't feel that you're my friend, you're all I have . . . you, and Joan. I am sorry about Josiane. I knew she was dead, and I used her and used you. I loved her too, Raymond. Although you don't think me capable of it, I grieved for her when I found out. . . ." Pfeiffer turned his head slightly, as if looking at someone who had just walked into the room. "Joan, thank you for everything. There's a story waiting for you at the bureau, my compliments. If this doesn't put you ahead of everyone else, nothing will. There's a stonewall on the news now, of course, but you won't have any trouble when it breaks. You're both safe; I've taken care of everything. That's all. Somehow... I suppose there's no way to make amends, Raymond; never will be. I'm sorry, and I love you. Goodbye...."

The image disappeared, and the room was quiet except for the ever-present thrumming of the engines and the creaking of expensive wood.

"Well," Joan asked, "what *did* you call yourself?"

"What?" Mantle asked, distracted. He was blaming himself for Pfeiffer's death, yet he *knew* there was nothing he could have done.

Joan moved closer to him.

"I think I called myself 'Hotlips Zymurgia.'"

Joan didn't smile. She was crying for Pfeiffer, or maybe for herself.

And, guiltily, Mantle realized that he was visualizing a new painting... that he wanted to paint again.

Joan and Mantle sat in the corner of the large, well-appointed Laurel Lounge, away from the other survivors who were watching the holographic tapes of the sinking of the *Titanic*. The images filled the large room with the ghostly past, and the survivors cheered each time there was a closeup of someone jumping overboard or slipping under the water.

"Where are the reporters?" Mantle asked.

"This room is restricted, at least for the time being," Joan said. "It was decided we needed a rest before the rush."

"I should imagine that keeping the audience in suspense is good business."

"This has become *the* biggest media event of the year," Joan said.

"And you were right in the middle of it."

"Yes, and I wish I'd never talked you into it, I—"

"*You* didn't talk me into anything," Mantle said, and then he became pensive, as if he were suddenly talking to himself. "Carl wanted me along for those last days. I suppose I'm all he had. He had no real friends; he scraped the bottom of the barrel with me...."

"I tried to be his friend," Joan said.

"Jesus, I can still see him," Mantle said; and then, as if he had just heard what Joan had said, he replied, "I know you tried to be his friend. I know.... But he had to hold Josiane in front of me as a carrot to get me to come along, to spend his last days with him. Only to tell me she was dead. Christ, how long had he been planning this?"

"And what about Josiane?" Joan asked, or rather blurted. She couldn't hold it back any longer. "In the room you acted as if you really believed that she's dead. Do you believe that ... now?" Joan looked at Mantle as if praying for the right answer.

"Yes," Mantle said, "I think I do."

And Joan's head lolled forward. She fell asleep right there, just as Mantle had once done when he found out that his mother would live. It was as if Mantle had exorcised all her dreams. Just then the doors swung open and a dozen reporters rushed into the room, followed by noisy entourages of technicians, makeup artists, camera people, and passengers.

But as Joan drifted into sleep, she thought she heard Mantle say, or think: "At least I'll try to believe...."

PART FOUR

Twenty-Six

The news of the fall of the government didn't break until Mantle and Joan were back home in New York City.

They took a glassite pod, which whizzed them through the transparent tubes of the city to Mantle's modular apartment on West Seventy-ninth Street. Mantle had kept his apartment plugged into the core tower, which rose several hundred stories through the grid that spiderwebbed the old undercity.

"Somehow I can't believe you lived here," Joan said to Mantle as they passed through a foyer. Rows of tables and chairs were placed against the walls. The marble floor tiles formed a dizzying geometric pattern, and the passageway was illuminated by available light streaming through a high, narrow, stained-glass window. Around the window and covering the walls were paintings, mirrors, and bric-a-brac.

"Why not?" Mantle asked as he led Joan into the living room, which was sparely furnished with low upholstered chairs and couches. The ceiling was lacquered, and a collection of ceramic and glass jars were displayed on the inside wall. The outside wall was transparent. The room seemed completely open to the city—the view was breathtaking—and yet it was also isolated, not cozy but protected, like some transparent womb.

"It's just so different from your home in Cannes... it doesn't seem like *you*."

"This *is* my home," Mantle said, looking around the room. A robot silently passed by the doorway as it carried their baggage into the bedroom. "It feels good to be back. I was afraid of returning."

"I can understand that."

"But that feeling of dread seemed to disappear as soon as we stepped out of the pod."

"Well, we should be happy about that," Joan said tightly.

"I know how uneasy you are right now," Mantle said. "I warned you, it can be quite disconcerting at first."

"I'll get used to it."

"If you can't, then we'll change it to suit *you*. I want you to know that."

"Thank you," Joan said, "but we'll have plenty of time to change whatever we like. It will be fine, I'm sure." And she put her arms around Mantle.

"There's something I have to show you," Mantle said. "Let's get everything over with at once."

"What do you mean?"

Mantle led her into the bedroom, which had a domed ceiling, large arched mirrors, ornamented walls of ceramic tile, and a deep red-and-blue oriental carpet. "I never allowed you into the master bedroom of my house in Cannes, remember?"

"Yes, of course I remember. You always kept the door locked."

"Well, this is the same bedroom exactly. I had it duplicated in Cannes, down to the last detail. I even had copies made of Josiane's letters and diary."

"Was this *her* room, then?" Joan asked.

"It was *our* room," Mantle said. "The other bedroom was for guests, I remember that. . . ."

Joan walked around the room, examining clothes, hollies, fax, and clippings that were strewn about.

"This room is just as Josiane left it," Mantle continued. "I thought that by keeping it as it was, it would help me to remember. That's why I recreated it in Cannes." When Joan did not respond, Mantle said, "I couldn't bring myself to share Josiane . . . until now. That's why you never saw this room in Cannes. But tomorrow we can have all this moved out, and you can decorate it any way you like."

"Are you sure you really want to give it up?" Joan asked. "It's early yet, so much has happened. . . . I wouldn't want you to do something you'd regret. You'd only blame me."

"No, I wouldn't blame you," Mantle said. "If it weren't for you, I don't know what I would have done." Mantle looked around the oriental, Mandarin room. "I've got to start somewhere, try again. You know, from everything I know about myself when I was with Josiane, from the tapes, I don't think I would like him . . . me."

"Now I can understand why you kept your bedroom door locked in Cannes. . . ."

"Is it because of Josiane that you dislike this—"

"That's a nasty way to put it, Ray," Joan said. "I have nothing against Josiane, for Christ's sake. My God—"

"I'm sorry, it was a wrong thought." Mantle fingered the objects on a bronze and onyx table, then wiped his hands on his trousers as if he had soiled them.

"There's something cloying about this room . . . this house. No, that's not quite what I mean. It's hard; it doesn't let anyone else in. It represents a whole world of isolation. It frightens me because I imagine that you and your sister were enough for each other—you didn't *need* the rest of the world."

"So I've been told."

"If you mean by Carl, I think he was jealous because your relationship was closed to him."

"I can't imagine a relationship more closed than his and Caroline's," Mantle said. They walked out of the bedroom, through the foyer, and into the living room.

"You were involved in a *ménage* with them," Joan said as she stared out through the transparent wall into the city. "How can you possibly consider it a closed—"

"It closed down almost immediately," Mantle said. "As soon as Carl felt secure enough to wall her away, so to speak."

"Perhaps that was a reaction to you and Josiane."

Mantle shrugged. "That was before—"

"I think it was obvious to everyone but, perhaps, you and Josiane of your feelings for each other."

"I have no way of knowing, but that's over with," Mantle said. "Now, I want to start my life again, fresh, with you."

Joan turned to him and said in a quavering voice, "Then have Josiane's things moved out of the bedroom. . . ."

Every day, Mantle expected it to hit him. But each day was calmness itself, and Mantle felt as if he had been born anew. He had no past—or a past that was clouded and dusty—and a clear present. He was home. Everything was familiar and comfortable and yet somehow new. Since he had redecorated the bedroom and had everything of Josiane's removed, he felt as if a great and terrible weight had been lifted from his shoulders.

Maybe there was hope, maybe he and Joan could make a life. . . .

What was happening to Mantle seemed to be symptomatic of the world, for Screamer attacks had stopped and the frantic anxiety that had overpowered nations was replaced by an uncertain calm. Everyone was waiting. The Crying Church was preaching that this was the promised calm before the storm, the time to make one's peace with the world before the final purging.

Mantle sat in the studio, the outermost room of the apartment, and painted. The smells of oil and turpentine were strong and satisfying. Mantle worked quickly with brush and cloth and knife upon a large canvas. It was ostensibly a painting of the *Titanic* floating on a cold, calm sea. The ship seemed to be floating in a gray heaven, for sky and sea were carefully merged. Images appeared and disappeared as one looked at the painting—a familiar technique of Mantle's. Finally, one would see a Dantean hell of men and women drowning while others were busy in the lifeboats. Parties were in full swing in watery staterooms; lovers kissed good-bye; sailors lowered collapsibles; and a dirigible floated above, its passengers pressing their faces to the tiny windows.

Mantle had two paintings in mind as he worked: *Swing Low, Sweet Chariot* by John McCrady, in which Satan and the angels battled in the evening sky over a shack where a black man lay dying, attended by his family; and *Night and the Sea* by Henry Mattson, a painting of angry green ocean, sky, and rocky coast. Every time Mantle had seen that painting, he felt his old fear of the sea, as if the sea were only for drowning.

When he was finished, he walked around the room and looked through the walls and floor at the city around him. Just below him were glassite rooms like his own, some opaqued, some transparent; and the passtubes spiderwebbed everywhere, like the transparent netting of a great crystal ship. It was still morning, and the city seemed filled with sunlight.

He walked back to the painting and stared at it. There was something wrong but he couldn't decide what it was.

But there was definitely something wrong.

He sat down in the comfortable chair in which he usually viewed his paintings and put a call through to Caroline, Pfeiffer's wife. It was time, he thought. He had waited long enough.

She appeared a comfortable distance away from him near the center of the canvas-filled room. Her blond hair was cut short, and she looked haggard, which was how Mantle expected her to look. After all, Pfeiffer had been her life for fifteen years.

"I was waiting for the obligatory Raymond Mantle call," she said; a faint smile formed and then disappeared.

"I'm sorry I waited, but—"

"You know better than that," Caroline said. "How is Joan?"

"Good," Mantle said, feeling awkward. "She's been working hard."

"So we've seen."

"Are you thinking about the poll?" Mantle asked.

"That, and the fact that she turned Carl's death into a sort of media event in itself. He would have liked that—if indeed he didn't plan it that way." She stopped talking, shook her head and said, "Christ, what's the use. I'm sorry, I've nothing against Joan, I've never even met the woman. The breakup was my fault, I wanted it . . . can you believe that?"

"Yes," Mantle said, "I can."

"I turned myself off to him, became like a dead thing. He couldn't live with that. He thought it was *his* fault. And I let him believe it."

"He deserved it, I think."

"No," she said, "he didn't deserve *that*. He loved me, even while he suffocated me. I wanted him to take care of me, make all the decisions, and then I didn't. I became strong enough to take care of myself, which left him with nothing. I should have made it easier for him, instead. . . ."

"I was with him on the ship."

"Ah," she said. "You certainly managed to slip through the cracks in the media."

"Friends in high places."

Her image wavered; she must have activated her scrambler. "He made a tape for me. I know he didn't kill himself on account of me. That *is* true, isn't it?"

Mantle nodded.

"He even planned that, the sonofabitch. . . . Ray?"

"Yes?"

"I hated him all the time, from the very first."

Jesus, Mantle thought, the poor sonofabitch. He was right to be paranoid and insecure. She *had* loathed him, as Mantle had. But still he loved him, as he supposed she did too.

"And I hate him for what he's done."

Mantle could only nod. "If you need me . . ."

"I'll be fine. Don't condescend."

"I—"

"He did tell me about your paintings, though."

"He had time for that?" Mantle asked, caught off guard.

"He wouldn't let that get by, you know Carl. He told me all about the wreath of cocks around my head in the painting." Again she smiled, that innocent, vulnerable smile. "At least you know *me*, in the quick."

"Jesus, Caroline, I—"

"You should know that Carl never leaves a stone unturned. Can I have the painting?"

"Not now, after all that's happened."

"Especially now, Ray. But it can wait until you return to Cannes. How long are you staying in New York?"

"I don't know."

"Come and visit, if you like."

"Yes, if—"

"I'm doing fine," Caroline said. "Really I am." Mantle could see fine lines around her mouth. Jesus, she's getting old, turning papery, washed out. "I'm so sorry about Josiane," she continued. "Are you able to talk about it, or should we hang up?"

"I can talk about it now," Mantle said. "What's the difference? I can't *remember* her, I still can't remember any of it."

"I don't believe he's dead, Ray." That came, it seemed, out of nowhere.

"What?"

"I don't believe he killed himself," Caroline said.

"But he *did*," Mantle insisted. "Christ, I was *there*."

"You didn't actually see him die."

"Caroline, I was there!"

She just looked at him. "I don't believe it, I can't," she

said after a pause. And then she faded away without a good-bye.

Mantle was shaken. Pfeiffer had been right: she would go over the edge. Mantle would have to visit her. He owed her that. Poor fucking Pfeiffer, he thought. She had really hated him. But he'd made sure he had the last laugh. Vengeful bastard. Yet, Mantle understood: she had collapsed Pfeiffer's world, and so Pfeiffer reached out to break hers.

Mantle stood up and examined the painting he had been working on. It was a good, technical job, he thought as he touched the raised surfaces of the paint that had already dried. He repressed an urge to scratch across the painting and remembered how he had gessoed over so many canvases in Cannes because he felt they were watching him, as if the paintings were conscious, alive, even when buried under the white paste. Mantle had that feeling now, and it unnerved him. He spread a drape over the painting and left the room, opaquing the walls, floor, and ceiling as he left. The room became a gray cell.

He walked into the living room and poured himself a drink from the bar. Perhaps a narcodrine would be better, a mild one. No, he told himself, taking a large gulp of Scotch. Not after Dramont with its hallucinogenic dust, not after scamming down on narcodrine reefer so long ago. . . .

He had a day to get through before Joan returned home from an assignment for Interfax. Mantle had finished his work for them and they were happy with it. His mirroring technique had become very hot with politicians, including the new media-sophisticated president. Interfax hadn't tried to press any new assignments on Mantle, but that would change when viewers got wise to the new subliminals, which inevitably they would. He sat down in a chair beside an ancient Chinese celadon jar on a pedestal and asked the computer for Pfeiffer's last work of fiction. He leaned back and the words were before him, hanging, as it were, in a cloud.

Mantle smiled: the novel was called *White Thought*. Pfeiffer never did have a sense of history, he told himself. What connotations this would have had a few hundred years ago. . . .

As he read, he discovered that he was one of the main characters in the novel. Caroline was right, of course: Pfeiffer would not leave a stone unturned.

* * *

When Joan returned, they celebrated by going downtown to the East Village to eat at the Old Merchant's House. It was a new restaurant in an antique building, one of the few antiques left in this area after the bombings and the Screamers. It was built in the nineteenth century and rebuilt toward the end of the twentieth, but the wrought-iron grilles and arcade entrance, which were its trademarks, were intact. Inside were great rooms, decorated in Empire styles. Joan and Mantle were seated in a large, formal dining room that was filled with other dinner-time guests. A Grandfather clock ticked slowly behind Mantle, as if to remind him that something was about to happen.

They ordered, and Mantle told Joan about Pfeiffer's novel.

"Well," she said, "it's only natural that he would use you as a character. He didn't use your name, did he?"

"No, of course not," Mantle said, toying with the empty snail shells on his plate. "The character didn't seem to be anything like me."

"Then why do you think he used you?" she asked between mouthfuls of salad.

"The protagonist had amnesia, isn't that enough?"

"What was it that he couldn't remember?"

"He never finds out."

"Tha doesn't seem to be much of a resolution."

"No, it resolves in its way."

"How?"

"The protagonist just goes his own way, settles down, has a decent life."

"Well . . . ?"

"It's what he doesn't know, what he can't remember having lived, that is the crux. He's content, and somehow *that's* the tragedy."

"Are you sure it's not your interpretation?" Joan asked. The waiter brought the food: pork Holstein topped with fried eggs, anchovies, and capers; grated potatoes; and buttered beans and peas. They had both ordered the same dish; it was the specialty of the house. Joan broke the yolks with her fork and pushed the anchovies aside. "Do you want the anchovies?" she asked. He didn't, and she continued: "Is that the way *you* feel?"

"Well...the thing is, I am happy."

"Don't protest too much or I won't believe you."

"I *am* happy," Mantle insisted.

"And you feel guilty about it, right?" Joan asked. "You can't afford to feel guilty about being content: that's crazy."

"I know," Mantle said.

"I think you still feel threatened by Carl, even now that he's dead. Why not let him go?"

"Pop-psych."

"Then I give up," Joan said, pushing her plate away. The waiter appeared an instant later with coffee and a deep, rich mocha pudding served in a ceramic double boiler.

"I still can't believe Carl's dead," Mantle said, leaning back in his chair.

"I know...."

"But the irony is that I can at least grieve for him, which is more than I can do for Josiane, whom I can't even remember."

"So...do you want to start the search again? Is that what you're trying to say?" Joan asked nervously.

"No. That's the crazy thing. No." Then, as if suddenly realizing that he really meant what he had said, he continued, "Please believe me, I am happy with you."

Joan nodded.

After a long pause, Mantle said, "I called Caroline."

"Is she well?"

"I think she's backsliding. Carl was right."

"Well, I'm sure something can be done."

"I'll have to go and see her."

"Do you think that will help?"

"Perhaps, perhaps not, but I feel a responsibility. I should have called her earlier, tried to help—"

"You can't blame yourself for *that*," Joan said. "*You* were in the process of getting well; that's all you could worry about."

"I don't know if you could call it getting well," Mantle said, toying with the food on his plate. The waiter kept glancing at their table as if annoyed because he couldn't take the plate away from Mantle and be done with this couple. "I still can't *remember*."

"That may come in time."

"I doubt that—and if it does, I don't want it!"

"Now *that* worries me," Joan said.

The waiter returned and asked Mantle if he wished coffee and dessert. When Mantle shook his head, the waiter quickly cleared the table. "Caroline doesn't believe that Carl's dead," Mantle said after the waiter left.

"Did you really expect her to?"

"I suppose not."

"She probably feels that *she's* the cause of his death. The best way out of that is not to believe he's dead. But why should that surprise you?"

"I don't really know," Mantle said. "I think what's bothering me is that I called her today."

"Maybe you felt ready, that—"

"I finished the *Titanic* painting."

"Yes, I saw it. I was wondering when you were finally going to get to that material. Actually, it seems quite right that you would call Caroline now."

"Did anything about the painting strike you as odd?" Mantle insisted.

"I didn't look at it closely, but no. I'll look at it later. Carefully. What's bothering you about it?"

"I don't know—that's just it. Maybe it ties in with why I called Caroline."

"Because you're working it out now. It's only natural that you'd call her. It does make sense, you know."

"But it feels wrong," Mantle said.

They credited the dinner check and walked to the Broadway "BB" rollway, which was crowded. Kliegs were on everywhere, and the passtubes and pods and towers above were all illuminated; the great weather dome that covered New York City seemed to contain the very stuff of light. The city reminded Mantle a bit of Paris, except that this was home. The atmosphere of the ways and streets had changed; the tension had eased—as much as it ever did in the great city. It was the same old New York that Mantle remembered: the same hustle, the rapid stream of shouting and huckstering, the same hot, sour air, pedestrians wearing designer noseplugs, prostitutes waiting at corners, police vans cruising, the robots in blue, beggars asking for small transfers of credit, religious fanatics begging a moment....

But Mantle was uncomfortable tonight.

"A penny for your thoughts?" Joan asked as they stepped off the rollway and onto the street platform.

"What?"

"A credit for your thoughts, how's that?" she asked, smiling. They crossed the street, which was crowded with shoppers searching for bargains. Now that it was safe, shopping in the streets was much cheaper than shopping by computer.

"I was thinking about you," Mantle said.

"Liar."

"I was thinking about us."

"You're still a liar, but that's better."

"I want everything to stay as it is," Mantle said.

And they took an elevator to their apartment.

Mantle walked directly to the studio to look at his *Titanic* painting.

"Ray?" Joan asked. She took the painting's drape from him; he was lost in thought, kneading the drape with both hands as if wiping them. "Tell me what you see?"

"What is it?" Mantle asked.

"Tell me what you see!"

In every lifeboat was a female figure, each a sublim wavering into and out of sight. Each one was Josiane.

Mantle unveiled other paintings, which were propped against the transparent far wall. They were painted in various mediums, ancient and modern.

It was as if the scales had dropped from Mantle's eyes. Now he could see what he had been doing for the last month. He had been painting Josiane over and over again. She was buried inside every painting. *She* was the ground upon which he was working. As if she were mocking him, her face stood out of every one of the boards and canvases.

He had not forgotten her.

He had not lost her.

Enraged at himself, he kicked and tore the canvases.

"What are you *doing*?" Joan shouted. She grabbed him, clinging. "Let me in, tell me—"

Startled, Mantle stopped tearing at his paintings and looked at her. She flinched as she felt the connection, the *circuit fantome*. This was what she had been waiting for.

But she had not wanted it to be like this! The light he turned on her had no warmth, and she remembered what Faon had said to her that morning in Dramont . . . that Mantle was promised.

And then the *circuit fantome* was broken as if a faulty switch had opened.

"It's Josiane," she said quietly, breaking away from Mantle.

"My God, I've been painting her . . . all along," Mantle said, as if to himself. "Jesus, I didn't even realize. . . ." Mantle shuddered and said, "Let's get out of this room." They walked into the living room, where Joan stood stiffly, as if she were as fragile and brittle as the jardiniere on the wall beside her. "Help me, Joan," Mantle pleaded as he put his arms around her. "I want *you*. Please believe that. I can't help what happened with those paintings."

"I expected something like this," Joan said. "No, I guess I didn't. I thought everything was going to be all right with us. After you were rescued, when the *circuit* closed, I tried to pretend that it would really reestablish itself, that you would want to be connected."

"I do."

"Then open yourself up to me; let me help you."

Mantle released her. "We've been over this before. You know I've tried, but the *circuit* has a will of its own."

"*You* closed it down a moment ago in the studio."

"I didn't, I swear it. The connection isn't everything; we don't have to be hooked in all the time. I love you, isn't that enough?"

"I don't know. . . ." Joan sat down on the couch and called the robot to bring her a narcodrine.

Mantle sat down beside her and said, "I saw something too, when the *circuit* flicked back on for that instant. . . . Like Faon, you think I'm promised, don't you?"

"No!" Joan said.

"I saw it."

"It's not true. I think no such thing."

"Then what do you have in mind? To pretend that everything is back to normal?" Mantle asked.

"Yes," Joan said. "And I want to make love. Now." She grabbed him urgently, and he could feel her fingernails piercing his flesh.

Mantle awoke in the middle of the night, as if he had been dropped from a height. He had been dreaming of Josiane. He dreamed that he had painted her over and over again, that he couldn't stop; and he dreamed of the dark spaces, of the black and silver, and the Screamers who were whispering to him, whispering words he couldn't understand, calling him. . . .

He was sweating, as was Joan, who was sleeping restlessly beside him. She groaned and shifted positions, reaching for the edge of the bed, perhaps dreaming that she was in the lifeboat again— or dreaming of the dark spaces as Mantle had done. Mantle was anxious and afraid; the darkness had that particular edge that it had during his transition crisis at Dramont. His hands were shaking.

He turned on the lights, and a soft white glow suffused the room, revealing arched opaqued windows, upholstered chairs, decorative Hansen wall lamps, chameleon carpeting which just now matched the ivory walls and bed, and a Louis Quinze bureau and console. He looked at Joan, who was lying on her back, and then caressed her face, which disturbed her breathing pattern. She expelled a short puff of breath and then, as if descending into deeper sleep, her breathing returned to its slow rhythm. Mantle remembered her frenetic, almost violent lovemaking: she wasn't used to narcodrines.

Looking at her now, he felt guilty about the *circuit fantome*. Mantle blamed himself. But he couldn't open himself up—the *circuit* either happened or it didn't, he told himself. He couldn't make it work. If there were any way to restore the broken connection, it was by ignoring it, not pressing for it. He had discovered that it was like peripheral vision: when he tried to see out of the corner of his eye, he couldn't. He just had to let it happen, as if by itself. The *circuit* was like a Zen thing, Joan had once said.

But although Joan desperately needed the connection, Mantle was afraid of it, afraid of being so exposed and vulnerable. He felt the guilt rise once again like bad food. He had used Joan, over and over. *He* had destroyed the connection, which had saved him on the lifeboat. Mantle lay back down beside Joan and let his mind wander, tried to drift into hypnogogic sleep where he could control his dreams. Perhaps he could restore the connection. It might just turn itself back on. And he owed her the connection. God, he owed her. . . .

She turned toward him, brushed an invisible spiderweb from her face, and rested her arm on his chest. As Mantle began to fall asleep, he tried to open the *circuit fantome*, tried to "let" it happen; but each time he tried, he would awaken with a jolt. Finally, he gave up—Joan was asleep, anyway. Even if he could connect with her, she probably wouldn't remember it in the morning, and he wanted her to know that he loved her. The idea almost came to him as a surprise: he *did* love her. In that instant, Mantle hated the very idea of Josiane . . . and he hated himself for painting her, for not giving up the dead.

He slept uneasily, dreaming of Josiane calling him, dreaming of Joan and the pool under the house in Dramont. And in the background, the Screamers seemed to be calling him, as if they had just awakened from a brief sleep and were now waiting, waiting for him. . . .

Joan groaned, turned her face back and forth against the pillow, waved her arms and kicked her legs as if trying to fend off an invisible attacker. Suddenly, she screamed and then fell back into deep sleep. Mantle almost awakened; but without realizing it, he had slipped into her mind. Her breathing once again became regular, and she settled down.

The *circuit fantome* was closed.

Together they traveled.

Mantle dreamed her dreams, her nightmares: snatches of swirling color, unrelated bits of the previous day, her anxieties about Mantle leaving her, her fear and love and hatred of him, and distant memories of other men, childhood terrors of being alone; and once again Mantle glimpsed the dark spaces, the cold corridors, the expanses which were as even and forbidding as deep ocean floor. She was being fed by so many connections—all subtle, unconscious, but flowing just the same—she was at once in the dark spaces and in the bright spaces, constructing them all into the fabric of a single dream, a nightmare woven out of silver thread and the whispers of Screamers. She too heard them. . . .

Mantle glimpsed a man in Joan's dream. He had a wide, fleshy face, high forehead, brown and gray hair which was thinning in the front but thick in the back and worn shoulder-length in the *boutade* fashion. The man looked to be about fifty; his pale, blotched skin was natural and wrinkled. Just a man growing old: a man who couldn't afford to, or didn't want to rejuvenate.

But there was something disquietly familiar about him. The man's image disappeared and reappeared in Joan's mind as if he were one of Mantle's painted subliminals. Mantle was awake now, barely, and he concentrated on this one thread of dream, blocking out everything else—all the good things he had wanted to say and think and feel about Joan: his feelings of love that he had wanted to reinforce in her dreaming mind.

Joan groaned, thrashed about for a few seconds, then became quiet again. In her dream, the man sat at a metal table in a shabby, dusty room, a kitchen. A soiled blue-and-white drape separated the kitchen from the bedroom/living room. The susurration of the ocean could be heard—close, by the sound of it—and there were paintings on the peeling walls, even in the kitchen. Perhaps they were holos....

But one of the paintings was Mantle's. It was a portrait of Josiane that he had painted years ago.

Mantle listened, privy to Joan's thoughts, and he could hear the workings of the man's mind in Joan's dream. The man was idly thinking about Josiane. Then he stopped writing and thought about Mantle for an instant. He felt a black rush of guilt....

Suddenly, Mantle realized who the man was. And Mantle was electrified. His heart beat so fast that it seemed to be in his throat.

The man in the dream was Pfeiffer! Pfeiffer was alive!

Even though Pfeiffer had had a face change, Joan knew him. She had a *circuit fantome* with *him*, too. She knew where he lived, where he walked, what he did. She knew the numbers on the streets, the webbings of his thoughts—all obscured, as if by distance.

Mantle tore out of the *circuit* like a disoriented patient waking up to find himself catheterized, pulling away in shock and pain. He sat bolt upright in bed. His breath was short; his sweat drew icy lines down his back. Beside him, Joan was curled up and making crying noises in her sleep, as if she were aware of what had just happened; but now that Mantle had pulled out, she settled down and seemed to be drifting deeper into unconscious, dreamless sleep.

She lied to me, tricked me, Mantle thought. She knew all along that Pfeiffer was alive. She was using *me* on his behalf, the bitch. Mantle could now only see Joan's face as it had looked when she rose out of the pool in Dramont to kill him. Everything was a lie but *that*. She wanted me dead,

Mantle told himself. But why? And why would Pfeiffer want me dead? Surely she was doing it for Pfeiffer. . . .

Everything, the whole world, had changed in an instant, switched from white to black, from day to the most bitter night.

Mantle flicked on the lights to *bright*, and Joan awakened with a start. "Whatisit . . . honey? Dim the lights. . . . "

"You knew all along, didn't you?" Mantle said. He was seething with coherent, directed hatred.

"What are you talking about?" Joan asked, propping herself against one of the pillows, wiping the sleep from her eyes; but Mantle slapped her hard in the face, then slapped her again. "My God, Ray, stop it, please. What's wrong, what's—"

Mantle felt as if he were distanced from himself, lost somewhere in the eye of a dark, emotional storm, caught in some purgatory between the bright and dark spaces, lost and helpless. "You knew about Pfeiffer all along. You knew he was alive. Why did he want you to kill me in Boulouris? Tell me *that*." And if Pfeiffer's still alive, what does he know about Josiane? Mantle asked himself. This must be about Josiane; it has to be.

"Ray, snap out of it!" Joan said, pleading. "What's come over you?" She reflexively moved away from him toward the other side of the bed for protection. "I don't know anything about Carl except that he's dead. You said you saw him die yourself. Darling, please try to come to grips with yourself. . . . You must have been dreaming. It was only a dream."

"I saw him in your mind!" Mantle said, stepping around the bed toward Joan. "That was no dream. Now tell me what's going on. Why didn't you tell me that Pfeiffer was alive. You *knew*!"

"Ray, please, I don't know what you're talking about," Joan said, stepping backward, away from Mantle. "Stop this, I'm frightened. . . . "

"Then tell me the truth!" Mantle grabbed her by the shoulders and shook her as if she were some sort of defective machine. She tried to break away from him, but he was out of control. He held her arm with one hand and slapped her face with the other. He slapped her over and over again until she collapsed on the bed; and then, as if it had a capricious life of its own, the *circuit* between Joan and Mantle was suddenly restored and Mantle saw into her, saw that she hadn't known about Pfeiffer until just now. It had all been buried in her mind, hidden. She had had some slight *circuit* with Pfeiffer but couldn't bring herself to recognize him, even in her dreams.

"Oh God, I'm sorry," Mantle said to Joan, who moaned and wiped her bleeding nose and mouth on the sleeve of her nightgown. She was crying and having trouble catching her breath. Mantle felt soiled, filled with guilt. He had wronged her *again*. What he had done could not be undone. He wanted to reach out to her, hold her, even though fear and revulsion were radiating from her like blistering heat.

Then everything seemed to cloud over and harden into silver and darkness. Mantle cocked his head to the side as he listened to a small voice whispering in his mind. . . . He was hearing Pfeiffer's thoughts, feeling Pfeiffer's emotions as Pfeiffer stood on the edge of a pool of pearly, viscous fluid and watched Josiane floating below. In that instant, Mantle realized that he too had a *circuit fantome* with Pfeiffer.

He remembered when he had smashed into Josiane in the dark spaces. Had he connected with Pfeiffer then, too . . . ?

Mantle was seeing Josiane through Pfeiffer's eyes, and Josiane was calling to him through Pfeiffer.

She was alive!

But what had Pfeiffer done to her?

Swept away by the violence of his emotions, Mantle grabbed his clothes and ran out of the room. Joan screamed for him to stop, and followed him, stumbling.

"Ray, I saw it, too," she shouted. "Please don't leave without me, don't shut me out again. . . . I'll go with you. . . ." But Mantle heard only the blood pumping in his head as he ran through the foyer, past the nineteen-thirties American prints and the ornate distorting mirrors on the walls, past the robot that stood eyeless as a statue, and out the sensor-lined door that opened onto the transpod platform outside his apartment. Mantle was overwhelmed with hatred for Pfeiffer and the need to find Josiane.

Joan followed him, but the *circuit fantome* between them had degenerated into a rushing noise in her head: Mantle had already blocked himself off to her so he could "hear" Pfeiffer.

Mantle climbed into a waiting transpod and punched in

random coordinates, just to get him away from Joan, who ran to the car and pounded on the transparent dome that enclosed him. "I'll be back."

But even as Mantle said that, he knew it was a lie. He *was* leaving Joan behind. In a way, he was promised... to Josiane. ...

Loathing himself, he opaqued the glass; and with a jolt, the car sped away from Joan into the machinery of the city.

But Mantle could still see Joan's agonized face, as if through the opaqued walls of the car. He could sense her in his mind, an agony. He blocked out her thoughts completely, as if he were a mason hastily patching over a broken wall.

His *circuit* with Pfeiffer, although it was faint, was still open. But now he knew where Pfeiffer lived: the undercity slums of Seagate, which had once been a walled village situated on the southernmost tip of Brooklyn.

The telepathic image of Pfeiffer watching Josiane floating in a pool still burned in Mantle's mind. What has he done with her? Mantle asked himself. Why did he lie to me? How could he *know* that Josiane was alive and not tell me...?

In a rage as cold and implacable as reason, Mantle punched in the proper coordinates.

Twenty-Seven

The pod sped down Broadway, over what had once been the Williamsburg Bridge, and then south to Coney Island. It slowed down until it clicked into a small, filthy transpod station. Mantle got out and walked through the empty, foul-smelling corridors that would take him to a rollway. He was afraid, for these corridors would normally be mobbed with people. And he smelled the stink of the *grido*, as his Neapolitan guide Melzi had called them. He sensed the slippery minds of unseen Screamers around him.

He heard voices calling him, whispering in his mind, talking too quickly to be understood, and it was as if he were walking through the black and silver corridors of the dark spaces.

If Mantle hadn't known where he was, he might almost think he was beneath the surface of the moon, lost in the tunnels of a liberated colony. But he was in undercity. What had once been sunlit and filled with those who had dreamed of retiring near the beach had become a klieg-lit cemetery for the living. Corridors widened into streets and avenues. A family of *boutades* hurried past Mantle.

Everything was baited. The world was about to be crushed.

Mantle took a rollway down Surf Avenue, which paralleled the sea, to the crumbling stone wall that divided Seagate from Coney Island. Seagate looked now, more than ever, like an ancient medieval village, a fortress that had been breached by time and by generations of those on the dole. Mantle stepped onto a rollway platform, which was deserted, and walked into Seagate.

Empty streets, as empty as Naples.

But he recognized where he was. He had followed Pfeiffer's spoor through that faint connection that Joan had not realized even existed. He sensed Pfeiffer as a direction, and right now he could sense that Pfeiffer was not in his apartment. Like Mantle, he was walking the undercity streets. . . .

Mantle kept going. Many of the kliegs were out, and the black ocean to his left was nothing but forbidding. Whitecaps crashed upon the filthy, littered beach, which was covered with shacks constructed out of garbage and oddments. Mantle felt he was being watched, as if by primitive natives, and his hand curled tightly around the heat weapon in his pocket.

He heard a faraway keening, and slowly the streets began to fill. Everyone was quiet, waiting . . . and Mantle remembered something Faon had once told him: when the Great Scream finally came, the dark spaces would descend upon everyone like a veil, like a dream. There would be no fear, simply the patience of death. . . .

He hurried to Pfeiffer's building. It had once been white, but years of grime and pollution had settled upon it until it was camouflaged, indistinguishable from the steel and concrete world that surrounded it. Its first and second-floor windows were bricked over, and broken stone perrons abutted the street. The building was sensor-protected: it would be impossible for Mantle to get past its sliding metal doors unless Pfeiffer was with him.

Mantle would wait for Pfeiffer to return. He stood in the shadows beside the perrons and kept himself out of sight, but the image of Pfeiffer watching Josiane in a pool of shimmering, viscous liquid kept playing in his mind like a film loop. Pfeiffer is a thief! he thought, shivering as if caught in an ice storm of his own pain and hatred. Pfeiffer had stolen Josiane . . . and he had taken Mantle's past away from him as a thief a purse.

Mantle hated Pfeiffer with all the dead weight of the years they had known each other. And he waited and watched and listened.

The air seemed filled with electricity. Mantle could feel the crowd on the street as if it were a thought, and he remembered something he had read in Boulouris about the crystal and the seed that turn the many into the One. Suddenly, Mantle jerked backward as if a cold blade had been thrust into his flesh. He gasped, and distinctly he heard Josiane call his name. "Josiane?" he whispered, but he was left in a wake of silence. As if he had been locked into himself. He couldn't even hear the crowd's pounding waves of thought.

Then he saw Pfeiffer making his way through the street. Even though Pfeiffer was wearing a different face, Mantle knew him. Pfeiffer was shabbily dressed—as soiled-looking and nondescript as the streets and buildings and people around him. He carried a tray of food canisters tightly under one arm. Mantle waited until Pfeiffer had climbed the few stone steps to the doorway and came up behind him. "Carl."

Pfeiffer quickly reached for the sensor beside the door, but Mantle grabbed his arm, pulling it down sharply. "I *know* it's you," Mantle said tightly.

"I was trying to deactivate the sensor," Pfeiffer said nervously. For an instant Mantle could see his fright, and then Pfeiffer took himself under control. "We certainly can't stand out here," he said calmly. "Can't you see what's brewing? It's all starting again."

Mantle followed him closely past the sensors and up a staircase to the second floor, which was divided into two apartments. Pfeiffer's apartment was the same one Mantle had seen in Joan's dream: used furniture, untidy crash-space, nothing more.

The first thing Pfeiffer did was tap into the computer console. A hollie appeared before him. It was a map of Europe; each area of disruption was a white number inside a black square. There was a chain of squares from Gibraltar to Palermo, all along the southern coastline. "Europe's falling to the Screamers," Pfeiffer said. "It's worse than I expected. It's going to happen here. Christ, I can feel it in the air . . . and those crowds. . . ." Only then did he take the canisters into the kitchen. When he came back into the living room, he took off his jacket and laid it carefully on the back of the green stuffed chair. "Could you believe I need food," he said, trying to make small talk. "I forgot to buy it—too many years of calling the Net for delivery, I suppose. But there's none of that down here." He tried to smile, but grimaced instead. "Can I fix you a drink?"

"You lied to me," Mantle said, and suddenly his thoughts were afire with static, other voices, and just on the edges of his perception he thought he could hear Josiane calling to him, over and over again; a constant, flooding whispering of his name. But the whispering, the jangle, the static of thought carried Mantle away, raised his anger and pain to a mind-crushing pitch. He was seething with it; but outwardly he was calm, as cold and dead as a machine.

"Of course I lied," Pfeiffer said. "I lied to you and Joan and everyone else I knew and loved. To protect them. What else could I do? I don't want to die, even if I have to live like this. But how did you find me?"

Mantle was standing beside a window that overlooked the street and the ocean beyond. He tried to clear his mind, calm himself. He looked out the window at the people milling around the building as if to get closer to Mantle, who heard them as a buzzing in his head. They were in his mind, every fleshy one of them a silvery thought. And Mantle was the crystal, the seed, the mirror. . . .

As if in response to Mantle's inward fury, a hutch had caught fire on the beach, and it was spreading through the garbage and debris to the other shacks around it.

Mantle pulled himself away from the window. "I found you through Joan," he said to Pfeiffer.

"What do you mean?" Once again Pfeiffer looked frightened.

"You gave yourself away when you connected with her."

"I—"

"You were so sure of yourself, as usual."

"There was no way she could have known," Pfeiffer insisted. "I used hypnodrugs and—"

"She learned later," Mantle said. "You had a *circuit fantome* with Joan and you still do, just as you have one with me."

Pfeiffer seemed to jerk backward ever so slightly. The look on his face was disgust . . . and fear. Mostly fear. In all of Mantle's experience with Pfeiffer, he had never seen him this way: cornered like a small animal. Even on the *Titanic* when Mantle had chased him, Pfeiffer was composed. Of course he was composed, Mantle told himself, he had planned it all out. . . .

"Tell me the truth about Josiane," Mantle demanded. "Tell me right now!" The buzzing inside his head became louder. Josiane's voice became clearer, magnified as if by a thousand voices . . . and then with a jolt Mantle remembered his encounter with the Screamers in Naples. His skin broke into a cold sweat, but it was too late to stop what he had put into motion.

"If we're connected, you should know everything. . . ." Pfeiffer mumbled.

"The connection's weak," Mantle said, almost shouting to hear himself over the din of dark, silvery voices screaming in his mind: Josiane screaming his name, calling him to her, taking him over. "Don't fuck around with me, not *now*!"

"I told you the truth on the ship," Pfeiffer said, backing away from Mantle. He moved toward his writing desk.

Mantle could *feel* Josiane's presence. "You're a *liar*!" Mantle said, shaking.

"I told you the truth," Pfeiffer said cautiously, but there was a slight whine in his voice. "I made a point of trying to help you so you could have a life with Joan, whom you've deserted . . . and at a time like this."

"You sonofabitch. Tell me what you've done with Josiane!" Mantle advanced toward Pfeiffer with every intention of beating the information out of him if he had to.

Then Pfeiffer suddenly turned toward the desk, yanked

open a drawer and reached inside for a weapon. Mantle rushed forward screaming and slammed the drawer on Pfeiffer's hand. They grappled with each other for a few seconds, but Pfeiffer broke free of Mantle and in a trice was out the door and into the hallway. He touched a sensor plate on the wall, and as the door unlatched, he flung himself into the apartment that was opposite his own.

But Mantle was right behind him, and Pfeiffer had no time to lock the door closed.

They fell to the floor together.

Mantle struggled with Pfeiffer, who was surprisingly strong. But Mantle overpowered him.

And just then Mantle heard a long, dark scream inside his head. He was hearing the thoughts of the Screamers who were tearing up the streets below.

The Great Scream had begun.

A bomb exploded, shaking the building. The door to the apartment started to slide closed, then stopped midway.

Something exploded in Mangle's mind. Although he had sensed it coming, he was instantly plunged into the dark spaces. He was part of the Great Scream. He was screaming for Josiane, and with every shout, he banged Pfeiffer's head against the floor. Pfeiffer still struggled, but to no avail; Mantle was on top of him.

"Stop, for God's sake, stop," Pfeiffer begged. "Please... I'll tell you, I—"

But Mantle was deaf and blind to Pfeiffer. Raging, overwhelmed by hatred, fueled by the Screamers below, he struck Pfeiffer furiously. He was completely out of control. It was as if *he* had become a Screamer... as if he were just another gray face screaming for salvation. He was paying back a debt for all the pain Pfeiffer had inflicted upon him, for every indiscretion of the past.

And the world was cheering him on.

One of Mantle's blows broke Pfeiffer's windpipe, and Pfeiffer thrashed about wildly, clutching his throat pathetically. Then it was over as suddenly as it had begun. As if jerking away from a terrible nightmare, Mantle found himself looking down at Pfeiffer, whose broken face was already turning black.

It wasn't Pfeiffer's face, but it was Pfeiffer....

Mantle felt numbing exhaustion and a wrenching isolation. The buzzing in his head had stopped. He had nothing but his own thoughts. He held Pfeiffer in his arms, whispered in Pfeiffer's ear: "I didn't mean to kill you. Oh my God, what have I done?" He sobbed and combed his hands through Pfeiffer's bloodied hair. "I'm sorry, but it wasn't my fault. It wasn't my fault. . . ."

Dazed, Mantle looked around the room. This place was so familiar. Pfeiffer had duplicated the apartment that they had once shared with Josiane in Syracuse . . . built it out of the past. Everything was here in this, the living room: the old green couch, the torn, stuffed red chair with the embroidered pillows they had all won at a country carnival. Josiane's ancient tapestry from New Zealand was even hanging on the wall.

Mantle was suddenly filled with longing and bitter nostalgia. He could almost see Josiane sitting on the floor under the tapestry. That had always been her favorite spot in the old apartment.

And suddenly he felt something open up inside him, uncoiling . . . something dark and silvery as thought.

The *circuit fantome* with Pfeiffer was strong and clear and sharp. Death became the very stuff of sight. Even in death they were locked together. . . .

It was a deep descent, a flowing. Mantle was sliding down a spiraling silver tunnel into undulating spaces, the dead places, and Pfeiffer was no more a presence than a shadow in the dark.

Silences, as Pfeiffer became weaker . . . as the icy darkness leached away his soul . . . and only then the taste of memories. Pfeiffer's memories. Pfeiffer's thoughts. And Mantle understood.

Pfeiffer loved Josiane too, had always loved her; and she, in her way, had loved him. But Pfeiffer burned for her, was consumed with the idea of possessing her completely. When he found her in a New York hospital after she had gone over the deep side and become a Screamer, she was in deep coma. He used his influence and a great deal of money to have her hospital records altered and had her taken to a place where she was immersed in a pool which would keep her alive. But she would remain in coma, a receptacle for Pfeiffer to plug-into. Pfeiffer couldn't bear to let her die, nor could he let her live without him, so he kept her in half-life. His own guilt-ridden life was centered around hooking into her; he was as much a junkie as an addict.

Then the sound and taste and feel of Pfeiffer's thoughts and memories became vague, as impressionistic as a painting. Only one thought remained clear . . . and that was a whisper.

Mantle heard Pfeiffer calling to Josiane, begging her to help him, even as Pfeiffer was dissolving into the dark spaces.

And Mantle realized that Josiane was *here*. In this apartment.

He could hear her calling. But she wasn't calling Pfeiffer. She was calling *him*.

Mantle followed Josiane's voice, as he had once followed Joan's. He stumbled through Pfeiffer's secret apartment from one dark room to the next—until he found a locked door. He burned away the lock with his heat weapon.

The door led into a large, dimly lit den that was soundproofed, by the look of it, and comfortably furnished. The only sound was the soughing of the filtration system.

In the center of the carpeted room was a small, oval pool, illuminated and very bright, and there floated Josiane in viscous fluid. It was just as he had dreamed . . . as he had seen through Pfeiffer's eyes. He felt her speaking to him, but could not yet make out the words, even as he looked down into the pool at her, even as she stared blindly up at him. She was so white, more dead than alive, and beautiful, as if made out of eternal stone.

His heart was pounding, and he was unable to stop himself from trembling.

He found a psyconductor beside the pool and, kneeling, placed the cowl over his head—he wasn't going to take any chances on a *circuit fantome*. There was a chair beside him where Pfeiffer used to sit when he hooked into Josiane.

Mantle was like a junkie giving himself an injection.

He felt the black and silver, for she was a Crier and could never return to the world of things and solidity. He felt her presence as a cold shock, and she overwhelmed him. It was as if he had been plunged into ice water.

"Josiane," he called, shivering as he was caught by her embrace as if he were twelve again, as if they were making love . . . soft ice cream. . . .

She was darkness and chill, and Mantle gasped, remembering.

He loved her. He had always loved her. They completed each other. There never could have been anyone else. He remembered, all the times revealed, all the special feelings and sensations and sights and sounds recaptured forever; the childhood and adult hungers and sharing, the anger, and the pain; and, finally, he was almost whole. And she led him down, deeper into himself, through the memories which spun like the blades of propellers. He heard her voice as if he were touching her cold skin, entering her over and over, deliciously, and she whispered, "It wasn't your fault, my darling, don't blame yourself. . . ." And finally he remembered how he had lost Josiane.

He screamed in terror.

He remembered the first Great Scream in New York: the crowds filling avenues and streets. Josiane had been out shopping; Mantle had been working in the apartment. Even in his soundproofed, insulated apartment, Mantle heard the scream. Frantic with worry for Josiane, he rushed out of his apartment and down into the streets. He too had been drawn by the Criers. Their scream was like the *ariara*; it was the rhythm of fire and transcendence and death, and it carried him with gale force to Josiane, who was trying to get home, who was struggling with the Screamers, with two husky *boutades* who were tearing at her. Mantle pushed his way through the crowd toward her. She saw him and called to him, pleading. But suddenly he felt silvery music, heard the dark, telepathic voices of the crowd, saw its thoughts, felt its longings and anger and jubilation. Its thoughts were becoming *his* thoughts. He was being swallowed by the crowd, and Josiane was danger and transformation and death. She was calling him deeper into the beast. If he tried to save her, he would lose himself. He turned and ran. He heard her screaming behind him, calling him desperately. She was being swallowed by the crowd, becoming a Screamer; and he didn't even turn around, lest he be dragged down, submerged in the undertow of minds.

Everything that had happened to Josiane was his fault. He had left her, left her for the Criers, for Pfeiffer, for this. . . .

Mantle couldn't bear the guilt and self-loathing, and Josiane whispered, 'It wasn't your fault.... It will pass....'

'But what about Carl?' Mantle thought. 'I've killed him.... I've *killed* him.'

"You've only helped him to the other side.... He's safe now.... The Criers are taking care of him. We'll all be together soon, and this time of our flesh will seem like only a bad dream....' She drew Mantle's mind deeper into the dark spaces, into cold comfort. She leached away his will, and Mantle felt her strength, reinforced by a thousand other dark minds, pulling him into the dark. 'It wasn't your fault,' they whispered, and the whisper echoed.

'We'll save you,' Josiane said, and she suddenly rose out of the opalescent fluid, grasped Mantle with her cold, powerful hands, and pulled him into the pool. She pulled him under, tried to drown him. Mantle broke away from her, but she pulled him down again, clinging to him like a parasite on hide. She held him under the surface, throttling him, and he felt her thoughts, her love, as a hail of ice-sharp silvery darts.

'Kill me,' she whispered. 'My brother, my love, take me into the dark spaces. We'll take each other....'

Everything darkened around Mantle. He was fighting for his life. But her thoughts were too strong. She commanded him, and he was helpless. Even as he snapped her neck, she called him into the dark spaces... held him under in the pool... was drowning him with sheer power of will.

And she had him. He was lost to life, following his sister through the silver corridors of death.

In death her hands were around his throat....

Then Mantle felt something open up in his mind, and a piercing scream suddenly shattered the dark spaces. In that instant, he broke away from Josiane's thoughts... broke away from the telepathic nets of the Screamers. He came awake and lurched backward, breaking the surface, gulping air. He felt light and warmth and living movement. He felt his lungs working and his blood coursing. Every heartbeat was a miracle.

And still he heard the scream.

It was Joan. She had found him.

He looked up at her from the pool. He blinked, still not certain of anything. He was dazed, his mind still filled with the silvery stuff of the dark spaces... with Josiane. For an instant he thought he was indeed dead. In the dark spaces. That this was a trick. But there was Joan standing near the edge of the pool and looking down at him.

Beside him, Josiane floated facedown in the warm liquid. Trembling, he pulled the skull fittings from his head.

Joan stopped screaming at him. But the horror and revulsion and terror she felt were unmistakable, palpable. Mantle felt her emotions as if she were burning with them. "I...I wanted to stop you," Joan said. Her voice quavered and she could not seem to catch her breath. She was crying as a child cries. "I *tried* to get through to you with the *circuit,* but you closed me out! But you couldn't close me out entirely. I could *feel* where you were; and, my God, I felt it when you killed Carl. It was as if we *both* killed him. And I could feel Josiane making you kill her and trying to kill you. My God, I'm too late, how could you... how could I... my God, my *God....*" Then her eyes rolled up and she started mumbling to herself. "It's not my fault... it is... it's too late...."

She turned and ran out of the room, almost falling as she did so. She ran toward the shouts and screams coming from the streets, toward the breaking of glass, the tearing and rending.

"Joan!" Mantle cried, coming fully to his senses, just as he had in the dolmen at Dramont Beach when the raiders attacked during the hook-in ceremomy. He saw Josiane submerged beside him in the pool, and jumped back reflexively, trying to get away from the ghost-white corpse. He remembered what happened, what he had done, and felt the full front of his self-loathing. Oh God, he told himself, I've killed her. It's Josiane floating dead beside me. My *sister*... my love. Yet for all his grief and remorse, he couldn't quite believe that the corpse floating beside him was his sister. It was as if she had died long ago.

Memories passed before his mind's eye, as if the past were alive once again. But now that he could remember, now that he finally had found his memories, he realized that he had changed. Although he felt grief and bone-crushing guilt over the loss of his sister, he was not in love with her. That passion was a shared childhood dream and would have been over long ago... but the Screamers took Josiane and locked Mantle out of his past.

And now, even now, he realized that he loved Joan.

But Joan was out on the streets... with the Screamers.

Resolving not to let the past repeat itself, Mantle pulled himself out of the pool. "I'm sorry, Josiane.... Forgive me," he whispered; and ran out of the room, down the stairs, and through the main sensor-guarded door that had been blown open by needle bombs. The street stank of sweat, blood, and burning. Frantic, he pushed his way past old men and children, past underside women wearing rags instead of the disposable clothes issued to them daily. Crowds filled Atlantic Avenue, the side streets, and the beaches. Rioters exploded needle bombs and gasoline bottles as people were crushed underfoot, beaten, and burned. Mantle saw a police platform laze about forty people before it was overturned and blown up in the road.

But he couldn't see Joan.

He *had* to find her. She would have no chance on the streets. Not in these crowds. His only hope was to open the *circuit fantome*, to find her telepathically....

Then the Great Scream shattered everything in his mind.

There was no escape, no haven from the explosions of telepathic fire and anger that became the dark cadences of transformation. Only the silvery music could carry him smoothly from flesh to death... to safety. All he had to do was give in for an instant.... A moment would given him eternity....

Mantle tried to protect himself from the Screamers who were randomly kicking and grabbing and punching anyone within reach. He tried to block out voices inside and outside his head, but the telepathic intensity of the crowd was overwhelming.

A voice called in his mind, pleading, breaking through. "Ray...." It was Joan, unmistakably. The *circuit fantome* was alive... as was Joan. She had not been caught by the Screamers. She had kept her mind closed to them and was hiding in the rubble of an old stone fortification on the beach. Mantle could hear the thunder of the ocean, for Joan was concentrating on the sound of waves breaking on a natural jetty of high, jagged rocks... transforming it into white noise... using it to close out the Screamers around her.

But Mantle could *see* where she was. He could see the ocean and jutting rocks, dark and cold as death. When she gazed upward, he could see the vertiginous webbing of the city above her. It ended several miles out to sea and gave off a dim, milky light, as if a thousand constellations of stars had been pressed together.

"Stay where you are," he called. "Keep yourself closed. I'll get to you." And Mantle pushed and kicked and elbowed his way across Atlantic Avenue toward the beach. He was in as much a frenzy as any Screamer. He would not let the Screamers take Joan. He had let them take Josiane. He would not let it happen again. He would redeem himself. They could take *him*, but not her.

"Close yourself up!" Joan said, but it was too late.

Mantle's thoughts had bled into the crowd.

The Screamers suddenly knew where Joan was.

He had given her away.

"No!" he screamed, trying to push his way past the agitated Screamers.

Suddenly, everything was deadly quiet. Everyone but Mantle stopped walking and shouting and babbling; they seemed asleep on their feet, each one dreaming the same dream, every head cocked slightly to one side or another, listening... listening. Mantle pressed between them, making the most of the moment. It was as if he were pushing his way through a throng of stinking, sweating statues. He could feel the telepathic current of the crowd. Something was about to break....

Thousands of Screamers turned at the same time... all caught in the same collective dream.

They turned toward the beach. Toward Joan. The fragmented groups of disoriented Screamers that were already wandering about on the beach suddenly gained purpose. They came together, then rushed Joan.

She tried to run, but it was too late. Several *boutades* and a middle-aged woman grabbed her and jerked her upright. Then one of the young *boutades* pushed her against a cement block and tore at her dress, tore at her while the crowd looked on.

She fought, but the others held her down... pinned her. She was helpless....

Mantle could see it all through Joan's mind and through the screaming mind of the crowd. The crowd was like an engine that had started again; and although nothing was engaged, it was roaring flat-out.

He screamed, as did the others; but he was screaming for Joan. He saw them take her and use her and soil her and make her public. It was a nightmare repeating itself.

He saw the white crust on the lip of the *boutade* who was raping her. He saw his narrow but guileless blue eyes. He felt Joan's pain and shock and horror... felt her last febrile thoughts before the Screamers devoured her exposed, vulnerable mind.

Still, he fought to reach her, to help her; but the crowd was now like a wall. He couldn't get close. But he *had* to save her. Nothing else mattered. He had killed Pfeiffer and Josiane. And now Joan. . . .

"Leave her alone," he screamed. "You can have *me!*"

But his screams were lost, and he was exposed.

Then, as they had with Joan, the Screamers turned on Mantle. Like a tidal wave, they washed over him.

They gave Joan back to him.

They *became* Joan. Each and every face was transformed. Every old woman and *boutade* and undercity urchin was Joan. Then, like chameleons, they changed again. Everyone took on Josiane's features. Every face turned into one face. Into Pfeiffer's. It was as if Pfeiffer were drowning him with his true face.

Mantle felt Pfeiffer's profound pain and sorrow magnified by every Screamer in the crowd. He couldn't stand the barrage of dark remorse, the cold melancholy of death.

He screamed. He poured out his spirit. He lost himself to the dead ghosts of those he had killed and wronged.

He died, even though his blood coursed and his heart pounded.

He was wrenched into the dark spaces.

As he made his passage, he electrified the crowd into unity.

A thousand voices joined him, and their screams spread like waves, until they became a sheet of noise, solid and dark and metallic, an outpouring of the dark spaces. The sound was coherent, a verbal lasing.

And Mantle was the insect around which the cocoon of sound had been woven. He had become the crystal when he killed Pfeiffer. When he killed Josiane. Now he was the seed.

Now he was the field, a field of black and silver upon which the many would turn into the One.

He was the dark spaces. *He* was the Great Scream.

He was the crowd. They were his thoughts.

He was death. . . .

Living and dying were the same now.

The crowd rushed toward the tanks and police platforms that had suddenly appeared and were now gliding down the streets, lasing everyone in their path. Hundreds were killed in seconds, only to be replaced by others who would scream their way into death.

One by one, the tanks and police platforms were overwhelmed by sheer numbers and crippled by needle bombs. The crowd took over the machines. The buildings on both sides of Atlantic Avenue were lased into rubble. A support tower fell, destroying a city block and creating havoc above, for the webbing of the city was delicate and much of undercity was the foundation for the upside world. The heat shock was tremendous. Streets were steaming, as if suddenly turned into a smoking jungle of plasteel and stone. Girders and hanging cable were the flora, just as the screaming crowd was the fauna of this new Amazon.

Mantle was the core of the soft machine that was intent on destroying itself and everything else, but as he ran he still screamed for Joan. "I'm sorry, Joan. . . ." He repeated the words over and over without comprehension, as if he were speaking in tongues.

He had no sense of self . . . no sense of place . . . no sense of time.

He was blind.

A sleeper between howling dreams.

As buildings exploded into white incandescence, and crystalline passtubes crashed around him, Mantle ran screaming through the burning undercity. But he felt no motion, heard no sound, saw nothing but endless darkness.

Yet, voices called him, whispered in his head until dreams began to form into icy patterns like frost on a cold, dark window.

And so Mantle dreamed . . . dreamed of his past, of Joan and Josiane and Pfeiffer, while silvery voices called him through the darkness. But one voice was clearer than the rest.

It was like a bright shaft of light.

It was Pfeiffer.

Pfeiffer was calling him, connecting from Screamer to Screamer, from *circuit* to *circuit*, reaching him through the dark spaces. Pfeiffer's thoughts, his very being, cut through the searing thoughts of distant Screamers.

Thus he wove his own bright skein from Joan to Mantle.

As the old *circuit fantome* flashed back to life, Mantle was electrified into consciousness. His lungs burned. His chest and arms felt as if they had been closed in a vise. If he didn't stop and break away from the screaming mob, he knew he would die. His heart would explode. He would be trampled, crushed by silver thoughts and bloody feet.

But he was still caught in the undertow of the dark spaces.

"Joan!" he called, sensing her presence. "Joan. . . ."

He focused his entire consciousness on the *circuit fantome*, drew strength from it, and broke away from the crowd.

He found himself on the beach, kneeling in cold, wet sand. Smoke from the burning buildings stung his throat, made his eyes water. The Screamers had left him behind. He could hear them roaring in the distance like armies clashing in battle, moving northward away from him into Coney Island Complex. The Net glowed dully above him—all that upside glass and plasteel reflecting the fires below. Around him, scattered like shells across the beach, were dead Screamers.

The beach surely seemed dead, deserted by the spirits of the Screamers.

Yet Mantle could sense Pfeiffer's presence. It was as if he too had been left behind. Two ghosts on the beach. "Carl, are you here?" Mantle asked. He held quite still, holding his breath for a few seconds, listening, then exhaling. All he could hear were waves breaking on rocks and steel . . . but he *felt* Pfeiffer's spirit. It was as if they were sharing old memories, a nostalgic sadness.

"Ray . . ." a voice called him; and Joan's thoughts washed over him like warm water . . . came to him as words and visions. She was alive and near and, through the *circuit* that was now as strong as sight, Mantle knew where she was. She whispered to him just as she had when he was adrift on a sea filled with ice and debris.

Mantle started back along the beach to find her.

Beside him, the ocean began to turn gray with wan morning light. The water was filled with debris and bodies. . . .

As before. . . .

Joan was waiting for him on the far end of a huge steel pier. It was a turn-of-the-century antique, a neodecadent grotesquerie that had in fact been built for a World's Fair. It had towers and girders and suspension cables like a bridge.

Mantle sat down beside Joan, and they huddled together in the dampness. They stared far out to sea, as if waiting for the RMS *Titanic* to appear resplendent over the horizon. They didn't speak for a time, didn't hold hands or embrace. They just leaned against each other, exhausted. The *circuit* was still alive but muffled, as if proximity had somehow put it out of focus.

"Do you want to go home?" Joan finally asked, breaking the silence.

Mantle didn't . . . couldn't answer.

"I can still feel Carl," she said, then suddenly laughed—a short, harsh cry. "The poor bastard had to get us in out of the rain even after—"

"Even after I killed him," Mantle said, feeling the old numbing isolation, reading her thoughts about the umbrella, the *ménage* with Pfeiffer.

"He broke loose from the dark spaces to get us away from the Screamers."

"Absolution," Mantle mumbled.

"But not for you, right?" Joan said harshly, and Mantle felt the full force of her anger through the *circuit*. He flinched. "You've got your past now," she continued. "Let's try to live with it. . . . Let's try to live."

Mantle felt something distant collapse, and a weight seemed to lift from him, releasing him.

Perhaps the Great Scream was breaking up.

He nodded, then embraced Joan awkwardly, gingerly, as if for the first time.

And Pfeifer dissipated like smoke into the open air. . . .

ABOUT THE AUTHOR

JACK DANN is the author or editor of fifteen books, including the novels *Junction* and *Starhiker*, and the collection *Timetipping*. He is the editor of the anthology *Wandering Stars*, one of the most acclaimed anthologies of the 1970's, and several other well-known anthologies, including the recently published *More Wandering Stars*. His short fiction has appeared in *Playboy*, *Penthouse*, *Omni*, *Gallery*, and most of the leading SF magazines and anthologies. He has been a Nebula Award finalist eight times, as well as a finalist for the World Fantasy Award and the British Science Fiction Association Award. His critical work has appeared in *The Washington Post*, *Starship*, *Nickelodeon*, *The Bulletin of the Science Fiction Writers of America*, *Empire*, *Future Life*, and *The Fiction Writers Handbook*, and he is the author of the chapbook, *Christs and Other Poems*. His most recent books are *The Man Who Melted*, a novel; and *Magicats!* and *Sorcerers!*, two anthologies edited in collaboration with Gardner Dozois. He is currently at work on another new novel, *Counting Coup*. Dann lives with his family in Binghamton, New York.

ELIZABETH SCARBOROUGH

☐ 25103	Bronwyn's Bane	$3.50
☐ 24441	The Harem of Aman Akbar	$2.95
☐ 24554	Song Of Sorcery	$2.95
☐ 22939	The Unicorn Creed	$3.50

URSULA LE GUIN

☐ 23906	Beginning Place	$2.75
☐ 23512	Compass Rose	$3.50
☐ 24258	Eye of the Heron	$2.95
☐ 24791	Orsinian Tales	$2.95
☐ 25396	Very Far Away From Anywhere Else	$2.50

ANNE McCAFFREY

☐ 23815	Dragondrums	$2.95
☐ 23459	Dragonsinger	$2.95
☐ 23460	Dragonsong	$2.95